BT

D1322152

Nina ~~~~~~ r
husb~~~~~~ ~~~~~~ren, ~~~~~~ a very rumbu~~~~~~ Yorkie.
~~~~~~ several years in the corpor~~~~~~ world she finally
followed the advice of family and friends to 'give the
writing a go, already'. She's oh-so-happy she did. When
not at her keyboard she likes to spend time on the
tennis court or golf course. Or immersed in a good read.

Helen Bianchin was encouraged by a friend to write
her own romance novel and she hasn't stopped writing
since! Helen's interests include a love of reading,
going to the movies, and watching selected television
programmes. She also enjoys catching up with friends,
usually over a long lunch! A lover of animals, especially
cats, she owns two beautiful Birmans. Helen lives in
Australia with her husband. Their three children and
six grandchildren live close by.

Scarlet Wilson wrote her first story aged eight and has
never stopped. She's worked in the health service for
twenty years, trained as a nurse and a health visitor.
Scarlet now works in public health and lives on the
West Coast of Scotland with her fiancé and their two
sons. Writing medical romances and contemporary
romances is a dream come true for her.

Island Escapes

Island Escapes: Hawaiian Nights

NINA SINGH

HELEN BIANCHIN

SCARLET WILSON

MILLS & BOON

First Published in Great Britain 2021
by Mills & Boon, an imprint of HarperCollins*Publishers* Ltd,
1 London Bridge Street, London, SE1 9GF

www.harpercollins.co.uk

HarperCollins*Publishers*
1st Floor, Watermarque Building,
Ringsend Road, Dublin 4, Ireland

ISLAND ESCAPES: HAWAIIAN NIGHTS © 2021 Harlequin Books S.A.

Tempted by Her Island Millionaire © 2018 Nilay Nina Singh
Alexei's Passionate Revenge © 2017 Helen Bianchin
Locked Down with the Army Doc © 2018 Scarlet Wilson

ISBN: 978-0-263-30246-2

MIX
Paper from
responsible sources
FSC™ C007454

This book is produced from independently certified FSC™ paper to ensure responsible forest management.

For more information visit: www.harpercollins.co.uk/green

Printed and bound in Spain
by CPI, Barcelona

TEMPTED BY HER ISLAND MILLIONAIRE

NINA SINGH

For my dear husband.
That was quite an impressive anniversary gift, hon.

And for my children.
Thank you for enduring bitter cold atop
a volcano, waiting for a sunrise with me.

CHAPTER ONE

His sister was starting to get on his nerves.

He loved her more than anyone else on this earth, but she had been pushing the boundaries of that love ever since she'd gotten engaged.

Clint held the cell phone to his ear, only partially listening to her latest panic-stricken rant. He knew better than to try and say anything to calm her down. The last time he'd tried that, he'd gotten an earful of colorful curse words streamed through the line that would have made his construction contractors blush.

He understood, or he was trying hard to anyway. She had a lot on her mind with the wedding fast approaching. In fact, his town car was dropping him off at the airport at this very moment on his way to sunny Maui where Lizzie and her fiancé would be tying the knot in a few short days. Only now she had some sort of pressing issue with a last-minute change, something to do with the catering. An issue she seemed to be taking way out of proportion. He'd simply learn who he had to pay to fix it once he got there. What was one more expense when it came to this wedding?

He'd be sure to take care of it after arrival. Again, he wasn't going to tell her that. Right now, Lizzie just needed to vent.

His sister had always been a bit overly dramatic. But this wedding was taking that penchant to a whole new level and making him wonder, for that matter, exactly how many women had been put on this earth simply to irritate him?

"Anyway, how are you doing? Anything new?" Lizzie surprised him by asking. Rant over somehow. Not that he wasn't grateful.

Did he dare tell her? That he was unexpectedly attending her wedding solo since the huge fallout with Maxine the other day. After she'd finally made one ultimatum too many.

He decided not to risk it. Lizzie would no doubt want the distraction and try to probe for all the details. Not something he wanted to get into right now. He'd tell her once he arrived at the resort.

"I'm doing fine," he answered honestly. In truth, it was a relief to have finally severed the relationship with the up-and-coming actress. Maxine had grown increasingly demanding and pouty over the past several months. The only frustration now was that he'd already paid for all her flights, excursions and accommodations. Not to mention a hefty spa-and-beauty package at the resort. Shameful waste. Though part of him couldn't help but wonder if it was worth it. "About to go check in for my flight as a matter of fact."

"I'll let you go then, big brother." She paused but didn't hang up. He knew what was coming and he appreciated it. But it still made him uneasy every time she did it. "And you know how much it means that you're doing all this for me," she said, her voice nearly breaking. "I mean it. Thank you."

So unnecessary. She was the only family he had. He'd been solely responsible for her since they were both barely teens, so of course, he would take care of her wedding. And anything else that would make up for the unfair lot they'd been dealt growing up. She didn't need to thank him for that. The wedding was just one more thing he considered his duty.

Unfortunately, so was having to listen to her mini breakdowns every time a snag occurred.

"You're welcome, Lizzie," he answered simply, then disconnected.

The morning didn't get any better after he'd checked in for his flight. With precision, he'd arrived with just enough time to answer any urgent emails and go over a new bid, then comfortably board without having to rush. The airline announced a delay before he'd even gotten a chance to pull his tablet out and log on to his company intranet.

Clint cursed under his breath. An hour, at least. As luck would have it, his private jet was being serviced. The timing was beyond inconvenient. Well, he wasn't going to sit here in this loud, crowded gate area. He'd go kill the time at the private executive suite the airport provided for certain clientele. Maybe he'd even get a chance to read a paper in some peace and quiet.

He swiped his card to get past the secure glass door to the exclusive suite and realized quickly that peace and quiet were not in the equation this morning.

This was, without question, one of the most embarrassing experiences of her whole life. Rita wanted to sink into the ground as she stammered to answer the airport employee who was very politely and professionally interrogating her. Not only had the other three people in the suite started to stare, she noticed from the corner of her vision that someone else had just walked in—a tall dark man with a leather briefcase. Wonderful. Yet one more person to witness her abject humiliation.

"I'm terribly sorry, miss. But there's no record of anyone sponsoring you to be in this room," the well-heeled, highly polished attendant repeated. Sheila, according to the gold name tag on her uniform. "I'm afraid you'll have to pay for your breakfast and then leave."

"Oh, um… I don't understand… I was told by my friend who's a member that I'd be allowed to hang out here if I wanted, and the flight was delayed. I just thought—" Her words were an incoherent mess. She'd never been good under pressure. And this haughty woman was making her feel like a piece of mud she was trying to brush off her Louboutins.

The attendant remained silent. Rita couldn't detect one iota of sympathy in her eyes.

Oh, what the hell. The mushroom omelet and mimosa weren't worth the trouble. Though it had to be the most delicious breakfast she'd ever been served.

"Fine, what do I owe you for the breakfast?" She reached for her wallet.

"With the drink, it will be seventy-five dollars."

She nearly dropped her purse when she heard the figure. "Seventy-five dollars?" How could that be? Had they personally flown in the mushrooms straight from Japan and had a master chef prepare the meal?

Sheila merely nodded in such a superior way that Rita knew she wasn't imagining her satisfied smirk of a smile. Satisfaction at her discomfort.

Currently between jobs, Rita had been trying hard to maintain a certain budget. A tight one. The loss of that kind of money had tears springing into her eyes. With shaky fingers, she reached for her credit card, which was already perilously close to the limit as she was about to spend a week in Hawaii. Most of her expenses were taken care of by the wedding party, but she'd still need money for extra meals or souvenirs. Why had she ever walked in here?

Suddenly, a wall in the form of a navy-blue silk shirt appeared in her vision. Someone had stepped between her and the employee, his back to Rita. The newcomer who'd walked in about thirty seconds ago. "Excuse me to inter-rupt, here. But I'd like to sponsor the young lady as my guest. Please put her breakfast charges on my account."

What?

Great. Now she was getting pity charity from strangers who wanted to pay for her breakfast. "That won't be necessary," she argued to the man's back. Lord, he was broad shouldered. She could see his toned muscles outlined under the finely tailored shirt. It was difficult to get around him to address the attendant.

"I insist," the stranger said to her over his shoulder.

"Certainly, sir. How nice to see you again," the attendant said to him. Rita dared a peek over his shoulder to look at her. It appeared that now Sheila was the one who looked somewhat uncomfortable, she noted with no small degree of satisfaction herself.

Still, she couldn't have random strangers pay for her breakfast. "I said that won't be necessary." She tried to step around him once more.

The man actually stretched his arm out to block her!

Of all the nerve. Granted, he was trying to do something incredibly nice for her but to actually stop her from having any say in the matter was a bit much. Nice or not, he had no right. It wasn't like she really needed his help. The amount would cause a dent in her bank account but she did have the means to pay it.

But it was too late. Sheila flashed him a bright smile, the smirk entirely gone. "I'll take care of it right away, Mr. Fallon."

Mr. Fallon. He turned to her as the attendant walked away. Rita blinked and did a double take as his deep brown eyes met hers. Recognition dawned with a sinking sensation as she realized exactly who he was—the dark hair, the familiar coloring and features.

"I didn't mean to insult you," he told her. "It's just that

I happened to have witnessed that particular employee's pettiness before. I might have to initiate some sort of formal complaint about her with the airport actually."

Oh, no. That wasn't what she wanted at all. "Please don't do that. I don't want to think about someone losing their job because of me."

He quirked an eyebrow in question. "No matter how badly they had it coming?"

She shook her head. "And it's not that I feel insulted."

"No?"

"No, not really." She blew out a breath. "I'm just a bit embarrassed. I wish I'd never walked in here in the first place."

His eyes narrowed on her. Rita couldn't quite read the expression on his face. "I'm actually really glad you did."

A small sensation tingled at the base of her spine. Was he trying to flirt with her now? Yep, definitely the most mortifying thing to ever happen to her. To make the whole thing so much worse, Clinton Fallon had no clue who she was. He didn't even remember her.

Clint wanted to tell the young lady he could relate. It hadn't been that long ago that people like Sheila had talked down to him in the same manner he'd just witnessed her being subjected to. Her embarrassed expression and obviously flustered state when he'd walked in had touched a nerve within him that he'd long since thought was dormant. Apparently, the universe decided he was due for a periodic reminder.

He was glad for it, as he'd just told her. He didn't want to get too complacent or take anything for granted.

"I guess I owe you a thank-you," she was saying.

Guessed? "Uh...you're welcome."

She reached for her carry-on. "I think I'll leave."

Clint stepped in front of her before she got far. Was she

confused? He'd just taken care of the matter so that she could stay. "You no longer have to."

Something flashed behind her eyes. It didn't strike him as gratitude. Far from it. He had offended her. Well, what was he supposed to have done? Let her get tossed out on her behind?

"Nevertheless. I'm not sure I want to stay in here any longer."

"You mentioned your flight was delayed. At least finish your breakfast."

"I'm sure it's cold now," she muttered, then blew out a breath. "I'm sorry. It's just—I've really been looking forward to this trip. And so far it hasn't exactly started off on the most positive note."

"I understand," he told her, a feeling of empathy settling deep within his chest. He did understand. More than she knew.

Rita adjusted her collar and tried to quell the shaking in her stomach. Clinton Fallon was standing before her without any clue as to who she was. Apparently, she hadn't made much of an impression on him all those years ago when she'd been at university with his sister. First, he'd witnessed her abject humiliation by the suite attendant. And now she was going to have to find a way to introduce herself.

Or reintroduce herself as the case may be. By contrast, she couldn't count the number of times she'd thought about him over the years. As if she hadn't felt silly enough about that small fact until this encounter.

She was trying to figure out a way to tell him exactly who she was when he extended his hand. "I'm Clinton—"

"I know who you are," she blurted out without really thinking.

He blinked. "You do?"

A small lump of disappointment settled in her gut. He

really had no inkling, no recollection whatsoever. Why was she surprised? Or even disappointed? People like him didn't take much note of ladies like her.

And exactly what kind of lady was she now? How would she begin to describe herself? Perhaps she could use the term *recent divorcée*. Or *unemployed veterinarian*. Or *failed daughter*. Unfortunately, any one of those could apply.

"Here. Let's give this a try." She removed a hair band from her wrist and quickly tied her thick dark hair in a loose ponytail. Then she removed a pair of thick glasses from her pocket and perched them on her nose.

Clint's only response was a completely blank look. Still nothing.

Rita sighed. Now she was just humiliating herself even more. He had no idea who she was. How often had she thought about him over the years? How often had she wondered where he was and what he was doing?

While he hadn't even given her a second thought, it seemed.

"I went to school with Lizzie," she told him. "You and I met in passing a few times at various school-sponsored family events." She extended her hand. "Rita Paul. I'm actually on my way to your sister's wedding myself."

His smile grew wide as he took it. "I'm sorry. I'm just so bad with faces."

"No need to apologize." Though she did appreciate the effort. An awkward moment passed as they limply shook hands. As if neither could decide who should let go first. Why was she behaving so loopily around this man? Finally, Rita pulled out of his grasp.

"It should have occurred to me that at least one or two of Lizzie's friends would be on this flight," Clint continued. "I'm not used to flying with the airlines. My private aircraft is undergoing some repairs."

"Did you really just say that your jet is in the shop?"

He gave her an embarrassed smile. "I guess I did."

He'd certainly come far. Though again, she wasn't surprised. The man she'd met all those years ago was clearly driven and talented. "You were just starting out in the construction business back when Lizzie and I were in school."

He nodded. "That's correct."

"You've just acquired a company, I believe."

"Correct again. The man I worked for was ready to retire. Said he trusted me more than anyone else to take over. Gave me quite a deal when he sold me the business."

"A deal you clearly made the most of then took to new astronomical heights."

He studied her. "I guess you could say that. Along with some well-placed investments, things have gone pretty well."

What an understatement. The man owned a private jet. She knew he'd single-handedly put his sister through school. No doubt, he was the one paying for this lavish destination wedding.

Clint Fallon represented the epitome of a self-made success story. She'd followed his life for a while in the local papers and news sites after graduating from school. Everyone was fascinated by a self-made man. But then her own life had gone completely awry. Unlike Clint and his string of successes, she'd only managed to accumulate one failure after another. Though heaven knew he'd been handed a much worse set of circumstances.

Well, this was her chance to get away from all that and try to forget. For the next few days anyway. This trip was all about Lizzie and her future husband and the love they shared.

She was trying to come up with a response when the airline announced they were finally boarding. "I should head out to the lobby," she told him. "I'm seated toward the back. I'll be one of the first they call."

But he reached for her arm to stop her from leaving. "Wait. I happen to know the seat next to me is free."

"But I thought this was a full flight. They were asking for volunteers to give up their spots."

"Fairly recent development. I didn't get a chance to update the airline. I was supposed to be, ah…traveling with someone. Their plans fell through at the last minute."

Understanding dawned. Pictures of Clint always showed him with a female companion. Always someone very glamorous and beautiful. None seemed to last for more than a few news cycles. The timing of his latest breakup appeared fairly inconvenient. He was going stag to his own sister's wedding.

"You can sit with me up in first class."

She had to decline. He'd already done more than enough by paying for her breakfast and vouching for her to stay in the lounge. "I appreciate that. But it's not necessary."

He blinked at her. "I could use the company," he countered, then pulled his phone out of his pocket. "It'll just take me a second."

Before she knew what he was up to, he was quickly on the phone with the airlines. Clearly, he had some kind of executive direct line that reached an employee right away.

Clint wasn't terribly good at reading her frustrated vibe.

He was already ending the call before she could protest any further. "You're all set. We can board together."

Rita clamped down on her annoyance. If she said anything further she would merely sound petulant and ungrateful. Never mind that she was trying to feel more in charge of herself, more in control of her life. This flight had literally been the first travel ticket she'd purchased for herself, paid for completely on her own. And Clint Fallon had just given it away and upgraded her to first class.

She knew it was illogical of her to be angry or to feel slighted. Clint had no idea of her circumstances. Or the silly symbolic meaning she'd put behind the whole trip.

Rita herself had only actually just now realized how much it meant to her.

It appeared Rita had not taken him seriously when he'd said he could use some company on the flight. Despite sitting right next to him, she'd barely spoken two words. The complete opposite of what he knew would have happened with Maxie. She would have no doubt talked his ear off about everything from her latest gig to the spa treatment she'd been scheduled for.

Something between the two extremes would have been nice.

He should have taken the opportunity to get some work done. But he'd found himself distracted by the delicate rose scent of her perfume. Her jet-black hair brushed against his shoulder when she shifted in her seat and he'd had to resist the urge to ask her if he could run his fingers through the thick silky strands.

How uncharacteristic of him.

Now, several hours later, she was just as quiet. They were finally approaching the Grande Maui resort in Kaanapali. And he was experiencing yet another silent ride. The woman had no interest in speaking to him.

The vehicle finally came to a stop and they both exited, then waited as the young driver pulled their bags out of the rear trunk.

He heard Lizzie's excited voice from behind before he could even reach for his luggage.

"You're here!" his sister shouted, her voice breathy with excitement. He found himself bear-hugged in her skinny arms a short second later. She noticed Rita standing next to them when she finally let go. "You're here too." Lizzie glanced at the town car. "You two came together?"

She didn't wait for an answer as she took Rita in her arms next. Clint watched as the two women also embraced, Rita's dark hair and olive skin a complete contrast to his sister's red coloring and fair complexion. There was true affection in their tight hug.

"I ran into Rita at the airport," he answered his sister over their heads.

"Oh, how fortunate," Lizzie exclaimed as they finally pulled apart.

"Yes. Very lucky for me," Rita began. "He paid for my breakfast, saved me from a very embarrassing situation at the executive lounge, then upgraded me to first class."

If she actually felt lucky about any of that, her tone distinctly said otherwise. Was she mad at him? Whatever for? The thought tugged at him. Usually, the women in his life made it more than clear whatever his transgressions against them might be. Maybe he was interpreting her tiredness after a long flight for sarcasm. Or perhaps he was hearing things; the large gushing stone fountain behind them was pretty loud after all.

"You'll both have to tell me exactly how you ran into each other," Lizzie said and peeked inside the still-waiting car. "But where's Maxie?"

Both ladies turned to him, awaiting his answer. He bit back a curse. This wasn't something he wanted to get into in front of Rita Paul. Though he'd be hard-pressed to say why that was so.

"Change of plans. I'll be unaccompanied on this trip," he told his sister, hoping beyond any real expectation that she'd let the matter drop.

She didn't. Lizzie's eyes grew wide and a huge grin spread across her lips. "I heard nothing of this change."

"Things didn't work out." And that's all he wanted to say on the matter.

His sister's smile grew wider. "You don't say!"

She'd never really taken to Maxie. Not that there'd been anyone he'd been with so far that she'd approved of. His sister kept telling him the women he dated were far too shallow.

Little did Lizzie know, at this point in his life, he wanted shallow. Particularly now, when he was no longer solely responsible for his sister.

Rita glanced from one of them to the other. Suddenly, Lizzie clamped a hand over her mouth; the smile completely disintegrated. "Oh, Rita, I don't mean to be insensitive. I'm so sorry things didn't work out between you and Jay."

A flash of regret seemed to pass through Rita's eyes, but it was gone in an instant. "It wasn't meant to be. Let's just focus on celebrating you and Jonathon."

"I missed you." The two women linked arms, then slowly started to walk toward the front desk. Clint hovered behind, tipping the bell steward who loaded their luggage onto a cart. His gaze remained on Rita as she walked away. He didn't know the woman from a passing acquaintance but he felt… He couldn't even describe what he felt.

He'd met her years ago and had somehow forgotten her. Which seemed unbelievable given his reaction to her now.

She was one of his sister's close friends. A bridesmaid in her wedding. Based on their conversation just now, she'd clearly just come out of what sounded like a serious relationship.

The last thing he wanted was any kind of meaningful relationship himself. Not for several years. He'd done all he could for his sister. She was a grown, educated, about-to-be-married woman. He intended this next period of his life to be all about his growing business and doing all the things he hadn't been able to do after he and Lizzie had been orphaned when he was merely sixteen. His sister had only been fourteen.

Lizzie turned and gave him a questioning look. He read it as "Hurry up, already." For the younger sibling, she could certainly be quite bossy, Clint thought as he strolled to where they now stood by the check-in desk.

"This is the man whose credit card is covering all these charges," Lizzie told the desk clerk as she pointed at him. "Including the expanded catering menu we discussed earlier."

The gentleman handed him a key card. "Mr. Fallon. Welcome. Your suite is ready and waiting for you. You'll find a chilled bottle of champagne and a basket of fruit."

Lizzie clapped her hands and turned to him. "Excellent, Rita and I will be snagging that champagne from you, big brother."

"Is that so? And why should I relinquish it to you two?"

Lizzie huffed with impatience, as if the answer should be obvious. "Because us girls are celebrating. More than just my upcoming nuptials."

"Fine. Consider it yours." He knew he could be too indulgent with her sometimes. But this was her wedding. "What else will you two be celebrating then?"

She draped her arm around Rita's shoulders. "We are also celebrating this young lady's newly found freedom."

Rita's eyes flickered downward. She looked far from celebratory at the moment.

Clint signed the paperwork he'd been handed and watched as the two women slowly made their way down the hall.

So who exactly was Jay? And was there any chance Rita was still hung up on him?

But there was no denying the real, much bigger question—why did Clint want to know so badly?

CHAPTER TWO

HER DIVORCE WAS hardly a cause for celebration.

Rita was just getting used to the idea that she was single again. The breakup had been her idea. She'd been the one who wanted out of her marriage. Still, it wasn't something she wanted to party over. Jay hadn't been a bad person. He hadn't even been a bad husband. In fact, he'd make someone else a fitting spouse one day. Just not her.

But Lizzie's heart was in the right place. So Rita figured she'd drink Clint's champagne with her. Speaking of, she hadn't missed Clint's curious glance in her direction when Lizzie had spoken of her breakup. Now, as they passed through the open-air lobby on the way to his suite, she could feel his intense gaze on her back. The knowledge sent a tingle of awareness along the surface of her skin.

Cut it out.

She was simply reacting to seeing her crush again after all these years. And that's all Clint had ever been: a crush.

"And it all starts tonight!" Lizzie chimed with excitement.

Rita was paying just enough attention to know Lizzie was rambling on about the various sightseeing tours and excursions planned for the wedding party. Apparently, it all kicked off with a traditional Hawaiian luau this evening.

Good thing one of them was talking; God bless her old friend for never being at a loss for words, as Rita wasn't feeling particularly chatty. Heaven knew she hadn't said much to Clint on the plane ride over. But what would she have talked about? Her stalled career? Her failed marriage? And she certainly didn't want to get into her currently very strained relationship with her parents.

At least she wasn't the only one here alone. Clint was also without a plus-one. Looked like they both were leaving some part of their pasts behind.

They finally reached his door and Clint used his card to let them in. Rita had to bite down a gasp as she stepped inside. His suite was the size of a small apartment. A wall of glass stood opposite them, the view a spectacular one of the ocean and the island mountain in the distance. Pity the woman who was supposed to be here and was now missing out on all this.

Among the other things she was missing out on.

Rita couldn't help but study Clint as he walked to the veranda and pulled the sliding door open. She'd certainly had good taste all those years ago when she'd first started crushing on the man. Tall and lean, he seemed to be quite fit. And he had the most striking facial features. Where his sister was fair with a patrician nose, Clint had more the look of a well-mixed genealogy. Lizzie had mentioned once that there was some Asian blood in their family ancestry. Though those genes hadn't found his sister, Clint clearly had what would be described as such characteristics. Overall, it made for a dashing, exotic look that definitely made him stand out in a crowd.

"They gave you the good stuff," Lizzie said as she pulled a green glass bottle out of the ice bucket.

"And I'm giving it to you two," Clint replied.

"I suppose we can let you have a glass. Not a big one though." Lizzie pinched her fingers in a demonstration of how much his pour would be. "We probably shouldn't have too much right now anyway. There'll be plenty of food and drink at the luau later this evening," she said, then glanced at Rita as if looking for agreement.

"Right."

"By the way—" Lizzie addressed her brother "—Tessa Campbell has been asking about you since she arrived. She happens to be your roommate, Rita."

Clint gave her a distracted nod as he stood staring at the majestic view in front of them. "Which one was she again?"

Lizzie gave an exaggerated roll of her eyes in Rita's direction, the effect so comical it made her giggle. "How can you not remember?" she asked her brother as she gave him the bottle to uncork. "She's been hitting on you since the tenth grade. Wait till she finds out you're here alone."

He actually groaned. "Now I remember. What are the chances I'll be able to avoid her?"

"Slim to none," his sister replied. "She is a member of the wedding party after all."

"Great."

Clint's tone held every hint of resignation. He was a man used to such attention. She wasn't surprised. It was all merely an annoyance for him. He deftly uncorked the bottle with a pop and grabbed two flutes off the serving table then began pouring. Tiny florescent bubbles floated through the air. He handed each of them a glass.

Lizzie suddenly let out a laugh that had her snorting bubbly champagne through her nose. The sight, in turn, made Rita laugh.

"What's so funny?" Clint wanted to know.

Lizzie rubbed the tip of her nose. "I just had an image of you ducking behind palm trees during the luau when you saw Tessa approaching."

Rita laughed harder at the visual that invoked. Clint glanced from one to the other, a resigned expression on his face. "I'm glad you two find this so amusing."

"I'm sorry," Rita told him but she couldn't seem to stop one last giggle. When was the last time she'd really laughed? The past few months had been an emotional hailstorm. She was so glad to be here, finally able to get away. To have it be for such a happy occasion was just icing on the cake. This chance to step back from her troubles for a while was exactly what she needed right now.

But then Clint focused those dark chestnut-brown eyes on her, his lips curved into a smile. She had to suck in a breath just as her stomach did a dive straight to her toes. Perhaps she'd found trouble yet again.

Clint's intention to get some rest before the luau with a quick nap was not going well. Every time he started to drift off, a set of dark brown eyes framed by silky jet-black hair sprang into his mind's eye and jolted him awake. What was wrong with him?

He was simply here to see his sister married off and to give her away. Not to explore a wayward attraction to a friend of hers.

A glance at the wall clock across the room told him the shuttle to take them into town for tonight's festivities would be arriving right about now. He had to get going. Lizzie didn't tolerate lateness. Not even from the big brother who was paying for this whole shindig. He didn't mind. Somehow his sister had escaped the cynicism spouted by their grandmother all those years. Bless her for it.

Maybe Lizzie would prove him and his grandmother wrong and make her marriage work. Maybe she'd be the one to break the Fallon chain of doomed relationships.

Lord knew, he wasn't going to be the one to try.

If that made him cynical, so be it. At least Lizzie had found love. Or what she thought was love. But then she'd always been the dreamer. While he'd had to be the responsible, serious one. He'd had no choice. With both parents gone and only an elderly, bitter matron in charge of them, the burden of responsibility had fallen solely on his shoulders.

He figured he'd done okay. They both had, he and his sister. Hokey as it sounded, he'd have to say he was proud of the woman his sister had become. And happy for her that she'd found someone. Jonathon was a good man. He'd make Lizzie a good husband. Someday, he'd make a good father.

Not that Clint was in any kind of hurry to become an uncle, he mused as he walked to the bathroom and turned on the shower. It would have to be a short one. Officially, Clint was the main host of this wedding. He couldn't be missing shuttles and ending up running late to the events. That also meant he had to be very cordial and very polite to every one of their guests.

So it galled him that there was only one in particular he was thinking of right now, wondering if they'd be seated anywhere near each other. Or maybe even together. He didn't know the full wedding party details; he had left Lizzie and Jonathon pretty much to their own devices when it came to planning.

Now he wished he'd been more involved. It might have avoided the whole fiasco at the airport when he couldn't even remember who Rita was. That had been wildly embarrassing. Had he apologized to her? He couldn't recall. If he didn't run into her tonight, he'd have to make it a point to find her and do so.

Right. And that would be the only reason for him to want to seek her out.

Damn it. Why couldn't he stop thinking about her?

Shutting off the water and toweling off, Clint realized he barely had time to make it downstairs in time for the shuttle bus. Throwing on a pair of khaki shorts and a Hawaiian shirt, he didn't bother to button it as he ran toward the hallway stairs that led to the lobby. Waiting for the elevator would be too risky.

In his hurry, Clint realized too late that someone else was on the stairway making their way down. The crash was unavoidable. Unable to stop himself at the speed he was going, he collided hard with an unsuspecting, soft body. He just barely managed to catch her in his arms and avoid what was sure to be a harrowing tumble down several sets of steps.

Turned out he wouldn't have to go looking for Rita after all.

"Oh, my—" Her words cut off as chocolate-brown eyes blinked at him with shock. Her gaze drooped down to his bare chest for a split second before snapping back up to his face.

"I'm so sorry," he began. "Are you all right?"

She blinked once more. "You're not even dressed."

Clint made himself release her in order to pull his shirt together. He began hastily buttoning. "Yeah, part of the reason for my rush. I'm running a little late."

"I guess *running* would be the operative word."

"And *colliding*. Don't forget *colliding*. You never answered my question."

"Question?"

"Are you all right? I didn't hurt you, did I?"

"I'm fine, just a little startled." She adjusted the hem of her sundress, which had shifted somewhat as a result of their collision. And what a pretty dress it was, a shiny number with thin straps that rested delicately on her toned shoulders. The navy blue of the fabric brought out the deep, rich hue of her silky, smooth skin.

Had he ever noticed a woman's dress before? Or how it brought out the color of her skin?

"I'm really sorry, Rita." To think, he'd intended earlier to apologize to her for something completely different: forgetting who she was. His mea culpas when it came to her were accumulating.

"Why are you taking the stairs?" he asked her. "Aren't you on a much higher floor?"

She shrugged. "I always take the stairs. It's better for you."

Well, she certainly was fit. And that dress made no bare bones about it. It showed off her long, toned legs and narrow waist.

This was getting ridiculous. He'd nearly caused her to wipe out down the stairs for heaven's sake. Not to mention he'd hauled her against his bare chest to keep her from falling. And now he couldn't stop ogling her. In a deserted stairway, no less.

"We should probably get down there," he said and motioned for her to go ahead down the final flight of steps. As he followed, he forced himself not to look at her shapely, rounded behind. Though it wasn't easy.

There was a whole pig twisting around on a spit. Head and hooves and all. Rita couldn't bear to look at the sight another second. She wasn't a strict vegetarian by any means. But her profession as a veterinarian made such a scene difficult to watch. In fact, she felt a bit queasy.

The rest of the crowd stood next to the open fire pit, oohing and aahing at the large animal about to be served as their dinner. A crowd that included the entire wedding party. She walked toward the water, away from the buffet area where the rest of the feast was being set up.

The party faced the sea, with a majestic view of the mountains on one side and crystal-blue water as far as the eye could see on the other. Banana-leaf-covered cabanas surrounded a large stage area in the center. Tables and tables of various dishes were already being set up.

Clint Fallon had spared no expense for his sister's wedding. Rita nudged the sand at her feet with her sandaled toe. She glanced over to where he stood with the rest of the crowd. Lizzie had been right about Tessa Campbell wanting to corner him. The woman had made a beeline to Clint's side as soon as they'd exited the shuttle bus. She'd been within two feet of him ever since. Several times, when Rita had ventured to look their way, Tessa had her hand on his arm or his shoulder. She'd definitely dominated his full attention so far.

Though Rita got the distinct feeling Clint was merely being polite. Actually, Clint looked somewhat uncomfortable with the constant touching.

Not that it would bother her if there was anything more than that developing between them. And the frustration she felt at that thought wasn't something she was going to dwell on. She thought of their near disaster on the stairs earlier. Like she'd fallen against a hard wall of pure male. She rubbed her cheek where it had landed against his bare chest when he'd barreled into her. Lord, he'd felt solid.

"Thought you'd taken off." A masculine voice sounded behind her and made her jump. Clint. Rita turned to find him no more than a few feet behind her, as if her thoughts had conjured him.

"Just wanted to admire the water for a bit."

He came to stand beside her, both of them facing the coastline. "You find it a much more palatable view than the one back there over by the fire pit."

He was an observant one. "Yes, well, there's that too." He must have been watching her. So maybe Tessa didn't have so much of his attention after all. "Was it that obvious?"

He smiled. "Your disdain was clear."

Oh, no. She hoped she wasn't coming off in that way. As if she were turning her nose up at the chosen venue or choice of entertainment. Sometimes her shyness was known to come off as a haughtiness. It had gotten her into trouble more than once. "It's just that when you spend your days taking care of animals, seeing one spinning above a fire pit that way is a little off-putting."

Something shifted behind Clint's eyes. Then he actually thwacked himself in the forehead with the palm of his hand. "It's you!"

"I beg your pardon?"

"Sarita. With the neon purple hair. Lizzie's roommate off and on during her school days. You were studying to be a veterinarian."

Ah, so now he was finally remembering. Took him long enough. "Wow, that didn't take you long at all," she said, her voice dripping with sarcasm.

He had the decency to duck his head as if chagrined. "I've been meaning to apologize for that." He spread his hands. "But you gotta cut me some slack. You never looked the same those few times I saw you. I mean, was your hair ever the same color?"

She had to give him that. Her puny attempts at college-girl rebellion centered around changing her hair constantly. Her father absolutely hated it. Which was the point, wasn't it? Still, Clint could have registered some recognition before now.

"And Rita's not your name," he declared. "That threw me off too."

"It's a shortened version of my name. As is yours."

He pursed his lips, as if that thought hadn't occurred to him. "I suppose you're right."

He supposed? Of course, she was right. Clint was short

for Clinton. How was that any different than shortening Sarita to Rita? She didn't get a chance to ask as they were interrupted.

"There you are! I lost track of you." Tessa ran up to Clint and wagged her finger at him.

Clint actually groaned out loud. Tessa didn't notice. Or she didn't really care. Then he shocked her by placing both his hands around Rita's waist. *That* Tessa definitely noticed. Her eyes grew wide with shock. And annoyance.

"I was just looking for Sarita. We ran into each other at the airport and I've been meaning to catch up with her ever since."

He was? Or was he just trying to use her to deflect Tessa's attentions? She wasn't sure how she felt about that last possibility. But when she glanced his way, his eyes implored her to go along.

His expression was so desperate, she almost felt sorry for him for a split second. "Yes, I'm hoping to hear about what Clint's been up to all these years since we've last seen each other."

Tessa would not be deterred. She crooked her hand into Clint's elbow. "Well, we can't have you two off by yourselves. This is a party after all."

"You know, you're absolutely right," Clint agreed with a wide smile that almost seemed genuine, even as he gently pulled his arm free. "We'll just be another minute."

Tessa's face fell. It was the first time Rita had actually observed such a physical embodiment of that expression. Tessa cleared her throat. "All right then. Don't take too long," she added before walking away.

"Very smooth, Mr. Fallon."

"What do you mean?"

"I mean the way you dismissed her while somehow agreeing with her. Very, very smooth."

"I told her the truth. I really do want to hear more about you. What better time than tonight? In this wonderful setting?"

She couldn't read too much into that comment. "Now that you finally remember who I am?"

He started to object but then apparently thought better of it. "And yes, I could use a break from Tessa, sweet as she is. Just stay by my side throughout the night and maybe she'll leave me alone."

"So I'm supposed to let you utilize our newly rediscovered friendship to allow you to avoid a potential suitor?"

He grabbed his chest in mock outrage. "That's only the secondary motive, remember?"

"Why?"

"Why what?"

"Why would I agree to do that?"

He quirked an eyebrow. "Because you can't resist my charm?"

Rita gave him a thumbs-down. "Try again."

"Because you've taken pity on me?"

This time she shook her head.

"Come on," he pleaded. "Just for tonight. So that I can maybe relax and enjoy this amazing dinner and the traditional performance."

She supposed he did at least have a right to that. Given that it was his sister's wedding they were all here for. Besides, she'd been thankful to Clint so many times in the past. Like when he'd bought his sister the car they'd both used to get from their off-campus dorm to their classes in the dead of winter. Or during junior year when their preferred choice of housing had fallen through and he'd pulled all sorts of strings to get them a place to stay.

Just admit that the prospect of spending the evening with him isn't exactly a turnoff.

She gave him a nonchalant shrug. "Why not?"

Somehow, against her better judgment, she'd just agreed to spend the evening close by Clint's side.

"I take it you won't be indulging in the main course," Clint said as he escorted Rita toward the numerous buffet tables laden with island food. So far, she was being a good sport about their earlier agreement to help him keep Tessa at bay. She'd stayed by his side and made sure to keep the conversation going between the two of them. Just generally staying in his company which he was enjoying way more than he should.

Truth be told, he hadn't been expecting to get much pleasure out of this evening. He wasn't exactly a luau type. Thanks to Rita, however, the evening was so far turning out quite differently than he'd imagined. In a very pleasant way.

The way the other woman was shooting daggers at him from across the serving area made it clear she'd noticed the camaraderie between them.

"You would be correct," Rita responded as they reached the first table.

Sarita. No wonder he hadn't recognized her. He could hardly be faulted for not realizing at first glance that she was the bespectacled, purple-haired, shy girl he'd see occasionally when he visited Lizzie at school. Hard to believe this was the same woman standing before him now.

"It's not like I'll go hungry," she added, breaking into his thoughts and motioning to the massive number of dishes laid out before them. He didn't even recognize half the plates. Tropical fruit, various pulled meats, grilled vegetables. In the center of every table sat a bowling-ball-sized bowl of some kind of pinkish pudding-like substance.

"Any idea what that is?" he asked her.

"I believe it's what's known as poi."

"Pa—what, now?"

She laughed as she handed him an empty plate, then grabbed one for herself. "Based on some reading I've done, it's made from some kind of native plant. It's supposed to be full of essential vitamins and minerals. It's supposed to be very good for you. Particularly for—" she paused midsentence "—um… Never mind."

Judging by the way she suddenly ducked her head, something had clearly made her uncomfortable.

"What were you going to say?"

"Nothing. Just an article I read."

"I'm a little hurt that you aren't willing to educate me. Perfectly okay that I'll remain woefully ignorant about whatever this *pwah* is."

She granted him a small laugh. "Poi. It's just very popular with the men in particular."

"Yeah, why's that?"

They both reached for the same serving spoon and the brush of her fingers against his sent a spark of awareness down to his center. Suddenly, he realized what she was referring to. The poi must be considered to lend some kind of boost to male performance.

She quickly pulled her hand away.

"I think I figured it out." He reached for the next item. "Not that someone like me would be concerned about that."

Why the hell had he just said that?

Damn it, now the air between them was awkward and strained. When they'd been having such a relaxed conversation earlier.

"That was just a joke," he said by way of explanation.

"Does that mean it's not true? That you could perhaps use the poi?"

"What? No! I mean, yes. I mean, of course it's true."

Saints above. It was like he didn't even know how to speak around this woman.

She popped a pineapple chunk into her mouth and winked at him with bemusement. He had to remind himself to breathe.

"Ha, ha."

Just to be funny, he scooped a ridiculous amount of the poi and dropped it in the center of his plate.

The show was just starting as they took their seats. He stole a glance at Rita next to him as she watched. She seemed thoroughly entranced by the story the performers were enacting on the stage. Tales about native islanders leaving their home to find more hospitable islands. Kings and queens leading their people to new lands, the culture and customs that they brought with them and how they mixed with inhabitants already living there.

Rita looked like she could be one of those queens. Or a regal princess adjusting to life on a new island. Her sundress swayed softly in the breeze. The glow of the lit torches brought out the dark golden specks of her eyes. Rather than wearing the flower lei they'd received upon arrival around her neck, she'd loosely wrapped it around the crown of her head. The overall effect was mesmerizing.

So much so that Clint barely noticed when the story depiction part of the show was over and the hula dancing had begun. Rhythmic drums filled the air as the dancers bounced to the music, their hips moving in ways that seemed to defy anatomical possibility. The dancers then formed a circle around the tables. Lizzie and Jonathon sat at the table next to them. The woman onstage spoke into her microphone. "I understand there are a bride and groom here celebrating with us."

One of the dancers extended a hand to Lizzie, who took it and then stood from the table. Jonathon stood as well with another dancer leading him by the elbow. All four started making their way toward the stage. Various other couples in the dining area were similarly led.

"Please come participate with us in a traditional celebratory dance," the woman said into the mic.

On her way to the stage, Lizzie suddenly stopped behind him. "Come on, big brother. I don't want you to miss out on this." She grabbed him by the crook of the elbow and pulled.

"Oh, no, you don't. I am not a dancer."

"Tonight you are." She tugged on his arm until he had no choice but to stand.

His sister wanted him to dance. Onstage. A traditional Hawaiian hula. Well, he wasn't going down alone.

"Rita? Care to join us?"

Her jaw fell. "Uh… I'll sit this one out."

"Come on. Don't make me suffer this alone." Before he could finish the sentence, the female dancer behind him took Rita by the hand and made her stand. Essentially making the decision for her. Clint decided he'd be forever indebted to the woman. They made their way toward the stage.

Once there, he found himself thrust in Rita's direction as everyone coupled up to dance, the women in front of the men. A dancer in the front led them, instructing how to move the hips just so. Rita did as instructed. And she seemed to have quite a knack for it. Her hips moved in swift circles in front of him and he thought perhaps his lungs would stop functioning.

Sweet heavens, perhaps he shouldn't have had any of the poi. Not that it would have made any kind of difference.

The early-morning jog along the beach was supposed to clear his head. But images from the previous evening kept invading Clint's mind as he ran at a punishing pace along the water. Rita's smile as she was teasing him about the local delicacy. The way she'd tried to avoid looking at the main dish.

How her hips had moved as she danced in front of him.

So he thought he must have been imaging it when he looked toward the horizon and saw her in the water climbing onto a surfboard, assisted by a tan, blond man. She appeared to be taking a surfing lesson. The man grabbed her about the waist as he held her steady on the waves.

How many times last night had his fingers itched to do the same thing? He couldn't count the number of times he'd awoken after midnight from a dream that prominently featured a dark-haired beauty with a flower lei adorning her head.

He watched her laugh as she toppled off the board and splashed in the water once more. The instructor immediately grabbed her and assisted her back on. Clint suddenly felt an irrationally intense dislike for the man.

This had to stop. He couldn't be having these thoughts. About her or anyone else. He didn't need any kind of disruption in his life right now. Didn't have time for it. He certainly didn't have the time or the inclination for a serious relationship with anyone, let alone a woman like Rita. She deserved nothing less than total commitment. Something he wasn't sure he'd ever be willing to give.

Good thing there were no group activities planned for today. He could use the time to clear his head. The next outing on the agenda wasn't until after midnight tonight, when they'd be picked up to go to Haleakala to see the sunrise atop the volcanic crater. He'd be sure to steer clear of her then.

You Fallon men have no idea how to fall in love without completely sacrificing your souls.

His grandmother was right. Not that he had any kind of notion that he was falling for Rita. It was simply the romantic mood of this wedding and the sensuous setting

of the tropical island. Still, he would have to make sure
not to let silly whims get the better of him from now on.
Asking Rita to pretend they were interested in getting to
know each other better had been a mistake. He would have
been better off just dodging Tessa's advances.

Much better off than what he was feeling now.

CHAPTER THREE

IF HER TEETH chattered any harder, Rita was sure to crack a molar. Given that they were supposed to be in one of the warmest climes on the planet, she hadn't expected it to be this chilly at any point during this trip. But being on top of one of the world's tallest volcanos, it made sense if one thought about it. Especially at about four thirty in the morning. Well, that particular bit of wisdom wasn't doing her any good at the moment.

Their tour bus driver said they had to get here this early or all the viewing spots would completely fill up. If she'd known about the biting chill, she might have argued to take the risk. People around her were bundled up in coats and scarves. A few had thick, plush blankets. Even members of the wedding party had somehow come prepared. Had they received some kind of memo she hadn't?

Probably not, Rita thought and hugged her sweatshirt tighter around herself. They had just somehow planned better than she had. Story of her life. It wasn't even a terribly thick sweatshirt.

She heard a shuffling behind her and turned to find Clint approaching. She knew it was him, though it was somewhat hard to see in the predawn darkness. He had a thick leather jacket on. Yet another person better prepared than she.

"You're shivering," he stated, noting the obvious.

"Ye-e-es. I—I a-a-am." Okay, so the stutter was a bit exaggerated. But not by much. Her lips were practically flapping together from the cold.

He started shrugging off his coat. "Here, take this."

She stopped him with a hand to his chest. "No way. I am not that s-selfish." The cold stutter made the word sound like she'd said *shellfish* and she had to stifle a laugh.

"I don't know you very well, but that's the last term I would use to describe you."

The words took her aback. In fact, she'd heard herself described that way countless times over the last several months. By people she cared for the most. When all she'd wanted to do was find her own way and discover what made her happy. Correction, she'd wanted to discover what made her *feel*.

Though she didn't want to examine exactly what it was she was feeling right now. Neither did she want to admit that she'd been hoping Clint would find her at some point on top of this mountain.

"I can't take your coat," she insisted through the chattering.

"Well, I can't take watching you succumb to frostbite."

Before she knew what he was up to, he'd stepped behind her and enveloped her in his embrace, the coat wrapped around them both. "Here. In the interest of compromise."

A cocoon of heat suddenly surrounded her, along with his woodsy masculine scent. In her desire for warmth, she didn't bother to stop him or step away. Right. Like that was the only desire driving her at the moment.

"This is supposed to be one of the most spectacular sunrises on the earth. You don't want to turn into a frozen popsicle before you get to see it, do you?"

"I suppose not." She resisted the urge to snuggle her back closer to his chest. "Thank you."

He shrugged against her. "It's the least I can do. After the way you helped me the other night."

"Ah, you mean your evasion mission."

"It seems to have worked. Ms. Campbell seems to be wrapped around one of the other groomsmen at this very moment."

The way he was wrapped around her. "I'm sure she's simply trying to stay warm too."

"No doubt."

"She wasn't terribly happy with me that night after the luau when she came in," she told him, remembering the slamming of the suite door as she was brushing her teeth. Rita had felt somewhat guilty. She had nothing against Tessa; they'd actually been study partners for some core subjects back in school. "I got a bit of the silent treatment before we both retired for the night."

"I think she may forgive you pretty soon. If she hasn't already. Judging by how she's moved on and all."

"I hope so. She did say one thing that night though."

She felt his warm breath against her cheek when he responded. "What's that?"

"She mentioned being surprised you were alone to begin with."

"So you guys were talking about me."

Uh-oh. "I won't deny it. Tessa said there had to be a story to explain why you were here stag at your own sister's wedding."

"Not really. Just one argument too many. Considering it wasn't a serious relationship, this seemed as good a time as any to end things. Rather than pretend during an island wedding full of activities. Some things simply aren't meant to be."

"I see. So it was mutual?" Rita wanted to bite her tongue as soon as the words left her mouth. She was giving Clint every indication that she was interested in his personal life. When she had absolutely no reason to be. No *logical* reason. She had to be careful. It would behoove her to be more guarded about such things, now that she was single again. "I'm sorry. It's not really any of my concern."

He remained silent at that. A strong gust of wind suddenly whipped through the air and she reflexively nestled closer against him.

Mistake.

A current of electricity shot through her core. She was no prude; she'd been a married woman for heaven's sake. But being in Clint's arms was triggering a reaction she hadn't been expecting. One she couldn't relate to anything else.

She'd loved Jay. She really had. But she couldn't recall feeling an electric jolt in the pit of her stomach when he held her. Not like she was feeling this very moment.

"What about you?" Clint surprised her by asking.

"Me?"

"If I recall, Lizzie mentioned a couple of years back attending a traditional Indian wedding. I believe you were the bride."

"You would be correct."

"But you're here alone."

"It's like you said, some things simply aren't meant to be."

He was silent for a moment, then she heard him take a deep breath. "I'm sorry."

"For?"

She felt his arms tighten around her. Sympathy? She certainly hoped not. "It's one thing when a short-term, frivolous relationship ends. A marriage failing is a bit more life altering."

He had no idea. The end of her marriage was only part of it. Someone like Clint would never understand. He could never grasp how someone like her had never truly felt untethered. She was a daughter first. Then a wife. Her identity had always been tied to someone else.

She'd never felt like just Rita. Just herself.

No, she wouldn't even bother to explain. There would be no point.

"Was it one particular thing?" he asked above her head. "That led to your split, I mean."

His question wasn't as simple as it appeared on the surface. There were so many particular smaller issues. And one major underlying one. "Yes. And no." It was the most honest answer she could give.

"So you're saying it's complicated."

She could repeat her answer and be correct once again. "Only in that we wanted different things." Things she was in no way ready for. While Jay wanted them more than anything. Things like a family, children, a house. Things she wouldn't be able to walk away from and then it would be too late, making her stay for all the wrong reasons. "So yes, in that way it was complicated."

She couldn't get into any more than that, despite Clint's charm and the effect he was having on her when he held her this way. How could she explain something that she hadn't fully grasped herself yet?

And what about him? What exactly was his story? The way he'd talked earlier about his relationships sounded as if he expected them all to come with predetermined expiration dates.

She was trying to come up with a way to ask when a small sliver of reddish-orange light broke through the surface of the clouds in the distance. The sun was finally beginning to rise. A collective hush suddenly fell over the murmuring crowd. In slow motion they all watched as more and more streaks of breathtaking hues of red broke over the sky.

The scene took her breath away. Any hint of her earlier

cold or discomfort was completely forgotten. This view, this image would stay with her forever.

As would the thought that she was unexplainably happy that she'd been able to share it with Clint. While he held her in his arms.

The woman pulled at him like a magnet. Clint had fully intended to stay away from her on this trip. He really had. But then he'd seen her shivering in the dark with nothing but a flimsy, hooded sweatshirt and some type of thin fleece headband. The windchill up here had to be below freezing at the least. How was he supposed to walk away?

He wasn't made of stone after all.

Now he was beyond happy that he'd ignored the warnings in his head and gone to her. He couldn't imagine taking in this scene any other way. Tomorrow he might think differently. But right now, watching the brilliant colors slowly explode across the dawn sky above the crater, he was more content than he could ever remember.

Spiritual. It was the one word that came to mind. The most spiritual thing he'd experienced in all his years. And he had the pleasure of doing so with the extraordinary woman who happened to be in his arms.

A few feet away, an elderly gentleman with long white hair dressed in traditional native garb began chanting.

"It's a prayer and salutation to the sun," Rita whispered below his ear. The chanter's deep, rich voice added yet another magical element to the extraordinary moment. Clint allowed himself to simply relax, to simply take in the majesty surrounding him. Rita was breathing steadily and deeply against his chest.

They remained that way several moments even after the sacred chant ended.

"That was amazing." Rita finally broke the silence but

made no effort to move out of his embrace. And he couldn't remember when he'd ever felt so at peace, so serene.

The sound of someone clearing their throat behind them made them both jump. Clint turned to see his sister and her groom both staring with their mouths agape. Reluctantly, he pulled his arms away and let Rita go.

"I was really cold," Rita offered by way of explanation.

Lizzie blinked, then focused her intense gaze on her brother's face.

"She was shivering."

"Right" was Lizzie's only response but she dragged out the word so long it was almost comical. His soon-to-be brother-in-law made a dramatic gesture of coughing into his hand in order to hide his laugh.

Rita adjusted her top and stepped away. "That was quite an amazing sight to behold."

Clint had to tighten his fists to keep from reaching for her again. As silly as that notion was under their current circumstances. But he couldn't deny that his fingers itched to do that very thing.

"Uh-huh. Sure was." Lizzie's double meaning was as clear as the new dawn sky behind them. He'd have to set the record straight with her at some point. Explain to her that he had no long-term sights on her school friend.

She really should know him better than that.

"So anyway," Jonathon finally said, "there's some hot chocolate and coffee waiting on the tour bus. The van with all the bikes is up here now. We'll be heading out shortly to ride." He tugged on his fiancée's hand. Lizzie finally moved and they both walked away.

Though Lizzie shot one more questioning look at him as they left.

"I'd almost forgotten," Rita said, not meeting his gaze. "About the biking."

Part of this excursion was to be a group bike ride back

down the mountain. Apparently, it was the thing to do when you came up here.

"All part of the adventure."

Rita bit down on her lip and glanced up at the road ahead. "I might have to skip that part of the experience."

That took him aback. "Whatever for? Can you ride?"

She nodded. "Yes, of course. But I've never actually ridden down a high, rugged mountain before."

He shrugged. "I'm guessing very few of us have."

She didn't respond.

"What will you do instead?" he asked her, suddenly beyond disappointed that she wouldn't be participating.

"I'll just ride down with the driver in the van."

He gave her a shrug. "I'm going to skip riding too then. I'll just drive down in the van with you."

"What? No. Why would you do that?"

"Well, I'm certainly not going to let you sit by yourself in the back of a van following the rest of us down as we ride. It's just not in my nature."

Her eyes clouded with concern. "I don't want to be the reason you miss out on this, Clint."

"Then reconsider. Come on, it will be fun."

Rita glanced at the road once more, apprehension clear in her expression.

"We'll go nice and slow."

She let out a deep sigh and rubbed her forehead. "All right. If you insist."

Clint couldn't help his smile of relief. He really hadn't been looking forward to the idea of being stuck in a van as everybody else got to enjoy the outdoor weather and mountainside sights. Not to mention, he figured he could use the physical exertion right about now.

Clint seemed to be exerting himself far more than the rest of them. Rita glanced behind her to check him once again.

He was barely keeping up with the group. She was glad he'd talked her into going. She wasn't even sure why she had hesitated back there. Bike riding wasn't a new experience for her. And she'd always been pretty adventurous. Though something had changed within her since the divorce, something that made her second-guess her decisions as well as her abilities. She'd have to work on that.

Now there was no denying that the fresh air and the physical activity were serving to clear her head and invigorate her spirit.

But Clint seemed to be struggling behind her. Despite pedaling furiously and clearly straining, he seemed to consistently lag behind them all.

That made no sense whatsoever; the man was clearly fit. He appeared that way. Though, she'd have to admit, she'd seen more than her fair share of large muscular dogs like pit bulls and Dobermans who lacked stamina and energy.

Great. Now she was comparing the man to various breeds of canine.

Still, it was quite surprising. Especially considering they were going downhill and all. He didn't strike her as the type to fall behind when it came to anything. Let alone a physical activity. But hey, looks are deceiving. She knew that firsthand.

He'd certainly felt lean and muscular earlier this morning. Her mind darted back to the feeling of being held in his arms, snuggled against his chest. *Stop it.* Blinking the images away, she took the next turn perilously close to the edge. She didn't dare look over the side. They'd been given a full safety and precaution lecture, but nothing could have adequately prepared her for just how harrowing a ride this would be.

She really just needed to focus on her own ride and staying steady on the path.

A gurgle of laughter floated over to her from the front

of the procession. She looked ahead to where Lizzie and Jonathon rode next to each other. They'd made some kind of game of trying to grab each other's hands, then letting go and quickly pedaling back to single file when the path became too narrow. How long the guide would let that continue was anybody's guess. But they seemed to be having a delightful time of it in the meantime.

Had she and Jay ever been that playful with each other? Had they ever shared such boisterous laughter? If so, she'd be hard-pressed to recall it.

That's what happened when you married out of a sense of loyalty rather than any kind of love or affection.

Clint had brought up her wedding. She hadn't thought about that day in ages. Though it had been a joyous occasion, she felt as though she'd sleepwalked throughout the entire ceremony and the events leading up to it. Her father had seemed so happy. Her mother the same simply by extension. A description that could pretty much summarize her parents' whole relationship.

Their families having been friends for years—since her father had immigrated—she and Jay had been thrust together pretty much their whole lives. He'd actually declared to her in third grade that he would take her as his wife. She'd stuck her tongue out at him.

And though her mom was as American as apple pie, Anna Paul had never questioned any of it. Again, another depiction that could define her mother's marriage to her father.

A grunt of noise behind her pulled her out of her thoughts. With a start, she realized it was Clint still straining to keep up. He'd broken out in a sheen of sweat. Was he ill?

A flash of concern shot through her chest. What if he wasn't feeling well? Maybe he was coming down with something. Luckily, the guide chose that moment to yell out that they'd be stopping for a water break at a rest area a few yards away.

Moments later, they had come to a complete stop.

"Are you okay?" she asked Clint when he finally pulled up next to her and disembarked from the bike.

"Must be the mountain air." He was as red as the sunset they'd just witnessed. "The brochure mentioned it might affect some people more than others."

"Maybe you should stop. Ask the guide to have the van come for you." No man she knew would go for that. They would take it as an insult to their very masculinity. But it was worth a try to make the suggestion.

"Maybe." To her surprise, Clint didn't immediately shoot down the idea.

Glancing over at his bike, Rita realized there was some kind of lever along the rails of his rear tire. One that wasn't there on hers. "Something's not right," she told him.

"What do you mean?"

"My back wheel looks different than yours."

He examined his bike, then studied hers. "You're right. Your bike's been running smooth?" he asked.

She nodded in reply. He bent and flipped some sort of gage on his back wheel. Something snapped in response on the bike's handlebars. Right then the guide came to stand next to them.

"Sorry, man. Mechanical malfunction. Looks like your brake was engaged this whole time."

Rita couldn't help it. Though she almost hated herself, she just couldn't help the bubble of laughter that erupted from deep within her chest.

"Oh, you think that's funny, do you?" Clint asked. But he wasn't trying to hide his own smile when he said it.

"I'm afraid so. I think it's hilarious."

Again surprising her, he threw his head back and laughed out loud himself.

Clint cursed out loud through his laughter. "Thank goodness you came along. Or I would have struggled with an engaged brake the whole time." He shook his head. "I can't believe it didn't occur to me to check that."

So the man could laugh at himself and didn't consider himself infallible. It was a novel experience for Rita to witness. She'd thought earlier about the lack of laughter between her and Jay. And here was yet another complete difference between the man before her now and the man she'd married. Jay would be taking the guide's name and information, making plans to call his superiors to complain about the oversight.

Enough. This wasn't some kind of schoolyard competition. She had to stop comparing this man she barely knew to her ex-husband.

Jay had been good to her. Even if some of his actions had felt patronizing and made her feel small, his heart had always been in the right place.

She really had no right to judge him so unfairly. Especially not after what she'd done to the man.

CHAPTER FOUR

TESSA WAS ALREADY in the shower when Rita got back to their room. And by the sound of things, she wasn't in there alone. Rita had to smile. Was there ever a time she herself had been that carefree? That determined to just go after what she wanted and just enjoy her life?

No, she never had. Maybe someday she'd reach that level of lightheartedness. Considering the way she'd grown up, it was going to take some time and some work.

As if on cue, her cell vibrated where she'd thrown it on the bed. A picture of her mother holding their shih tzu appeared on the small screen.

Opening the glass sliding door and stepping onto the balcony, she clicked on to answer the call. "Hey, Ma."

A family with three small children was playing some kind of tossing game in the yard right below their room. The gleam of the ocean shimmered in the distance. She tried to focus on those images rather than the expression that was sure to be on her mother's face an ocean away.

"Hello, dear. I finally got tired of waiting for you to call." Of course, the impetus was on her to be the first one to call. As always.

"Things have been very busy. Lizzie's packed a lot of activities into the schedule."

Rita could hear the notes of some bouncy hip-hop tune

in the background. For as straitlaced and matronly as her mother was, she had some very eclectic tastes in music. Much to her father's chagrin. In so many ways, they were complete opposites. Maybe that was the secret of their success.

"How is dear Lizzie?" her mother asked. "Any wedding jitters?"

Rita thought about their playfulness during the bike ride. On the contrary, Lizzie and Jonathon seemed like they couldn't wait to tie the knot. "I haven't noticed any."

"Good. That's good to hear. I hope the two of them can make it work." The words *unlike you* hung unspoken in the air.

Rita bit back the response that popped into her head. Lizzie and Jonathon were so very different than she and Jay. For one, they'd actually chosen each other. "I think they will. All signs point in that direction."

"Good," her mom repeated. An awkward silence ensued in which all Rita could hear were some very racy lyrics about going to "da club." There was no way her father was home. Else he was on a completely different floor or puttering around in his garden outside.

"Jay came by the other day," her mother suddenly announced. "He asked about you."

A pang of sensation stirred within her chest. They had no business being married, but she missed Jay. She really did. One of the hardest things about the divorce was the fact that she'd felt like she lost a lifelong friend. Maybe over time they could become close that way once more. Another endeavor that was sure to take time, if it was possible at all.

"How is he doing?"

"He still seems quite morose, to be honest." A heavy pause followed which Rita figured she was supposed to fill. But what could she say to that? They'd gone over this before. The notion that perhaps Rita had been too hasty to end her marriage. Jay had pleaded with her to keep trying, claimed complete shock that she was ready to walk out. But she'd held firm. No reason to draw out the inevitable after all. Her husband showed no inclination to change. And she didn't know how.

Finally, her mother relented. After a long sigh, she continued, "His research is going well, at least. Said he was close to another patent. I get the impression he's thrown himself deeply into his work."

That made sense. There were times she hadn't seen him for days at a time. He'd disappear into the lab early and come home late. A slight wave of guilt hit her when she recalled how she'd mostly felt relieved those days, relishing the solitude and having the town house to herself. Jay had a very large personality. When he was around, there was no solitude to be found. "I'm glad he's doing well. On the professional front anyway. I know the rest will follow for him."

She heard her mother take a deep breath. "And what about you, love? Are you really doing well?"

She was. This trip away was exactly what she needed. Seeing Lizzie again, enjoying the majestic beauty of the island. Simply being in an environment so different from home, not to mention all the activities. She really hadn't anticipated enjoying a group bike ride down a rugged mountain. Clint had convinced her otherwise.

Clint. She couldn't deny she was enjoying his company. Perhaps more than she should have.

"Yes, Mom. I'm having a lot of fun here."

"Of course, you are, dear. But what about after?"

"After?"

"You're in paradise now, sweetie. What happens when you return and reality descends? I don't want you to regret your decisions. Now that it's too late to rectify any mistakes."

There was that word again. Some of the most important decisions she'd made in her life were ones her parents considered as her mistakes.

Rita rubbed her temple. Was it too much to ask just to live day by day? Did she always have to be focused on some future point off in the distance? "I'll be too busy to wallow, Ma. I have a lot to do when I get back."

For one, she'd have to look for another job. Perhaps she might finally find somewhere she could really make a difference. Although she loved the animals, she'd had her fill of the bureaucracy and constant focus on profit margins at her last position. She'd only taken the job to make Jay happy. Well, as happy as he was going to be when it came to her career.

"Your dad's threatening to retire. Again." Her mom suddenly changed the topic.

Speaking of people she missed. Though she'd seen her father plenty of times since the divorce, there seemed to be so much emotional distance between them now. Even more so than usual. "I'll believe it when I see it," she responded with a smile. Dad made that claim once or twice a year. Usually around wintertime, when he dreaded facing driving in the snow to his downtown office.

"He misses you." Rita sucked in a breath at her mother's words. The woman had always been very astute. And straightforward.

"I miss him too, Ma." She felt her eyes moisten with tears as she continued, "But I know I've disappointed him. Again."

"Oh, honey. He's your father."

"I think we'll just need some time. To find our way again with each other. I'm sure it will happen."

Sometimes, it was best just to tell her mother what she wanted to hear.

* * *

Clint watched from his balcony as a solitary figure made her way toward the water, strolling slowly, her head down. Even from this distance, there was no mistaking who it was. Rita. The slump of her shoulders and the drag in her step told him she wasn't exactly enjoying her slow walk along the beach. Something was on her mind.

It was none of his business really. This was one of the rare nights that Lizzie and Jonathon didn't have anything scheduled on an otherwise ridiculously packed itinerary. Good thing too. The excursion planned for tomorrow was a whole-day event: a ride down the Road to Hana, which apparently took several hours as a driver took them around the island and showed them many of the pertinent sights. So tomorrow would be completely spent.

And Clint had work to do. He'd already been away from his office for two straight days; there were a slew of emails waiting for him and several items that needed the CEO's signature.

The wise and prudent thing for him to do would be to pour himself a beer from the minibar, order some room service for dinner and fire up his laptop. But his eyes couldn't tear away from where Rita stood off in the distance. An unfamiliar tingle stirred in his chest. If he didn't know better, he'd think it was concern. Which made absolutely no sense. Aside from Lizzie, he'd never really been personally concerned about anyone's emotional state. Sure, he cared for his employees and made sure to take care of them, particularly the more loyal workers who had been with him from the beginning. It was those employees who deserved some of his attention right now in the form of email responses and returned phone calls. He was too hands-on not to be missed when away from the office.

Plus, as sweet as she was, he really had no business worrying about Rita Paul's mood.

He tore his gaze away from where she stood and turned back into the room. As soon as he booted up his computer, several messages scrolled across the scene. Clint rubbed his eyes. Yeah, it would be a long night of correspondence and directives. So he had to focus, which meant he had to keep his mind from drifting. Without meaning to, he looked up to glance toward the beach once more.

She'd moved. He could no longer see her. Had she gone back to her room? Walked farther along?

Damn. It didn't matter. He had work to do.

Clint clicked on the first message and began to type.

She had to get used to this, Rita thought as she perused the menu she'd been handed. Being a single woman now, she had to get used to dining alone. What better time to start than a beachside seafood restaurant on exotic Maui?

At the table next to her sat a family of five with three young children. As frenzied as the parents looked, they posed a perfect picture of a happy unit. As the mom explained something on the menu to her preteen, her husband slowly rubbed a gentle hand down her back. True affection was clear in his absentminded movements. Rita forced herself to look away. Perhaps she'd have that someday. But that day was far-off.

As painful as it was, moments like this made her realize how right she'd been to end her marriage. She and Jay would never have been that couple sitting next to her right now. He may have loved her, but Jay wasn't the type to ever display affection in public. It seemed such a small thing, but small things sometimes made all the difference. She hadn't been able to explain that to him, or her parents for that matter, without feeling like she was being petty and childish. Rita thought back to the phone call earlier with her mother. Maybe they would never understand. Her ex-husband certainly didn't seem to still.

She found herself eavesdropping on the conversation at the next table. Having settled in with their appetizer as their children colored with fat, stubby crayons, the parents were now discussing the prospect of moving to a larger house. Rita watched as the man listened intently to his wife's thoughts and concerns on the matter. He reassured her they would make the correct decision when the time came. She responded with a small kiss to his cheek.

So different from any major discussion she'd ever had with Jay. In fact, when they were first engaged, her ex-husband had declared unequivocally that he had no intention of moving out of the condo he rented close to the university where he worked. It was understood that she would have to make herself at home at his place. She'd just accepted it. Then she'd been miserable. There'd been nothing overtly wrong with the place, but Rita had never felt like she truly belonged there. Her attempts at redecorating had been met with resistance and resentment.

Jay liked his environment the way it was.

In retrospect, she had to admit that perhaps she should have held her ground, tried harder to exert her desires. But it hadn't seemed worth the effort. Her heart was never quite in it. Pulling her thoughts away from the past and from the conversation she had no business listening in on, she took a sip of her lemon water. No, her marriage had never been a true partnership, not like the one sitting at the next table anyway.

Was there a chance she would find that someday? Would she even have the gumption to risk her heart again? An unbidden image of chestnut-brown eyes and a dashing smile clouded her vision. Rita made herself blink it away and focus on her menu.

She honestly didn't know the answers. In the meantime, it looked like she'd be dining alone for a while.

* * *

He absolutely had to stay here and get some more of these emails answered. Clint stared at the screen until the words became a jumble of blurry swirls in his vision.

Focus.

He'd barely gone through a dozen or so messages. He had no business wondering about Rita and where she'd been heading. He absolutely could not go find her. It made no sense. And he was all about being logical and sensible.

So why did he suddenly stand and grab his shirt and sandals rather than clicking on the reply button of the message he'd been staring at for the past twenty minutes? Why was he out the door, making his way downstairs and outside before he could give it any more thought?

It didn't take long to spot her; she hadn't been moving very quickly after all. Clint watched as she went up to the maître d' podium of an outdoor restaurant, then was led away to one of the outer tables.

She sat down with a smile to the waitress, opened up her menu and seemingly ordered a drink. In a sea of tables, Rita sat by herself. When her drink arrived—some fruity concoction with an umbrella—she just stared at it for several moments. She was the only one eating solitary.

Damn.

This was silly. He couldn't very well just stand here staring at her any longer. How much time had passed anyway? Without allowing himself any further debate, he made his way to where she sat.

So deep in thought, she didn't seem to even hear him approach.

"A lei for your thoughts?" he said, clearly startling her out of her reverie.

"Clint." She gave him such a welcoming, radiant smile that it almost had his knees buckling with pleasure. Then she tucked a strand of hair that was blowing in her face behind her ear. It immediately escaped again from the wind. "I just thought I'd grab a bite."

"Are you waiting for someone?" he asked, though he was pretty sure he knew the answer.

She shook her head. "No, it's just me. What about you?" she asked. "How did you decide to come here?"

He didn't have it in him to lie. "I saw you out here and thought maybe you could use some company. You seem a bit…melancholy. If you don't mind my saying."

She didn't answer right away, instead turning to stare off into the distance. "You're a very observant gentleman, Clint Fallon."

And she was downright beautiful. The sinking sun made her dark hair shimmer around her face; her lashes went on forever over piercing brown eyes. Clint had to suck in a breath and turn away to keep from staring at her.

"Have you eaten? I think I owe you a dinner," she suddenly proclaimed.

"Not yet. But I don't see why you would owe me anything."

"You saved me from certain frostbite early this morning. Remember?"

He'd been right about what he'd witnessed from the balcony. She was definitely nursing some kind of hurt. Her tone sounded down and defeated.

He'd never been accused of being the most attentive listener, but he could certainly lend an ear when he needed to, when the situation called for it. He heard a clear calling right now.

"I don't typically turn down pretty ladies who want to feed me." He pulled out the chair across the table from her and sat down.

A smile tugged at her mouth. "Does that happen to you often?"

"Not often enough."

"I find that hard to believe."

She motioned to the menu that sat in front of him. "This place is supposed to be one of the best eateries in town. The concierge mentioned they have the best *hula* pies on the island."

"Moola pies? Sounds expensive."

Feeble a joke as it was, her smile grew wider. "*Hula* pies."

"What exactly is *hula* pie?"

"You'll have to experience it yourself."

"Thank you for the recommendation, ma'am. I look forward to it."

Sooner than he would have thought, the restaurant started to fill. They'd timed it right; the place was just on the verge of welcoming the evening dinner crowd and gradually becoming busier and busier.

In no time at all, almost every table was full and a line had formed outside the door all the way down to the beach.

"That was lucky. Timing it so that we don't have to wait for a table."

"If you're feeling lucky now, wait till you taste this pie." Her tone was whimsical but the merriment didn't quite reach her eyes.

What in the world could have brought her so down since their bike ride earlier today? He hoped she had grown comfortable enough with him to tell him whatever it was.

The waitress arrived to take their order. Clint ordered the *poke*, apparently some sushi dish that the menu said was the freshest this side of the sea, and a beer.

"I'll have the *hula* pie, please," Rita told her.

"Yes, miss. And for dinner?"

"I'm going with that as my dinner."

The waitress gave her an indulgent wink, then took their menus and left before returning with Clint's drink.

Clint chuckled. "Ice cream, chocolate, coconut and nuts. I suppose that covers most of the food groups."

"Sometimes a girl's just looking to have dessert."

"One of those afternoons?"

"You could say that."

"Please don't tell me my sister's pulling some bridezilla moves and hassling her bridesmaids."

She shook her head. "No, nothing like that. I haven't even seen Lizzie since this morning's bike ride."

"Phew, I didn't want to have to reprimand her at her own wedding."

She gave him a curious look at that statement, then reached for her cocktail. He tried not to focus too closely on her lips when she lifted the cherry and popped it in her mouth. "Just a phone call from back home. I let it affect me more than I should have."

"Must have been one heck of a phone call. You just ordered dessert for dinner. Not that there's anything wrong with that."

"There are people who might not agree with you on that point. They'd see plenty wrong with it."

The ex. She had to be talking about him. Perhaps that had been who her misbegotten call had been with. He clenched his fists on the table and had to take a swig of his beer. The idea that she stayed in touch still with her former husband left a bad taste in his mouth. But again, none of his business.

"Anyone in particular we're talking about?"

She took another sip of her drink, looked out over the horizon at the setting sun. Though the scene held no comparison to the breathtaking visual of the sunrise they'd watched this morning, the sheer magnitude of vibrant color in the Hawaiian sky was a sight to behold.

"Could easily apply to several people actually. People who are very focused on rules and structure and propriety."

Oh, yeah. She definitely had something on her mind. "Nothing wrong with rules and structure," he told her. "As long as those rules serve a purpose and make sense."

"I suppose you're right."

"I think so. I wouldn't be able to run an international construction firm if I didn't adhere to some type of structure and follow it rigidly."

"Run a tight ship, do you?" She asked with a hint of a smile.

No doubt about it. Not when his reputation and livelihood were on the line. The slightest mistake could cost big. Both in terms of dollars and time. Not to mention, the risk to lives if proper safety protocols weren't followed. When it came to his company, Clint kept as much as feasible under his tight control. Down to the specific types of screws and nails to be used at all of his sites. "I have to run a tight ship. A lot can go wrong on a construction site. Especially when you're talking tall buildings. Can't leave anything to chance."

She chuckled at that and started fidgeting with her napkin. "You sound very much like someone else I know. That's a favorite phrase of his." Raising her glass in a mock salute, she cleared her throat. "You can't leave anything to chance." Her tone was exaggeratingly deep.

"Sounds like a wise man. Want to tell me who you might be referring to?" Though he could guess. It didn't take a mind reading ability to figure who she meant.

"I will tell you. Probably because I've had half of this very strong drink on an empty stomach."

He doubted the fruity cocktail—complete with a paper umbrella—could be that potent. She was clearly a lightweight. "Maybe you should slow down."

"I'm talking about my ex," she said, ignoring his warning. "More than once, he tried to teach me a lesson about why I should be more disciplined and not leave things to chance."

Taught her a lesson? The hair on the back of Clint's neck stood up as a bolt of fury shot through him. His vision blurred. If that pitiful excuse for a man had so much as harmed a hair on her, he'd make it a life goal to find him and do some score settling.

"Rita. Did he hurt you in any way?" he asked steadily through tightly clenched teeth.

She blinked. "What? No. That's not what I mean," she said with a dismissive wave of her hand.

Clint let out the breath that had caught in his throat. "Then what do you mean exactly? About teaching you a lesson?"

"Exactly that. Jay's a medical researcher at a prominent university. He's used to controlling every variable. I'm a bit more carefree. He simply took some pains to show me why his way was right and mine was foolish."

"I don't follow."

She leaned forward on the table, steepled her fingers. "There was the time we were grocery shopping. I walked away down another aisle. I left my purse in the cart. I knew exactly what I was going to get and where it was." She glanced off to the side, as if recalling the exact memory. "When I got back to the cart moments later, my purse was gone."

He was starting to see where this might be going. "Let me guess, he'd warned you repeatedly not to leave your bag unattended."

She raised her glass. "A toast to you for the right answer. I got a scathing lecture about how right he'd been. How reckless and senseless it was of me to walk away from the cart that held my wallet, my keys, my money."

All right. It sounded like it might have been harsh for

her to hear. But many husbands would have reacted the same way.

But Rita's hands were trembling as she recalled the story.

"I was panicked," she continued. "My phone, my license. Everything was in that bag."

"I guess he could have been a bit more understanding." Still, it hardly seemed like an unforgivable reaction. She had been rather careless to leave the purse unattended.

She laughed but it sounded less than jovial. "There's a surprise ending to this story."

"What's that?"

Her fingers tightened on the stem of her glass. "He's the one who'd taken it. He'd walked all the way back to the parking lot and to our car and thrown it in the trunk."

That *was* a surprise ending. Clint had definitely not seen that twist coming. Words failed him. Who would do something like that?

"What happened?" he finally managed to utter.

"After several minutes of panicked searching, during which he coldly stood by and watched by the way, I finally asked for his phone so I could notify the authorities about the theft of my personal belongings. That's when he finally told me he'd had it the whole time."

Clint downed the rest of his beer. He couldn't imagine doing such a thing to another person, especially someone he supposedly loved. It seemed so... *Petty* was the one word that came to mind.

"That was just one example," Rita added, polishing off her drink, as well.

"There was more?"

She nodded. "Little things. He insisted on being in charge of my online passwords because I didn't change them often enough. He kept asking how I planned to be a responsible mother one day if I couldn't keep track of little details such as security codes. So, ultimately, I decided that I wasn't even ready to be a wife. Let alone a mother."

Clint needed another drink. But the waitress was nowhere to be found. To think, this accomplished, intelligent, talented woman before him was thought to be careless and in need of strict guidance by the man she'd married.

"I had to walk away. The controlling became too much," she said on a sigh.

He couldn't help himself. He reached across the table and took her hand in his. "I'd say that behavior sounds a bit beyond controlling." Much more. In fact, the word *belittling* came to mind.

CHAPTER FIVE

HER HEAD POUNDED like a slow hammer when she awoke the next morning. There was a reason she generally tried to stay away from hard liquor. If she'd only stuck with her usual cabernet, she wouldn't be feeling so foolish this morning.

Though she couldn't bring herself to regret a single moment of it. Sitting there with Clint in that restaurant, she could almost pretend she was a regular young adult on an exciting date with a new man. Not a recent divorcée who was just sharing a meal with her friend's brother. Her friend's handsome, charming and beyond alluring brother.

A smile touched her lips when she thought of the joy that had flooded her chest when she'd looked up to find he'd followed her, that she wouldn't have to eat alone after all. A silly girlish giggle escaped her lips before she bit down on it. How foolish of her.

In any case, she should have definitely gone easier on the mixed drinks. But no, she'd had to indulge. And look where it had gotten her. She'd ended up letting her tongue loose and way oversharing with Clint Fallon. A man she had nothing in common with. A man she would probably never see again after this wedding was over.

And in the meantime, she had to spend a whole day with him and the rest of the wedding party in a large van as they traveled the Road to Hana.

He'd caught her at a vulnerable time, she thought as she summoned the elevator—this time unable to face the stairs—to take her down to the front entrance where the shuttle would be picking everyone up. Phone calls from her mother tended to put her in such a state. She'd simply meant to take a walk along the beach to shake off the doldrums of her conversation, then check out the restaurant she'd heard so much about since arriving.

But then he'd shown up.

Rita stepped into the glass elevator and watched the scenery outside as the unit began to descend to the first-floor lobby. There was no denying her immediate reaction upon seeing him last night though. There was no denying her reaction to him in general.

The truth was, a wave of pleasure had bloomed in her chest when she'd seen him arrive to eat with her last night. Electricity had crackled between them all during dinner, even after she'd overconfided.

And how foolish was that? They were from two different worlds. He'd accomplished so much and her life was in complete shambles. Before she could even think about any kind of attempt at a relationship, she had to repair everything that had gone so wrong these past couple of years.

Starting with repairing the relationship with her father.

The only sound thing to do today would be to avoid Clint Fallon altogether. She would appreciate the sights, take lots of photos, talk to everybody else and try to enjoy herself. With a sigh of relief about her decision, she stepped outside through the sliding doors of the front hotel entrance.

The bus was almost completely full by the time she got on. She passed Lizzie and Jonathon in the front row. They were too engrossed with each other to take any notice of her. Seat after seat was taken.

The only one she didn't see yet was Clint. Rita continued slowly making her way to the back of the bus. Tessa smiled at her from one of the middle seats, next to a groomsman Rita didn't know by name. Probably the shower buddy from the other night. Still no Clint. There was definitely a pattern. Every seat held a man/woman pairing. Looked like there was a lot of hooking up going on.

Oh, great, she could see where this was headed.

There were times Rita was sure the universe was simply laughing at her. This was clearly one of those times.

She found Clint in the final row. With the only open spot left on the bus next to him. He scooted over and gestured for her to sit. Like she had a choice. "Looks like everyone has paired up," he said as he scooted over. "Kind of leaves you and I as odd men out."

Which essentially had the effect of pairing them up as well, Rita thought, trying not to groan out loud.

So much for the Fallon-avoidance plan.

Within an hour, they'd reached their first stop. Somehow, the day had grown cloudy with a slight mist of rain. The change in weather did nothing to diminish the sight however. They were on top of a lookout that showcased several majestic waterfalls.

The pairing on the bus didn't disperse as everyone exited the vehicle. Several of the couples held hands. More than a few relationships had apparently formed over the short time they'd been in Hawaii.

She walked over to one of the railings and leaned on the metal, simply taking in the view. Sure enough, Clint appeared beside her within moments. He leaned over the banister, as well.

"If you want some alone time, just let me know."

She couldn't even be sure if that's what she wanted. Her emotions and feelings were just a mishmash of confusion right now.

"But it seems a shame not to share the beauty of this experience with someone else," Clint added.

He was right, of course. This was silly. They were both adults. They might even be considered friends.

She gave him a slight smile, not turning away from the view. "I thought maybe you'd be tired of my rambling. I did somewhat talk your ear off last night."

"Do you really believe that?"

No, she didn't. Clint was genuine and attentive. He'd listened to her and sympathized last night. Not once had she felt a hint of judgment on his part. Exactly what someone would want if they were looking for a confidant.

She hadn't realized how much she needed that, just to have someone listen. Without any criticism, unlike her parents whenever the matter came up. Her girlfriends were all too quick to try to reassure her that the divorce was for the best, just like Lizzie had the day of arrival. Hard to believe Clint Fallon was the first person to give her a chance to finally get some of the turmoil off her chest. It was more than just the drink. She'd found Clint surprisingly easy to talk to, to confide in.

Still, thinking back on the exchange now, she felt raw and exposed. "I didn't mean to share that much," she admitted.

He waited a while before answering. "I'm really glad you did."

Clint resisted the urge to gently nudge Rita's head onto his shoulder. She'd fallen asleep as they drove to their next stop on the tour. She didn't look terribly comfortable with her head bent at an odd angle against the seat. He wasn't sure how she'd react, given how regretful she seemed about their time together last night at dinner. She couldn't think he thought any less of her because of what she'd told him about her failed marriage. If anything, he'd been struck by her strength and resilience in the face of such a situation. Someone should have really told her that at some point.

He was spared further internal debate about moving her when they finally reached their next destination: one of the Seven Sacred Pools of 'Ohe'o. He gave Rita a soft tap on the shoulder to wake her up. She opened her eyes with a start.

"Sorry. But we're here. I didn't think you'd want to sleep through the Seven Sacred Pools visit."

Rubbing her eyes, she stood and stretched out her legs. The innocent gesture sent a bolt of awareness through him. He gave himself a mental snap. Resilient or not, the woman was reeling from a broken relationship. He had no business staring at and appreciating her legs. Shapely and alluring as they may be.

"Thanks. Guess I was more tired than I realized. Did I miss anything along the ride?"

Clint shook his head, then stood to join her in the aisle of the van. "Only an interesting dissertation about lava tunnels from our expert tour guide/driver. He seems to know quite a bit. Both about the geography and folklore. Said he was born and raised on Maui." Okay, he was clearly rambling. But they'd already had a few moments of awkwardness between them so far this morning. He found himself missing the easy camaraderie of the previous evening. It couldn't have been totally alcohol driven, could it?

"You'll have to fill me in on the rest at some point," she said as they exited the van.

This was one of the spots they'd been told to pack bathing suits for. A lush green mountainside with several small waterfalls surrounded a pool of crystal-blue water. It was apparently one of the most popular spots for tourists to take a dip in. A few of the visitors already there were jumping into the water off some of the lower cliffs.

"This is one of the seven legendary pools," their tour

guide and driver said to their quickly dispersing crowd, raising his voice to be heard. "It is said that a dip in these pools will lead to good fortune and the finding of true love." He scanned the wedding party. Several couples were already in the water, giggling and splashing around. Tessa had jumped onto her groomsman's back as he playfully ducked under the water to get her wet. Jonathon had his arms wrapped around Lizzie's waist as they waded into the pool.

"Then again, it looks like you all might not need it," the tour guide added with a light chuckle.

A heady idea suddenly occurred to Clint. He turned to Rita standing next to him. "Would you like to come with me?"

She gave him a questioning look. "To swim?"

"Sort of. I think we should try jumping off a cliff."

Rita was determined to make the best of the way this day was turning out. Clearly, she and Clint were the only people in the wedding party who hadn't hooked up, so to speak. Well, good for them. As for her, she was going to make the most of this adventure, enjoy the company of the man saddled with her for now and try to just enjoy herself in general.

Though she hadn't exactly planned to start with a jump into a deep pool of water off a rocky cliff. Some of which didn't seem terribly high, but still.

"Are you with me?" he asked her. "You can swim, right?"

"It's not the swimming part that I'm grappling with."

"Come on. It'll be fun. I'll lead the way and stay with you the whole time." With that, he took her hand and they started making their way along the slippery, wet rocks surrounding the edge of the water. She'd never seen such greenery, such lush plant life. She'd never cliff jumped before.

But despite her apprehension, she'd be a fool to miss out on any of this. If just for today, she was going to forget about the shambles her life had become, forget about the depressing phone call with her mother yesterday and try to fully immerse herself in this adventure.

To his credit, Clint kept to his word and steadied her the whole way up. If he would do a cliff jump with her, he'd probably follow her anywhere. Pretty soon, they found themselves perched on the precipice of a jutting boulder along the side of the mountain about ten feet above the water.

"Is this a good spot?" Clint asked.

"Well, I'm not going up any farther, if that's what you mean." Though now she was looking down, she wasn't quite sure even this was too high.

Clint chuckled. "We can jump in together, if you'd like," he said, taking her hand once more. Her fingers reflexively curled around his. She'd been trying not to look at him too closely after he'd taken his shirt off earlier. The man was fit. A solid chest, taught, defined muscles, skin already a deep rich tan.

"Are you having second thoughts about this?"

More like I'm having unwanted thoughts about you.

She shook her head. "I think maybe we should just jump before I start to though."

"You're sure you're comfortable in the water?"

"Oh, yes." The water part wasn't the issue. It was the whole launching herself off a cliff thing. How in the world had she allowed herself to get talked into this? Why did she get the impression she wouldn't even be attempting it if Clint wasn't by her side? And what exactly did that mean for her mental state when it came to him?

This was so not the time to contemplate it.

"In that case—" He didn't finish, just tugged her along with him as they both jumped off.

Rita felt herself hit the water with a resounding splash. Exhilaration pumped through her veins as she broke the surface, laughter erupting in her throat.

Clint still held on to her hand.

"That was amazing."

"Hope I didn't take you by surprise, tugging you in like that."

"Oh, but you did." She playfully splashed him. "And you don't regret it at all, do you?"

He laughed in return. "Figured you didn't need too much time to think about it."

She dived under the surface, allowing the coolness of the water to refresh her both in body and spirit. If she had to work hard to have fun and forget her troubles for a while, then so be it. Though she had to admit, having Clint around was making the endeavor easier than it otherwise would have been. Too easy.

All too soon, the guide signaled that their party should probably start toweling off and return to the van. Reluctantly, Rita followed as Clint guided her toward the edge of the pool and helped her out. Their guide handed them thick towels.

"Thanks for doing that with me." Clint rubbed the towel around his head to dry off his hair. The strands were a mess of spikes around his head when he was done. Somehow the look did nothing to diminish the rugged handsomeness of his face. The wetness turned his locks from a dark brown to jet-black that brought out the golden specks in his eyes.

Rita looked away and focused on getting herself dry. But she couldn't hide the shiver than ran over her skin, only partially due to the chill of being wet. The sun had poked through a thick cloud while they'd been swimming but it was still somewhat overcast.

"Here." Clint stepped over to her and draped his towel over her shoulders.

"Thanks—you keep helping me to stay warm, it seems." Not to mention, the exciting things he'd been convincing her to try. As if something happened to her cautious inhibitions around this man.

The clap of the guide to summon them cut off Clint's response. He followed her to the van and they both got on board.

"You may be wondering why these pools are full of fresh water when they touch the sea," the guide began, using a microphone to address his many passengers. Part of the experience of the tour was a continuing commentary about the island and the sites they were visiting. Rita found it charming. The driver was personable and well-spoken, a good fit for the job he was in. "There are many theories, some more scientific than others."

"We want to hear one of the nonscientific theories," Lizzie declared from the front and Rita saw Jonathon give her shoulders an indulgent squeeze. A collective shout of agreement chorused from the others.

"Anything for the customer," the guide said into his mic. "There's a particularly sad legend about a princess and her lost love."

Rita settled back into her seat; Clint's warmth next to her and the deep voice of the driver lulled her into a meditative state of relaxation that she more than welcomed.

The man proceeded to tell a wrenching story that had to be based on at least some truth—that thought made her heart ache—about a princess who fell deeply in love with one of her guards. But she was honor and duty bound to marry a prince from another neighboring native tribe, one her father had picked for her.

The princess turned her back on her true love in order to perform her expected duties and married a man she didn't care for. He turned out to be cruel and vicious. In a fit of rage and jealousy, he killed the princess when he thought she was being unfaithful. He had incorrectly mistaken one of her handmaidens for another man as both male and female islanders wore their hair long past their hips. Finding out about his error made him irrationally even angrier.

So just for good measure, he searched out the man who had first claimed the princess's heart and brutally murdered him, as well.

"So every night, the ghost of the poor princess sheds enough fresh tears into the pools to flood out all the salt water." With that, the guide rehung his mic into its slot on the dashboard.

A quietness settled over the cabin of the van. The overall mood had definitely turned to the somber side.

Rita knew it was simply a story, most likely based on generations of native folklore. But the lesson and theme was a universal one and she found herself instinctively nestling closer to the man sitting next to her.

"Next stop is Black Sand Beach." The driver's voice crackled through the vehicle's intercom system and pulled Rita out of her thoughts. She'd been thinking about the sorrowful story of the princess since they'd left the last location.

"Ready for the next adventure?" Clint asked as they pulled to a stop. Another breathtaking scene of visual magic greeted them when they disembarked.

A wide pathway led to a steep stairway that took them down to a beach unlike any she'd seen before.

The sand, the pebbles, the boulders that met the crashing waves were all completely black. As if some divine hand had taken a tub of ebony paint and brushed wide strokes over the entire area.

"Amazing, isn't it?" Clint asked her.

"I don't have the words." She turned to him. "Thank you for this. Really. I would have never seen any of this if it hadn't been for you. And Lizzie."

He ducked his head like a small boy almost. She'd embarrassed him. "More so Lizzie. She and Jonathon coordinated with a planner and booked every tour and excursion."

He wasn't going to take any of the credit, even if he was bankrolling the whole thing. As far as big brothers went, Lizzie had hit the jackpot.

"There's a cave over there." Clint changed the subject before she could say any more about his part in all the wonder they were experiencing. "I say we go explore."

Without waiting for an answer. He pulled her behind him and led her into the mouth of a cavern. Not that she would have said no in any case.

It was like stepping into another dimension. All the noises outside went suddenly mute. Other than the opening, the area around them was pitch-black. The walls shimmered with moisture. A sudden cold wetness ran over her sandaled feet. The unexpected sensation jolted her; she lost her balance and startled to topple backward.

A set of steel-hard arms immediately wrapped around her waist and pulled her upright. She found herself hauled against a hard, broad chest.

"We've got to stop meeting like this," Clint said hoarsely against her ear. The heat of his breath sent a tingle along her skin. It would be so easy to turn to him, to totally succumb to the warmth and security of his embrace.

"You seem to keep rescuing me. Starting at the airport."

She felt him chuckle more than she heard it. "You're hardly the type of woman who needs rescuing, Rita."

Did he really mean that? Did he see her that way? As someone strong? Independent?

She felt heady at the thought. So many times in her life, the people she loved the most made sure to point out all the ways she was *less*. So often, Rita had spent all her energy trying to simply prove them wrong. But this man before her now seemed to think otherwise, he seemed to see her as *more*. It was a new experience.

A peal of laughter from outside the cave spiked through the air and pulled her back to reality.

"We should go with the others," she said.

Clint hesitated a beat but slowly let her go. "Yeah, you're right."

Rita sucked in a breath of air as she followed and gave herself a mental shake. She had to keep her bearings about her. The exotic location and all the excitement was making her act with uncharacteristic recklessness. For one insane moment, she'd thought about kissing him. Her fingers went to her lips as she wondered what that might have felt like, what he might have tasted like.

No. She had to accept that this was part of some dreamlike fantasy that she was unlikely to encounter again. Reality would return soon enough and she had to be ready for it.

But she would never forget the things he'd said to her, the way he'd made her feel for the brief moment when it was just the two of them in this empty cave. She reached down and picked up one of the small black rocks from the ground. Turning it in the palm of her hand, she slipped it into the pocket of her jean shorts.

No, she would never forget standing in a tight, dark cave with Clint nor the feelings the close proximity elicited within her. But she wanted a memento nevertheless.

CHAPTER SIX

CLINT DESPERATELY WANTED a shower. Preferably a cold one. The colder the better. Then he was going to find an aged bottle of fine bourbon and spend the night on his balcony drinking and willing away the thoughts that were sure to plague him after the day he'd just spent.

With Rita.

He would have to try hard not to think about all the times her leg had brushed along his in the seat during the drive. All the times the car had gone around a curve and her delicious, supple body had slid up against him.

And he absolutely could not think about the way she'd felt in his arms after they'd jumped into the sacred pool together. She'd almost said no to that. Just as she'd originally balked at the bike ride. Rita must have taken quite a hit to her confidence these past few months. She just needed a nudge to show her how capable and competent she was. A small hint of pride sparked in his chest that he'd been the one she'd allowed in enough to do so.

He'd wanted so badly to kiss her in that secluded cave. He could imagine even now how she would taste.

It was going to be a hell of a night.

Right now, they were all spilling into the lobby after several hours spent seeing the sights and attractions along the Road to Hana. It had been a long day. Fun but tiring. The kind of day that would normally end for him with a

cold drink in his hand and a warm body in his bed. An unbidden image of dark chocolate eyes and silky black hair
popped into his mind before he pushed it away.

He'd had way too much fun with Rita. Every stop made
more enjoyable with her accompanying him. So much so
that he didn't want it to end. But it would have to. If she
was anyone else, he'd ask her to join him on that balcony.
To share that drink with him and let the rest of the evening
take its natural course.

But no. Not this time. Not with this woman.

He didn't do long-term relationships and she wasn't the
kind to have a fling with. Especially considering she was
still licking her wounds after a recent divorce.

Oh, and there was also that whole thing about her being
a close friend of his younger sister's. There were all sorts
of ways a careless move with Rita could get messy and
complicated.

Logic dictated that he simply bid her good-night and
hope he'd see her again tomorrow morning. He turned
to do just that but was abruptly cut off by Lizzie's angry
shriek from across the lobby.

"How could you say something like that?" she demanded
of her fiancé, her cheeks blazing red with fury. "You can
be such an ass sometimes."

"What did you just call me?" For his part, Jonathon
looked equally as enraged.

"You heard me."

Clint debated going over there to pull one or the other
to the side. They'd started to attract the attention of other
guests. The night manager behind the desk looked as if he
was trying to decide the same thing. The man had gone
pale and swallowed hard.

"I would hate to have to burden you with an ass for a
husband," Jonathon fired back.

Lizzie's eyes narrowed on Jonathon's face. "What's that

supposed to mean? What exactly is it that you're trying to say?"

Clint uttered a curse under his breath. He really wished she hadn't asked him that. Jonathon's reply was exactly what he'd feared it might be.

This did not bode well.

"Maybe this is a mistake, Lizzie," Jonathon bit out through clenched teeth. "Maybe we should call off the whole thing."

Lizzie's gasp of horror was audible; she visibly bit back a sob. Clint started forward but felt a small hand grab him about the wrist. He turned to see Rita shaking her head slowly at him, a clear warning in her eyes.

His sister brushed past him as she fled the lobby. Jonathon stomped off in the opposite direction, leaving everyone else in the lobby staring agape.

Several bridesmaids and groomsmen turned to him, as if awaiting some sort of explanation. Like he had any idea what had set the whole argument off. Last he'd seen, the two had been all over each other on the bus.

"Show's over, folks," he said to the collective crowd. Several moments passed but eventually, one by one, everyone started to disperse.

All except for Rita.

She cleared her throat next to him. "I hope you understand why I stopped you from going to them."

He sighed. "Yes. You were right. Nothing would have been gained by me getting in the middle of that." He turned to look her straight in the eye. "I owe you a thank-you for averting it." He could have very well made things much worse. Though it looked bad enough already.

"They probably both just need some time," Rita said. "Weddings can be really stressful. Once they've had a chance to cool off, I'm sure they'll both be ready to make up."

He certainly hoped so. Otherwise, he'd have a huge

mess on his hands. All the pending arrivals would need to be notified. Contracts would need to be canceled. There was no way he'd see any kind of refund for anything. Not at this late stage.

Not that any of that mattered. Lizzie would be miserable and that tugged at his heart. She deserved to be happy.

The manager appeared by them, his cheeks a slight pink. "Any way I may be of service, Mr. Fallon?"

"Yes, please. Send a bottle of your house merlot and some snacks to my sister's room. Please add a card that says she knows where to find me if she needs."

"Right away, sir."

Clint turned to see Rita eyeing him, a curious glint in her expression. "What?" he asked.

She shook her head. A soft smile graced her lips. "I think you could use a drink yourself. Can I interest you in joining me for one?"

All his earlier intentions of avoidance fled in that very instant. Nothing in the world could have possessed him to turn her down in that moment, not when she was looking at him like that.

"I'd be very interested," he told her, ignoring the cry of warning in his head.

The moon cast silver light on the sand next to their table at the outdoor bar of the resort. Foamy waves crashed against land a few feet away from where they sat. Rita ran her finger around the rim of her wineglass. She didn't really want the drink, felt tired down to her bones after the day they'd just had.

There was no denying that Lizzie and Jonathon's argument had shaken her. They'd seemed so happy together just a few short hours ago. The thought of the two of them breaking up just before their wedding was almost too much to bear. There was no way she would be able to fall asleep with all that on her mind.

Plus, she had to admit she didn't want to say goodbye to Clint just yet. There was nothing scheduled for tomorrow. No excursions, no meals with the wedding party.

She realized she dreaded the idea that the whole day might go by without seeing him. That thought sent a surge of guilt through her chest. She should be worrying about her friend and the possibility her engagement may have ended just days before she was due to be married. Instead, here Rita sat, overly concerned about spending time with that friend's brother.

What was it about this particular man that called to her so strongly? Her friends had warned about being on the rebound and falling too quickly for someone. But this didn't feel like a rebound scenario. Not that she could really know for sure. All of this was so new to her.

She hadn't really dated anyone seriously. And as soon as she was old enough, her father had subtly pushed her toward Jay in so many nuanced and not-so-nuanced ways.

If ever there was someone who should tread carefully when it came to the opposite sex, she would be the poster child.

"I wonder what triggered that whole thing," Clint said after taking a small sip from his drink. The thick amber liquid in his glass told her it was something strong which would probably make a lightweight like her gag if she tried it.

"Lizzie and Jonathon's argument, you mean?"

He nodded. "I'm guessing it was something she was being stubborn about. She can be a little self-centered." He sighed and looked out toward ocean. In the distance the water looked as black as the cave they'd been in earlier. The cave where she'd fallen into Clint's strong arms when he'd caught her before she could fall.

Don't go there.

"I blame myself for that," he added. "For how stubborn and self-centered my little sister can be."

"I think you're giving yourself too much credit. Or fault, in this case."

He shrugged. "Maybe. But I was the one responsible for her."

"You're not that much older than her, Clint."

"That may be so. But after our parents died, there was no one else."

Rita knew a bit about their struggles as teens after the passing of their mom and dad. They'd been sent to live with a maternal grandmother who was way past the age of being able to care for two grieving and active teenagers. Lizzie hadn't really talked about it much at school, but there'd been enough times when she'd opened up.

From what Rita understood, Clint had started working as soon as he was of age to help care for himself and his sister. By the time Rita had met her, Lizzie's brother was already on his way to becoming a multimillionaire tycoon with his own construction firm with satellites all over the nation.

Quite extraordinary if one thought about it.

"Oh, Clint," she began, unable to keep the sudden emotion out of her voice. "You had to grow up pretty fast, didn't you?"

He looked off into the distance toward the water. "Not by choice."

He was so wrong about that. "You did have a choice. You could have left Lizzie to her own devices. Or tried to get your grandmother to step up."

He laughed at the idea. "Yeah. That wasn't going to happen. It was clear within months of us moving in with her."

"What do you mean?"

"Nothing specific. Just that money was always tight.

My parents didn't exactly save for a rainy day. Too busy spending it all on their travels and adventures. What little they left, my grandmother put away. Never let us touch it. We were in a new school, the kids ready to pounce at our clear disadvantages. The girls were particularly hard on Lizzie. For having to wear the same clothing and shoes to school almost every day."

"What did you do?"

He rubbed a hand down his face. "It's not important."

She leaned closer across the table. "Please tell me."

He hesitated so long, Rita thought he might not answer. Finally, he let out a deep sigh. "What could I do? I got several odd jobs so that we could have some kind of spending money. It wasn't much, just tips from busing tables at a restaurant and lawn mowing money. But it was something."

She thought of the boy he must have been, the sheer effort and discipline it must have taken for him to rise to where he was.

An urge to go to him, wrap her arms around his shoulders to comfort and soothe him almost overwhelmed her. She fought it. Hard.

"Thanks again for making sure I didn't get in the middle of their argument," he told her. "I wasn't even sure what I would have said. Or which one of them I would have said it to."

"It never works out well when a third party tries to intervene in a relationship."

Clint didn't say anything for several beats, just studied her face. "You sound like you're speaking from experience."

She allowed herself a laugh that held no real humor. "I suppose I am. To this day, both my parents seem to think I was the one who managed to ruin a good marriage. My mom is a bit more vocal about it but my father's feelings have been made clear, as well. Many times."

He reached for her hand across the table and held it tightly in his. The warmth of his skin sent a tingling sensation up her arm and straight to her heart. "I'm sorry you had to deal with that, Rita. You deserve so much more."

"Thank you for that." She ducked her head. "I wouldn't want either Lizzie or Jonathon to feel that way. Not even for a moment."

He gave her hand another squeeze before slowly letting it go.

"I just hope they figure it out soon." He let out a small chuckle and rubbed a hand down his face. "Who knows. Maybe this is happening because someone didn't pay heed to the curse our tour guide warned us about."

"Curse? I didn't hear anything about a curse." Just that terribly sad story about the heartbroken princess who'd tried to do right by her family and tribe only to be murdered.

Clint polished off his drink. "You might have been sleeping. He said nothing should be removed from any of the beaches we visited. Not even so much as a pebble. Or it would lead to doom and bad luck."

Rita felt a slow sinking in her chest. She'd taken that small rock. But surely it was just a silly superstitious story. She'd simply wanted a small souvenir.

Her small transgression could absolutely *not* be the reason the bride and groom were fighting at this very moment. And threatening to call off the wedding.

"It sounds like mere superstition," Rita said, voicing her thoughts, just as their waitress appeared. "Island folklore."

Their server smiled at them. "What folk story are you referring to?" The young lady asked with a friendly smile. Her name tag said Tanna in curly black lettering. "I come from several generations of native Hawaiians. I may know it."

"The superstition that says removing anything from Black Sand Beach will result in misfortune."

Tanna shook her head vehemently. "Oh, no. That one's real. Those beaches are sacred. Nothing is to be removed It's absolutely bad luck."

Rita felt her stomach drop. This was just silly. She hadn't even known she was doing anything wrong!

Tanna continued, "It is very easy to anger the spirits. Every pebble, every rock, every grain of sand is exactly where it is supposed to be. The slightest intentional human disruption will lead to disorder and make the spirits very unhappy."

"It's like a more eerie version of the butterfly effect," Clint told her.

"What's that?" Tanna wanted to know.

"There's a theory stateside that even the interruption of a butterfly flapping its wings can have a ripple effect and cause devastating changes throughout eternity."

Tanna studied his face for a moment. "That's heavy." Then she eyed them both before continuing, "Can I tell you two something?"

They both nodded as Tanna leaned in and lowered her voice. "This very resort was built on sacred ceremonial ground. My *tutu* keeps imploring me to quit this job. I could tell you stories from guests that would make you want to check out right now." A silence settled in the air between them. Suddenly, Tanna straightened. "Anyway, can I get you anything else?" she asked, indicating Clint's empty glass.

"No, thanks."

Great. Just great. Rita grabbed her still-full goblet and downed the glass of wine she suddenly decided she wanted. As if she didn't have enough on her mind. Now she had to worry that she may have inadvertently jinxed Lizzie's wedding.

A bubble of laughter crawled up her throat as she realized how silly that notion was. Curses. Spirits. She was essentially a scientist by trade, trained as an animal veterinarian. She didn't believe in anything so fanciful.

But a nagging sensation ran over the back of her neck as they stood to leave. She could have sworn the breeze picked up just then, enough to whip a nasty gust of sand into her face.

Rita punched her pillow for what had to be the hundredth time in the past two hours. The digital clock next to her bed read 3:10 a.m. Would she ever get any sleep tonight? As exhausted as she was, she desperately needed it. But what her muscles were craving, a sound night of rest, her mind just didn't seem to be in the mood for. And her mind could be quite stubborn.

Rather than allowing her to succumb to much-needed slumber, her mind insisted on replaying the scenes of the day on a repeat loop. Clint's smile as he pulled her off the cliff to jump with him. The way he pointed out the glorious mountains in the distance during the drive. How he'd held her in the cave. Each moment of remembrance sent a tingle of awareness down her spine.

Oh, and there was also that thoughtful, kind gesture he'd made to his sister when he'd sent her room service after the fight. Not to mention, all that he'd shared with her about the difficulties he and Lizzie had endured growing up.

She had to stop thinking about him.

Only when she forced her mind away from the enigmatic man who seemed to be haunting her thoughts, it turned to a disturbing mishmash of angry spirits and a crying dead princess.

Get a grip, already.

She tossed onto her back with a frustrated sigh and stared at the blinking light of the fire alarm on the ceiling. Tessa was breathing evenly in the twin bed next to hers. Surprisingly, her roommate had made it in alone and at a decent hour last night. The epic fight between bride and groom that everyone witnessed in the lobby no doubt cast a pall on more than one partygoer's plans.

She counted seventy-five blinks on the alarm, then forced herself to close her eyes. If sleep was going to elude her all night, then she'd just have to stare at the inside of her eyelids for a while. Only now she could see the blinking light in her head, so she started counting again. Some people counted sheep. She got enough of animals during her waking hours. She found other things to count. She made it to eighty this time when she felt the air shift at the foot of her bed. Now she was disrupting her roommate's sleep with her constant tossing and turning.

"Sorry, Tessa. Bad case of insomnia. It's why I'm moving around so much and rustling the sheets."

But the responding mumble from Tessa came from the other side of the room. Where she was apparently still in bed. Rita's eyelids flew open. A shadow moved from the foot of her bed to the side and then to the sliding glass door of the balcony.

Rita's mouth went dry and her heart pounded in her chest. She was not imagining it. Clicking on the small night-light above the headboard, she bolted upright.

Nothing.

There was no one there.

Rita blew out a long sigh of relief. Talk about getting a grip. She was letting all the ghost stories get to her. There was no such thing as a crying princess spirit. There was no such thing as a vengeful one who wanted to keep all his rocks on his beach. Really, she had to stop taking everything people told her to heart. Also, putting an end to any kind of late-night drinking would probably be wise, as well.

Throwing the covers off, she rose out of bed to get a glass of water from the bathroom. A crumpled piece of fabric lay on the floor by the bathroom door. She kicked it aside before realizing what it was.

But it couldn't be.

With dread, Rita bent to pick up the item to make sure. Her mouth went dry when she saw what it was she held. Her jean shorts. The ones with the rock in the pocket. She was one hundred percent certain she'd thrown those in the closet atop her other worn clothing when she'd walked in this evening. In fact, the rock had been completely forgotten after the emotional tug of the fight between Lizzie and Jonathon. She hadn't given it a second thought until all the talk of curses and spirits.

The added weight of the fabric told her it was still in there. Was she losing her mind? Had she pulled it out and forgotten somehow? There had to be a logical explanation.

She'd never been one to entertain superstition. But her father had grown up believing in various gods and guiding spirits. He wasn't terribly traditional but he'd definitely carried over some beliefs with him.

Even as a child, she'd always scoffed at his stories, along with her mother. They were both convinced that he couldn't really believe all the things he was spouting. It all seemed the stuff of fairy tales and lore, though Papa insisted it was all real.

In a stunned daze, Rita made her way back to bed. The night-light was going to stay on for the remainder of the night. One thing was certain, she had lost all hope of getting any sleep.

CHAPTER SEVEN

CLINT FOUND IT impossible to sleep.

Now as a result of a restless, frustrating night he'd started his jog ridiculously early. The term *predawn* came to mind. Rita. She'd been all he could think about. The whole day spent with her yesterday was magical. One he'd never forget. But she'd gone suddenly quiet after their nightcap. He had been about to suggest a walk along the beach when she'd abruptly bidden him good-night and then practically run to the elevator.

Was it something he'd said?

He hadn't meant to get into all that about his grandmother and the loss of his parents. Those weren't topics he normally entertained or liked to talk about. Not with anyone. But the more he got to know Rita, the more he felt able to open up. Even about his childhood. And she'd seemed genuinely interested, asked him to confide in her. Which had been far too easy. He'd never felt so comfortable around a woman, so at ease with just being himself.

But something had definitely spooked her at the end. Served him right. The past was better left behind where it belonged.

Then there was the worry about his sister. He'd not heard from her at all after that little display in the lobby other than a quick text.

Thank you for the wine and chocolate, big brother. Just need some time alone. Time to think.

Women. He would never understand them. It was why he was going to stay single for as long as he could. Perhaps even as long as he lived. A set of dreamy dark chocolate eyes framed by long lashes flashed into his mind. He pounded the sand even harder.

By the time he made it back to the entrance of the hotel lobby, he'd only hammered out a fraction of his frustration. But it was better than nothing. The resort was still quiet. Only maintenance and servicemen were up and about.

So he figured he was seeing things when he spotted Rita at the outside bellhop stand. Clint squinted against the early sun rays. Yeah, it was definitely her. What in the world was she doing out here at this time of morning?

One way to find out.

The bellhop was typing something out for her on his handheld tablet when Clint tapped her on the shoulder. She jumped and clapped a hand to her chest.

"Clint. What are you doing here?"

He made a show of looking down at his workout clothes and lifted the cell phone in his hands, then pointed to the wireless earbuds in his ears.

"Right. How was your run?"

He ignored that. He also tried hard to ignore her shapely, toned legs in the black capri leggings she was wearing. Or the way the white tank beneath her jean jacket came up just above her cleavage.

"Going somewhere?"

"As a matter of fact, I am. I was going to try to text Lizzie later. Both to check in and to see how she was doing."

She was going to text Lizzie. Had no intention of contacting him. Why that thought stung was beyond him. She certainly didn't need to okay her whereabouts with him. Though it would have been nice.

"She told me last night she just wanted some time to think. Alone. Where?"

"Huh?"

"Where are you planning to go?"

She bit down on her lower lip. "I'd rather not say."

The bellhop's gaze bounced from one to the other, as if he was watching a slow, yet gripping, tennis match.

Clint was in no mood for this. Between concern for his sister, worry that they might end up canceling this whole soiree and trying to figure out the rapidly changing mood of the woman before him, Clint figured he was swiftly reaching his outer limits.

"I have a real problem with that," he declared.

Rita blinked at him. "I beg your pardon?"

"I have a real issue with your refusal to tell me where you're going."

Anger flashed through her eyes. Rather than heed the warning, Clint stepped in closer.

"You have an issue with my refusal to tell you something that's none of your business in the first place?"

"That's where you're wrong. I think it's plenty my business."

Her chin lifted with defiance. "I utterly fail to see how."

"Let me explain then," he said, knowing he was being a bit of a heel given his tone and his wording. But he couldn't seem to help himself. She was about to take off in the wee hours of the morning without a word to anyone. Her plan only to drop a text to his sister later. A sister who was plenty distracted and might not even be looking at her phone for countless reasons. "I'm responsible for this event and for the wedding party here to attend it."

"You certainly aren't responsible for me."

"You're here for this wedding aren't you? The one we're having for my sister?"

She leaned back and crossed her arms in front of her chest. "I'm sorry. Does that somehow mean I have given up my free will?"

"What? Of course not. I'd just rather have an idea where my guests may be." *And, in her case, feel assured that they're safe and secure.*

The bellhop cleared his throat behind them. "Ms. Paul, if you'll excuse me. I'm afraid the only cars available are smaller hatchbacks. I wouldn't recommend one of those on the drive to Hana. Would you like me to see if there's a tour I can book you on?"

Rita threw the man a hard glare. "No, thank you. That won't be necessary."

Clint wanted to shake the man's hand. Now he knew where she was going. He just couldn't guess why.

"You enjoy the tour that much?" Clint asked. "Have to go back the next day?"

"Don't be silly. I only want to get to one spot."

"What spot could possibly be so intriguing?"

But she ignored him. "I'll take one of the hatchbacks," she told the bellhop, who now seemed a little afraid, judging by the way he took a step backward.

Was she nuts? She was going to try to drive that rugged terrain in a hatchback? Some of those roads were downright treacherous. Never mind the winding curves that required the stability of a much larger vehicle.

The thought made him shudder. He knew firsthand how a seemingly frivolous decision during a trip could alter one's fate. His parents had made just such a decision and it had cost them their lives.

"Right away, miss." He picked up the tablet.

"What are you doing?" he demanded to know. "Don't you remember all those cars we saw rotted out at the bottom as we drove on some of those mountain roads? What are you thinking?"

"I'm thinking I'm an excellent driver. Please go forward with the car," she directed the bellhop once more.

Clint held up a hand to stop him. "Hold off, please."

Rita practically jumped on her heels in protest. "I am trying to secure a car which I need to get somewhere. You have no say in this."

"Just stop," he told her before she could continue the takedown she was so prepared for. Of him. "That won't be necessary."

Drawing a steadying breath, he focused back on her face. Her lips were pursed, her eyes held a hardened glint. He knew determination when he saw it. She was going to her destination whether he wanted her to or not. "I always make sure to rent a car when I travel. Usually a late-model SUV. I've done so this time. It's available to you if you want it."

That took the wind out of her sails. She visibly relaxed and lowered her shoulders.

"But I'm going to ask to come with you," he added before she relaxed too much. "I'd really rather you not travel that route alone."

"What if I say no? Will you revoke the offer of your car?"

"No, it's still yours if you want it."

A slight softening showed behind her eyes but then swiftly disappeared at his next words. "I'll just follow you if I have to."

Her lips tightened into a thin line once more. "How? You've given me your car."

He shrugged. "Guess I'll have to take one of those death-trap hatchbacks. Just hope and pray I don't plummet to the bottom of Mount Name-I-Can't-Pronounce to my untimely and tragic death." Hard to believe he could joke about such a thing, but there it was.

A smile tugged at the corners of her mouth. He could see her lips trembling in an attempt to control it from fully blossoming. Throwing her hands up, she rolled her eyes. "Fine. Come with me if you insist. But you're probably just going to laugh and call me all kinds of foolish." She looked him over, from his sweaty forehead to the grains of sand on his running shoes. "I suppose you're going to want to get cleaned up first."

"If it's not too much of an imposition," he said with mock seriousness, then bowed.

Rita simply shook her head slowly, then turned on her heel and walked back into the lobby of the hotel. Taking a moment to breathe a sigh of relief, he gave the bellhop a nod of thanks. The other man wiggled his eyebrows at him, his meaning clear. Yeah, Clint had his hands full. With another silent nod of agreement, he turned to follow her.

When he thought about how much of a coincidental fluke it was that he'd run into her in the first place, he cursed out loud. Thank the heavens he'd started his jog early. Or she could very well have been puttering up a mountain right now in a rackety small hatchback.

Whatever her reasons for wanting this so badly, he couldn't even venture to guess. One could only hope they were good ones. But he couldn't help but wonder which one of them was really the fool in all this.

Clint keyed the necessary information into the GPS and pulled the midsize Range Rover onto the road leading out of the resort. He and Rita had decided to take turns driving and he'd won the coin toss to determine who'd go first. Or maybe he'd lost, he couldn't even be sure. He didn't seem to know which way was up when it came to this particular woman.

So why did he find that intriguing when he ought to be downright annoyed about it instead?

He slid his gaze to the passenger seat where she sat next to him, fiercely studying the view from the window. Her legs were crossed, one shapely calve over the other. He'd touched her enough times to know her skin was soft and smooth. Her legs would probably feel that way too under the palm of his hand.

He gripped the steering wheel tighter and pulled his attention to the road.

She was completely different from any woman he'd previously dated. He had thought he preferred blondes, but he seemed to be enamored with her dark silky hair. She wore it up in some type of loose bun at the moment; wispy tendrils framed her face. The effect lent a soft, angelic quality to her features.

Whereas most of his previous dates were curvy, Rita was lithe and toned. And unlike Maxine, his most recent terminated relationship, Rita wore very minimal makeup.

"Are we heading the same way we did yesterday?" she asked, pulling him out of his somewhat inappropriate musings about her body and her hair.

"Yes. But you're eventually going to have to tell me what our ultimate destination is. Unless you plan on blindfolding me at some point."

That notion brought up all sorts of inappropriate thoughts dancing in his brain. He made himself focus on the road; they hadn't even left the city yet. It was going to be another long day. For some reason, that idea didn't fill him with dread the way it should have.

She slowly folded the map, rubbed her forehead. "I'm trying to rectify a mistake I made yesterday. Or think I made. I don't even know."

That made no sense whatsoever. He waited for her to continue.

"I took something I shouldn't have."

She couldn't mean what he thought she meant. The idea was a preposterous one. "Are you saying you took something from one of the souvenir shops? Without paying for it?"

She gasped and shifted in her seat to stare at him, her mouth agape. "What? No! How could you even think that?"

"I didn't really. I mean—I don't know what I mean. I'm just trying to understand what's happening."

"I didn't steal anything, Clint. I'm not a thief!" she declared on a huff.

"Then what are you talking about? Why are we retracing our route from yesterday?"

"I took a rock, okay? I need to get back to Black Sand Beach."

He couldn't have heard her right. A rock?

She blew out a breath. "I think it's my fault Lizzie and Jonathon are fighting."

Okay. Maybe Rita *had* hit her head when they'd jumped off that cliff and he'd missed it. Clint thought about turning around and finding the nearest medical clinic instead of continuing on their current route. But she'd been pretty coherent the rest of the day after that.

"Because the spirits are angry," she added.

Angry spirits…? Understanding slowly dawned as he recalled the waitress from last night and her dire warnings about curses and spirits. Rita was staring at him with expectation.

"Huh" was all he could muster.

"That's it?" she asked. "That's all you have to say to what I just told you?"

"You think you picked up a cursed rock and now you want to return it. In case it has something to do with the sudden threat to Lizzie's nuptials. Does that about summarize it?"

She nodded slowly, still hadn't shut her mouth completely. And what a luscious, beckoning mouth it was. Full lips just slightly pink above a rounded, feminine jaw.

"Yes," she replied. "It's why I want to go back to Black Sand Beach."

Now, why was it so hard for her to have told him that? Honestly, he couldn't figure her out at all.

"All right. Let's hope we make good time. It looks cloudier today than yesterday. We might be a bit chilled."

She gave her head a shake. "You're not even going to try to tell me I'm being silly? That going through all this trouble for a supposed curse is a downright waste of time?"

"Why would I do that?"

She let out a small chuckle. "I know you're not saying you believe it, that something like a lifted rock can have any kind of effect on a wedding." She rubbed her brow. "Sheesh, when I say it out loud, it sounds even more outlandish."

He shrugged. "I know you believe it. That's enough."

"It is?"

"It is for me." He turned onto the Hana Highway.

The thing was, Rita wasn't even sure if she did believe in the curse. In fact, she was almost certain that she didn't give it much credence at all.

She just didn't want to risk it. Not after whatever it was that she'd seen last night. And she still couldn't explain how her shorts had ended up out of the closet and on the floor.

She fingered the object in question inside her jacket pocket. The rock felt smooth and sleek under her skin. As small as a pebble. Hard to believe it could cause any kind of trouble. Well, it was too late to back out now. If Clint thought she was crazy, he was doing a good job of keeping that to himself.

The ride went by in comfortable silence. For the most part anyway. It certainly wasn't comfortable that she was so very aware of him.

He'd changed into navy-blue sailing shorts and a white V-neck tee that brought out his newly tanned skin. A silver-and-gold watch clasped on his right wrist had the most complicated face on it she'd ever seen, with three different dials and four hands. His hair was still wet and combed back to reveal his strong, square jaw.

Even dressed island casual, the man looked like he could grace the cover of *Executive Today* magazine.

Rita forced her attention to the road ahead. It was indeed quite curvy, perilously close to the edge in several spots. But Clint was effortlessly navigating the car in such a smooth way, her stomach hadn't dipped once. So unlike the ride yesterday.

"Are you getting tired of driving yet?" she asked, hoping the answer would be no. For all her protests earlier, she was quite enjoying being able to sit back and enjoy the scenery. No way she'd ever share that bit with him though.

"I think I'm good. No real good spots to stop anyway. Not for a while."

Nodding, Rita turned to stare at the sapphire-blue water beyond the mountain road they were driving on. She'd tried to stay angry, she really had, about the way he'd commandeered the whole endeavor. But how upset could she really be? He hadn't made fun of her. In fact, he hadn't so much as even smirked. He'd provided her with a steady and reliable car for the trip, and spared her from having to make the ride on her own.

Even if he had been a little domineering in the process.

No one was perfect, right?

Between her overbearing father and control-loving ex-husband, it was been-there-done-that as far as she was concerned. Regardless of his well-intentioned motivations,

Clint had definitely shown a similar quality earlier today when he'd found her at the bellhop podium

Moot point. It wasn't like she was committing herself for life to the man. She had just accepted his gracious offer to assist her with her mission. Nothing more.

With what seemed like great time, they finally pulled up to a gravel road. A large wooden sign at the entry said Wai'anapanapa State Park. Rita felt like months had gone by since they'd been here. Hard to believe it had been less than a day. So much had happened since. Clint pulled into one of the parking spots and they both got out of the car. Except, where Rita's limbs felt sore and stiff, Clint seemed to be able to bounce out of the SUV and easily stride to where she stood. Athletic and agile.

"All right. Let's go get uncursed," he said.

She tried to hide her trepidation. What if it didn't work that way? What if the spirits were unforgiving types that didn't care about attempts at restitution after the fact?

She'd never forgive herself if Lizzie and Jonathon broke up for good and there was even the slightest possibility she'd caused it. Even indirectly.

"Let's go." She started walking to the concrete steps that led down to the beach area. "I'll show you where I picked it up."

Clint had been right about today's weather being cloudier and more windy. These waves were definitely harsher than yesterday's. Angry water pounded on the boulders and sent splashes of foam high into the air. A mist of salt water fanned her face when they reached the bottom step.

"I picked it up in the cave," she told him and navigated around two jeans-clad teenagers taking selfies.

"Guess I shouldn't have pulled you in there yesterday," Clint responded.

But he *had* pulled her in. And they'd been merely inches

apart. And she couldn't forget that she'd actually imagined him kissing her, had wanted him to.

"I'm the one who picked up the rock."

"Which is why we're here." He led her toward the crashing waves and to the mouth of the cave in a replay of yesterday. It occurred to her that today there'd be no one to yell at them to come out, to tell them they needed to leave. A shiver of apprehension traveled up her spine. Or maybe it was more anticipation.

She stepped inside and he followed closely behind her. "I guess I should try to put it exactly where I found it on the ground. Or as close as possible."

"Right. So he can be reunited with all his little pebble friends."

"Ha ha." Rita bent down and gently deposited the rock, then straightened. Already, a sense of calm and relief settled over her. Superstition or not, she definitely felt a sense of unburdening.

"Ready?" Clint asked.

She nodded. "Seems anticlimactic somehow."

"You were expecting drama? Or perhaps that the spirits would descend all of a sudden and bestow you with thanks and praise?"

She smiled. "It's the least they could do, you know. They've put us through a lot of trouble."

He fished out his phone. Looked back up at her, eyes wide with shock. "You're not gonna believe this. Lizzie just texted that she and Jonathon have completely made up. Just this very moment."

Rita felt her jaw drop with disbelief. "Oh, my God! You're kidding?"

He waited a beat, then grinned. "Yeah, I am." He slid his phone back in his pocket. "I'm not even getting cell reception."

He was teasing her! Of all times. She reached over and gave him a useless shove. "That was mean."

The laughter died in her throat at his expression. Clint's gaze dropped to where her hand touched his shoulder. To her surprise, he wrapped his fingers around her own. His skin felt warm, strong against hers.

"You almost fell yesterday in here. Remember?" he asked, his voice near a whisper.

Rita's mouth went dry. If he only knew. Yes, she remembered. She'd been thinking about it ever since. The way he'd grabbed her to keep her upright. The solid wall of muscle against her back as he'd held her steady against him. "Guess I should thank you for that too."

His gaze fell to her mouth. "Maybe you can show me."

There it was. A clear invitation. All pretense gone.

And he'd made sure it would be her decision. The ball was fully in her court.

What would he taste like? How would his lips feel against hers? She'd thought so often about kissing him before, when she was merely a besotted coed with a crush. It had never occurred to her back then that she would ever get the opportunity. Yet, here it was. As if she was in some sort of fairy tale or dream. Their time together on Maui had only served to heighten her attraction. She'd grown increasingly more aware of him every moment they spent together. All too often on this trip, her imagination had created scenarios of the two of them together. Intimately. Scenarios, through some miracle, exactly like the one she found herself in now.

Rita had the distinct impression reality would be even better than the products of her imagination. She could guess what he would taste like: masculine and bold. His lips would be firm against hers, just as she'd so often dreamed.

It would be so easy to find out once and for all, to just lean into him and take him up on his tempting offer.

But could she? Could she tune out all the warnings, the red flags? All her life, she'd tried so hard to do what was expected of her, what others told her was the right thing. This one time, did she have the courage to simply do exactly what she wanted?

And she so desperately wanted.

Clint's breath caught as he watched Rita's inner struggle. He knew what she wanted; her eyes had clouded with desire. He had no doubt about that. Whether she would act on it was a completely different question. He willed himself not to move so much as a muscle. As badly as he wanted to lean into her and finally take those lush, tempting lips with his own, the next step would have to be hers. Whatever happened next between them had to be completely on her own terms.

It was only fair.

Not that he was trying to be honorable. The only real honorable thing to do would be to walk away, if he was being honest. Relationships weren't his thing. Not long-term ones. Fallon men couldn't be trusted with real commitment. History told that it never went well. Between his parents' fatal accident and his grandfather's self-inflicted untimely death, Clint determined long ago that he was never meant to be a family man.

He wouldn't lead someone like Rita on. But he could no longer deny his attraction. Nor hide it.

"I don't think that's such a good idea," she finally answered with a breathy rasp. A bolt of disappointment stabbed through his center. He felt the loss like a physical blow. A blow that wasn't the least lessened by the fact that she was right. Of course she was.

"It's not that I don't want to."

Well, that was something at least. It helped, though not much.

"It's just…" She thrust a hand through the hair at her crown. "I'm not sure exactly who I am at this very moment in time. I know it sounds silly."

Clint wanted desperately to wrap her tight in his arms, to kiss away the tension and angst clear in every muscle in her face. "It doesn't sound silly, Rita."

"I wish I could explain."

She didn't get a chance to try. A boisterous family of four appeared in the entryway and made their way inside.

"Ooh, spooky," the teenage girl said, her eyes glancing around the dark cave walls.

"You're a wuss" came the reply from her smaller brother, who stepped around her to go farther inside.

Clint cursed under his breath while Rita smiled politely at the intruders.

"We should go," he told Rita and gently took her by the elbow. "It's getting crowded in here," he added in a lower voice only she could hear.

"You all have a good day," the woman said pleasantly as they stepped out.

It occurred to Clint just how they must have looked, like a besotted couple who'd been interrupted as they stole a private moment in a beachside cavern.

So far from the truth it caused a pang in his gut.

"We've traveled quite a distance. It would be a shame just to turn around and go back." Clint opened the car door for Rita and waited as she crawled inside. It wasn't easy acting like nothing had just happened between them before the family had come in. Although, technically, nothing actually *had* happened.

Entering the car, he shut his door a little too hard. Rita winced slightly next to him.

"What did you have in mind?" she asked.

"A few stops I've heard about that the driver didn't take us to yesterday. Off the beaten path, so to speak. Are you hungry?"

Her stomach answered for her. As soon as he asked the question, he heard a soft grumbling coming from her midsection.

"Take a guess," she said in a giggle.

"There's supposedly a roadside hut that serves the best banana bread on the island. Or so I've been told."

"Sold. But only if it's my treat." She seemed genuinely excited. He hoped at least part of that came from not wanting their private little outing to end just yet. Maybe he was fooling himself. She was simply hungry. Still, he'd take it.

"It's a deal." He put the car in gear and began to drive.

Within minutes, they'd reached the stand and were handed tinfoil-wrapped loaves of aromatic bread that made his mouth water. Rita began tearing at the foil.

"Uh-uh." He stopped her by placing his hand on hers. "Not yet."

She glared at him. "Why not? I want my lunch."

Her outrage made him laugh. "Patience. We can eat it at the next stop."

She reluctantly lowered the bread. "We're still off the beaten path then?"

"Let's go." He'd been thinking about taking her to this next stop all day. Hoped it would live up to expectations. From what he'd been told, the spot was a well-kept secret among the locals who didn't want it overrun with campy tourists the way the state properties usually were.

Rita seemed the type who would appreciate a place like that.

He had his answer when they reached the isolated beach about half an hour later. She gasped as he pulled up along the side of the road and put the car in gear. Before he could turn off the ignition, she'd already exited and started running toward the small stretch of beach.

"Oh, Clint!"

"What do you think?"

"It's pink! I've never seen anything like it. The sand is actually pink! I thought the black sand was impressive."

Before them lay a crystal-blue pool of water surrounded by sand the likes of which he'd never seen before. Rita was partly right as far as he was concerned. He'd describe the color as more of a ruby red, depending on where the light hit it.

"This is otherworldly." She bent down and scooped some of the sand into her palm before letting it slowly sift through her fingers.

"I figured we'd have our banana bread lunch here. Make a picnic out of it."

The smile she flashed him gave him the response he wanted. It also nearly took his breath away. An almost giddy sense of pleasure hit him at how happy she was to be here.

What a schoolboy with a crush he was acting like.

They sat down on a large boulder between the road and water and began to eat.

"Looks like we have company." Clint swallowed the bite he had in his mouth as a large lanky dog jogged toward them. It stopped about six inches away and started sniffing at the food. Clint's food to be more accurate. Rita had impressed him by finishing first.

"Hey, baby." She stood and held her hand to the dog's nose to sniff.

"Is it a stray?"

"I don't think so. No collar but it seems taken care of. Well-fed, no signs of emaciation."

Right. She was a vet after all. The dog licked her finger, then turned back to Clint, eyeing the bread again.

He pulled the loaf back. "This is mine."

Rita squatted in front of the animal. "Are you lost, girl? Let's take a look at you." Placing her fingers along the dog's jaw, she slowly pried its mouth open.

Clint stopped chewing. "Um…is that wise?"

She ignored the question. "Teeth look good. Relatively clean for what I'd guess is her age. She seems to be some type of pit bull–mix breed. Definitely some other terrier in there too."

"So she's not lost?"

Rita looked up to glance at the road behind them. "There are some houses back there. I'm guessing she's just out wandering."

"I think she smelled banana and came looking." He could have sworn the dog actually nodded at that statement. Then it lifted a paw and dropped it onto Clint's knee.

There was barely one morsel left.

"She likes you," Rita declared, clearly laughing at his displeasure.

"She wants my lunch."

Again, he could swear the dog was nodding. He suddenly felt guilty. "Should I give her some?"

Rita seemed to think. "Probably not. It shouldn't harm her but it is pretty sweet. Sugar sometimes upsets their digestive tract."

Guilt evaporated, Clint popped the last piece of bread into his mouth, then leaned over to rub the dog's head. "Sorry, pal. You heard the doc."

He got a sharp bark in response. "Hey, you should be thanking me. I just spared you an upset tummy."

"And diarrhea," Rita added.

Well, now things were getting romantic. The dog gave him one more derisive look, then dropped its paw and started to walk away. Rita followed for a few feet and watched it cross the road.

"She seems to be heading toward that brown house at the turn," she told him over her shoulder.

Sure enough, they both watched as their former visitor walked through the yard and jumped through what appeared to be a puppy door by the side of the house.

Clint heard Rita's sigh of relief. He had the distinct feeling she would have followed that dog until she made sure it had a home and had reached it safely.

"What a cutie," she said and returned to her spot next to him on the boulder. "Do you have any pets?"

Clint shook his head. "I'm never home long enough. The poor thing would starve. I imagine you have a few."

"Not right now. Jay had allergies. He'd react even to the hypoallergenic breeds. So we never bothered to get one."

"Couldn't you have gotten one of those hairless cats or something?"

She bit out a short laugh. "Sphynx cats? Believe it or not, people have reactions to those too."

"My sister wanted one of those, though I'll never understand why. I personally think they look like deflated balloons. With a face." He picked a small pink pebble, thought about throwing it into the water and dropped it back down. In case the curse applied to more than just Black Sand Beach.

And since when did he give any credence to curses and such? He hardly recognized himself on this trip. Now here he was sitting on a magical beach with the most beautiful, alluring woman and so far they'd talked about canine diarrhea and hairless cats.

"But she never got one," he continued. "We didn't have any pets growing up."

"Oh?"

"My grandmother wouldn't allow it. She said she had enough on her hands being strapped with two teenagers to bring up at her late stage in life. Wouldn't budge even though we swore we'd be the ones taking care of any animal she'd let us get." He stared off into the water. "Heck, Lizzie would have settled for a goldfish."

"That's too bad. I think pets serve to teach children a great deal. Particularly a good sense of responsibility."

"Other than that, Grams was all about responsibility." Especially when it came to him. "Our grandmother made no secret of the fact that she'd disapproved of my parents' marriage," he added, not quite certain why he was ready to share so much with her. These were things he'd never spoken out loud about with anyone. Not even Lizzie. "Almost seemed to take it as a personal affront. I got the impression I was somehow supposed to make up for their transgressions to her."

She touched his knee in sympathy. An electric current shot through from the point of contact straight through his chest.

"That's a lot to process for a teenage boy."

"Past history." He shrugged, ready to change the subject. "So what was the last pet you owned?"

"My parents always had one or two dogs. This past year was the first time in my life I didn't have an animal to come home to."

"Good thing you get enough animal contact through your work then, huh?"

She bit her bottom lip, looked out over the water. "I'm not practicing right now."

Whatever the reason, she didn't seem happy about it. He got the impression her sabbatical wasn't by choice. Not her choice, in any case.

"Why's that?"

"Long story. Jay asked me to quit when we first got married. He wanted to focus on a family. I'd only taken the job to make him happy anyway."

"I don't understand."

"My original goal out of college was to try to start my own practice, set up shop somewhere. Or to work with one of the local animal shelters. But both those options would have taken countless grueling hours and total commitment. Jay wasn't too keen on that idea. I let him convince me to try for a clinic instead. He had some help from my parents in the convincing department. They'd never understood my career choice anyway." Her laugh was not a genuine one. "Neither my mother or father could figure out why I'd want to go through all that schooling and training and not become an actual doctor." She used air quotes to emphasize the last two words.

Clint continued to play with the sand at his feet. Staying silent seemed to be the best course of action right now. To just let her continue.

"Anyway, I ended up at a chain practice where they controlled everything from my schedule to the length of my patient visits."

"That doesn't sound like a good fit for you."

"It wasn't. It got to the point where I started spending more time filling out forms to prove profit contribution to the clinic than I did actually treating pets. So when Jay asked me to quit…"

"You quit to make him happy."

"I guess I did."

"And now?"

She tucked a strand of hair behind her ear. "What do you mean?"

He thought his meaning should be obvious, but she was looking at him expectantly. "What's stopping you now from going after that original goal?"

She blinked, then looked away into the distance. "I don't know if I even have the same goals anymore. A lot has happened since I got my degree."

"Sure it has. You've gained even more experience in

your field." He thought of the way she'd handled the wandering dog just now, the pure contentment and energy in her eyes as she tended to it. "You're clearly good at what you do."

She smiled. "I suppose. I just don't know if I have it in me any longer to pursue such grand endeavors. Right now, I just need to settle into a quiet, comfortable routine."

"Sounds a bit boring."

Her chuckle was half-hearted. "I could do with a little boring at this point in time."

More likely, she was scared. Based on the little bit she'd confided, her decisions had been questioned so often and so thoroughly, she was probably hesitant about making any more major ones. Clint would keep all that to himself. Who was he to try to analyze her choices?

"Yet one more thing to figure out, I guess," she added, not tearing her gaze away from the horizon.

He didn't say anything else, though he desperately wanted to. He simply reached for the hand she still had on his knee and gave it a tight squeeze. They sat in silence for long enough that he actually lost track of the time. Five minutes or an hour could have gone by before Rita spoke again.

"Clint." The way she said his name made his heart hammer.

"Yeah?"

"I've changed my mind."

He lifted an eyebrow in question. Then sucked in a breath at her next words.

"I would like you to kiss me. In fact, I'd like it very much."

Rita couldn't recall ever being so bold. She'd asked before she could let herself think too much longer about doing so. And now she couldn't think at all.

Clint's kiss was gentle at first, like a soft breeze on a warm summer evening. But then something turned. He took her by the waist, pulled her closer, her body tight up against his. His mouth grew demanding, delving deeper and asking for more. She was oh, so ready to give it. Shivers ran down her whole body, desire racked her core. She'd never felt such intense longing for a man, simply from his kiss.

A thrill shot through her chest at the knowledge that he wanted her, as well. There was no doubt, not given the way he held her, the way he was plundering her mouth with his own.

So this was what true passion felt like, what all the books and movies and love songs were always referring to. All these years, she'd had no idea until this very moment. With this one man.

Her hands moved up his arms to his shoulders. She wanted him closer somehow, would never get close enough. Her heart hammered in her chest as she molded her body against his. Nothing in her past dreams could have prepared her for the reality of being in his arms, tasting him like this. Her fantasies hadn't done him justice. He was making her burn through to her very soul. An exquisite, enticing burn she'd never get enough of. He tasted like sin and pure masculinity. And banana bread.

That random thought served to pull her out of the spell. Enough to let all the warning cries in. Abruptly, she made herself tear away from his grasp. The loss felt like a bucket of cold water splashed into her face.

She shouldn't be doing this. Couldn't be doing this.

She'd made too many mistakes in these past few years. It would take her years to recover from them.

She couldn't make another one by losing her heart to Clint. There would be no recovering from that.

Clint Fallon wasn't the type of man a girl got over. Ever.

CHAPTER EIGHT

THE RIDE BACK was mostly silent save for the luau music playing on the radio. She'd noticed Clint had gradually turned up the volume higher and higher, as if it somehow refuted the lack of conversation between them. Neither one seemed to know what to say to each other.

Rita felt like a wound-up ball of emotion by the time they returned to the resort and went their separate ways. Her distraction was the reason it took her a minute to realize what she'd walked in on after she opened the door to her room and switched on the light.

She quickly shut if off again as soon as her eyes adjusted and she realized what she was seeing.

"Rita!" Tessa's surprised voice shouted across the room from her bed, immediately followed by the low rumble of a man's chuckle. It appeared Tessa and the groomsman had taken their friendship to the next level.

"It's o-okay," Rita stammered and tried to walk quickly backward out the door. Her jacket pocket caught on the doorknob and yanked her to a halt.

Tessa appeared at the door, wrapped in a sheet. Which had to mean the groomsman wasn't covered at the moment. She made sure to quickly avert her gaze.

"I'm really sorry, Rita. I guess I wasn't expecting you back. You've been gone all day."

"We were exploring the island."

Tessa gave a nod. "With Clint, right? You've both been gone. I just assumed "

Rita could guess what she'd assumed. "It's okay. I didn't mean to interrupt." It didn't quite feel right that she was the one apologizing but somehow she felt the need.

Tessa blew a tuft of hair off her forehead. "I mean," she said, dropping her voice to a whisper, "Rob and I have been really hitting it off, you know. It's like—I've never felt so attracted to someone. Hasn't that ever happened to you?"

She didn't know how to answer that. It had happened, so very recently. It *was* happening. And she didn't know how to cope with it.

"I'm happy for you," Rita blurted out, not even sure if it was an appropriate response for this moment.

"Thanks. I guess I kinda figured you'd sort of be occupied too."

An image flashed through her mind of exactly what Tessa was referring to. In that picture, it was her and Clint wrapped up in each other under the sheets in a dark room.

She sucked in a breath and forced her mind to focus on Tessa's face.

"Listen, it's okay. You guys…uh…you guys have fun."

Tessa squealed a small laugh. "Oh, we are."

"How about you just drop me a text when it's safe for me to return?"

Tessa leaned over to give her a one-armed hug, the other hand holding tight to the sheet. "Thanks, Rita! You're the best. I'll call you as soon as… Well, you know."

Rita backed away into the hallway as the door shut. The squeal she heard from Tessa in the next instant sounded nothing like the one from before.

Making her way to the ground-floor lounge, she settled on the couch and adjusted a cushion behind her, trying to get comfortable. She almost envied her roommate. To be that bold, to feel that liberated had to be so freeing in so many ways. Tessa obviously didn't give much thought to long-term ramifications. While planning for the future had been a constant theme in the way Rita lived her life. Look how that had turned out. Rita sighed and closed her eyes, willing for at least a few moments of sleep before she could go back to the room.

Tessa's text never came.

He'd become quite the wanderer in Hawaii. Clint made his way down the stairs and past the lobby. He'd gotten tired of tossing and turning, trying to get to sleep. It wasn't early in the evening but it certainly wasn't late by any means. He and Rita had gotten back less than three hours ago.

He couldn't stop thinking about her. Or the way she'd kissed him.

More than that, she'd opened up to him. Though it had been difficult to hear about her former husband. Just the thought that she'd belonged to another man not so long ago made him want to punch a wall. How utterly Neanderthal-like. He wasn't proud of his reaction.

Rita and her ex sounded like two completely different people, totally incompatible. Rita was warm, genuine and fully appreciative of everything around her. Her ex-husband seemed the stoic and serious type. He blew out a frustrated breath. What did he know about it? He'd never even met the man. In fact, he'd never felt such a strong dislike for someone he'd never laid eyes on.

He halted in his tracks as he approached the sitting area by the ground-floor lounge. Great. Now he was starting to see her everywhere. That couldn't really be her sprawled out on one of the couches.

He drew closer to find it was indeed her.

"Rita?" He gently tapped her on the shoulder. Once, twice. Nothing. Leaning in, he gave her arm a gentle squeeze. Finally, she started to stir.

"Clint?"

"Yeah. Hey, what are you doing here? Do you sleepwalk or something?" he asked, not even certain if he was joking.

She winced as she shifted to a sitting position, must have been lying there long enough to have her limbs go stiff.

"I was waiting for Tessa to get back to me."

"About what?"

She arched her back in a stretch, spreading her arms out. Clint had to look away from the scene of her long, graceful neck and the tempting curves under her tank top.

"Tessa had company when I walked in. She said she would call me when they were...you know, finished."

"I see." He glanced down at his watch. "It's past midnight. Way past."

"Guess she forgot."

More likely, they weren't yet "finished." "Do you want to try calling her?"

Nodding, she pulled her cell out of her pocket and dialed. Several beats passed then Clint heard Tessa's voice through the tiny speaker saying she couldn't answer.

"Straight to voice mail." Rita tossed her phone on the coffee table in front of them. "Guess I'll be enjoying the open-air lounge for a while longer."

"Why don't you just go back to your room. Tell them they've had enough time."

Her eyes grew wide. "No way. That was embarrassing enough the first time."

"Embarrassing how?"

"I sort of walked in on them."

Clint slapped a hand to his mouth, but not before he could stifle the burst of laughter.

Rita narrowed her eyes on him; her lips formed a tight line. "Ha ha. I'm glad you think that's funny."

"I'm sorry. It is pretty funny, knowing what I know of

you." No doubt in the world Rita had turned redder than the woman who'd actually been caught in flagrante.

"What's that supposed to mean?"

"Never mind. It's not important."

"I think you might have just implied I'm a prude."

"If the shoe fits...yada yada."

She glared at him. "I'm going to choose to ignore that by changing the subject. How's Lizzie? Have you heard anything?"

Quite a deft way to change the subject, at that. Thankfully, there was at least some good news on that front. "I called her a little while after we returned. Looks like she and Jonathon went to dinner together. Crisis averted apparently."

"Thank goodness."

"Now for your crisis." He motioned to her and then around to the couches.

"I'd hardly consider this a crisis. I can always go ask for another room."

"Are you kidding? This place is continually booked. We had to reserve our rooms months ago."

Her shoulders sagged with defeat. Turning behind her, she punched the seat cushion and leaned back against it. "Looks like I'll have to make myself comfortable here awhile longer."

Like he would allow that to happen in a thousand years. Standing, he offered her his arm. "That's silly. Come with me."

She blinked up at him. He felt a resounding sense of relief when she finally stood up and took his hand. "Where to?"

"Just follow me." He knew she wasn't going to go along with his idea easily, but they could argue along the way.

"Where are we going? I'd like to know," she insisted even as she trailed behind him.

"I'm not going to let you sleep here all night. Not when there's a perfectly good suite we can share."

If she was counting, she would have to acknowledge all the times that Clint had come through for her in the few short days since he'd walked into that airport executive lounge. A nagging voice repeated in her head that none of it boded very well for her newly avowed goal to live more independently, reliant on her own devices.

Clint must have sensed her hesitation.

"It's a two-room suite. One bedroom and one living room complete with a long sofa and a connected door that can be closed."

"I'm not so sure that's a good idea."

"You'll have all the privacy you need."

Rita inhaled deeply as she contemplated his words. It made total sense. Definitely more sense than trying to get any sleep out here in an open lounge area. And frankly, she was exhausted between all the activity of the past few days and her sleepless night. Not to mention, she didn't want to be out here alone in case there were any visitors. Especially incorporeal ones like from the night before.

"It has been a rather long day." Two days, in fact. "And I would kill to wash my face and brush my teeth." Two routine tasks she'd really rather not wait until morning for.

"We can pick up some sundries from the night manager. I'll even let you have the bed."

She shook her head. "No way. If I do this, I insist on sleeping on the couch."

"Suit yourself."

"I haven't actually agreed."

Despite her words, he must have sensed her capitulation, as Clint further pleaded his case. "We have an all-day snorkeling adventure tomorrow. You'll need to be rested up."

Rita rubbed at her forehead, trying to release some of

the tension that had suddenly gathered there and knotted itself under her scalp. She had no good reason to say no. And she was so bone tired. Her only options were to sleep out here, kick a sleeping man out of a warm bed that he was sharing with a warm body. Or she could take Clint up on his offer. Maybe she was too exhausted to think straight, because only one of those options seemed to make sense at the moment. Besides, they were both adults. Technically, she'd known him for years. They'd just spent the whole day together. Quite an enjoyable day, in fact. Well, except for the awkwardness toward the end that came after that soul-shattering kiss.

And that was it right there. She'd be following him to his room right this very minute ready to fall fast asleep, if it wasn't for that blasted kiss. Could she really be that close to him, practically in the same room, all the while knowing what it felt like to be held by him? The way he'd tasted. Her skin tingled as she recalled the way his hands had gripped her around the waist, held her tight up against him.

"Rita. Come on. Show some compassion."

"Compassion?"

"Do it for me. I will get absolutely zero sleep knowing you're out here by yourself. Plus, I think there's some heavy rain due later tonight."

"I'm pretty sure you just made that up. About the rain."

"I might have." He gave her a small smile. "You have to know you can trust me," Clint added, throwing down the proverbial gauntlet and making it almost impossible to say no.

She did trust him. Without any qualms or hesitation. She just wasn't so sure how much she trusted herself.

The man looked like sin. Rita adjusted the waistband of her swimsuit and tried to avert her gaze from where Clint stood on the deck of the boat. Beyond him the water of the

Pacific Ocean gleamed like a sea of blue-green emeralds under the bright, shining mandarin-orange sun.

He'd been right about last night. Despite her heightened awareness of him in the next room, her tiredness had won out in the end and she'd fallen asleep as soon as she'd collapsed on his couch. Hadn't even heard him when he'd come to throw the extra blanket over her. He'd also let her oversleep, so her run to the room to get her tankini for this snorkeling jaunt had been frantic and rushed.

Despite the unexpected lie-in, Rita felt like she could use several more hours of sleep.

No doubt, a set of puffy dark circles framed her bloodshot eyes. Well, it hardly mattered—her face would be under a mask, then submerged in water most of the day. Clint, by contrast, appeared awake and alert. He stood against the railing, bouncing on his heels to the rhythmic reggae music the captain had playing. A jovial crew ran around them, prepping for the first snorkeling stop.

For two people who had spent the night in the same suite, they were doing an impressive job of avoiding talking to each other.

The truth was, she'd been the one avoiding him. But it was for her own self-preservation. Every time she glanced at his face, her gaze fell to his lips and triggered a tingling sensation in hers. Dreams of their kiss yesterday had haunted slumber all night. Images of her locked in his embrace framed against a backdrop of glimmering blue water and sparkling pink sand.

Stop it.

Well, she couldn't keep up the avoidance for long. The wedding wasn't for two more days still. Their paths were sure to cross at some point.

Bending down to reach for her mask, she came face-to-face with a set of sparkling blue eyes when she straightened.

"Hi, Tessa."

"Oh, my God, Rita. I'm so sorry I didn't text you last night. We fell asleep. We were just so tired."

"I kind of figured."

"I'm guessing you found a place to crash." She gestured to where Clint still stood, his tanned muscular back to them.

"Yes, I did," Rita simply replied. There would be no use in trying to correct Tessa's misguided insinuation. Nothing had actually happened between her and Clint overnight. Only in her dreams.

Tessa clapped her hands in front of her chest. "I figured you might." The woman was just too giddy this time of the day. She gave her a sly wink. "So it won't be a problem if Rob and I have the room to ourselves again tonight?"

Was she serious?

"I'm not so sure—"

Tessa's face fell, the smile dropping from her lips. She looked like a wounded puppy. Rita felt her jaw clench as she inwardly cursed. She had no reason to feel guilty. It was her room too.

"What about Rob's room? Perhaps you two can take turns," she offered.

Tessa pursed her lips. "His roommate apparently picked up the perky, smiley waitress at the cabana down the beach. Already told Rob he called dibs on the room."

What in the world? How was everyone in the wedding party so great at hooking up? And here she was, a fluttering, quivering mess just because Clint had kissed her on the beach. In fairness however, she'd never been kissed that way before. And it would probably never happen again. That notion had her heart sinking. Her eyes automatically found him once more. Her breath caught in her throat.

Tessa looked from one of them to the other. "I don't understand. I mean, clearly you two are—"

Rita cut her off. "We're not. Really, we're just friends."

Tessa didn't bother to hide her eye roll. "You could have fooled me. The way you two keep looking at each other."

Rita felt her cheeks flame with heat. Was she that obvious? Could the whole world tell that she was attracted like crazy to the bride's brother? How utterly horrifying.

"I'm sorry for assuming," Tessa continued. "I'll tell Rob he's out of luck tonight. Though I don't know where the poor guy is going to crash if his roommate brings the waitress there with him again."

There was a lounge area on the ground floor that wasn't terribly comfortable but could be considered an option, she almost told her. Rita sighed. It was like a domino effect. She felt herself capitulating. It wasn't like she didn't have a place to stay. Clint's suite did have ample room. And once she shut the door, it was like they weren't even sharing a space.

She studied Tessa's face. Her expression held more than disappointment. Much more. Rita got the feeling she was witnessing more than an island fling.

"You're falling for him, aren't you?"

To her utter surprise, the other woman's eyes started glistening with tears. "I've never felt this way before about anyone. He's gentle and sweet. And he makes me laugh. I can't bear to think about what's going to happen when we leave here. He lives on the opposite coast after all."

Rita took the other woman's hand in her own. "Oh, Tessa. I'm sure you two will figure something out."

"Do you really think so?" Hope shone through her eyes.

"I really do."

"Thanks." She sniffled. "I really hope we can."

"I'll be rooting for you." That comment earned her a wide smile.

Rita sighed with resignation. In the meantime, she could let them have these few remaining nights together. At least one of them had found their chance at happiness and love.

Who was she to stand in the way? Tessa started to stand but she stopped her. "Consider the room all yours."

Clint couldn't really keep up with what Rita was trying to tell him. Something about the waitress from the poolside cabana bar and Tessa living on the opposite coast. And also something about Rob What's-His-Name who was one of the groomsmen and how much Tessa liked him.

In Clint's defense, it was hard to concentrate on her words when the sun was shining on her hair and making it glisten like liquid black silk. Her cheeks were touched by just enough tan that they'd turned an intriguing rosy color he'd be hard-pressed to describe. And don't even get him started on the bathing suit she was wearing. Modest by most standards, it showed just enough of her midriff to scream temptation. The rich scarlet color of the fabric complimented her skin tone in a way that had him losing his train of thought.

A thin gold chain around her ankle made him want to reach down and run his fingers over the charms she wore on it. Then he'd work his way slowly up her calves. Then higher.

He gave his head a shake.

He had to pay attention. She was trying to tell him something important. But all he could focus on was the fact that it appeared she would be staying with him again tonight. That's all he really needed to hear.

They were disembarking off the catamaran after a full day of snorkeling. All in all, not a bad way to spend several hours off the sunny coast of Hawaii. Only it didn't compare to the pleasant enjoyment of yesterday, when he'd had Rita to himself.

"So I guess I'll just come by after dinner sometime. As soon as Rob shows up. You don't mind, do you? I feel kind of awkward asking."

"It's no trouble at all, Rita."

She still looked apprehensive and stopped him as they walked along the beach back to the resort. "Please don't read anything into this."

Something sparked in his chest. After all the experiences they'd shared together so far on this trip, all the ways he'd opened up to her and vice versa, she felt the need to warn him about making assumptions. The notion stung more than he cared to admit.

"Why would I? I'd like to think you're not the type to be coy when it comes to asking directly for what you want from a man."

Her gasp of surprise told him his comment had hit home. Good, he'd meant for it to.

"Maybe this isn't such a great idea after all." Her voice held a plethora of doubt.

What did she expect? Was he also not supposed to read anything into the way she'd reacted to his touch? Or the way she'd moaned softly into his lips as he'd kissed her?

He didn't get a chance to respond as Lizzie stormed past them followed by Jonathon hot on her heels. Lizzie's anger was palpable, the steam rising from her almost a tangible sight.

Not again.

"Huh." Rita spoke behind him. "We returned the rock and everything."

Clint resisted the urge to go after them both and tell them to get it together already, that the attendees didn't have time for this childish behavior from the bride and groom. But he had his own ire to contend with.

"What do you mean exactly?"

She blinked up in surprise. "Clearly Lizzie and Jonathon are fighting again."

"I know that. What do you mean about me not reading into things when it comes to you?"

Rita stomped past him without answering, her footsteps splashing water onto his legs. Well, he wasn't about to let her get away. Catching up to her, he gently but firmly took her by the elbow.

"Care to answer?"

"I don't think I do. Forget about me staying in your suite tonight. Forget I even mentioned it."

"It's a little too late for that, don't you think? You've already told Tessa she could have the room."

She pulled her arm free. "I'll think of something."

Clint rubbed a hand down his face with frustration. "What is it with you?"

"I don't know what you mean."

"It means I noticed how you've been avoiding me the whole day. Barely spoke two words to me even though we've been on the same boat for the past several hours."

"I was enjoying the scenery."

"Sure, you were. You practically pulled a muscle trying to get sunscreen lotion on your back by yourself."

Her jaw dropped. "Are you actually saying you're upset because you wanted to rub lotion on my back and I didn't ask?"

Well, when she put it that way...

He ignored that and continued, "Then as we're disembarking, you finally remember my name and ask about staying in my suite. Only I better not get any high hopes that it might mean something."

"I'm sorry."

"And another thing—wait... What did you say?"

"I apologize. I shouldn't have ignored you. It's just hard to know what to say to you now."

Because he'd kissed her. She was clearly conflicted about it.

Well, so was he. But he refused to regret that it happened and very much hoped she didn't regret it either.

"This is all taking me a bit by surprise." She said it so softly, with such a wistful sadness in her voice. There was no denying the truth in her statement. He suddenly felt like a heel for the way he'd just behaved, making her feel the need to apologize to him.

"Yeah, I know. Apology accepted. And I'd love to have you as a suite mate again."

She finally smiled. "Maybe we can make a whole event of it. Rent a movie and do each other's hair. Like a real sleepover."

As far as jokes went, it was a pretty lame one. But Clint appreciated the attempt to lighten the mood.

He wasn't going to tell her just how impossible it had been to sleep last night, knowing she was only a few feet away. This thing between them, whatever it was, had him spinning and twisting about inside. He'd never felt anything like it.

How in the world was he supposed to ignore that for the next several days until they both went back to their regular, daily lives? He had no doubt Rita was just as bothered as he was. That kiss yesterday in the cave proved it. He wanted to make the most of the time they had here together still. In a way that wasn't awkward or strained.

He watched the remaining members of the wedding party as they slowly strolled past, some holding hands. Tessa and Rob were particularly engrossed in each other as they made their way along the beach. Rita sighed as they walked by.

"You were right yesterday, about everyone coupling up on this trip," Rita stated, echoing his thoughts. "It's not just my roommate and her groomsman."

Without allowing himself to think, he crooked a finger under her chin and lifted her face to look up at him. "Maybe we should too."

He'd shocked her. She visibly retreated as he said the

words. "Oh, Clint. You have to understand. The timing is just so wrong."

Didn't she see that was his whole point? "It doesn't have to be, Rita. We have four more days on this island. We can make the most of it." Boldly, he stepped closer to her. "I know I want to kiss you again. I want to feel what I felt in that cave when you were in my arms. As often as I can before we have to bid our goodbyes once this is over."

The struggle behind her eyes was clear and tangible.

"Think about it." He dropped his hand. "In the meantime, my couch is yours tonight if you need it."

They were both silent as they slowly made their way back to the hotel lobby. Rita dared a glance at Clint's profile. The sleek, stylish sunglasses he had on made it difficult to gauge his expression. Dear Lord, he'd essentially just asked her to consider a mindless fling. He'd just thrown it out there, as if it was the most trivial thing in the world. Like asking her what she wanted to do for lunch later.

To his credit, he was being brutally honest. A heaviness settled into her chest. He wanted nothing more than a light, swift affair. His exact words were *before we have to bid our goodbyes*.

She'd be foolish to read anything more into his proposal.

Did she have the nerve to take him up on it? For just the next few days, could she really put aside her concerns and reservations and just enjoy herself? Live in this fantasy she found herself in?

Think about it, he'd said. As if she'd be able to think about anything else.

CHAPTER NINE

As FAR AS finally getting some sleep, tonight was no different than the previous two.

Clint threw his arm over his head and muttered a curse in the dark. Funny, he'd never been plagued by such relentless insomnia before this trip. Then again, never before had he ever had a woman so close yet so out of his reach.

The timing is just so wrong. The words Rita had spoken to him on the beach echoed through his head.

He grunted out loud. With thoughts like that floating through his mind, it was no wonder he couldn't sleep. A slight movement outside the glass door of the patio suddenly drew his attention. Apparently, he wasn't the only one who couldn't sleep. After crawling out of bed, he tugged the sheer curtain aside to see Rita standing by the railing, staring up at the moonlit sky. He opened the door slowly so as not to startle her.

"Decided to do some stargazing?"

She smiled at him as he walked closer to stand by her side. "It's very pretty. The sky is so clear, the moon so bright."

"Mmm-hmm."

"Why are you up?"

He shrugged. "Couldn't sleep."

"I hope I wasn't making too much noise out here." She reached up, started rubbing the back of her neck.

"You didn't wake me. Stiff?"

She rolled her head back and forth, working out some sort of kink. "No, it's not that."

"You didn't hurt yourself snorkeling, did you?"

He heard her laugh. "Only when I scraped by knee against the rough coral when I foolishly dived under and got too close. Just really wanted a better look."

That didn't explain what was wrong with her neck. Then he realized. "It's the couch. You can't be very comfortable on that thing."

"It's fine, Clint. I just fell asleep at an odd angle. It'll be all right once I knead out the knot at the base of my neck."

"Here." Without giving her a chance to protest, he reached over and started to massage the spot she'd been working. "Better?"

She sighed with satisfaction and Clint felt his mouth grow dry. For heaven's sake, he had to stop reacting to this woman's every movement. What in the world was wrong with him?

"Much better. In fact, I'm gonna go lie down again. Good night," she said with a small wave.

"Rita, wait."

She turned on her heel. "Yes."

Clearing his throat, he decided to just blurt it out. "The bed is huge. Too big for one person. Even with someone my size in it."

"Clint. I'm not sure it's wise for us to share a bed."

The proposal he'd made to her earlier on the beach sat like a proverbial elephant in the room. Maybe he should have never done it. What had he been thinking? Rita wasn't the type to have a meaningless fling. She deserved more from a man than what he'd offered her.

"Listen, if you're concerned that I'll take your sleeping in the bed as some sort of answer to what I proposed earlier, you don't have to worry about that."

"But you did propose it, Clint."

"And now it's totally in your hands. Whatever you decide, whenever you decide it. The ball is completely in your court."

She chewed her bottom lip. "We'll only be sharing the bed in the interest of comfort and practicality?"

He nodded. "I honestly don't see why we can't. I'd offer to take the couch myself if I thought for one instant that you'd allow it." But that was not the way she was wired.

Rita was the type of woman who tried to sleep in a lobby lounge chair so her roommate could have some privacy. She was the type to make sure a wandering dog wasn't a stray and that it made it back to its home safely. She was the kind of woman any man would be proud to have in his life.

Any man who deserved her. And he certainly didn't qualify. She warranted more than he'd ever be willing or able to give. And if that didn't make him selfish for the way he'd casually asked her for a fling, he didn't know what would.

"If it makes you feel better, I can't seem to fall asleep anyway," he told her. "I fully intended to power up the laptop and try to get some work done."

"All night?"

"I've done it before." More often than he could count, particularly those early days when he was getting his business off the ground as well as working ten-hour shifts to lend a hand at the various construction sites.

She glanced behind him into the room. "It does appear rather large."

"A California king they called it when they sold me the package. It would be a shame to let it go to waste."

"Are you sure I'm not kicking you out of your bed?"

She remained where she stood.

"You're not," he offered in as reassuring a tone as he could muster.

"All right, then. I could use the rest."

He stepped over to the door and held it open for her, trying to ignore the enticing citrus-and-coconut smell of her skin as she walked past.

The chances of him actually getting any work done were almost zero.

She could hear him breathing deeply in the other room. He'd set up his laptop and gotten to work, all right. But then he'd promptly fallen asleep. She could tell by the steady rhythm of his breath. On the same uncomfortable couch he'd rescued her from.

How was she supposed to relax knowing he was out there and she was in here on a nice comfortable mattress?

Sighing, she lifted away the covers and walked over to the other room.

Yep, out cold. Clint was sprawled on the couch with his legs and arms dangling off the ends. It was way too small for him. His head was bent on the back cushion at the same odd angle she'd woken up in earlier. As it was, she'd barely avoided a nasty tension headache due to the awkward position. She didn't want the same for Clint, especially considering it would be her fault.

She gave him a gentle nudge on the arm and quietly called his name.

He opened his eyes almost immediately. It took a few blinks but eventually she watched as he focused on her face. "What's wrong? Are you all right? Your neck hurt again?"

An odd sensation stirred in the pit of her stomach. His first reaction upon wakening had been concern for her. How many people in her life could she say that about?

Only her mother came to mind. When she wasn't soundly disappointed in her. Which was all too often.

"I'm fine," she responded, touched even further when he blew out a relieved breath. "But I think we should make this a true slumber party."

He sat up and rubbed his eyes. "Huh?"

"We can share the bed. Like a real sleepover. What do you say?"

With a groggy smile, he got up and followed her to the bed.

"Thanks," Clint whispered once they'd both crawled under the covers. She could smell the subtle scent of his aftershave even though it was now hours old. She'd taken a whiff of the bottle in the bathroom earlier, recognized the scent now.

"Please don't thank me for letting you sleep in your own bed, Clint. It makes me feel quite guilty."

"Sorry."

Now he was apologizing; that was somehow even worse. "Good night."

"Good night, sweet Rita."

The endearment evoked a small spark of pleasure in her chest. Would he have ever spoken that way if he wasn't half-asleep? Doubtful. "Get some sleep."

She heard him yawn beside her then turn to his side. Eventually, his breathing seemed to return to the same steady rhythm she'd heard earlier when he'd been asleep. So it surprised her when he spoke again a few moments later. Even more shocking were his words.

"Did you love him, Rita? You must have loved him deeply if you married him, right?"

Clint realized with a start that he'd actually voiced the question out loud. Damn his sleep-fogged brain and the tongue it had set loose. Rita's gasp of surprise left no doubt that she was now stunned and uncomfortable. Probably regretted inviting him into the bed for their "sleepover" as she called it.

They were both wide-awake now.

"That's quite the question."

"I'm sorry," he replied, with genuine regret. It wasn't like he actually wanted to know the answer. "It's none of my business."

"I married him. We both took vows to love and cherish each other."

Her words felt like individual blows to his gut. He'd been right; he hadn't really wanted to know. To top it off, Rita's tone held a strange tightness. He'd insulted her. After all, his question insinuated she may have married a man she wasn't in love with.

Clint wished he'd never even opened the can of worms. "I'm sorry it didn't work out," he lied.

The truth was, he wasn't sorry one bit that she was here solo. This trip would have been a far less memorable experience sans the time they'd spent together. He supposed that made him selfish, considering he had no claim to her. He'd probably only see her in passing, if ever, once they left this island.

"Jay and I grew up as childhood friends. In a way, we've always loved each other."

The blows kept coming. The tightening in his gut had him cringing. He had to acknowledge it as jealousy. As if he had the right.

"But it wasn't the type of love that should have led to marriage."

That threw him for a loop. Was she implying they were just friends? If so, why would they have tied the knot? There didn't seem to be any kind of financial reason, and she didn't seem the type of woman who would let something like a financial concern influence any kind of decision. Let alone a commitment like marriage. He knew about her father's cultural roots. Had that had something to do with it?

The questions hammered through his brain. As much as he wanted the answers, he resisted asking. She would share if she was ready. He'd done enough prying.

Enough time went by that he figured she wasn't ready. But then she surprised him by turning to face him. Her hands cupped under her cheek, the intensity in her eyes shone even through the darkened night.

"Someone like you wouldn't understand."

She was right about that. He didn't understand any of it. Nor could he explain his own reaction to it all. "I'd really like to."

"I didn't grow up the way most American girls do. In many ways, my family was very typical. In others, not so much."

So, it was cultural.

"My father didn't want to leave anything to chance when it came to his little girl, his only child."

"That actually sounds like pretty much any decent American dad."

He heard her inhale deeply. "Yes. And no." She blew out a breath. "He could be confusing as a parent."

Outside the glass wall, the moon slowly faded behind a cloud, casting longer darker shadows through the room.

"How so?"

"Well, for one, he made sure to instill a fierce sense of independence and strength in me. Made sure I knew how capable I was."

That much was clear in her every action, every nuance.

"But by the same token, there were all these decisions he'd made himself that he just wanted me to accept."

"Like marrying the man he'd chosen for you."

"Yes."

"What else?"

"My choice of vocation. He really grappled with the fact that I wanted to spend my life taking care of animals."

"Where was your mother in all this? Did she have any opinions?"

"My mom grew up in the Midwest. A rancher's daughter with five older brothers. Let's just say she made it a life goal to be a dutiful wife. A quality she seemed shocked that I didn't inherit from her."

"Wow. That is shocking."

"What? That I'm so different from my mother?"

"That you have five uncles," he joked, hoping it would lend a little levity to such a serious conversation. To his surprise, the remark earned him a small laugh.

"Yeah, I have like a million cousins. Holidays are fun."

"I guess my holidays will be different going forward too. Now that Lizzie's getting married. Jonathon's also got a large family." Clint only now realized the notion had been on his mind for a while, he'd just never brought it out into the forefront until now. His life was about to change almost as much as his sister's.

"You're going to make a great uncle yourself someday."

He groaned and rubbed a hand over his face. "Not anytime soon, I hope. I need some time to prep my embarrassing uncle game."

Her laugh echoed like a song through the darkness. "Why do I get the feeling you're more likely to be the uncle who shows up with armloads of gifts, spoils the kids rotten, then leaves a ridiculous mess for the parents to clean up after he's left?"

"I shall aspire to such greatness." Clint chuckled. The humor was short-lived.

"Sorry to say, my next family gathering will be as awkward and trying as the last one," Rita said, her voice so low it was barely a soft whisper.

"How come?"

"My father has barely said more than a few words to me since the divorce."

"He's angry?"

"No. Worse. He's disappointed." Maybe he'd imagined it, but he thought she might have wiped at her cheek. The thought of her crying made him wince inside.

"He's convinced I made a foolish decision in ending my marriage. That Jay and I were meant for each other and I blew it. For no discernible reason as far as he's concerned."

"Maybe you should explain your reasons then."

Her response was a long sigh. "My father isn't an easy man to talk to. I'm not sure exactly what I would say."

"I think it will come to you."

"You think so, huh?"

"I do. You still have a chance to try."

She shifted ever so slightly. "You're thinking of your own parents, aren't you?"

"I guess I am. My folks were gone often but when they were around, it was a completely different dynamic."

"In what way?"

"The world just felt whole, complete. Then suddenly it wasn't. And I had to accept the fact that life would never feel that way again."

"You were so strong, Clint."

Touching as it was, he chose to ignore her praise. He'd had no choice but to act strong. "Perhaps your dad just needs a nudge. If he's the man you've described so far, he'll come around."

"I hope so." She shifted closer to him; he could feel her sweet breath against his chin. "I've never discussed any of this with anybody before. I want you to know that."

Clint couldn't help reaching for her. He ran a gentle knuckle down her cheek, then down lower to her long graceful neck, felt her swallow under the tip of his finger. Electricity shot through his arm straight down to his feet.

"I don't know if you and your ex belonged together or not. But I can't imagine being the man who had to let you go."

Her only response was a sharp intake of breath. Clint wanted desperately to pull her to him, to rub the tension in her shoulders, tension so palpable he could see it despite the dark. He clenched his fists; he wouldn't touch her. It would be wrong to do so. She'd confided in him just now. He wouldn't betray that confidence by giving in to the desire he'd felt for her since they'd first laid eyes on each other.

His subconscious must have had other plans.

When they woke up the next morning, she was in his arms, head nuzzled against his neck. Her hair fanned like a dark silk scarf around his chest and shoulders. He didn't move a muscle for fear of waking her.

Unwilling to let her go just yet.

CHAPTER TEN

RITA SEEMED TO LIKE her showers extremely hot, judging by the steam wafting out from the bottom of the bathroom door. He tried not to imagine her behind that door, inside the shower stall, her smooth bare skin under the hot water. Was she lathering up right now, running a bar of soap over her curves?

Oh, man, he had it pretty bad.

He had to step away, before he gave in to the urge to knock and ask if she wanted company. Grabbing the pot of coffee he'd ordered earlier from room service, he poured a cup and walked onto the balcony to take in the early-morning weather. Another gorgeous day it looked like. Was there anything on the schedule wedding related? He couldn't even keep track anymore. Plus, he'd been a little distracted. In the distance, the ocean waves crashed gently along the sand of the beach. The vacant mountain was partially covered in fog, the top quarter not even visible.

The shrill sound of his cell phone in his pocket interrupted his thoughts. He pulled it out and clicked without looking at the screen. Most likely, it was Lizzie calling to give him an update. He'd left her several voice mail messages to check on her yesterday.

He was wrong. A husky, rich feminine voice greeted him when he answered.

"Did I wake you?" Maxine asked with her usual purr.

An urge to disconnect and pretend the call was dropped entered his mind. But he immediately nixed that idea. As much as he wanted to avoid this conversation, running was not his style.

"No. I've been up for a while."

She hesitated before speaking again, perhaps sensing the lack of enthusiasm in his voice. "How are things down there?"

"Fine. Everything's fine."

"And our bride? How's Lizzie faring?"

Our? Clint didn't miss the subtle meaning behind the use of the word. So now Lizzie was somehow her relation, as well. He rubbed his forehead. There was no doubt why she'd called and where this phone call was headed. Not that he'd had any doubt to begin with.

A pang of regret settled in his gut. Maxine wasn't a bad person. She really wasn't. But this thing between them had run its course.

"I've had a nightmare of a week," she told him.

Ah, so that explained the sudden call. Maxine needed a sounding board for the latest professional rejection. And someone to tell her how great she was, that whoever had turned her down was a bumbling fool of an idiot to do so.

He just didn't have the patience right now. "I'm sorry to hear that, Maxie. Hope it gets better for you."

He could almost feel her surprise bounce off the satellite and into the small speaker. "That's all you have to say? Don't you want to hear what happened? It was just awful, Clint."

He didn't have to respond. She continued without giving him a chance to, "The studio said they loved me when I went in and read. But I never even got a call back. Turns out, they've decided to go with that new Australian model who wants to break into the US movie market. I can't even believe they'd make that decision..."

Clint lost focus as she went on. Not that he didn't feel bad for her, he really did. But this was a pattern for her. A complete immersion in melancholy until the next gig came along. She had beauty, talent and connections. The next one always came along. Which is what he would have normally told her back in the United States.

Today, he didn't have the will for it. Nor the desire.

"Sorry, Maxie. You're a talented actress."

"Do you really think so?"

"I do."

He heard her sigh across the line. "You're so good for me, Clint." She paused for several beats. "I miss you."

There it was. He couldn't bring himself to answer, to lie to her. So he did the best he could. "Thank you."

Her gasp of outrage was unmistakable. "Thank you? That's what you're going to say to me?" Her question came through like the demand that it was. Demand that he apologize and thank his lucky stars that she'd deemed him worthy of the contact and this phone call.

Hard to believe a few short days ago he would have gone along, would have played the little game. Now he couldn't believe he'd ever had the patience for it.

"Sorry, Maxie," he repeated, more than ready to have this call over with.

"I accept your apology," she said with a breathless huff. "Now, I have great news for you."

"What's that?"

"I've decided I have to see you. Soon. I'm having my assistant arrange a flight right now."

Damn it. He should have seen that coming. The water shut off in the bathroom and he heard the shower stall click open. An immediate image of Rita dripping wet and naked flashed in his mind and he had to lean over the balcony railing to keep from doubling over.

Whatever Maxine was saying was a stream of static;

he couldn't even focus on her words. "Max, I don't think that's a good idea. I think we both need to move on. Individually."

"I don't understand."

Oh, honey. Sighing, he tried to wrangle his calmest, most soothing voice. "I think you do."

After listening to a stream of curse words and several insults hinting at his questionable heritage, Clint finally figured Maxine was spent for now. He told her goodbye as gently as he could and clicked off the call.

Up until a few days ago, he'd sworn all he'd ever want from a relationship was some idle companionship and a little fun. He couldn't be so certain of that conviction now. He'd shared parts of himself with Rita that he'd never opened up to anyone else. Her face was the first thing he pictured upon wakening in the morning. And the last image he had before falling asleep at night. He heard her laughter in his head and couldn't stop thinking about her when they weren't together.

Now, watching Rita as she stepped out of the bathroom with a thick terry-cloth towel wrapped around her middle and her glorious hair piled high atop her head, a wave of doubt made him wonder. About his feelings for Rita. About what he'd proposed to her on the beach after snorkeling, essentially a short-term, casual relationship for the duration of this trip. Up until now, he'd been all about such casual and meaningless relationships.

When it came to Rita, was that really enough? Or did he in fact want more?

Clint tried for the umpteenth time to focus on the column of figures his administrative assistant had emailed that morning. Rita had gone ahead to breakfast. Having been woefully negligent in answering any business emails, Clint regretfully told her he'd meet her there after responding to the more urgent messages.

A knock on the door waylaid his next attempt at concentration.

Must be the bellhop. He'd asked the front desk to bring all of Rita's stuff to his suite as soon as feasible. So she wouldn't have to keep returning to her room to retrieve various articles of clothing. It occurred to him before opening the door that he'd never actually gotten a chance to tell her about her things being moved. Well, it would be a pleasant surprise.

But the man standing across the threshold wasn't the bellhop. It was his future brother-in-law.

"Clint. We gotta talk, man."

Rita couldn't decide if the steam surrounding her was coming from the pot of hot water at the center of her table or directly out of her ears.

The man had some kind of nerve.

Clint hadn't made it down to join her yet. Which was probably not a good thing for him because the longer she sat here, the angrier she was getting. Finally, she watched him descend down the winding staircase and toward the dining area. He made a beeline when he saw her, his smile wide and cheery.

That wouldn't last.

"Hey, beautiful. Did you start without me?"

"Have a seat, Clint."

The smile faded. Pulling out a chair, he sat and folded his arms in front of him. "Something wrong?"

"As a matter of fact, there is."

"What's the matter? You look mad."

Wasn't he observant. She resisted the urge to sarcastically clap to congratulate him on it. "That's because I am."

"At me? Whatever for?"

He really had no idea. Well, she would explain then. "I went to my room before coming down for breakfast, wanting to drop off my nightclothes."

Understanding dawned in his eyes; his Adam's apple bobbed up and down as he swallowed. "And your stuff wasn't there."

"That's right. Tessa said a hotel employee had come in and asked her to gather everything that was mine. He'd been told to take it elsewhere. By you."

"Yes, I asked them to deliver it all to my suite."

"I caught the man in the hallway before he got to your door," Rita bit out, recalling how flustered the poor employee had been. Torn between following earlier directives or listening to the agitated woman telling him not to.

"I don't see the problem. I was simply trying to spare you from having to run back and forth every morning."

"That wasn't your decision. And it certainly wasn't one for you to make without even discussing it with me."

"It slipped my mind, okay? For what it's worth, it wasn't due to any kind of assumption about what I asked you yesterday."

The sudden further surge of anger had her gripping the table. "It absolutely better not have been."

"I just told you it wasn't. Why is this such a big deal?"

Did he really not see why? For heaven's sake, she'd gone to her room to find all of her things gone. Without anyone telling her why.

Their server appeared right then, sparing him the reply Rita was about to deliver.

"What can I get for you both?"

Her appetite had evaporated but she needed something to calm the queasy waves in her stomach. "Just toast for me, thanks."

Clint ordered a meat-and-cheese omelet, then turned his attention back to her. "I'm sorry if I made an incorrect assumption," he told Rita after the woman had left. "I just figured you'd be staying with me the rest of the trip."

His words carried an intimacy they weren't quite ready for. She hadn't even given him an answer yet. More accurately, she knew *he* wasn't ready. That's why the whole fiasco with her possessions had her so wound up. He was making assumptions about the two of them, without any hint of awareness on his part. Evidently, he didn't see that.

"I simply would have appreciated some consultation before you went ahead and made decisions on my behalf."

"You are blowing this way out of proportion." His voice was hard, firm. He leaned over, rested his forearms on the table. For a moment, she felt a twinge of apprehension at the hardened glint in his eyes. Right now, he seemed irked, as well. Escalation was never a good thing.

But her point had to be made. She wasn't about to back down.

"They are my things. I decide where they stay. And nothing said I was going to spend another night in your room. I told Tessa we would make that call day to day."

"You don't want to stay in the room, just say so."

She flung her napkin on the table. "This has nothing to do with where I'm sleeping at night. That's not the point. Not at all."

"I guess I'm missing your point. Exactly what is it?"

How much clearer could she be? "Don't make decisions on my behalf. No one gave you such a right nor a claim."

His eyes grew wide. Without an answer, he pushed his chair back and stood to leave. "I've lost my appetite." Well, that made two of them.

"My door is open if you need tonight. Without any expectations whatsoever. Bring your things, don't bring them. Totally up to you."

Rita's jaw clenched with frustration. "That's my whole point."

He shook his head. "Whatever you decide, have a pleasant day."

Turning to leave, Clint only made it about one step from his chair. His sister ran down the stairs at that very moment and made her way to their table, her eyes blazing.

"Oh, no, you don't, big brother. You're not going anywhere." Lizzie pulled his chair back out. "Have a seat. We need to talk."

Okay. Rita glanced from one sibling to the other. This was something of a new, unexpected development. Looked like her own tiff with Clint was going to have to wait.

Things did not appear to be going his way this morning.

She started to get up. "I should probably give you two some privacy."

Lizzie held up a hand to stop her. "No, Rita. Please stay. I'd kind of like a third party here. It might keep me from causing too much of a scene."

Seemed a little late for that, but Rita figured she wouldn't voice that out loud.

Even given her displeasure with him at the moment, Rita shot Clint a questioning look. She wasn't going to stay if it made him uncomfortable. He gave her a small affirmative nod.

"What exactly did you say to my fiancé this morning?" Lizzie demanded of her brother.

"Hey, settle your tone there, sis."

"Just tell me what you said to him."

"He came down to talk to me. Maybe you should be having a conversation with him. Whatever it's about."

Rita found herself fascinated. An only child, she had no firsthand knowledge of sibling angst. Whatever Clint had said to Jonathon, it appeared Lizzie was ready to thrash him for it.

"Oh, I did talk to him," Lizzie said. "It seems he's working for you now."

"So?"

Lizzie slammed both hands on the table. The couple at the neighboring table gave them a startled glance. "So? Why would you offer my fiancé a job? First of all, he's an attorney. You own a construction firm. How blatantly obvious that it's nothing more than a nepotistic gesture."

"I consult with attorneys all the time."

"International law attorneys? You need one of those in-house, do you?"

"Look," Clint began, "he came to me to say he's been edgy and worried. It's why he's been snapping at you. Things aren't going well at work for him. He thinks his days at the law firm may be numbered."

"I know all that."

That seemed to take Clint aback. "You do?"

"Of course, I do. He's my fiancé. We actually share our fears and joys and concerns with each other."

"Then why did he come to see me?"

"Not to ask you for a job!"

"Then what?"

"Nothing. He wasn't asking you for anything. He simply wanted to explain to his fiancée's brother why he might be behaving on edge lately."

Clint squinted against the sun. "Huh."

"But somehow you offered him a job and I'm guessing you didn't take no for an answer."

"Hold on. That's not how it went down."

Lizzie's mouth tightened. "Right. Because you're never overbearing and assuming at all." Sarcasm dripped from her lips.

"If he didn't want the job, he could have just said so."

"Clint. He said he tried. But you just acted like you'd solved everything and showed him the door. Guess what, bro?"

"What?"

"He doesn't want to work for his brother-in-law. He wants to find his own way out of this."

Rita didn't miss the clear sense of pride in Lizzie's voice. Clint must have heard it too. It was hard to miss.

"But now he has all sorts of doubts. Thanks to you."

"What? Why?"

"Now he can't help but think maybe he should take your offer. Because how would he feel if nothing panned out for him and he'd turned you down?"

Clint shrugged, gave his sister a look like she was missing something terribly obvious. "Just tell him the offer stands whenever he wants it."

Wow. Rita wanted to grab his shoulders and give him a hard shake. Not only had he missed the point, it had blown right past him without even entering the strike zone. Lizzie visibly deflated in her chair.

"Oh, Clint," his sister began. "Don't you know what telling him that would do to him? How much worse it would make all this?"

Clint threw his hands up with exasperation. "Fine, go tell him the offer is rescinded. To forget I ever made it."

He really didn't get it, Rita thought. An unwelcome twinge of sympathy stirred in her heart. At this point, she couldn't tell if she felt worse for him or Lizzie. Or even Jonathon. Clint was somehow internally programed to solve any issue he came across. Whether people wanted solutions from him or not.

Lizzie slowly stood, every inch of her dripping resignation. "Enjoy your breakfast, big brother."

She gave Rita a small wave and turned on her heel to leave.

Clint watched her back for several moments before clearing his throat.

Rita scrambled for something to say. Anything. The words failed her. Lizzie was right; she knew that. But there was something so defeated in Clint as he'd watched his sister leave, Rita couldn't help but feel moved by it. Her earlier anger at him notwithstanding.

"You'll have to excuse me," he told her, then stood and walked away in the opposite direction. Away from his sister.

And away from her.

It took all his will not to punch a hole in the wall when Clint got back to his room. Was every female in his orbit put there just to vex him? He plopped himself down on the unmade bed and tried to clear the fog of confusion from his head. Just a few short hours ago, he was lying in this very spot with Rita's soft, supple body nestled against him.

Now he wasn't even sure if they were on speaking terms. And for what? Because he hadn't wanted her inconvenienced.

As for his sister, he couldn't even fathom that one. He really thought Jonathon had come to him looking for help with his next position. How was he supposed to know the man simply needed to vent?

Usually when people came to him directly it was absolutely because they needed something. And unlike Rita, when he did something he thought was considerate, usually they were thankful. Not ready to bite his head off like she'd clearly wanted to.

He needed to get out of here. Out of this room, away from this resort. Though the sun was already bright and hot and it was probably way too steamy for a run, he figured he needed it. Or he really would punch a wall.

Pulling on his running shoes, he made his way out of the hotel and onto the beach. The next forty-five minutes was a grueling stretch of self-torture. Clint was near heaving for breath by the time he made it back. It was worth it. Every ounce of exertion had helped to vent his frustration and clear his head. He'd almost been able to eradicate the image of Rita shooting proverbial daggers at him this morning. Almost.

Despite his good intentions, she was rip-roaring mad at him. And so was his sister.

Clint rubbed the sweat off his forehand with the back of his arm and made his way to the elevator. He had to go see Lizzie. Then he had to clear things up with Jonathon. He couldn't have this hanging over their heads during the wedding. He'd do a mea culpa, even if he couldn't quite grasp exactly what his transgression was.

With reluctance but determination, he punched the floor Lizzie's room was on and knocked on her door moments later.

"Come in. It's not locked."

He wondered if she would be granting entry if she knew it was him. Opening the door, he hesitantly ducked his head in. "You sure I'm welcome?"

His sister sat at a vanity, her arms outstretched in front of her. Several bowls of liquid sat in front of her along with a variety of brushes and colored pencils like he'd never seen before. Lizzie motioned for him to come inside. He did so and shut the door behind him.

Then stopped in his tracks when Rita suddenly walked out of the bathroom. What was she doing here? She carried a glass bowl with some type of reddish pudding concoction.

She quirked an eyebrow at him when she saw him.

"Am I interrupting something?" Clint asked. "You doing each other's nails?" Great, maybe they were bonding over their mutual disgust of all things Clint Fallon.

"Rita's giving me henna tattoos. A bridal design in honor of my wedding."

"A hen of *what*?"

Rita shot an exaggerated eye roll in his direction. "A henna. Tattoo."

As if that cleared it up. "Right."

"Here, I'll show you," Lizzie said and lifted her foot.

He drew closer to see an elaborate array of designs adorning her right ankle. It was a complicated design of swirls and patterns, drawn in some type of orange-reddish ink. He'd never seen anything like it.

"You did that?" he asked Rita, incredulous.

"She sure did," Lizzie answered. "She's going to do my hands next."

He was beyond impressed. Considering the skin on a human foot wasn't the smoothest, particularly around the ankle, the design showed a tremendous amount of detail and a very steady hand. Though, he shouldn't be surprised. After all, part of her profession was performing surgery on small animals. But the pattern on his sister's foot said she also had a striking amount of artistic skill.

"Wow." It was the only word he could summon.

"Amazing, isn't she?"

Yeah, she certainly was. Every time he turned around, she seemed to do something or say something that drove that point home. He studied her now as she sat down on the velvet seat of a short metal stool in front of his sister. She dipped one of the wooden sticks in the bowl of pudding and began to work on Lizzie's right hand.

"You're very sweaty." Rita finally addressed him, throwing the comment over her shoulder without looking at him.

"Yeah, I, uh, went for a run."

"Did it help?"

"Yes. It helped a lot. Which is why I'm here." Clint focused his gaze on his sister's face. "Look, the last thing I want is to have you upset with me as I'm walking you down the aisle."

Lizzie pursed her lips, as if she were holding back a sob. Damn it. He didn't need that. He could handle her anger way better than he could deal with her sadness. "I don't want that either, big brother."

"I'll clear the air with Jonathon. I'll find him later and buy him a beer. Or maybe one of those Hawaiian mai tais."

"The ones they bring out all aflame?"

He grinned, relieved that things seemed to be smoothing over. "Yeah. Those ones. Better yet, I'll make him buy me one."

"I think he'd like that, Clint."

"Good. Don't give the whole job thing another thought, all right?"

"It's a deal." She suddenly smiled wide and looked down to where Rita was painstakingly drawing on her hand. "Hey, I think Clint needs a henna tattoo also. What do you think?"

Uh-oh. What had he just walked into here? Rita stopped what she was doing.

"I suppose. It's not typically something men have done."

"My brother is far from typical. Have a seat," she ordered. "She'll do you as soon as she's finished with mine."

Turned out, that didn't take long. Lizzie jumped up when she was finished and admired the artwork. "I'm going to go find Jonathon and show him. Do Clint's now," she directed before leaving the room.

An awkward silence hung in the air when it was just the two of them. Clint blew out a breath. "I don't know. I've never had a henna tattoo before. Don't think I really want one now. But what the bride wants…"

"The bride gets," Rita finished for him. "Here." She motioned for him to sit.

"That looks really sharp," Clint commented on the wooden stick she'd picked up.

"Don't worry. I'm not planning on stabbing you with it. Though the thought has occurred to me."

"Um…thanks?"

"Let's just say it's a good thing you knew enough to make amends with Lizzie just now."

He tried not to react as her soft, warm fingers moved over his skin while she worked. Sweet heavens. How was he supposed to sit still and resist the temptation to turn around and yank her into his arms when she was touching him like this?

He tried to focus on the conversation. "At the risk of a stab, I'm going to admit that my apology was more to regain the peace than any kind of actual understanding about what I did that was so wrong."

Her fingers stilled. "You honestly don't know?"

"I thought I was helping, Rita."

Her voice was soft when she spoke again as she resumed slowly working on his back. "That's not what Jonathon came to you for. Nor what he needed."

"How was I supposed to know that?"

She leaned closer, her tempting breath hot against his ear. "Perhaps you could have listened."

"I thought I had. And what I heard was that he needed a more secure job. Why would I not offer that to him when I can?"

"Because it only served to make you feel better."

Harsh.

"You're used to taking over," Rita continued. "You're used to exerting control in order to fix things. Whether the situation calls for it or not. You did the same thing when you thought I needed my things to be moved into your suite."

Why was that so wrong? "Yeah, well, I guess I had to learn from a young age that someone had to take the lead when things needed fixing. My parents were gone and the grandmother in charge of us could barely take care of herself." He bit out a curse. The last thing he wanted was to sound defensive. She wouldn't understand. For all their faults, Rita had grown up with two very involved parents—perhaps overly involved—who made sure to give her stability and structure. He'd done his best to do the same for his sister, for better or worse. "Lizzie never fully appreciated what it took to just survive back in those days." Which was fine with him. It was bad enough that one of them was terrified about the uncertainty of their future. Lizzie was too busy grieving to fully comprehend exactly how tenuous their reality had become. He'd had to be the one to plan for their future, to make sure they'd be safe and secure. Their grandmother certainly couldn't be counted on. All the burden had fallen like a ton of bricks securely on Clint's shoulders. No, he'd never talked to Lizzie back then about all the nights he'd lain awake, fighting off near-crippling anxiety. And Lord knew there wasn't anyone else to talk to.

Several beats passed before Rita answered, "Perhaps she would have understood, if you'd bothered to ever tell her."

He hadn't seen any point in that. "She had enough to contend with. I didn't want her bothered with anything more than she had to."

"Hmm. And despite that tendency of yours, Lizzie has still managed to turn into quite a competent and mature young lady."

Clint gave his head a shake. Despite? "What's that supposed to mean?"

She released a deep sigh and he could feel her warm breath against his shoulder and upper back. "It means that you were an incredibly competent guardian for your sister. Anyone can see that, Clint."

"But?"

"But people need room to grow and make their own

mistakes. And often all they're looking for is some reassurance and emotional support."

He couldn't come up with a response to that. Of course she had a point. But he didn't have many choices back then. He could only do what he thought was right. No one had been there to guide him after all. And what did any of it matter now anyway? All past history not worth revisiting.

It took about another half hour for her to finish, where she mostly worked in silence. Half an hour of divine torture and temptation. Her fingers deftly moving over his skin. The warm touch of her hands on his back.

Finally, she stood. "You're done."

"Thanks."

He stole a look in the mirror. His jaw dropped.

"Not what you were expecting?"

She'd drawn an elaborate rendering of…of all things… a butterfly. He groaned out loud. "Great. This will look wonderful on the beach. I'll feel so manly as I sport my fresh butterfly tattoo."

She had the audacity to giggle. "You'll get used to it. Maybe after a year or two."

A year! Or two!

"Whoa. Wait a minute. This is permanent?"

"I thought you knew."

Clint felt a moment of panic, then noticed the smile tugging at the corners of her lips. She was a lousy actress. "Sorry, couldn't resist."

"Ha ha. Can we say we're even then?"

"Even?"

She had to know what he meant. He wanted to put the argument of the morning behind them as well as the whole conversation they'd just had. He wanted to go back to the moment they'd woken up with her embraced in his arms.

A soft sigh escaped her lips. "You're a tough man to stay angry at, Clint Fallon. Yes, I suppose we're even."

* * *

That was definitely her up there.

Clint squinted up into the sun at the top of the rock cliff on the edge of the resort property. The same rock cliff that the resort guests jumped off into the ocean. It had taken him several beats to make sure but that was definitely Rita climbing to the top. Apparently, today was the day she made the jump herself. He couldn't help but recall the afternoon three days ago when they'd held hands and launched themselves together into one of the Seven Sacred Pools.

Looked like she wanted to do this one alone.

He'd been looking for Jonathon, who was supposed to be out on the beach somewhere, soaking up some last rays of sun as a free man before he said his vows tomorrow. But Clint's eyes had inexplicably been drawn to the rock wall, as if he'd sensed her presence there. Now she was gracefully ambling closer to the top. All thoughts of Jonathon forgotten, Clint made his way closer to the wall. There was a line of people waiting on top of it to go before her. Hopefully, that would give him enough time to reach a spot where he could watch her jump from fairly close by. A ridiculous part of him wished she'd asked him to go with her, wished that he was up there right now waiting to take the plunge with her in the way they had that day at the Seven Sacred Pools.

Well, he'd take the next best thing. He'd surprise her by greeting her with a dry, ready towel when she swam out afterward. Taking a quick detour to a resort shack, he grabbed two beach towels. He reached the side of the beach wall just as the person in front of Rita jumped in.

Her turn. Even from this distance he could see her anticipation; excitement was visible in her stance and posture. Taking a step back, he watched as she held her arms in front of her in an arch above her head. In the next instant, she launched herself headfirst into the water. A clean dive that hardly made a splash. If he wasn't worried about looking foolish to the beachgoers around him, he would have actually clapped.

Nothing was going to stop him from giving her a round of applause when she came out. Which didn't seem to be anytime soon. Clint waited as several moments went by. He still didn't see anyone out there who could be Rita. Had she broken the surface further down and he'd missed her?

That didn't seem likely. He'd been watching carefully for her.

A worrisome spike of apprehension stabbed his heart. He knew she was a good swimmer but what was taking so long? Even jumpers who'd gone in after her were already out and swimming to shore.

Deep breaths. He had to get a grip here. She hadn't been under that long. And she'd proven herself more than comfortable in the water both during their snorkeling adventure and when they'd swum at various spots on the Road to Hana.

But the nagging sensation in his chest persisted. He had to do something. He'd never forgive himself if something had gone wrong with her jump and he was just standing here like a dolt.

The wall was rough and jagged. It had to be that way under the water too. Rita could have very well hit her head.

The idea of that possibility and the image it evoked made up his mind. Kicking his sandals off, he dropped the towels and made a mad rush toward the water. He swam several feet faster than he would have thought possible then dived under when he got closer to the diving spot.

No sign of her.

Clint's heart pounded in his chest. He'd waited too long. He should have jumped as soon as it had occurred to him that she might be hurt. Sucking in a deep breath he dived under once more. Salt water stung his eyes and burned his throat as he stayed under too long to keep searching.

This couldn't be happening to him twice in one lifetime. To lose his parents in a boating accident was more than tragic enough. Fate couldn't be so utterly, shatteringly cruel.

He had to break the surface again, needed another lungful of air. There was nothing for it. Panic set in his veins, his heart hammering from exertion and fear.

It seemed to take forever to kick back to the top. A familiar face met him when he finally got there.

"Hey, Clint." She flashed him a brilliant smile. "I thought that was you. Did you see me jump?"

The sudden surge of relief he felt was almost instantaneously replaced with a blazingly intense fury.

"What the hell were you thinking?" Without waiting for an answer, he swam back toward the beach.

She was fast on his heels when he got there. "What exactly is your problem?" she asked.

Clint grabbed one of the towels he'd dropped on the sand earlier and handed it to her. She grasped it none too gently out of his hand even as she uttered a begrudging thank-you.

Leaning down, he grabbed the second one for himself. It was covered in grainy sand now—thanks to the wind—and the chafing sensation as he tried to dry off only served to irritate his nerves even further.

"I asked you what your problem is," Rita repeated. "Is there a reason you came into the water to yell at me?"

"My problem is that I thought you might be floating out to sea about to become a tasty morsel of shark food."

She stalled in the act of towel drying her hair. "What? Why in the world would you think that?"

"Because you didn't come up. Do you have any idea how long you were under?"

She gave a slight shrug. "I stayed under as long as I could."

"Whatever for?" To give him a heart attack perhaps?

Her jaw clenched. "I appreciate that you were worried. But you needn't keep yelling at me. As you can see, I'm perfectly fine. There was no reason for you to come after me. And no reason at all for the way you're behaving now."

Clint sucked in a breath trying to calm himself. It didn't work. She had no idea how much of a scare she'd just caused.

The thought of her hurt, struggling under the water had unnerved him unlike anything else he could recall.

She really had no clue.

"Why would you even do such a thing by yourself?" He realized people were starting to stare but he couldn't seem to lower his voice. The panic still pounded through his system.

"Not that I owe you an explanation. But I've been wanting to do that jump for days and there weren't that many people up there for once." She crossed her arms in front of her chest. "And frankly, I'm starting to feel a little resentful at your tone. It's really none of your business who I jump with, if anyone at all."

Resentful? None of his business?

That was it. Between her inflated reaction this morning to the moved luggage and the vitriol she was feeding him right now, he'd had it.

"You know what, Rita? I believe you're right." He picked up his shirt and sandals. "Feel free to spend the night in the suite if you want. Or not. It's up to you. If not, I guess I'll see you at the wedding."

He didn't give her a chance to respond.

Of all the...

Rita watched Clint's retreating back as he stomped away down the beach. All she'd wanted to do was take a refreshing plunge into the water. Then, as she was under, a glorious sea turtle had swum by, so close she could have reached out and touched it. A truly magnificent, breathtaking beauty of a creature she didn't want to stop admiring. So she'd stayed down there as long as she could. Until her lungs had started to squeeze in her chest and her cells had begun to cry out in protest for oxygen.

Okay, so maybe it had been a little long. But if Clint had just taken the time to listen, she could have explained all that. She might have even asked him to go back in with her so that they could look for it together. Maybe she would have confided that he was the first person she thought of sharing the experience with, had even felt a pang of longing to have him there with her. He hadn't even given her a chance to speak.

Instead, he'd chosen to stand on a public beach, in front of countless people, and loudly chastise her.

In fact, it had been his first reaction. To be domineering and overbearing, two traits she'd had more than her fair share of in her life up until now. Way more than enough.

No more.

She hadn't gone through the trauma of divorce and the sorrow of estrangement with her father to turn around and embrace more of the same from someone else.

So why was she fighting such a strong urge to run and catch up to him? To grab him by the arm and tell him she was sorry he'd been so worried about her.

Why did her eyes suddenly sting and a painful lump form in her throat?

Because she was a fanciful nitwit who'd gone and developed feelings for a man who was utterly wrong for her. At a time when she shouldn't even be entertaining such a notion.

She'd been trying so hard to deny it. But she'd been unable to think of anything or anyone else since she'd woken up in his arms this morning.

The feel of his body wrapped around hers elicited emotions and longings she had no business feeling.

And all afternoon, her mind had replayed the hour in Lizzie's room when she'd drawn on his shoulder. The feel of his skin under her fingers. The woodsy, masculine scent of him mixed with the salty air he'd just been running in.

His surprised and bemused face when he'd realized what she'd tattooed on him. The butterfly had been a whim. He'd spoken of the butterfly effect that night before they'd traveled alone together down the Road to Hana to return the rock.

He hadn't made the connection. And why should he? She'd obviously given it way too much thought. Spent too much time analyzing what would have happened if she'd never walked into that lounge at the airport. Or if he'd flown down in a private aircraft as per his usual routine. So many variables could have been even slightly altered and they would never have even crossed paths until the first wedding excursion. He most likely wouldn't have given her a second glance.

The same way he hadn't all those years ago when she'd first met him as a college coed.

CHAPTER ELEVEN

THE BEACH CHAIR wasn't so bad. At least as comfortable as the couch in Clint's suite. But definitely not as comfortable as his bed. Not that Rita was going to allow herself to think about being in his bed right now. Spending the night there was absolutely not an option this time. Not after their little exchange this afternoon due to her cliff-jumping adventure. Her pride would not allow it.

This was just fine; it wasn't even that cold out here on the beach. Only when the wind blew really hard did it get a little chilly. She could deal with that. For the next few hours she would just lie here with a big beach towel wrapped around her until Tessa's text let her know she could return to their room.

This time, she'd made Tessa promise not to fall asleep and forget.

Who needed Clint Fallon? Certainly not her.

She clung to that thought as the temperature gradually dipped lower over the next hour and a half. Her patience wearing thin, she double-checked her phone in case she'd missed Tessa's message.

Nothing.

All right. That was it. Tessa would get a few more minutes tops. Half an hour at the most. Then she was going to her room whether the other woman liked it or not. At this point, she didn't even care if Rob was still in there with her.

She was so tired and sleepy, she probably wouldn't even be able to stay awake long enough to witness anything.

Somehow, despite the chattering of her teeth, she managed to doze off. She wasn't even sure how much time had gone by when a set of strong, warm arms suddenly reached around her middle. She felt herself being hoisted up, then nestled against a hard, blessedly warm chest. She immediately recognized his scent, even through the haze of groggy slumber.

Clint. Of course. "Hey."

"Hi, sweetheart."

"How did you find me?"

"I checked the lounge area but you weren't there. Then I just knew."

"You did?"

He shrugged, lifting her slightly higher and tighter against him. "Yeah, I don't really know how to explain it. It was like something led me directly to where you were."

"Huh."

"I know it's hard to believe."

Rita recalled the night after she'd picked up the rock. The eerie sensation that someone, or something, was there with her in that room. Trying to tell her something almost. How her shorts had ended up on the floor outside her closet. "I do believe you," she told him.

She leaned into his chest and snuggled further into his welcome warmth.

"Babe, I'm sorry." Clint spoke in her ear, his hot breath warming her cheek. "I want to kick myself that you felt the need to sleep out here."

"I wasn't going to all night. I was going to demand the use of my bed in just a few minutes. As soon as Tessa and Rob are finished." She stifled a giggle, not even sure what she was amused by. Now she was just downright giddy.

"You don't need to do that."

What was he referring to? Between being so cold and half-asleep, it was so hard to focus. "Do what?"

"Demand the use of your bed. You'll be sleeping in mine."

The whole first floor of the resort was deserted when they walked through. Before she knew it, they were somehow in Clint's suite and he was gently depositing her on the bed. She snuggled deep into the soft pillow as he tucked the covers around her.

"I'm sorry," she whispered into the darkness. "For earlier. For scaring you."

"Oh, sweetheart. I should have handled it better."

"You were angry."

She sensed more than saw him shaking his head. "It was more that I was scared."

Something had been nagging at her all evening. She should have thought about Clint's history, the way he'd lost his parents. She felt like a selfish, inconsiderate brat. No wonder he'd been so upset. "Your mom and dad died in a boating accident, didn't they?"

He blew out a breath. "Yeah, they were vacationing off the coast of Greece. Got caught in an unpredicted Mediterranean squall." He flinched as he softly recounted the memories. "They were always off somewhere, exploring the world. Just the two of them."

While their two children were foisted on a grandmother who didn't want them around, Rita thought. Only to be stuck with them permanently when tragedy hit.

"And one day they left and never returned."

"I'm so sorry you and Lizzie had to endure that."

He rubbed a hand down his face. "Ironically, that was the year Lizzie had a starring role in the middle school play. She'd begged them not to go."

Rita felt a surge of tenderness for her friend. The loss of her mother and father at such a critical age must have been unbearable. And what of poor Clint? In many ways, being the older sibling, he had it so much harder. Her heart ached for the young man he must have been. A young man suddenly stranded with more responsibility than he could have dreamed. And he'd accepted it with grace and dignity.

"Lizzie mentioned what happened two or three times while we were at school," she told him. "I didn't push for details. I got the impression she didn't really like talking about it."

"She doesn't. And I can't say as I blame her. We both had to deal with their loss and move on as best we could."

He made it sound so simple. Perhaps deep down, he really believed it actually was.

"The adults you and Lizzie have both turned into despite all that is beyond impressive. Commendable."

"Thank you for saying that, sweet Rita."

Suddenly, Clint stood and turned to go.

She didn't want him to. "Clint, wait."

"Yeah?"

"Where are you going?"

He leaned over her to brush a loose strand of hair off her forehead, let his hand linger at her temple. "I'll go sleep on the couch. You know, in the interest of harmony."

She took his hand in hers before he could pull it away. "Stay."

It was the perfect day and setting for a wedding.

Rita followed the rest of the bridal procession to an archway covered in gorgeous tropical flowers on the beach. A small band behind them consisting of ukuleles and various drums played an island version of the wedding theme. All in all, the scene could have been out of a bridal magazine. Or a young girl's fantasy. When they reached the front, the groomsmen broke off to one side, while she and the other bridesmaids went to stand opposite.

Then Clint walked out with his sister from a covered canopy, leading her down the aisle. Rita had to remind herself to breathe. She hadn't seen Clint since this morning when they'd woken up in each other's arms again after having easily fallen asleep together the night before. Then the hectic pace of wedding preparation had immediately taken hold of them all. Now looking at him in a form-fitting tux with a Hawaiian flower in the lapel, she almost felt light-headed.

He had to be the most handsome, alluring man she'd ever known. And she'd have to say goodbye to him in about forty-eight hours.

Rita swallowed down the lump of sadness that settled in her throat. All fantasies came to an end. There was no use in wallowing. Served her right for letting her guard down and falling for a man who wanted nothing but freedom. On the heels of a failed marriage no less. Well, it seemed to follow a pattern of awful timing she'd somehow fallen into. Her first goal upon returning home would have to be to break out of it.

Lizzie beamed as she approached her groom, her smile as bright as the glowing Hawaiian sun above. Her dress was a delicate lacy piece that seemed to float around her as she walked. A tiara of beautiful flowers adorned her head and framed her angelic face. When they reached the archway, Clint gave his sister a soft peck on the cheek before putting her hand into Jonathon's outstretched one. As he walked toward the other groomsmen, he looked up to catch Rita's eye. The depth of emotion she saw in his gaze almost made her knees buckle.

How in the world was she supposed to go back to any semblance of a normal life after this? How was she supposed to live day to day as if none of this happened? While thinking of him every moment? For she had no doubt she'd be doing just that.

She'd gone and fallen in love with him. Who knew, perhaps it had been years in the making, since she'd first laid eyes on the man all those years ago. Now, with all the time they'd spent together in such close quarters, her feelings had developed into so much more.

She hadn't given him an answer. They still had two more days on Maui. To his credit, Clint hadn't even brought up the proposition he'd so casually made the other day. But she hadn't forgotten. She had no doubt he hadn't forgotten either.

The rest of the ceremony seemed to go by in a daze.

She watched Clint clap as the officiator finally pronounced Lizzie and Jonathon man and wife. He'd done so well by his sister, Rita thought. From a young age he'd taken care of her, made sure she prospered and thrived. Now he'd given her the most dreamlike wedding.

He was sure to make his own bride a very lucky lady one day. Though he swore he wanted to remain single, there was no question that someday someone would come along who refused to let him go. A wise, clever woman would make it her life's goal to figure out how to snare him for good. Rita couldn't help but envy her.

In the meantime, did she have it in her to take the little he was willing to give?

"May I have the honor of this dance?"

Rita looked up to find Clint holding out his arm to her as she sat watching the bride and groom canoodling at the head table. The reception was in full swing now. Even random strangers walking along the beach had joined in the revelry. A couple of local residents were doing an impressive luau dance, their hips moving so fast it made Rita's pelvis hurt just watching them.

Taking Clint's hand, she followed him out to the dance floor. As if by fate, the bouncy rhythmic reggae number that had been playing suddenly switched to a slow Hawaiian love song.

Clint took her gently by the waist and pulled her tight against him. A curl of heat unwound deep in her belly and moved in every which direction.

"Hard to believe they're finally married," she offered by way of conversation.

He laughed against her cheek. "I was really worried for a while there that it might not happen."

"I always had faith," she countered. "In those two and in the spirits."

"Is that so?"

"Mmm-hmm. I knew the spirits wouldn't let us down." Not when it came to the wedding anyway. As far as her heart, the spirits had apparently decided she was on her own. It had been slowly breaking since she'd run into Clint back on the mainland.

She nodded against his neck, resisted the urge to nestle closer and inhale deeply of his scent. She wouldn't be able to enjoy it much longer.

She pulled back to look him in the eye. "Clint, I haven't forgotten what you asked me."

He merely nodded, waiting for her to continue.

"I know I haven't given you an answer yet. I'm not sure that I can, even after all this time."

"Which is in itself answer enough, isn't it?"

Rita swallowed past the painful lump that suddenly formed at the base of her throat. This was so much harder than she'd expected. The truth was, she just couldn't do it, she couldn't have a casual affair. Not with him. Her heart was already lost to Clint Fallon. She couldn't bear to turn her soul over to him, as well. For that's what accepting his offer would do. She would never recover afterward, not when she had to walk away from him as if none of it mattered.

For several quiet moments, they just held each other, swaying softly to the music. Rita didn't trust herself to speak.

"So what's next for you, Sarita Paul?" he surprised her by asking. "Once we all return to reality, I mean."

"I guess I've got a lot to figure out."

"Well, if you're ever in the area," he said against her cheek. "You know the rest."

Something broke in the vicinity of her heart, an actual sensation of snapping that had her struggling for breath. How could he be so casual, so matter-of-fact about whether he would ever see her again? She had to get away before she made a fool of herself by sobbing into his chest.

She slipped out of his grasp and ran toward the crashing waves of the water. It didn't surprise her when his footsteps sounded in the sand behind her seconds later.

"Rita." He spoke her name softly, like a whisper on the wind.

"I'd like to be alone for a while."

"There are some things we should discuss, don't you think?"

She didn't dare turn to face him, afraid of what her face might give away. "Like what? Like how I should look you up when I'm in town? Is that what you'd like to discuss?" she asked over her shoulder.

It was no use. He came to clasp her by the shoulders and turned her to face him.

"You have a lot to figure out. You said so yourself. It would be selfish of me to stand in the way of that."

"Don't pretend that's why you're doing this, Clint. Please give me more credit than that."

He blinked at her.

"Why would you say that?" He seemed genuinely perplexed. For such a smart, accomplished man, he really could be very obtuse. Or he was working really hard at it.

"You're letting yourself off the hook by pretending this is all about me."

He let go of her shoulders and shoved his hands into his pockets. The action had the effect of pulling his shirt tight against the toned muscles of his chest and widening the V at his collar where he'd undone two buttons. The overall look was so devilishly handsome, she wanted nothing more than to forget this conversation and fling herself into his arms.

But that would only serve to prolong the inevitable.

"It's really more about you. And how scared you are."

He didn't meet her gaze, stared at the sand beneath their feet. "What exactly do you think I'm so afraid of, Rita? Please enlighten me."

She ignored the snark in his tone. "Of loving someone and then losing them. It's why you strive so hard to control what's around you. Who's around you. But you can't control human beings, Clint. Nor their feelings."

He looked up, off to the horizon and the setting sun behind her. His next words proved she was right about everything she'd just said.

"You may have a point. It doesn't change anything."

"How can you say that?" she pleaded, hating the sobbing quality of her voice.

"I was clear from the beginning, sweetheart. This was one week on an exotic tropical island. Reality is what it is."

The breaking in her chest she'd felt earlier turned into a violent shatter. "So that's it then? You're going to let fear and uncertainty keep you from moving forward? You're so ready to just turn your back on any feelings that you may find inconvenient."

His eyes narrowed on her face. "And what about you, Rita?"

"What about me?"

"You're not exactly in a position to cast stones."

What was he talking about? She wasn't the one ready to walk away from what they were beginning to feel for each other. Feelings she knew he had to be experiencing also. Or else what did that say about her?

"I have no idea what you mean."

"You really don't see it?"

"See what?"

"Let me ask you something. Exactly how have you moved forward since your divorce?"

What did Jay or her divorce have to do with anything? "What are you insinuating? Maybe you should just come out and say it."

He bit out a curse. "Fine. You're stuck in a holding pattern. Too afraid to move, too afraid to risk another chance at letting others down."

She sucked in some much-needed air. "You have no idea what you're saying. You don't know what it took to sever my marriage, the pain and anguish it caused me and to those around me."

"You're right. It did take a lot of courage. So now what?"

Rita wanted to slam her hands up against her ears. Suddenly, this conversation had turned into one about her. And all her shortcomings as far as Clint was concerned.

The way he saw her was breaking her heart.

He didn't wait for a response. Shaking his head, he continued, "You said you'd thought years ago about opening your own practice. Or maybe working for an animal shelter. Yet you plan on looking for another small office to join when you return. How is that any different than what you were originally trying to get away from?"

"It's very different."

He shrugged. "Is it? Perhaps. I guess I wouldn't know. But it's not what you really want."

"I'm trying to figure out what I want."

"So you say."

She willed the tears that now stung her eyes to keep from falling. He thought she was indecisive and weak. It hurt more than she would have thought.

"And what about your father?" he demanded to know.

"What about him?"

"You've stood up to him. And your relationship suffered. What are you going to do about it now?"

"We just need time," she cried out.

"And it will all miraculously work itself out?" he said with a questioning shrug. "Face it. You're stuck and it's because you've chosen to be. Both in terms of your career and your relationships."

"You have no idea what you're saying."

"I think I do. It's like you've made the climb up onto that cliff. But you're still just standing there, not ready to jump but not willing to climb back down."

So that's how he really saw her. The revelation felt like a physical blow. Lifting her chin, she summoned her voice despite the pain, despite the anger. "At least I made the climb, Clint. Look around you and see if you can say the same."

Something shifted behind his eyes; they suddenly grew darker. She thought he started to reach for her, but it was too late. Rita stepped away and strode past him as far as she could before she had to catch her breath. Maybe it made her a coward but she had to flee. Before he could hurt her anymore.

Clint glanced at his watch and scanned the outdoor reception area once more. There was no sign of her. She'd stormed away from him about two hours ago. And now it was almost midnight and he hadn't seen her since.

He'd already checked her room and tried calling her repeatedly. Man, he really shouldn't have gone off on her like that. Now that he'd cooled down, he figured he should find her and try to apologize. But she was nowhere to be found.

As much as he didn't want to worry his sister on her wedding night, he was going to have to ask her if she knew where Rita was. Either that or he was ready to call the authorities and round up a search party.

He approached Lizzie where she stood by a buffet table feeding Jonathon various pieces of fruit.

"Hey, sis, got a sec?"

"For my big brother? Always."

"You're leaving me here alone?" Jonathon petulantly asked. "It's our wedding night. I thought we might retire soon."

Lizzie gave him a hard kiss on the lips. "I won't be long. You wait right here for me."

Clint bit down on the nausea that little exchange invoked and pulled his sister to the side.

"Sorry for the interruption. And I don't want to worry you, but I haven't seen Rita in several hours. She's not answering her phone. Have you heard from her?"

Lizzie's smile faded and her face fell. "Oh, Clint. You don't know?"

A bad feeling started to bloom in his chest. "Know what?"

"Rita decided she'd been away from home too long. Asked if I'd mind if she left a couple days early."

"She's gone?"

Lizzie nodded; lines of sympathy etched her eyes. "Now that the reception is over, I told her it was fine. Apparently, there are some pressing matters she needs to address back home. She's taking the red-eye out. You two didn't discuss it?"

He could only shake his head.

"I'm surprised she didn't say anything to you."

"Not a thing." Not directly anyway. Indirectly, she'd

told him everything he needed to know. And then she'd just up and left. Without so much as a word of goodbye.

Well, what did he expect? After the way he'd confronted her earlier, she would have had every right to slap him before storming off. And he would have deserved it.

"I'm sorry, big brother." He could barely hear Lizzie over the sudden roaring in his ears. "If I'd realized you didn't know, I would have come to find you right away."

Rita was gone. "It's not your fault. You should get back to your groom."

"What about you?"

He shrugged. "I'll be fine, just need some salty air." Turning, Clint made his way toward the beach, toward the spot he'd stood arguing with Rita. Was that the last spot he would ever see her? The notion sent a painful stab in the area of his chest.

Lizzie was following him. He turned around to give her a questioning look. They'd reached the beach.

"What happened between you two?"

"Nothing you need to concern yourself with. Not now of all times. You just got married for heaven's sake."

"That may be so. But I'll always have time for my big brother."

Clint forced a smile and crouched down in front of the crashing waves. To his surprise, Lizzie dropped down next to him, sitting right on her bottom in the sand. She pulled her wedding dress tighter around her as a small gust of wind carried over from the water.

"I've known Rita for years," she began. "She's one in a million. Whatever went wrong, I'm guessing it was completely the result of you being your usual foolhardy and rigid self."

His sister could be quite blunt. "My only defense is I never tried to lead her to believe otherwise."

"I see. And you think that absolves you somehow?"

He rubbed a hand down his face. "I don't know what I think," he answered truthfully. "This was all supposed to be so simple, so straightforward."

"And all within your control."

He gave her a side-eye glare. "Don't start, Lizzie. I don't want to fight with you too."

"So, you two did have a fight then."

Could it even be called that? Apparently, he and Rita had both been making all sorts of observations about each other. While failing to look within themselves. "More of a heated discussion. Rita felt compelled to point out a few things that she thought I was missing. About my behavior. I sort of returned the salvo."

"I see. What did Rita have to say?"

"I'm sure you can guess."

"That you insist on taking charge because you think if you control as many circumstances as you can, you can spare yourself?"

"Did you two compare notes?"

"You're not exactly an enigma, big brother."

He humphed at that.

She remained silent for a while, played with the sand around her. When she spoke again, the change in topic threw him for a loop. "Jonathon and I decided we'd like a very big family. Like his. And we want to start right away."

Clint didn't bother to stifle his groan. Hadn't he been through enough tonight? "Is that your very uncouth way of telling me that you're going back to your groom now?"

She laughed. "No, I just want you to think about what that means. For you in particular."

"For me?" Where in the world could she possibly be going with this. He honestly had no clue.

"When you become an uncle. Are you going to avoid my children? For fear of growing too affectionate of them?"

"Of course not, especially if they're lucky enough to resemble their uncle."

"Ha ha. The simple truth is that you'll love them and cherish them from the moment they arrive in this world until your very last day. That's just who you are."

"Of course, I will." What was the point of this conversation she was leading him down? Now of all times. And here of all places, on the beach after her wedding.

"And what about me? Did you ever think it'd be easier just to write me off when I became an adult? You never stopped caring about me."

"Are you getting to some kind of point? You're my sister. Your children will be my nieces and nephews. How in the world would I have any choice in the matter when it came to loving them or caring about them? Or you?"

She actually had the gall to throw sand in his direction. He closed his eyes just in time but couldn't avoid several grains landing directly into his mouth.

"You have no clue, do you?"

Clint made an exaggerated show of spitting out the offending sand. "About what?"

"Don't be dense. From where I'm standing, it's patently clear that you have no choice when it comes to Rita either."

Rita pulled out her boarding pass and reconfirmed her seat as she made it to the sitting area of terminal twenty at Kahului Airport. To think, just a few short days ago she'd been in a different airport ready to board a different flight, completely unaware that she was about to come face-to-face with the man she would fall in love with.

For that's exactly what had happened. She could no longer deny it. She'd fallen head over heels for Clint Fallon. But she couldn't manage to figure out a way to reach him. Hard to believe, but this was so much worse than her marriage failing. Her divorce had led to feelings of sadness and profound failure.

When it came to Clint, she felt absolute, sharp, nearly unbearable pain.

Biting back tears, she made her way to one of the many empty chairs to wait for boarding. What was Clint doing at this very moment? Had he even noticed she'd gone?

She felt a small twinge of guilt about leaving him back there without so much as a word. But what was there left to say?

You've made the climb up onto that cliff. But you're still just standing there...

His words were so unkind. So unfair.

She'd taken a giant leap by insisting on splitting from Jay. Hadn't she? Of course she had. Look at the ramifications it had led to, the hit her relationship with her father had taken.

And what had she done about that? Nothing so far. As Clint had made sure to point out.

Without giving herself time to think, she pulled her phone out of her pocket and called up her parents' number. What time was it on the East Coast? Early morning, but she didn't care. Not right now.

Her mother picked up on the second ring. "Rita, is everything all right? It's awfully early."

"I'm sorry. I just wanted to talk to Dad. Is he up?"

"You know he is. He always wakes up at the crack of dawn. What's this about, dear? Are you sure everything's all right?"

No, she wanted to wail out. And it would never be all right again. "Yes, Ma. I promise."

Her mother hesitated a few moments before Rita heard shuffling on the other end of the line. Seconds later, her father's rich baritone and mild accent greeted her with concern.

"Sarita? What's this about? Do you need help? Where are you?"

The concern in his voice brought tears to her eyes. She knew he cared about her; he loved her deeply. But it was no longer enough. She wanted more from him. And she was ready to ask for it.

"Everything's fine, Pa. I just wanted to tell you that I love you."

Dead air. Finally, her father cleared his throat. "I...love you too, sweetheart. You have me quite concerned though, dear one. Do you need to be picked up?"

Rita swallowed down the lump in her throat and forced herself to keep talking. "No, I'm fine. I just need you to talk to me. To be my father."

"I don't understand."

No, he didn't. But she would do everything in her power to make him understand. "And I want you to be proud to be my father. But it can't be solely on your terms, Papa."

Then she could no longer hold the tears back at all.

CHAPTER TWELVE

IF RITA CLOSED her eyes and concentrated long enough, she could easily imagine she was back in Hawaii sitting in a lounge chair on the beach. She could almost feel the salty air against her face and the sun shining bright and hot, warming up her skin.

Hard to believe it was only two weeks since she'd returned. Rather than a sandy beach, she was sitting behind a desk trying to put the final pieces in place to kick off the annual fund-raiser for the Greater Westport Animal Shelter. Not that she was complaining. Somehow, she'd landed her dream job within days of getting back from Lizzie and Jonathon's wedding. Who was she kidding? If it wasn't for Clint and the way he'd confronted her about moving forward with her life, she would have never had the gumption to apply for it.

Even her father was impressed. He'd actually taken her out to lunch to celebrate when she'd told her parents the news last week. Rita's eyes stung as she recalled her father's efforts that afternoon. They'd never, ever sat down together one-on-one just to talk. He'd actually said he was proud of her and her newfound position. She couldn't have been more surprised if he'd jumped on the diner counter and started doing a step dance.

His words echoed in her head still. *You've always had the sheer will and strength to go after what you wanted.*

There was at least one exception, Rita thought. Those qualities her father touted had failed her perhaps when it mattered the most. And she would have to live with that for the rest of her life.

Thank goodness for how demanding the new job was. It was keeping her just busy enough that memories of Clint Fallon only plagued her at night. Except for those moments during the day when a pair of dark brown eyes flashed in her vision, or she thought she smelled the woodsy scent of Clint's aftershave.

Rita threw her pen down on the desk in disgust. Who was she kidding? Hardly a moment went by that he wasn't in her thoughts. Every time her cell rang, her heart leaped to her throat. Until she saw on the screen who it was. Never him.

So far she'd resisted the urge to call her friend under the pretense of asking about her newly married life just to get info on her brother.

But she wouldn't allow herself to stoop to that level.

A sudden knock on the door was followed by her vet technician popping her head in. "I'm really sorry about the interruption, Dr. Paul. But there's a man out here who insists he needs to see you before he'll sign off on his adoption. Refuses to speak with anyone else."

Rita looked up from the paperwork she'd been shuffling. She had to get through it all so that she could start her rounds with the animals. But it had been hard to focus.

"I'd ask him to leave," Val continued. "But he seems really interested in one of the pups. I'd hate for the little fella to miss a chance at adoption."

"That doesn't explain why he needs to see me specifically."

"Should I get Frank from the auto parts shop next door to show him out?" Val asked.

Rita let out a long sigh. Looked like the paperwork and

the animals were going to have to wait a little longer. "No, it's okay. I'll talk to him. Thanks."

She did a double take when the visitor entered the room.

Rita rubbed her eyes. Maybe this wasn't real. Maybe she was simply seeing what she wanted to see. But then he spoke. And all doubt fled. Her heart fluttered like a hummingbird in her chest.

"Hey, remember me?"

"Clint?"

"Hi, sweetheart."

"What are you doing here?"

He shrugged, shut the door behind him as Val stepped away. Rita thought she heard the younger woman giggle. "I wanted to show you something."

This was surreal. All this time she'd been willing the phone to ring. Just to be able to hear his voice would have sent her soaring with happiness. But here he was. In the flesh.

She wasn't sure how her mouth was working but somehow she managed to speak. "Show me what?"

Her jaw dropped when he started unbuttoning his shirt, then shrugged it off. Suddenly, Clint Fallon was standing in her newly gained office, shirtless and smiling. How many surprises could she be dealt today?

"My tattoo," he answered her.

Turning, he pointed to his back above the shoulder blade. Rita's vision clouded as she realized what she was looking at. He'd gone and made her butterfly permanent after all. "I had the tattoo artist trace your design before it could fade."

"Oh, Clint." Without thinking, she flung out of her chair and into his embrace. His strong arms went immediately around her. He smelled the same.

"Does that mean you like it?"

She couldn't summon the words to express what she felt.

"I haven't stopped thinking about you," he whispered as he dropped devastating kisses along her temple, down her cheek. Then he took her lips brutally with his. Rita felt the kiss down to her core. "I missed you."

She pulled away. "Oh, Clint. I missed you too. What took you so long?"

"I wanted to make sure to give you enough time, then I couldn't wait any longer. I've barely been functioning these past few weeks." He paused to look around her office. "Whereas you've clearly been busy. I read about your new post online. Congratulations, babe."

She sniffled. "It was a long shot. I didn't think I was qualified for the director position, of all things."

"Oh, Rita."

"But then I thought about what you said. About just jumping off the rock cliff."

"I'm sorry about that night. I'm so sorry I said all those things."

She hugged him tighter. "Please don't apologize. I needed to hear it all. I needed to hear it from you."

He sniffed her hair. "But I should have also told you how extraordinary I think you are."

"You do?"

"Oh, babe. You're warm, witty, generous. You make sure a wandering dog isn't a stray and that it's well taken care of. You're a staunchly loyal friend. You don't think twice about driving up a harrowing mountain to return a rock which may be jinxing your friend's wedding, just in case it's real."

She had to chuckle at that. "Some men might call that feckless and silly."

"Not this man." He shuddered in her arms. "But please don't try anything like that again. Not without me."

He had no idea. She didn't want to do much of anything these days without him by her side.

"I won't. And as far as loyalty, you have it in spades yourself, Mr. Fallon."

"Huh?" he studied her.

"Oh, Clint. Don't you know how impressive it is? The way you made sure to not only take care of your sister from such a young age but also to help her thrive. And look at all you've accomplished. Completely on your own. I've been in awe of you since the day I met you at school move-in day." She inhaled deeply, decided to make yet another jump. "And now, after all these years, I've gone and fallen in love with you."

He actually lifted her off the ground. Did a mini spin. "Well, that happens to work out, Dr. Paul. Because I've fallen madly, irreversibly in love with you too. We should really do something about that."

He took her lips once more, delved deeply into her mouth. Rita had to catch her breath when he finally pulled away.

"You love me?"

"As sure as the sun rises over that freezing-cold crater every morning."

Rita was certain her heart had burst in her chest. This was beyond any fantasy she'd dreamed up.

"Oh, by the way, I plan on adopting that poor, ridiculously tiny Chihuahua out there."

She couldn't help but laugh. "The Chihuahua? Really? I would have pegged you for a…larger, more rugged breed."

He shrugged and flashed her a smile that sent heat simmering over her skin. "What can I say? You don't seem to have any of those hairless cats."

"They're called Sphynx cats," she reminded him.

"Whatever. The little fella called to me. Plus, your staff told me that he's been here the longest."

A wealth of emotion flooded her chest and threatened to split her heart open. She was completely, steadfastly, head over heels in love with this man. Perhaps she'd loved him since she'd first laid eyes on him as a young college student. Back then, he had seemed beyond her reach, someone to dream about. Now, all these years later, here he was, making her dreams a reality.

"Then he's yours," she vowed, laughing some more when he picked her up and sat her on the desk. "I shall personally vouch for you."

"Good. Guess what?"

"What?"

"You're mine too."

EPILOGUE

One year later

"You know, it's our anniversary too," Clint informed her as he turned onto the roadway leading to Wai'anapanapa State Park.

"Is that so?"

"You bet. It was exactly one year ago that I kissed you for the first time. I don't suppose you remember."

Rita waited for him to park and got out of the car before she answered. "I remember everything about that trip." The statement earned her a deep kiss that had her toes curling. The effect Clint had on her senses had not diminished in the slightest in the year since they'd been on this island for Lizzie's wedding. They'd joined the couple here for a celebratory trip in honor of their first anniversary. Never would Rita have guessed back then that she'd be here with Clint for such an occasion a year later.

A strange sense of déjà vu overcame her as they walked down the steps leading to Black Sand Beach. It was hard not to feel slightly silly when she thought about the superstitious reason behind the need she'd felt to return a silly rock. Superstition could be a powerful thing, it turned out.

Clint held her hand as they made it to the bottom. The waves were quieter today than that morning a year ago. The dark sand was the color of black onyx, just as she remembered. They walked farther toward the water. Though he hadn't come out and said so, Rita knew where he was taking her, touched that he'd thought to do so. He'd obviously been planning.

There it was. The cave where she'd first touched him, where she'd first asked him to kiss her.

"Do you think you'd recognize it?" he asked in a light, teasing voice. "Your rock?"

"I have no doubt. It was a very special one that called to me."

They stepped inside the opening and immediately all the warm memories came flooding back. She wrapped her arms around his neck and gave in to the desire to kiss him.

"I, for one, am glad you picked it up all those months ago," Clint said against her mouth. "Or else I would have never gotten you in here alone."

"Very true."

He winked at her. "See if you can find it."

He was serious. "That's ridiculous, Clint. It was a year ago. It's probably nowhere near here anymore."

"It was magical, remember? Look around. You never know."

Rita let out a resigned groan. Just to humor him, she looked down along the ground, then stood upright. "It's not here."

Clint shook his head. "You didn't even try. Look again. At exactly the spot you left it last year."

Why was he doing this? All she wanted to do was enjoy the scenery and then go indulge in some of that delicious banana bread she'd been thinking about all day.

"If you insist."

Stooping lower, she searched the spot where she remembered dropping the rock so many months ago. Not that she really knew for sure what to look for. All the rocks looked exactly the same.

A small speck of white caught her eye on the ground near the cave wall. She bent to pick it up.

"What is that?" Clint asked, taking her hand to study it.

"A flower. Or half of one. How'd a broken flower get in a beachside cave?"

Clint shrugged. "It doesn't appear to be any old flower."

Rita looked closer. He was right. Upon closer inspection, it appeared the flower hadn't been torn in half at all. "It looks like it somehow bloomed that way, only half a flower. I've never seen anything like it."

"It's beautiful. You know, now that I think about it, I've heard about these flowers. They're native to Hawaii."

"You have?"

"Yes. It's coming back to me. The story behind it. It's called a *naupaka* flower."

Rita narrowed her gaze on his face. Something was up. Clint wasn't normally the type to pay attention to legends or stories. Even if he had indulged her last year when she'd felt the urgent need to return a displaced pebble. And he certainly wasn't the type to remember the name of a flower.

"What's this story?" she asked him.

"More a legend really. About a princess."

"Another sad story about a princess?"

Clint pursed his lips and nodded. "I'm afraid so. Apparently, she fell in love with a man who was already spoken for. He felt the same way about her but the gods decreed they were not meant to be. Since she couldn't give him her heart, she took a flower from her hair and tore it in half. Until their deaths, they each carried half the flower with them always. It's been blooming that way ever since."

Rita didn't know quite what to say. It really was a beautiful, touching story. But it still didn't explain how the flower had gotten here. Or why Clint knew so much about it.

He continued with the rest of the legend. "It's said that

when the two halves of the flower find each other, then true love blossoms."

He hadn't finished uttering the last word when Clint suddenly bent down on his knee before her. Reaching in his pocket, he pulled out two items. One a small velvet box.

The world spun around her head. She forgot to breathe.

And then she realized what the other item he held was—the other half of the flower. He must have been planning this for so long. All of it for her. Tears stung her eyes as she looked into the love that showed in his. How in the world had she gotten to be so fortunate?

"Sarita Ann Paul," he began. He took her hand and opened the box to reveal a breathtaking stone set in a glittering band. It was the most exquisite ring she'd ever seen.

"Would you do me the honor of marrying me?"

Rita barely heard him over the roaring in her ears and the overwhelming joy in her heart. As much as she'd dreamed, nothing could have prepared her for what was happening. Clint Fallon had just asked her to be his wife.

Somehow, she found her voice despite the flood of emotion pouring out of her soul. "Yes. A million times over. Yes!"

* * * * *

ALEXEI'S
PASSIONATE
REVENGE

HELEN BIANCHIN

For my daughter, Lucia, with all my love.

CHAPTER ONE

'GIVE ME A few minutes, then send her in.'

Alexei ended the call, slid the smartphone into the inside pocket of his jacket and stood in reflective silence as he studied the scene beyond the tinted plate-glass window.

Viewed from a high floor in an inner city office building, it appeared picture-postcard perfect with sparkling blue harbour waters against a backdrop of partially dark shrub-covered rock face showcasing glimpses of expensive real estate.

Sydney. The iconic Opera House, the expansive harbour bridge.

A large cosmopolitan city he'd departed beneath a deliberately fabricated cloud.

A city he'd vowed to return to in vastly different circumstances.

Which he had.

With a plan.

One which covered all the bases, and every possible contingency.

Five years ago he'd stood in this office space, denounced and discredited by Roman Montgomery, the owner of Montgomery Electronics, for daring to conduct a covert affair with Roman's daughter, Natalya.

A young woman who had enjoyed a life of wealth and

privilege since birth. Intelligent, having graduated from
university with an MBA degree with honours…savvy, and
employed as her father's PA.

A life in which a thirty-year-old American *nobody* of
Greek origin could never be a contender. As an added
insult, Roman Montgomery had laughed at Alexei's expressed honourable intentions, written out a cheque in lieu
of notice and issued an immediate dismissal, adding the
rider Natalya had merely been amusing herself with a temporary fling. What followed became an orchestrated farce
as Alexei's calls, emails and texts to Natalya were ignored,
and within a matter of hours he discovered all her contact
numbers had changed to an unlisted category.

Security guards posted in the main lobby of her apartment building ensured Alexei was denied access, and a
determined attempt to reach her involving mild force resulted in a Restraining Order issued against him.

Which Alexei disregarded…to his folly.

The appearance of two police officers at his apartment
with an arrest warrant provided a sobering experience at
best. Invoking his right to legal representation ensured
Alexei's incarceration was brief.

The desire to vent at what he perceived to be an injus-
tice had been eased…*slightly*…by a harsh soul-destructive
session with a punching bag at a local gym. He could still
recall the cautionary shout from a fellow member nearby…
'Hey, man, you aiming to kill that thing?'…resulting in one
final vicious hit before he steadied the bag, tore off his
boxing gloves, then turned and strode towards the changing rooms without so much as a word.

'Better a punching bag than Roman Montgomery's jaw,'
he muttered beneath his breath as he stood beneath a hot
shower to dispense the sweat from his body before switch-

ing the dial to cold in a bid to cool off physically, mentally and emotionally.

Within a matter of days Alexei had boarded a flight to New York, reconnected with his widowed mother, his two brothers in Washington and worked every waking hour, prepared to do anything within the bounds of the law—and a few that hovered on the fringes—in order to establish the foundation of an empire to rival others in the world of electronics.

And he had, exceeding his own expectations, aided by a new invention embraced worldwide that had elevated him to billionaire status.

During the past five years success and wealth had provided Alexei with much. Real estate in several countries, including a Paris apartment, a vineyard nestled on the slopes of northern Italy, an apartment in Washington, a Santorini villa inherited from his paternal grandfather.

Women? He'd bedded his share…a selected few of whom he continued to regard with affection. Yet not one of them had captured and held his heart.

While innate ruthlessness had ensured Alexei gained control of Montgomery Electronics, Roman Montgomery's daughter fitted another category entirely.

Five years of planning, negotiating, dealing, had been with one goal in mind. To make Montgomery Electronics his own via the Australian arm of his global ADE Conglomerate.

No money had been spared in implementing state-of-the-art equipment at the electronics plant situated at one of Sydney's industrial sites, together with complete refurbishment of downtown city offices previously leased to Montgomery Electronics.

The media had featured the coup, speculated on the new owner's identity, and relayed Roman Montgomery's

failing health, financial mismanagement and the global
recession as the reason for sending Montgomery Electronics to the wall.

CVs and performance reports of existing employees
had been examined, decisions made, with employment
contracts prepared…currently in the process of being offered by Marc Adamson, Alexei's legal advisor, to selected
employees for signature.

Among whom was Roman Montgomery's daughter,
Natalya.

An act of vengeance?

Against Natalya's father? *Without doubt.*

Natalya?

The decision was personal.

Make that *very* personal.

CHAPTER TWO

THE MEETING WITH the new company's CEO was a mere formality, Natalya assured herself as she left Marc Adamson's office and made her way along a wide corridor with strategically placed alcoves featuring magnificent floral displays on glass-topped stands. Professional renovations, individual reception areas bearing luxe new carpeting, expensive leather seating, artwork gracing the walls.

A major upgrade from the old-school style her father had favoured.

A faint smile curved her generous mouth. New owner, new vibe.

From a personal perspective, there was a sense of satisfaction in having been offered the position as the new company owner's PA. The plus aspect being a very satisfactory salary package.

It would be interesting to discover how many office staff employed by her father had been retained.

As yet the new owner's identity hadn't been disclosed, with one media-projected rumour referring to an American-based billionaire.

If correct, she mentally sketched him as being over fifty, maybe older, with access to inherited family money. Of average height, possibly bearing a paunch, together with thinning hair or a toupee.

A new broom sweeping clean…or perhaps a figurehead content to delegate and spend time schmoozing at various functions with the city's social elite?

Whatever…first impressions were key, and she tamped down the faint onset of nerves as she approached the CEO's executive area.

'We're not fully operational until Monday. Just knock on the door and walk right in,' Marc Adamson had instructed.

Okay, no problem.

She had a signed contract as proof the position was hers. All she had to do was smile, be professional and relax.

What could possibly go wrong?

Natalya curled fingers into her palm, rapped a firm double knock against the open heavily panelled door and entered a spacious office containing high quality furniture, floor-to-ceiling bookcases along one wall.

A quick glance revealed a wide custom-made desk bearing a laptop, various electronic devices, in front of which there were four single studded leather chairs spread out in a spacious semi-circle.

Within scant seconds it made a statement—wealth, excellent taste and power.

It was then she registered the tall broad-shouldered male frame silhouetted against a wall of reinforced plate-glass, affording an angled glimpse of strong features, a firm jawline, dark groomed hair.

A corporate wolf in his mid to late thirties clothed in black designer jeans, open-necked white shirt and a black soft leather jacket was vastly different from her preconceived image of the new company CEO.

A swift unbidden curl of sensation deep within surprised her, and was immediately discounted as a ridiculous flight of imagination.

Alexei held the advantage, one he used without compunction as he slowly turned to face the young woman who'd once shared a part of his life.

Dark almost black eyes regarded her steadily...waiting for the moment recognition hit.

As it did within a few fleeting seconds, and Alexei took pleasure in witnessing the faint widening of her eyes, the way her mouth parted, the quick swallow as if a sudden lump had risen in her throat as she visibly fought to school her expression into a polite mask.

Alexei? *Here?*

Coherent words momentarily failed her big-time, as she struggled to control the feeling she'd been hit by a force-ful, if metaphorical, punch in the solar plexus.

Breathe, she bade herself silently as emotions rose to the surface, a gamut almost defying description, for how often had she attempted to cast aside images from their shared past?

Too many times to count.

Nights, on the edge of sleep, were the worst.

For it was then the memories returned to haunt her...the way his smile affected each and every pulse in her body; the gentle trail of his fingers down her cheek to trace her soft trembling lips. His mouth savouring her own, teasing, tasting, as he drove her wild with wanting *more*. The heat in his dark gleaming eyes a prelude to mind-blowing intimacy.

Five years on there was no warmth apparent in his de-meanour, just an inflexibility that sent a chill scudding down her spine.

What did you expect...a romantic reunion?

Seriously?

After five years... Are you insane?

From a time when she'd been able to accurately define his every expression, now she felt as if she'd been flung into a maelstrom of wild conjecture where nothing made any sense as he allowed the ensuing seconds to weigh heavily in the electrified air permeating the room.

Her mind reeled with unvoiced questions. Initially, his motive to buy out the firm formerly owned by her father?

Rapidly followed by…how could Alexei Delandros have accumulated so much wealth in the space of five years?

Groomed designer stubble shadowed his jaw, adding an edgy quality, and there was a hardness apparent which didn't equate with the man she'd once known…and loved.

Natalya kept her eyes fixed on his in a determined effort not to escape his steady gaze. An act of defiance…or a mix of self-preservation and stubborn pride?

Both, she conceded.

Alexei took a degree of dispassionate interest as he examined Natalya's slender curves, narrow waist, slim hips, showcased in a black tailored business suit, with killer heels emphasising toned legs encased in sheer hose.

Subtle use of cosmetics enhanced her delicately boned face, emphasising expressive dark eyes and generously curved mouth.

The length of brunette hair styled into a sleek chignon made his fingers itch to free the pins to allow the thick waves to frame her face.

Professional cool…successfully achieved, Alexei admitted.

Absent was the vibrant, fun-loving girl who'd once embraced the world and all it had to offer. The sweet curve of her mouth parting in a laughing smile…eyes sparkling with teasing humour. The touch of her mouth on his own, magical, incredibly sensual as passion transcended to intimacy.

Alexei lifted one dark eyebrow in a gesture of musing cynicism. 'Nothing to say, Natalya?'

Where would you like me to begin? presented a tempting start.

Instead, she cut straight to the point. 'If this is some kind of sick game,' she offered with controlled calm, 'I refuse to be a part of it.'

He'd expected no less of her, given his deliberate act to conceal the new owner's identity from the media.

He inclined his head in silent mockery, enlightening, 'I prefer…a calculated strategy.'

Any sense of calm was discarded as anger rose to the surface, almost robbing her of speech as she fought the desire to slap his face hard.

'What else from a man such as you?'

Dark eyes speared her own. 'You have no knowledge of the man I've become.'

So very different from the Alexei she'd once known as memories flashed through her mind…hauntingly real for a few heart-stopping seconds as she recalled her body beneath his…supple, avid, in a manner that drove her wild.

For him, only him.

Dear God in heaven…*stop*.

Reflection in any form was a madness she could ill afford.

Almost as if he knew the passage of her thoughts he indicated the nest of chairs framing the front of his desk. 'Take a seat.'

Natalya spared him a dark glare, which had no effect whatsoever. 'I prefer to stand.'

He merely inclined his head…and waited.

An action which ramped her animosity up a notch, and her eyes speared his as she sought a measure of calm. 'The employment contract your henchman presented for my signature bears no mention of your name.'

'*Henchman*, Natalya?' The query held a vague musing

quality. 'Marc Adamson is ADE's legal consultant.' He eased his lengthy frame against the edge of his desk as he spelled it out. *'Alexei Delandros Electronics.'*

'Very cleverly disguised in the contract I signed,' she accused as she reached into her satchel, removed the folded document, ripped it in half, then tossed the pages onto his desk, quietly pleased when a few of the torn pieces fluttered onto the carpet.

She wanted to hurt him, as she had been hurt by his abrupt disappearance from her life. Days when she could barely function. Nights where sleep eluded her until the early dawn hours.

Weeks, dammit, spent examining every possible reason he could have left without a word.

An inexplicable action which compounded when she woke one morning feeling queasy and had to make a mad dash into the en suite bathroom. Something she ate became less likely when a second early morning bathroom dash occurred the following day, and the next. A positive pregnancy test had tipped her into a state of shock…they'd always used protection, so *how?*…until she recalled a night when need had obliterated common sense.

A rapid calculation of pertinent dates had merely confirmed a distinct possibility, followed by a host of scattered emotions that briefly pitched her between delight and despair, and the inevitable…*this can't be happening.* Except a further three pregnancy tests over several days had eliminated any vestige of doubt.

Vivid images swirled unbidden through her mind of times shared, long nights together, the joy of love and quietly spoken plans for their future…then nothing, no word as to why Alexei had seemed to disappear like smoke in the wind.

The energy she expended attempting to track him down

without success. Details of staff employed by Montgomery Electronics revealed Alexei's file had been deleted but she had no idea who by or why.

It appeared he'd intentionally slipped off the radar...but for what possible reason?

She'd lain awake for nights searching for an answer... *any* answer. Only to come up with a few scenarios, none of which seemed to fit the man she thought she'd known so well.

Was she that desperate to locate the father of her unborn child, when he'd presumably taken steps to disappear? And what if she *did* manage to make contact? Would he be someone with whom she'd want to do battle over shared custody?

Seeking medical confirmation was a given, providing the reality of early pregnancy, closely followed by her determination to carry the child to full term. The only person in whom she'd confide was her mother...except she needed the right words, the chosen moment.

Only to have the decision taken out of her hands when she'd suffered a miscarriage just six weeks into the pregnancy.

A tiny foetus not meant to develop and take life's first breath.

There was little solace in medical opinion a second pregnancy would need to be carefully monitored with ongoing blood tests during the initial three months of pregnancy. Facts which didn't begin to equate with Natalya's emotional distress, until Ivana took action by booking flights and accommodation for a ten-day vacation on Queensland's Hamilton Island.

On reflection, they'd shared a lovely apartment with views over tropical waters, restaurants, time to relax and enjoy what the resort had to offer, indulging in facials, body massage, treatments at the Island's Resort Spa.

Sunshine, soft warm breezes, an idyllic beach. A healing period which strengthened their mother-daughter bond.

'Love you, darling,' Ivana had offered quietly as they exchanged hugs while the cab driver transferred Natalya's travel bag from the vehicle's boot. 'Are you sure you don't want me to come in with you?'

'I'm fine. Really,' Natalya assured her, aware once she settled into her apartment and resumed work as her father's PA life would assume its normal pattern...or as close to a facsimile of it.

And it had, over time.

All of which now flashed painfully through Natalya's mind, and served to heighten her anger as she rose to her feet, choosing to icily indicate the destroyed paperwork lying on the carpeted floor of Alexei's office.

'Not even a million-dollar salary would convince me to work for you.'

There was nothing she could gain from his expression, or his demeanour, then one eyebrow lifted to form a slight arch as he queried silkily,

'Are you done?'

Courage...she owned it in spades, Alexei acknowledged. Together with a flash of temper, which showed for a brief instant before she visibly gathered it in.

'Yes.' Succinct, and final.

Natalya turned to leave, and he waited until she reached the door before relaying with drawled intent, 'I strongly suggest you change your mind.'

He watched her shoulders stiffen, their slight lift as she took a calming breath before she swung back to face him.

With determined effort she took in his sculptured facial features accented by scrupulously groomed designer stubble...impossibly sexy, highlighting a raw edgy quality she found disturbing.

Dark eyes...not warm as she remembered, but cool, analytical. The faint groove bracketing each cheek seemed a little deeper, and the mouth which had caressed her own, devoured and taken, was now set in firm lines.

His shoulders...had they been so broad? His hair, so silky she'd exulted in ruffling it into disorder. Matching the dark promise in his eyes, a soft throaty chuckle an instant before he claimed her mouth, her heart...her soul.

Then.

Not now...and it rankled more than she would ever admit to how much the admission had the power to hurt.

She was over him. *Way* over.

Alexei Delandros belonged in a previous chapter of her life. One she had absolutely no intention of revisiting. Only a degree of stubborn pride ensured she remained facing him...when every cell in her body urged she should simply turn and leave. *So why didn't she?*

Because it was the easy way out. And she didn't do easy.

Like she'd even consider working for the man who had ruthlessly set out to destroy her father's business empire?

Natalya lifted her chin and threw him a fulminating glare. 'As far as I'm concerned, you can take your employment contract and shove it.'

She was either a very good actress, Alexei conceded, or she genuinely had no inkling of the verbal bombshell he was about to deliver.

'You might consider leaving your options open.'

Her eyes never left his own. Dignity and sarcasm didn't mesh, but she really didn't care. 'Please don't hesitate to enlighten me as to why?'

Family values had been her strong point. One he'd admired...until he'd dug deep into her father's business and private affairs and uncovered a number of discrepancies revealing the antithesis of the man Roman Montgomery managed to portray.

Had Natalya been aware of her father's transgressions? Possibly not, given Roman's penchant for subterfuge.

There was no point in sugar-coating the facts, nor did he feel inclined to soften his words.

'My accounting team have uncovered an elaborate scheme involving several bogus offshore accounts created by your father for the illegal transfer of Montgomery company funds.'

Alexei watched her eyes sharpen with disbelief. 'There's no way my father would commit fraud.'

It was a gut reaction and, on the surface, genuine, he perceived. Although she'd managed to fool him in the past.

'You're so sure of that?'

'I'd stake my life on it,' Natalya voiced emphatically, ignoring the folder Alexei extended towards her.

'I suggest you examine the paperwork.'

'And if I choose not to?'

He studied her features as she ran a pale lacquered nail over the folder's seam, noted the soft pink colouring of her cheeks, the defensive spark in the depths of her eyes, and for a brief moment he almost felt sorry for her.

Almost.

'The report details dates, account numbers, the series of complicated layers deliberately created to prevent detection.'

Natalya cast him a withering look, only to witness it had no effect whatsoever, and she tossed the report, unread, onto his desk.

'You can't be serious.'

The silence became an almost palpable entity as she refused to shift her gaze. Difficult, when a host of conflicting thoughts swirled through her mind.

If...and in her opinion it was a vastly improbable if... the report held a grain of accuracy, the question had to be what Alexei intended to do with it.

At best the details would reveal any fraud had occurred without her father's knowledge.

At worst...she wasn't prepared to give that thought any credibility.

'Read the report.'

Only a fool would fail to recognise the steely intent beneath his silky drawl, and she shot him a baleful glare as she picked up the proffered folder and flipped aside the covering page.

The first thing she noted was the name of the firm who'd compiled the data...and recognised it as one of the foremost sources well known worldwide for its excellent reputation.

Why did she have the instinctive feeling the goal posts had suddenly undergone a subtle shift, when it was she who'd determined to maintain control during this brief... *very* brief encounter?

A small ball of tension manifested itself in the region of her mid-section, and she took a calming breath before she began skimming the range of figures, dates, only to slow down as growing alarm escalated with each turn of the page. Detailed entries tracking each amount as it passed through an elaborate tracery of accounts.

A trail initiated by direct instructions from Roman Montgomery.

Amounting to millions of dollars.

Natalya felt as if she needed to sit down, and she froze for a few heart-stopping seconds as reality hit home.

If the report was brought to the notice of relevant authorities, her father would face restitution, penalties incurred for tax evasion, and probable jail time.

It was beyond belief.

She lifted her head and looked at Alexei with undisguised incredulity for a few unguarded seconds, before reassembling her features into a taut mask as realisation hit.

'There's more.'

Natalya's eyes flashed dark fire as they fixed on his own. 'How can there be *more*?'

Alexei reached behind him, collected a second folder from his desk and handed it to her.

Her reluctance to examine the contents was apparent, and he watched in silence as her shoulders stiffened before she turned her attention to the written details, the photographs, and caught the moment irrefutable proof led to the only possible conclusion.

Roman Montgomery led a double life and had been doing so for many years.

There was an apartment in Paris, occupied by a mistress. A London apartment in fashionable Notting Hill housed a second mistress. Each of whom were maintained by Roman, whose visits coincided over the years with so-called business trips to both cities.

Deeds to both properties were buried beneath a list of subsidiary companies, ultimately tracing back to one man…her father.

Disbelief, together with emotions she was loath to name, coalesced into anger she fought hard to control.

The burning question had to be *why* had Alexei Delandros hired accredited investigators to delve deep into Roman Montgomery's business affairs and his personal life?

Why expend so much time, effort and money?

To do *what*?

Blackmail?

Her father? *Her?*

On the surface, such conjecture appeared unconscionable.

It took considerable effort to remain relatively calm, when her overwhelming desire was to toss both folders onto Alexei's desk and walk out, take the elevator down to basement car park level and exit with a squeal of tyre rubber.

Not the best idea...but incredibly satisfying. Provided she maintained control and didn't crash the car. Or worse, suffer an injury or three.

Her eyes darkened as they fused with his own.

'What do you intend to do with this information?'

Alexei regarded her thoughtfully, noted the tension evident in the way she stood, the straight back, squared shoulders, her eyes fixed intently on his own.

'That depends on you.'

The only visible indication apparent was a slight narrowing of her eyes, followed seconds later by an increased pulse-beat at the base of her throat.

A vivid reminder of past occasions when he'd touched his lips to that pulse, savoured it, before kissing it gently with his mouth. Her soft husky groan followed by a faint gasp as he used his teeth to tease and nibble a little.

Almost as if his body remembered, he felt its damning response, and silently cursed as he shifted position, using the moment to transfer a slim document and pen from his desk and extend it towards her.

Natalya's eyes flashed with fine fury as she recognised it as a duplicate of the contract she'd just destroyed.

'I have no intention of attaching my signature to a document representing *any* company involving your name.'

'That's your final decision?'

'Yes.'

'You might care to consider the fallout if I disclose the information I have on your father to the relevant authorities and the media.'

He'd do that?

The answer was clearly apparent in the chilling darkness in his gaze, and her mind reeled at the impact the exposure would have on her parents, their lives, *her mother* once Roman's infidelity became known.

Anger burned her throat. 'You *bastard*.'

'Language,' Alexei chided mildly.

For a brief moment she wanted to cause him physical harm, unaware how well he was able to read her.

Silence filled the room…ominous, intrusive, threatening.

'Decision time, Natalya.'

The silky warning apparent in his voice acted as a reality check, and earned him a baleful glare.

'I need to consider my options.'

'There are two.' His gaze seared her own. 'You sign, or you don't.' He waited a beat, then added with irrefutable inflexibility, 'It's a simple no-brainer.'

Her father's indiscretions made public. Worse, much worse…her mother's humiliation and heartbreak.

The mere thought of the snide whispers, the disdain as the social elite tore her mother's marriage, her very life to shreds…

A silent curse rose and died in her throat. She couldn't do that to a caring, loving woman who in no way deserved such denigration.

Natalya subjected Alexei to a killing look which should have felled him on the spot, and gritted her teeth in sheer frustration when he displayed no reaction whatsoever.

'Give me the damn paperwork.'

Seconds later she tore it from his extended hand and began reading the various clauses. Carefully checking no word or phrase had been changed from the contract she'd initially signed.

Every detail was clearly defined, stating as his PA she'd be on call twenty-four-seven when necessary, and available to accompany him on business trips within Australia and overseas. The contract would be valid for one year... renewable by mutual agreement.

While a term of one year had seemed perfectly reasonable, *now* it stretched way too long. 'I insist renegotiating the one-year term down to three months.'

'No.'

His unequivocal refusal ramped up her anger to boiling point. 'Revenge or blackmail?' she demanded tightly. 'Which?'

'Neither.'

He expected her to believe that? 'And the moon is a ball of blue cheese,' she offered with deliberate disparagement.

If he displayed so much as a glimmer of humour, she would hit him and be damned to the consequences. Only a forward flash of reality provided her saving grace, and she forced herself to mentally calm down, breathe, and stick to the basics.

'What guarantee do I have you won't go public?'

Alexei spared her a steely look. 'My word.'

'Not good enough,' Natalya dismissed with a retaliatory edge, and glimpsed his eyes harden at her temerity.

'The original certified documentation is held in a bank's locked security box.'

She didn't hesitate in issuing a cool demand. 'Copies?'

'Returned to the bank's security holding after you've signed a new employment contract.'

'I'll require a certified bank receipt in confirmation.'

He leant back against the desk, seemingly relaxed, but only a fool would ignore the restrained power apparent, or doubt his intent to use it. 'Done.'

Her eyes silently warred with his own, her mouth tight

as she fought for a semblance of control as Alexei handed her a pen.

A mesh of angry pride caused her to hesitate for a few seconds before taking it from him.

'Just for the record... I hate you.'

'An emotion which should make for an interesting relationship.' His voice was a smooth drawl which did little to improve her anger level.

'Business-related *only*.' The emphasis was fiercely stressed with finality as she attached her signature to a copy of the contract, watched as he countersigned, then she stood to her feet, walked out of his office, and took the lift down to the basement car park.

Alexei was intent on playing hardball, expecting her to meekly comply?

Comply, yes.

There really wasn't an option.

But meekly?

Not a chance...

CHAPTER THREE

NATALYA ENTERED HER HOME, greeted Ollie, her beautiful Birman cat, caught him close for a customary cuddle, gave a light laugh at his plaintive miaow as she made her way into the kitchen.

'Okay, I get it. Dinner time.' She toed off her stilettos, dropped her bag onto the marble-topped servery, then moved to the walk-in pantry.

'Chicken or fish?'

Unable to answer, Ollie merely butted his head against her chin and began to purr.

'Chicken,' Natalya decided as she extracted the appropriate tin, removed the seal, spooned the contents into the cat dish and placed it on Ollie's food mat. 'There you go.'

Her apartment was one of two situated in a large two-level converted family home in an exclusive bayside suburb overlooking a sweeping promenade bordered by a stand of tall Norfolk pine trees along the seafront.

Inherited from her maternal grandmother three years ago, the home rested high on a sloping hill with sweeping views over the bay and neighbouring suburbs.

Renovated into two beautifully decorated apartments, one of which she leased to a responsible tenant, the property represented a valuable investment, providing Natalya with a place where there were no memories of her shared time with Alexei to haunt her.

Except now he was back.

Food held no interest whatsoever, and she reached for the remote, activated the TV, checked local and international newscast, and scrolled through the host of programmes until she found something that might provide a distraction.

A night in was a conscious choice. Not that she was a social butterfly, although there were a few very good friends whose company she enjoyed...live theatre, movies, social events for worthy charity causes; lingering over a shared coffee, and there was a sports complex she frequently visited with an indoor swimming pool, and several large rooms hosting a variety of exercise equipment. None of which held immediate appeal.

She wanted out of her clothes, a leisurely shower, then she'd slip into something comfortable and carefully examine her copy of the employment contract in the unlikely event she'd discover a possible loophole.

An hour later she tossed the contract aside, aware there appeared no evident room to manoeuvre within the skilfully crafted legalese.

Food was a requisite, and having nibbled without appetite she settled into a comfortable chair and channel-surfed the TV for a while, noticed a much-viewed programme, only to discover it was a repeat episode she'd already seen.

What next? Phone a friend? Skype? Flip through the pages of a current magazine?

Indecision wasn't one of her usual traits, so she decided to retire to bed with a good book. Ollie merely tilted his head in silent askance at this change in his mistress's usual evening routine, and leapt onto the bed when it became apparent Natalya intended to settle in comfort.

Half an hour in, the written word failed to capture her complete attention, given her mind seemed intent on reliving events of the day.

No matter how hard she tried to focus on the story, Alexei's image kept intruding, until she simply gave up, closed the bed lamp, and attempted to sleep...with no success whatsoever.

Emotional reflection eventually tipped her back into a place which transported her back six years to a time when she first met Alexei...at an end-of-year social gathering for employees of her father's affiliate firm responsible for the manufacture of electronic components.

Tall, dark-haired and ruggedly attractive, he'd stood apart from the rest of the men present. For a heart-stopping moment she'd become acutely aware of every breath she took, unable to look away as he turned slightly as if drawn by her attention.

Dark gleaming eyes met her own, lingered, before returning to the young woman who clung to his side. Understandable, Natalya conceded, given he possessed the wow factor in spades.

She could, if she was so inclined, cross to his side and effect an introduction. Hadn't she slowly circled the room achieving the social etiquette required of the boss's daughter separately, and at her mother's side, as the evening progressed?

Except she'd been forestalled by one of her father's foremen, intent on introducing his son, and when she moved on the object of her attention was nowhere in sight.

Shame, she mused, aware she'd probably never see him again.

Yet she did, days later, when she entered a suburban supermarket to purchase a few groceries needed to replenish her fridge and pantry. And there he was, in the same aisle. Their eyes met, and they both exchanged a smile at the coincidence, whereupon Alexei introduced himself, and Natalya did likewise. Coffee, the universal suggestion, worked, and led to conversation and the exchange of phone numbers.

What followed rose to the surface, intact and in glorious Technicolor...a relationship so special, caring, so attuned to each other there had been no need for words. Just the touch of his hand, the warmth of his smile, dear heaven, his mouth as it possessed her own. The hard strength of his body, aroused emotions taking them both to a place where they existed in a sensual world of their own. Erotic, exquisite, mind-blowing.

A time when she'd felt so happy...so *alive*, in mind, body, and soul. Sure in her heart they were destined to share a life together.

Only to wake one morning to find herself alone in her flat, no explanatory note, only a brief text message on her cell phone later in the day indicating little, and not followed up at all.

'The number you are dialling has been disconnected', a disembodied robot had intoned, sending her reeling with alarm. Worse, the crushing news he no longer worked at her father's electronics plant.

Five years, with no satisfactory explanation.

For all she knew he'd disappeared off the face of the Earth, followed by months of her agonising *why*. Ultimately, the realisation he didn't want to be found.

Now he was back. Not the man she'd once known and imagined she'd loved, but a hard, resolute stranger bent on revenge—no holds barred. Bent on destroying her father, using her as a tool.

Blackmail...no other word suited as well.

She wanted to hit out...verbally, physically.

Silently didn't begin to cut it.

Getting physical, however, did.

First up, her apartment, which she cleaned to within a whisker of perfection.

A long session at the local squash centre expended excess energy, and there was a certain satisfaction in continuously slamming a ball against the wall, especially as she mentally imposed Alexei's body centre front and deliberately aimed to hit target every time.

Revenge of sorts for his physical image which had entered uninvited in dream form throughout the night, providing vivid memories she assured herself she'd long forgotten.

And knew she lied.

'Why so aggressive?'

Oh, hell.

Natalya closed her eyes, then opened them again as she turned towards her squash partner and endeavoured to catch her breath.

'There has to be a reason.'

Aaron offered her a penetrating look. 'Spill.'

One of the pitfalls of a good friendship being they knew each other too well.

Initially they'd met at a social gathering hosted by her father. A partner in a prominent law firm and the eldest son of a wealthy family, Aaron was sophisticated, charming and considered to be a very good catch in the matrimonial stakes. Only a chosen few knew he maintained a relationship with a long-term same-sex partner.

'Nothing I can't handle,' Natalya assured him as they emerged from the court.

Aaron read her better than most, a good friend who'd provided unstinting support when she'd needed it most.

Such as now, when his teasing anecdotes would do

much to help lighten the dark mood threatening to destroy her composure.

'Share dinner with me this evening.' The invitation was tempting, yet she hesitated as she collected a towel from the neatly folded stack adjacent the locker rooms.

'I'll make a reservation and collect you at seven.' His smile held a tinge of humour. 'Enlighten me or not, your choice.'

She didn't, because she couldn't bear to drag into the open how deeply Alexei's presence affected her. Or revive memories too breathtakingly real to share.

Instead they kept the conversation light, touching on the ordinary, and simply enjoyed fine food, a little wine, and the relaxed benefit of good friendship.

It was a pleasant evening, and Natalya thanked him as he deposited her outside the entrance to her home.

Surprisingly she slept well and woke early, pulled on a Lycra body suit, added a singlet top, affixed earbuds to channel music and took her customary morning run...at a more gruelling pace than was her norm.

Following a shower, she dressed, munched on an apple as she collected keys, shouldered her bag and drove to the nearest mall to stock up on essentials.

As she drove to her parents' home later that day to share Sunday lunch she couldn't help but silently question what was *real*, as opposed to what had been a superbly acted sham on her father's part, given he'd managed to fool her so well. There were no incidents she could recall to indicate her parents' marriage had been anything other than a devoted union. There had been the odd private meeting while in London when her presence as his PA was not required. Likewise Paris.

The knowledge refreshed memories of her father taking time out for a relaxing massage. Personal shopping time. The supposed private business meetings he attended alone.

How naive had she been?

Worse, did her mother suspect?

Doubtful, given Roman had provided the perfect cover by employing Natalya as his PA, ensuring his daughter accompanied him to interstate and overseas business meetings.

A string of silent castigations didn't come close to easing the anger she felt at her father's deceit. There was a part of her that wanted to confront him, rail her fists against his chest and demand to know how he could have put his marriage, dammit, his life, in jeopardy by such selfish careless actions.

Play nice, Natalya cautioned as she eased her car into the driveway leading to her parents' modern home set in beautifully tended grounds.

Smile, chat, and pretend nothing has changed.

Except it had, and the conscious effort to maintain a façade affected her appetite.

It was during dessert the question arose regarding her future plans.

'Darling,' Ivana broached with interest. 'Are you going to take a break before applying for another position?'

Oh, my. Evade the issue, or aim for the partial truth? It had to be the latter…

'No break, unfortunately,' she managed with a credible smile.

'Really?' Disappointment was apparent in her mother's voice. 'I was hoping we might share some girl time. Lunch, shop. Book a massage, facial, mani-pedi.'

'Who will you be working for?' Roman queried, direct and to the point, as ever.

There was no easy way to break the news, other than

to make the truth as simple as possible…then wait for the inevitable fallout.

Natalya met her father's narrowed gaze with outward calm. 'The ADE Conglomerate.'

His eyes hardened, so did the tone of his voice. 'You intend to work for the firm who bought me out?'

Natalya chose not to remind him that technically the bank had foreclosed.

'Is that a problem?'

Roman's features darkened. 'You're aware of the CEO's identity?'

'My interview was conducted by a legal representative.' Initially it had been, and not precisely an untruth.

The media presses would run overnight for newspapers delivered at dawn. In a matter of hours the news would become public knowledge.

'Alexei Delandros *is* ADE Conglomerate.'

'Delandros?' Roman's face grew dark with a mixture of anger and disbelief. *'Alexei* Delandros? What the hell are you *thinking*?'

Of my mother… Except the words never left her lips. Instead she lifted her chin a little and met his anger with determined spirit.

'He made an offer I couldn't refuse.' The truth…just not all of it.

Dark, almost black eyes hardened, and she saw his mouth thin to an ominous line as he made a visible attempt to rein in his wrath. 'How could you even *consider* working for Delandros?'

Because there's no alternative.

'In what position?' The demand was palpable.

With no easy way to break the news…except tell it as it was. 'PA.'

Roman regarded her with disbelief for several long seconds, then he slammed a fist onto the table, sending crockery rattling in protest. 'I'm calling my lawyer.'

'Who'll only confirm the contract was signed without duress and therefore legally valid.'

A telling silence reigned as Roman processed the inevitable. 'I hope you know what you're doing,' he warned heavily.

Her eyes didn't waver from his own for several seconds, then she discarded her dessert fork and pushed the plate aside. The thought of taking another bite of food made her feel slightly ill.

For as long as she could remember, she'd prided herself on being part of a close loving family worthy of her implicit trust.

Now she was forced to recognise the father she had adored was not the man she'd believed him to be, and the pain of betrayal was almost a physical ache.

The desire to leave was uppermost...now, before she uttered words that, once said, couldn't be retracted.

Another hour, that was all, then she could escape.

Consequently Natalya accepted coffee, lingered over it, and accepted Ivana's invitation to admire her treasured garden.

Together they moved outdoors, leaving Roman to add a generous snifter of brandy to his coffee, and smoke a cigar, presumably in the hope the alcohol and nicotine hit would soothe his temper.

Scrupulously tended and picture perfect no matter the season, the beautifully sculptured shrubbery and numerous borders were Ivana's pride and joy. While a part-time gardener took care of the heavy work, Ivana was very hands-on with the choice of plants and succulents designed to provide a glorious balance of symmetry and colour.

'Darling, I'm very concerned for you,' Ivana said quietly as they wandered through the grounds. 'Having to sell Montgomery Electronics was a blow to your father's pride and self-esteem,' Ivana added. 'It doesn't sit easily on his conscience he needs to rely on the money and investments I inherited from my late mother's estate.'

Natalya's grandmother had expressed a dislike of Roman Montgomery from the onset, and had been fiercely against the marriage, ensuring each and every one of her assets on Ivana's demise would pass directly to Natalya.

Natalya had adored her *babushka*, the regular visits with her mother, the joy and the laughter, tales relayed of an early childhood in another land, the treasures representative of a different country and culture...the division between wealth and poverty.

Ivana caught Natalya's hand and brought it to her lips. 'Will you find it difficult working with Alexei?'

The answer could only be an unspoken yes. 'I'm no longer the lovesick young girl of five years ago, *Mama*,' Natalya reminded her.

'Perhaps not. But...'

'I've moved on.'

You have? Like the initial encounter with Alexei Delandros was totally impartial and devoid of any emotion?

'I hope so,' Ivana opined evenly. 'For your sake.'

It was easy to offer a smile and brush lips to her mother's cheek. 'I'm fine.'

Little white lies and pretence. Not something she favoured, but forgivable in the circumstances...surely?

She lingered a while as they leisurely wandered through the structured pebbled paths, pausing to admire numerous plants, commenting on the subtle scent of roses, while listening to gardening tips Ivana chose to share.

There was a sense of relief when they reached the silver BMW parked in the pebbled forecourt.

'Come inside, darling, and have a refreshing drink.'

'Another time, *Mama*, if you don't mind.'

'You're leaving so soon?'

'New job,' she managed lightly. 'I need to check my wardrobe, laptop, and grab an early night.' She leant forward and hugged her mother close. 'Love you. Thanks for lunch.' A quick movement released the BMW's locking mechanism. 'I'll phone during the week.' She slid behind the wheel, fired the ignition, and blew a customary kiss as she eased the car forward.

Not the most convivial lunch, Natalya perceived wryly as she traversed the main road en route to her own home.

Tomorrow was likely to be a whole lot worse.

Working in close proximity to Alexei Delandros featured way down at the end of her choose-to-do list. So how did she prepare to meet her nemesis?

Perfectly groomed, elegantly attired, immaculate make-up, heels to die for…and presenting solicitous professionalism together with a degree of unruffled cool.

Something she achieved following two attempts to acquire the desired effect with her make-up.

Laptop, iPad, leather satchel, smartphone, car fob… *check*.

Minutes later Natalya joined early Monday morning traffic into the city, fought the long delays at numerous controlled intersections before entering the underground parking area assigned to the building housing ADE Conglomerate.

Easier said than done to tamp down the onset of nerves as she rode the lift to a high floor.

She'd been her father's PA for several years, she knew what the position entailed. There might be a few adjustments, but how difficult could it be?

CHAPTER FOUR

NATALYA ENTERED THE ADE reception and was met by a personable young woman who moved forward to offer a polite greeting.

'Natalya?' A hand was extended, which Natalya accepted.

'Marcie,' the blonde enlightened by introduction. The smile was genuine, which helped ease any preconceived tension. 'I'll take you through to your office suite.'

A comfortably large room, Natalya perceived, executive fittings, new state-of-the-art electronic equipment.

'Louise is your assistant, whose office is to your right, separated by a shared lounge,' Marcie offered with a smile. 'I'll introduce you, when we're finished with the tour.'

So far, so good.

'Alexei is at the industrial plant today. His office is to your left, accessed via his assistant's office, and their shared lounge.'

A reprieve, Natalya accorded, aware the day just became a little better.

Space, lots of it with room to move. Comfort, synchronised professional privacy...and far different from her father's former set-up.

Introductions completed, Marcie indicated Natalya's office. 'I'll provide a brief overview of Alexei's schedule for the current week, and answer any questions you might care to raise before I leave to take a mid-evening flight back to the States.'

Efficient, capable and very clear re the CEO's schedule. One which Natalya reluctantly admitted appeared daunting.

Did the man sleep?

Not a wise thought, given it led to imagining if anyone shared his bed, and, if so, whom?

So what do you care?

You hate him, remember?

Focus, she admonished.

'I've printed out notes you may find helpful.' The attractive blonde bestowed a conciliatory smile. 'I'm confident you'll be fine.'

Natalya was sure she would be even if it killed her. For no way would she permit Alexei Delandros to have any reason to find fault with her performance.

As to her emotional heart…it was guarded in self-imposed lockdown. Deliberately sought, to regain a sense of purpose. Sure, she'd indulged in a social life, even flirted a little…if you counted a pleasant smile, intelligent conversation, light laughter.

Did anyone see beneath the façade? Detect her broken heart had been figuratively stitched together, never to be torn apart again? Healed, resolute, as she fought for contentment…and thought she'd achieved it, until a few days ago when Alexei Delandros reappeared on the scene and any pretence of contentment went out of the window.

Worse…unless she was wildly wrong, he'd deliberately taken advantage of her father's misdeeds to place her between a rock and a hard place.

Damn him.

He sought to play hardball?

Then so would she.

'Are you okay with that?'

Marcie's intrusion wrenched Natalya back into the here and now.

Schedule, overview. 'Got it.' At least she thought she had, and, failing that, there was Plan B… Marcie's printed notes.

Besides, she knew the electronics business well. Her father's list of contacts was on speed dial, and saved in her computer's email address file.

How difficult or different could it be?

Different, Natalya discovered soon after she entered the offices of Alexei Delandros Electronics the following morning.

Absent was the relaxed, almost laid-back atmosphere generated during her father's regime. Instead there was a fast-paced vibe as she passed through Reception. The receptionist's usual warm friendly smile was absent, replaced by a slightly harried look, and Natalya arched an eyebrow in silent query, only to receive an expressive eye-roll in return.

Alexei Delandros was in the building, and obviously bent on ensuring everyone followed a high-powered work ethic.

Which indicated she should merely offer a smile in return and walk on through to her office…instead she paused to indulge in a brief post-weekend chat.

Staff camaraderie had always been an important factor during Roman Montgomery's reign…

At that moment her smartphone buzzed and she retrieved and answered it, only to hear Alexei's secretary's voice.

'Natalya. Mr Delandros expects you in his office.'

Now…was an unspoken directive holding a slightly ominous tone.

'Two minutes,' she advised patiently, and fluttered her fingers at the receptionist before heading down the corridor.

A brief stop off in her office to deposit her bag and laptop, then she collected her iPad, breathed in deep and tapped on Alexei's door.

She could do this…and fervently wishing otherwise wasn't going to change a thing.

So ignore the man, smile, be so efficiently professional he'll have no cause for complaint.

Easy in theory…difficult in practice when all it took was a glance at Alexei's arresting features for her heartbeat to quicken. Worse, the sudden spear of sensation arrowing deep within her belly.

What was with that?

Her body out of sync with her brain. Granted, her polite smile didn't waver as she met his impenetrable expression.

The dark superbly tailored three-piece business suit, crisp dark blue shirt and perfectly knotted silk tie did little to tame the predator image.

If that was Alexei's aim…he'd unequivocally nailed it.

Cool, professional, remember? 'Good morning.'

One eyebrow lifted slightly. 'Your lateness is an oversight?'

Natalya checked her watch. Three minutes past eight. 'My usual start time is nine,' she managed civilly.

'I gather you failed to check your smartphone for messages…or your laptop?'

She had. Last night. Not this morning.

'Twenty-four-seven contact,' Alexei reminded her.

'Ultimatum,' she corrected without missing a beat, ignoring the silken warning apparent in his dark gaze.

He rested back a little in his chair and regarded her with a steady appraisal. If she was bent on a confrontational path…he was a few steps ahead of her.

'Written into your employment contract and specifically drawn to your attention during Friday's interview.'

Tough. While she had every intention of being the quintessential PA, and polite in the presence of others, any pretence when they were alone went out of the window.

She was something else, Alexei conceded as he took in her groomed appearance, the smooth chignon, skilfully applied make-up, red lipstick which matched the jacket she wore over a pencil-slim black skirt.

He experienced an urge to ruffle her composure, to dig beneath the professional façade. Then what? Rattle her cage?

His body stirred with sensual adrenalin, unwanted and inconceivable, but *there*. A *need* to pull her close and ravish her mouth…to remind her of what they'd once shared.

To what end? Play it forward to rumpled bed sheets and hot sex? Simply to satisfy an urge?

Evidence he unsettled her could be detected in the fast-beating pulse at the base of her throat, the edge of tension whenever he entered her personal space.

He had never aimed for the grab-and-conquer method with a woman. Mutual attraction and mutual need were his requisite for sex.

Natalya? Why this instinctive feeling there was a missing link? One only she could provide?

Patience. And time…the latter of which he had plenty.

Alexei indicated the structured curve of studded leather armchairs. 'Take a seat. I'll outline the day's schedule.'

Extensive, Natalya breathed as she noted appointments, calls to be made, two afternoon meetings to arrange…and lunch with a business associate.

'Book a table for one o'clock,' Alexei instructed, naming a restaurant with inner harbour views and known for its excellent cuisine. 'Contact Paul, my driver, and arrange to have my car waiting outside the main entrance at twelve forty-five.' His eyes didn't waver from her own. 'Naturally, you'll accompany me.'

Hadn't she attended many business lunches with her father? So why would this be any different? Professionalism ruled as she held his gaze. 'It would be helpful if you could reveal who'll be joining us.'

'Elle Johanssen and her PA.'

Natalya maintained a polite expression. Eleanor, or Elle as she insisted on being called, held a reputation for winning, by whatever means it took. Those among the business sector who'd parried with her and lost were known to refer to the woman as Hell-Jo…an unflattering but self-explanatory term.

Elle Johanssen, the noted ball-buster, locking heads with Alexei Delandros?

A woman associate with whom Roman Montgomery had refused to do business following one scalding episode that had left him red-faced and publicly humiliated.

Lunch should be *interesting*, to say the least.

She could do this, Natalya assured herself silently a few hours later as she rode the elevator with Alexei to the ground floor.

So why did she feel conscious of every breath she took, together with an incredibly heightened awareness that threatened to destroy her hard-won composure.

He radiated male sexuality, too much for any woman to ignore. Especially her, having known how it felt to be possessed by him. Sensual heaven…and then some.

Even now, when she had every reason to hate him, he still held the power to affect her emotions.

Five years…during which time she'd attempted to convince herself she was over him…disappeared like mist beneath rays of the sun.

Not good. Not good at all.

So much for self-survival skills.

And this was only day two in her contracted employ.

So…suck it up.

Which she did. Although there was a moment when Alexei indicated they share the rear seat of the chauffeur-driven limousine.

A deliberate ploy to unsettle her?

Who could tell?

She could analyse it to hell and back, and still not arrive at a definitive answer…so why even try?

The key being to adhere to the rules…a faultless PA during business hours, amenable and highly professional, even if it killed her, for no way would she allow him to glimpse so much as a chink in her emotional armour.

Consequently Natalya entered the restaurant at Alexei's side, where the maître d' offered a deferential greeting and led the way to their table.

Not the bar, which had been her father's preferred starting point. Or, she perceived in retrospect, where Roman plied his guests with alcohol before adjourning to a table where he ordered fine wine with no regard to cost. By which time, business, as such, became a secondary consideration.

Elle Johanssen made her entrance a fashionable five minutes late, offered a faux smile, apologised briefly as she slid into the seat politely held for her to grace it, and took control by ordering wine.

A female shark baring her teeth, Natalya mused, all too aware of the woman's reputation for shrewd deals tailored to her advantage.

In a contest of strong wills, Elle most often won out, her gritty formidability legend. So, too, was her intolerance for fools.

Natalya sat still, aware, alert...and prepared to watch the play between two business titans, each of whom were determined to win.

A little wine, which did nothing to soften Elle's forceful tactics...and the wheeling and dealing began.

It was quite something to watch, as Alexei simply listened while Elle outlined her terms, declared them non-negotiable...only to stiffen defensively as Alexei discounted all but one of them, before stating *his* terms.

Stalemate.

'You're new in town,' Elle dismissed haughtily, only for Alexei to qualify,

'But not new to business dealings.'

'My terms cannot be bettered.'

Alexei merely lifted an eyebrow. 'I disagree.'

'Really? By whom? A firm who'll use a superior to broker the deal, then pass the client on to a less experienced staff member?'

'No.'

Natalya saw Elle's eyes narrow in speculation. The ADE Conglomerate was huge. To have Alexei as a client would be a very large feather in the woman's cap.

It would be interesting to tell which card Elle would play.

'Then there is nothing more to say.'

Alexei's shoulders lifted in a negligible shrug. 'So it would seem.'

The word-play game had just moved up a notch.

A waiter delivered their entrees, which were eaten in supposedly companionable silence.

Was this the final act in negotiations, and, if not, who would concede?

Natalya's money was on Elle, given it was Alexei who held the power.

Conversation during the main course centred on world economics, a subject in which both Alexei and Elle were well-versed.

Dessert was declined, and Alexei chose not to linger over coffee, stating the meeting concluded.

That was it?

Unbelievable.

Alexei indicated Natalya take care of the bill with ADE's corporate card...which she did, following him from the restaurant to witness Alexei's limousine sliding to a smooth halt at the kerb.

It was then Elle moved a few steps to his side.

'Have your lawyer email me a copy of your terms.'

Alexei didn't miss a beat. 'There's no point.'

'I'm prepared to consider a few adjustments.'

Really? Natalya mused as she heeded the faint pressure of Alexei's hand at the back of her waist as Paul appeared and opened the limousine's rear door.

Alexei refrained from making any comment as he followed Natalya into the rear seat and gave Paul instructions to leave.

'Checkmate?' Natalya offered with a tinge of cynicism, and incurred his measured glance.

Wednesday morning there was a courier delivery from Elle Johanssen containing an amended list of Alexei's terms. All of which, with the exception of three relatively minor clauses, Natalya noted, had been accepted.

'Return to sender,' Alexei instructed within minutes of perusing the document. 'With an attached letter rejecting the amendments, reaffirming ADE no longer require her services.'

Natalya keyed the relevant words into her iPad, glanced up and caught his slightly raised eyebrow.

'The three clauses are quite minor.'

Alexei's gaze was impossible to discern. 'I was unaware I requested your opinion.'

Was it her imagination, or did the room temperature suddenly drop a few degrees?

'You were present when Elle Johanssen requested a list of my terms,' he reminded. 'My parting statement to her was clear, was it not?'

'Perfectly. But she's…'

'Playing me.' His eyes seared her own. 'Something I refuse to allow anyone to do…under *any* circumstance,' he added in silky dismissal.

Okay, duly noted. Natalya collected the paperwork. 'I'll ensure this is returned today.'

'Via courier.'

Natalya inclined her head. 'Of course.'

'No further input you'd like to add?'

She didn't miss a beat. 'Nothing you'd want to hear.' Not the best exit line…yet there was a small degree of satisfaction in having had the last word.

And in doing so, she failed to see Alexei's lips quirk with mild amusement.

Natalya Montgomery was the antithesis of the carefree young woman he'd once known. Now she rarely smiled in his presence, which shouldn't concern him, yet it did, for he could too easily recall the way her voice would subside into a husky purr as he pleasured her. The sweet slide of her mouth when she caressed his body, teasing, tasting with such delicacy it drove him mad…until he took control, and it was she who gasped as he used his mouth to trace a tortuous path to the apex between her thighs, edging them gently apart to savour the acutely sensitive clitoris, using his tongue to drive her wild with need as she begged for his possession. And cried out as he moved over her and surged in deep as they both became swept up in the throes of a passion so intense there was only them… devoid of sense of time or place. So completely lost in an acutely sensual climax.

Alexei had contemplated for ever, his ring on her finger, a home, children…the complete package.

Only for everything to suddenly and inexplicably change.

Alexei leant back in his office chair and idly took in the cityscape, brilliantly clear on a mild summer morning. Beyond the many varied buildings the sky and sea appeared to meld as one.

The past couldn't be changed. There was only the present, and the future. Together with a plan…one he was determined to win.

CHAPTER FIVE

IT WASN'T SURPRISING the media channelled social and business reports around Alexei's every move...or so it appeared.

He was the new man in town. Successful mogul, ruggedly attractive with a dark earthy quality that had the social set flooding him with invitations.

Very few of which he chose to accept, preferring two prominent events, the proceeds of which aided worthy children's charities.

Both events drew national media attention, and resulted in photographic evidence of his presence with a different glamorous socialite clinging to his side. Each almost visibly simpering at having gained his notice.

Instructions for flowers...specifically roses...to be despatched to each socialite with the following message...

My personal appreciation for an enjoyable evening.

Really?

How personal was personal?

As if Natalya cared.

Although he did, in her eyes, redeem himself slightly by gifting a sizable donation to each nominated charity.

Laudable, Natalya conceded, or calculated...and mentally derided the latter as prejudicial, in spite of the fact he ranked *numero uno* on her list of least favourite people.

On the other hand she had to admit he worked long hours, for it soon became apparent he was the first to arrive each morning and the last to leave. No one could achieve what he managed on a nine-to-five schedule. A factor which had obviously enabled him to reach his current level of success.

His prominence in the business sector seemed to grow with each passing day, as did the respect of his peers.

Everything her father could…and should have had if he'd paid more attention to business instead of frittering company funds with magnanimous abandon.

Three weeks in, Natalya had managed to assume an admirable professionalism—no matter what Alexei threw at her.

And he did. Frequently, without warning.

If he was bent on testing her, she managed to rise to the occasion, and derived a certain satisfaction in holding her own…*professionally.*

Personally? Not so much.

As hard as she tried, she couldn't fault him. And she wanted to, badly.

Staff admired his business nous…especially the men. While the female staff sprang to sparkling attention every time Alexei appeared within sight.

Something Natalya chose to ignore, without much success. A fact which irked her unbearably.

She was over him. Had been for years.

So why did he enter her dreams and force a vivid reminder of what they'd once shared?

It was crazy.

This Alexei bore little resemblance to the man to whom she'd gifted her body…dammit, her soul.

Then he'd surrounded her with his warmth, his affection. *Love*, she amended, prepared to stake her life on it.

A time when she'd thought to hold the world in her arms, when nothing and no one could take it away.

Yet he had. And she hadn't been able to pick up the shattered pieces of her life.

The many nights she'd lain awake in tears searching helplessly for a reason *why*. Hoping, praying for a phone call, text, email…*any* form of contact that would provide an explanation.

Yet none had appeared, and slowly she'd managed to rebuild her life. Vowing she'd never let another man get close enough to melt her frozen heart.

There were friends, the trusted, tried and true kind, of whom Aaron was one. Ivana, her mother, another she'd trust with her life. Leisl, her BFF, who had married and now lived with her husband in Austria, with whom she kept in regular contact via social media, Anja, registered nurse and cosmetician to a leading Sydney dermatologist.

Acquaintances, of whom there were many, but not one of with whom she would lay bare her innermost thoughts.

The insistent ring of her smartphone dismissed any further reflection as she checked caller ID, picked up and briskly intoned, 'Natalya.'

'I'll require your presence this evening.'

Alexei issuing a statement, not a request. And there was no reason whatsoever for the faint shivery sensation feathering down her spine at the sound of his voice.

'I may have made other arrangements.' *May* ensured it wasn't exactly a fabrication. She even managed to sound suitably regretful.

'Cancel them.'

Just like that? 'If you'd given me more notice,' she began, only to have him cut her words short.

'Have you neglected to recall the terms of your salary package?'

Really? As if she could forget. 'Is it too much to expect a degree of courtesy?' Sweet she could do, albeit with a touch of saccharine.

For an instant she braced herself for his comment, only to feel slightly disappointed when he didn't rise to the bait.

'My car will be waiting outside your home at seven.'

Her chin tilted a little, a response ready...only to have him intercede before she managed so much as a word.

'Business, Natalya,' he relayed with an edge of mockery, and named a restaurant. 'Arrange a table for six between seven-thirty and eight.' Business...*naturally.* What else would it be? 'Of course.'

Selecting what to wear wouldn't be a problem, given her wardrobe included clothes suitable for every occasion.

Nevertheless she changed her mind a few times before settling for elegant evening trousers and camisole in deep jade, and teamed the outfit with black killer heels.

Understated make-up, emphasis on the eyes, a light gloss covering her lips, her hair loose framing her face, and she was done.

Her iPad was a given, satchel, smartphone, keys, a fine cashmere black wrap folded over one arm, and she was good to go with five minutes to spare.

Limousine and driver were waiting out front when Natalya checked, and she smiled as Paul crossed to open the rear passenger door.

'Thanks.'

She moved close, saw Alexei already seated, and bade a polite good evening as she slid in beside him.

The night was warm, the air-conditioning within the car set at a comfortable level, and she forced herself to relax as the limousine purred through suburban streets towards the city.

There was a moment caught up at a controlled traffic intersection when Natalya caught a glimpse of Alexei's profile outlined in sharp relief.

An attempt to be analytical failed miserably as she skimmed those strong features. The firm jaw, broad cheekbones, eyes as dark as slate, his mouth…

Don't go there.

Except it was impossible to still the sudden flare of emotion in vivid recall of the way his mouth had wrought havoc on every intimate inch of her body. In the name of heaven…get a grip!

She did, in spite of the effort it cost her, and she offered him a cool glance.

'Do you have anything to add relevant to this evening's meeting?'

All she had was a business dinner for six, time and venue.

'No.'

Great. There was nothing like being unprepared…

'No comeback?'

She shot him a steady glance. 'No.'

For a brief second she thought she sensed a fleeting smile, then it was gone.

The car eased into a sweeping curve and slid to a halt immediately adjacent the entry foyer of one of Sydney's upmarket boutique hotels.

Alexei's associates were already seated as she entered the Bar Lounge at Alexei's side.

Four men of varying ages…three of whom she knew by reputation. And Jason Tremayne, son of one of the city's wealthy scions, who'd come on to her in the past… charming in company, the reverse in private, as she'd discovered to her cost.

The tension racked up another notch.

'Natalya.' Jason's voice was almost as fake as his smile. 'How *fortunate* you were able to score the position of ADE CEO's PA.' He waited a beat. 'But of course, you're old friends.'

The subtle emphasis didn't escape her, yet she managed a cool smile as she took a seat and ordered sparkling mineral water from an attentive waiter.

The evening's focus was business, and she assumed the expected role for which she was employed. A pleasant meal, during which her conversational input would be minimal. A few hours, then she'd return home.

Simple.

Except she hadn't factored in Jason's slightly raised eyebrow, the faint curl of his lip on occasion in a subtle reminder of a reckless mistake in judgment. Hers to have accepted his invitation almost four years ago at a time when she was most vulnerable.

Sydney's social elite were intensely active, organising and attending numerous charitable events for various reputable causes. A scene her parents had once been a part of for as long as Natalya could remember. Roman had considered Jason's late father as a business and social equal. There had even been talk at the time that a marriage between Natalya and Jason would prove a valuable business advantage. Something Natalya had refused to contemplate.

Until one evening, a few too many flutes of fine champagne, a starry night, and a determined need to move on with her life…the result had been a close encounter of the not wanted kind, ending with Jason's harsh words, a few hurtful bruises, and her desperate escape.

Something Jason had never let her forget, nor Roman's fall from grace in the business sector.

Alexei's reappearance in Sydney and his coup in acquiring Montgomery Electronics raised conjecture... So what if Alexei was flavour of the month and the rumour mill shifted up a gear?

Beating herself up about it wasn't going to change a thing.

'Indulging in a little mind-wandering, Natalya?'

Without pause she spared Jason a measured look and recounted a concise review of her condensed notes. 'I believe that covers it?'

She offered the three men a brief smile as the waiter appeared to request a preference for tea or coffee.

It was impossible to ignore Alexei's presence, or the effect it had on her emotions. A contradiction in terms given she had every reason to hate him...and she did. Unequivocally.

So why this simmering awareness? For no matter how strong her denial, her body possessed too many vivid memories to be easily dismissed.

Alexei Delandros was in her face...encroaching her space during working hours, and invading her dreams at night.

She was over him. At least she'd thought she was...until a few weeks ago when she entered the new CEO's office and discovered she'd walked into a living nightmare manipulated by a man she'd once loved so deeply, nothing, no one could possibly come between them.

So much for blind faith.

It was a relief when Alexei called time on the evening, and issued instructions to summon his driver.

'I'll take a cab,' she managed quietly.

'Not an option.'

Why, when the meeting was done and she was on her own time?

With the practicalities taken care of, Alexei's guests exchanged courteous pleasantries and made their way from the restaurant.

Natalya gathered her satchel. 'An emailed copy of my notations will be available on your laptop prior to the start of tomorrow's business day.' Professional efficiency delivered with firm politeness could hardly be ignored…surely?

Alexei pocketed his smartphone as he moved from the table and indicated the main exit. 'My limousine has just pulled into the kerb.'

'I've ordered a cab.'

He turned slightly and shot her a measured look. 'Cancel it.'

'No.'

If he brought up the twenty-four-seven thing again, she'd be strongly tempted to verbally lash out at him. It had been a long day, fraught with delays and interruptions beyond her control…throw in Jason Tremayne, and her composure was beginning to shred. More than anything she wanted the familiarity of her home and a blissful night's sleep.

'Do you particularly want to cause a scene?' His voice was a dangerously soft drawl, and she silently challenged him for several seconds, unwilling to capitulate.

The sight of a cab swooping to a halt directly behind the limousine proved perfect timing.

'There's my ride,' she indicated with polite civility, only to see Alexei cross to the cab, pay the driver, then return to the waiting limousine and indicate the open rear passenger door.

If a look could kill, he should have collapsed onto the pavement. As that didn't happen, she had to content herself with a flame-fuelled stare…one which, much to her mounting anger, he met with glittering dark eyes and held for what seemed a ridiculous length of time.

'Get in the car.' His voice was quiet. Yet only a fool would ignore the steel beneath the deceptive calm.

She tilted her head a little, for even in killer heels her height didn't come close to his own. 'You neglected to add please.'

Are you *crazy*? The answer had to be a definite yes.

He held the balance of power, and thwarting him to any degree was the height of folly.

For years, *hell*, most of her life, she'd complied, content to fit in. Happiness equated to family, good friends, satisfying job, and a pleasant lifestyle. Not that she didn't possess views, nor was she afraid to voice them when the occasion warranted it.

Easygoing, fun, joyful…until five years ago when everything had fallen apart.

Since then she'd toughened up…on the inside. Outwardly there appeared little change in her demeanour. As far as anyone knew, she'd survived and regained her former easygoing persona.

Only she knew it to be a protective shell. There were nights when vivid dreams haunted her sleep, occasionally so painful and stark she'd awake with tears dampening each cheek, emotionally and mentally exhausted by painful images.

'Natalya.'

Okay, enough with the hissy fit. One of them had to give in, and it was clear it wasn't going to be Alexei. Conceivably, how long could they remain standing here, Paul and the limousine waiting, in a deliberate face-off?

She gave Alexei a look that should have seared his soul.

'Go to hell.' The words were quietly spoken, but there was little doubt of the heartfelt meaning as she moved past him and slid into the rear seat, reached for the seatbelt, fastened it, and steadfastly ignored Alexei's presence as he joined her.

Silence is golden?

Really? It felt like a thick fog encompassed the car's interior as it moved quietly through the city streets.

She wanted to lash out at him in verbal rage...so much so it became a palpable entity.

'Nothing further you'd like to add?'

Natalya spared him a hard brief glance. The temptation to tell him precisely what she thought of his macho tactics was almost irresistible. 'Not at the present time.'

For a millisecond she imagined the gleam of humour in his dark eyes, and her own narrowed at the thought he might be amused.

She was tempted to take him up on it. Although the joke would be on her if it could have simply been a trick of reflected light in the car's dim interior.

Focussing her attention on the passing traffic, the bright neon billboards, worked for a few scant minutes, until unbidden memories rose to the surface.

Remembering too well vivid images of his mouth on her own. The way his tongue sought, teased in wicked exploration, and possessed until she became totally lost in the magic of his touch...and the response it evoked as she matched the sensual fervour to a point when foreplay ceased to be enough...

The images came to a sudden screeching halt as her mind went into involuntary shutdown.

She was so not going there.

Couldn't, if she was to retain a shred of sanity.

At least she managed to exert strict control during her waking hours...

Now he was there, five days out of every seven, invading her space, a constant reminder of what they'd once shared.

A deliberate manoeuvre in his plan for revenge.

Against her father…without question.

Her? How many times had she lain awake in the dark of night emotionally agonising for a possible answer?

Too many times to count.

Alexei had done his homework too well, ensuring Natalya's one way out would involve irreparably breaking her mother's heart, and she hated him for it.

Worse, the all-consuming emotional war was gradually tearing her apart.

Had that also been part of his plan?

It said much for her resolve that she managed to regain a semblance of apparent calm until Paul turned off the main thoroughfare and eased to a halt outside her home.

Natalya unclipped her seatbelt, offered a polite goodnight, and made her exit, assuming a normal pace as she walked the path to the front door, inserted the key, entered the foyer, then closed the door behind her.

Inside the car, the driver spared his employer a questioning glance via the rear mirror. 'Seaforth, Alexei?'

He inclined his head, and issued a brief affirmative. Home was a beautiful mansion high on a promontory with enviable views. Professionally decorated and furnished, with staff to cater to his slightest whim.

Hard work, long hours, a penchant for electronic design…add the three Ds, determination, dedication and desire…had seen him succeed beyond his wildest dreams.

Some of his contemporaries had described him as *driven*. Only *he* knew the true reason why he'd deliberately chosen to bring Roman Montgomery to his knees, and make Natalya pay.

There was a personal need to push the boundaries… which surprised him. So, too, did Natalya's concerted intention to become the quintessential PA.

Absent was her smile, replaced by an efficiency he couldn't fault.

Had she changed so much from the beautiful young woman in mind and spirit with whom he'd once fallen in love?

Haunting memories teased his sleep on occasion, and left him wondering if there was a missing link he'd failed to discover.

Yet he'd employed one of the best investigative teams to uncover fact, down to the most minuscule detail.

For a brief second he considered calling one of the few young women he'd dated socially, each one of whom had pressed a note with their smartphone number into his hand, issuing a sultry smile and breathing an inviting call me, any time.

Sex for the sake of it?

He'd taken his share. Indulged in short-term relationships that weren't destined to go anywhere.

Alexei checked his wristwatch, noted the time, aware the workforce on the other side of the world had begun, and there was data he needed to check, calls to make.

'Yes,' he conceded.

CHAPTER SIX

ALEXEI'S PREDICTION OF a full day fell short of the reality, as scheduled meetings ran late; an important presentation was held up due to an unforeseen delay, and there were occasions when the air in the conference room of an affiliate firm could have been cut with a knife.

The pace was relentless. A restless seemingly sleepless night meant Natalya needed to maintain focus, and as the afternoon wore on it took concentrated effort to keep up.

'Did you get that?'

Natalya met Alexei's studied gaze without so much as a blink. 'Of course.'

She did her work, executing each assignment with dedicated professionalism. No one was aware she downed painkillers for a persistent headache, or that her body became limp with relief when Alexei called an end to the afternoon meetings, issuing a curt demand to a contemporary associate to supply the relevant information within three hours or the deal was off.

Then he closed his laptop, gathered his briefcase, spared three associates a brief nod, and strode from the room with Natalya at his side.

Alexei's limousine was stationary in a temporary parking bay as they exited the building, and she slid into the rear seat, leaned back against the cushioned rest and appreciated the silence during the relatively brief ride while Alexei checked messages on his smartphone.

All too soon the limousine slid to a halt in the forecourt of their office block, where within minutes they reached the bank of elevators to take the first available one to their designated floor.

'Have Louise send in coffee, and arrange for food to be delivered here at six,' Alexei instructed, shooting her a glance as they approached his office. 'If you've made arrangements for tonight…cancel them. We'll be working late.'

'Tonight isn't convenient for me.' It was a retaliatory answer, despite being politely couched. More than anything she wanted to finish what was left of the working day, drive home, soak in a hot bath, then crawl into bed.

'Make it convenient.' Without a further word he moved to his desk and opened his laptop.

She was *so* tempted to utter a comeback, and almost did. Instead she turned away, effected an expressive eye-roll, stepped into her office and summoned Louise, who raised an eyebrow and offered, 'You look ready to slay dragons.'

For a few seconds she contemplated her weapon of choice…not that it changed anything, but the image of winning provided momentary satisfaction.

'The CEO requests coffee asap.'

'Hot, black, strong. Got it. Anything else?'

'Dinner for two, to be delivered here at six p.m.'

Louise glanced up, pen poised over her iPad. 'Sourced from where? Preferences?'

Natalya named a nearby restaurant, specified orders, and waited until Louise retreated before allowing herself a faint smile.

Choosing Alexei's least favourite food would afford a slight victory of sorts…and if challenged, she had the perfect answer.

Meanwhile she compiled notes on an extensive report, and transferred it to Alexei's laptop.

Dedication was key, and it said much for her stoicism that she achieved an enviable workload. What was more, she managed cool…albeit polite cool.

By five-thirty most of the office staff had departed for the day, and promptly at six an alert came through announcing their dinner delivery.

Natalya checked the foyer camera onscreen, cleared the delivery, then went to Reception. Minutes later she collected two containers of food, paid the delivery guy, returned to her office and alerted Alexei.

'Take it through to the staff room. We'll eat there.'

Not if she could help it. 'I'll take a half-hour break at my desk.' Plus strong coffee and more painkillers.

Alexei spared her a brief glance as she deposited his food within reach, inclined his head in acknowledgment, and returned his attention to the screen.

Witnessing his reaction when he checked his meal would have been a plus. Although the visual aspect was less important than the deed itself.

The evening ran longer than anticipated, the pace full on…so much so, she began to suspect deliberate payback. Yet she refused to bend, achieving everything he threw at her until enough was enough.

With care she closed her laptop, stood to her feet and extracted her bag.

'You have a problem?' His voice was pure silk. 'We're not finished.'

Her gaze met his, fearless, unequivocal. 'I am.'

The air appeared to chill a little, and she stiffened her shoulders against the icy finger feathering down her spine.

'Angling for dismissal?' Alexei posed quietly as she stepped towards the door.

'Be my guest.' A foolhardy response, but right at that precise moment she didn't care.

'We both know that isn't going to happen.'

Natalya swung round to face him, and for an infinitesimal instant the atmosphere became electric. Her eyes met his in open defiance, silently daring him to react.

His eyes hardened, and a muscle bunched at the edge of his jaw. 'Think before you indulge in a war of words.'

'Really? *Why?*'

He waited a beat. 'Give it up, Natalya.'

'And if I don't?'

He didn't answer. There was no need.

She could plead exhaustion, a throbbing headache… she should probably apologise.

Instead she did neither, supremely conscious with every passing second of being alone with him in an empty suite of offices…no phones ringing, smartphones chirping or the buzz of background noise.

Were there others working in the building, putting in the hours? Who would know?

'Fifteen minutes should wrap it up for the night.'

Refuse or comply? The reality being comply…which she did, with a measure of reluctance. 'Fifteen. Not a minute more.'

Natalya caught his studied appraisal, met it briefly, checked her watch, then she returned to her office.

Precisely fifteen minutes later she shut down her laptop, pushed it into her satchel, gathered her bag, closed her office, stepped along the corridor…and found Alexei waiting in Reception.

'Thank you.'

It was an unexpected courtesy, and she found herself examining his tone for any hint of an edge, discovered none apparent, and merely inclined her head as she pro-

ceeded through the entry foyer to summon the elevator...
which, despite a silent prayer, failed to appear within seconds, and left her little option but to share as Alexei ap
peared at her side.

Fate chose that precise second for the lift doors to open.
Of course...what else?

Alexei stepped into the electronic cubicle and indicated
the instrument panel. 'Which basement level?'

'Three.'

The small confines merely emphasised their isolation,
and she hated his close proximity, the subtle aftershave
which, unbidden and unwanted, succeeded in heighten-
ing her senses.

Nothing more than a temporary madness, she dismissed, more relieved than she was prepared to admit
when the elevator slid to a halt.

The level was well lit and almost empty, given most of
the building's staff had vacated hours ago.

With a brief goodnight, Natalya moved quickly towards
her BMW, aware he remained at her side, and she pressed
the remote button to deactivate the car's locking system,
heard the resultant chirp and leant forward to open the
door at the same time as Alexei did.

The touch of his hand on her own sent heat searing
through her veins, and she quickly snatched her hand free,
shaken by her reaction.

Worse, the unwanted flare of emotion deep within.

Get real. You have every reason to hate him, remember?
And she did, *really* she did.

So why was she temporarily locked into immobility?

Without a word she slid in behind the wheel, inclined
her head in silent thanks as he closed her door, and she ig-
nited the engine, eased the car out of the parking bay and
resisted the desire to speed.

'Idiot,' she muttered beneath her breath, unsure whether the castigation was against Alexei or herself.

Both, she decided as she reached street level and joined the stream of traffic.

Ollie offered a plaintive miaow as Natalya unlocked the front door, and she scooped up his furry body, ran a gentle finger down his throat, sensed rather than heard his responsive purr, latched the door, then entered the kitchen, checked his dry food feeder and water bowl.

Stilettos off, briefcase deposited in her home office, then she headed through her bedroom to the adjoining en suite bathroom.

A leisurely shower, pyjamas, channel-surfing the TV, then hitting the bed were all on her agenda.

It had been a long day...not so much in hours, per se, but the pace. Achieving in one day what would have taken a minimum of several days during her father's regime, interrupted by over-long lunches, time out for one innocuous reason or another.

With hindsight it had been she who'd attempted to adopt a more businesslike attitude in preceding months leading towards the forced sale of Montgomery Electronics.

Takeover, she mentally corrected. Engineered by Alexei via an agent.

Payback. Undoubtedly justifiable revenge on Alexei's part...from his perspective.

How many nights had she lain awake wondering how their lives might have been if she'd been able to reach him when she first discovered her pregnancy?

Five years had passed, time during which she'd carried on with her life, and managed just fine, she added silently...until Alexei reappeared on the scene.

Disturbing her peace of mind, her emotions.

In a deliberate ploy to unsettle her? Subtly remind her of what they'd once shared? The passion...the love.

A time when she could read him so well. The teasing gleam in his eyes, the curve of his mouth when he smiled. The barely disguised passion...a reminder of what they'd shared, and would again. *Soon.*

The light touch of his fingers as he trailed them down her cheek to cup her jaw, the slight pressure as his eyes darkened with passion...the light brush of his lips as they teased her own. The moment *teasing* became more...so much more there was no sense of time or place. Only pleasure of the senses, escalating until clothes became an unwanted restriction to be discarded at will...slowly, tortuously. Or almost torn with urgent hands until they each stood naked, exulting in the magic freedom of skin against skin and the mutual delight of touch to explore, tantalise and exult in mutual passion.

Natalya closed her eyes in a bid to dispense the memory, only to fail miserably.

Alexei's image was there, embedded in her mind, surfacing from a past for which there could be no return. Even now...especially now, there was a part of her that ached for what they had shared.

A past where she could read him so well, aware of the simplicity of curling her hand into his, the subtle trail of his fingers as they brushed her cheek.

Dear heaven, the quiet promise of how their day would end, the love they'd shared—so deep and all-consuming neither had any doubt it was the for ever kind.

Only for Alexei to suddenly disappear...and her world turned upside down, when hope died, together with the fact she needed to get on with her life.

During the past four years Natalya had studied advancement potential in existing technology—projecting how it could and would aid production. Increasing her knowledge in the field of electronics, creating ideas for media attention, publicity via donations to worthy charities…in each of which Roman showed little interest.

Her suggestion she join the directorial board had been dismissed out of hand. Reason being Roman was inured in the theory he had everything under control, and when he chose to retire, the lead role would justifiably be filled by a man.

Women, while delightful creatures, inevitably became tied up in relationships and/or marriage and children. Ergo, their attention became divided.

Natalya's rebuttal in naming women with high profiles worldwide who successfully managed both with admirable acclaim had been airily dismissed, followed by a reassuring pat on her shoulder and the words…together we make a good team. Why change?

Because if you don't, the firm will become vulnerable.

Words she had uttered at the time, to no effect whatsoever.

Never going to happen, Roman had assured her.

How wrong her father had been, Natalya reflected as weariness won and sleep provided a blissful escape.

Reflection served no purpose, Natalya decided as she guided the BMW through heavy traffic clogging main arterial roads leading from the city at another day's end.

A day fraught with action, demands which tested her ability to keep up with Alexei's instructions…so much so, tense didn't begin to cover it.

The man was a machine, geared into top form and take no prisoners mode. So chillingly calm, it sent figurative ice tricking down her spine…together with a degree of sympathy for whoever was his target.

If Alexei's motive had been an exercise in trialling the limits of her professional endurance…he'd positively nailed it.

There was the need for distraction, preferably something physical, where she could don boxing gloves and rid some excess anger against a punching ball…replacing the ball with a figurative image of him. There was a gym bag packed with clean gear in the boot of her car in readiness for a spontaneous workout should the mood take her…as it did now.

A flyer for a new women's only gym in a relatively new complex not far from her home had recently popped into her mailbox, and on the spur of the moment she decided to give it a trial.

Attractive signage, she acknowledged as she parked the car and retrieved her gym bag. Uncluttered reception area, boutique style with strategically placed mirrors, an attractive receptionist who took details, offered a friendly spiel, and alerted an attendant to escort Natalya on a explanatory tour of the premises.

Great state-of-the-art equipment, where a few participants played…the only word Natalya could think of, wearing the latest design in imported gym wear, full make-up, hair artfully tied back, at a pace aimed deliberately to avoid a sweat.

Seriously?

Her own dark grey sweat pants and matching sports top would stand out like a sore thumb.

Then she spotted a woman with a camera, and realised an infomercial was in progress.

'They're nearly done,' the attendant relayed quietly as she indicated a passage. 'The change rooms are accessed to the left. Each cubicle has an individual lock, a cabinet for your personal effects and an adjoining shower.' She handed over a key, offered a friendly smile. 'Enjoy your time here. Any questions, just ask.'

Feminine and functional…a pleasant combination, Natalya approved and she donned gym wear, executed a set of warm-up exercises before hitting the gym itself, initially setting a moderate pace before gradually increasing to near professional speed, maintaining it, then easing off. Taking time to hydrate, before moving on to a rowing machine.

Physical exercise, endorphins helped ease stress and tension…a clinical fact, Natalya acknowledged with gratitude as she took a leisurely shower more than an hour later, emerging refreshed, equilibrium somewhat restored by provided liquid lotions, clean casual clothes.

Natalya offered the receptionist a brief smile as she handed in the locker key.

'That was some workout,' the attractive blonde relayed with a degree of admiration. 'I hope you'll decide to take advantage of our membership.'

Maybe. The venue had high-end equipment, the facilities were fine, and it was close to home. There was no reason why she couldn't split her exercise regime between her regular gym and this one.

She was almost out of the door when her smartphone beeped with an incoming text, and she checked the screen, recognised the sender's number, and muttered something unprintable as she reached her car, aimed the remote, heard the resultant chirp, then slid in behind the wheel to check the message.

Current Passport USA Visa departure next week, destination NY. A.

Okay, she got it. Business, with scheduling details to follow.

CHAPTER SEVEN

THE REMAINDER OF the week progressed without a hitch as Natalya dealt with work, meetings, together with Alexei's seemingly incessant instructions. If, as she suspected, he sought to see her fall in a heap as he ramped up the pressure, she took satisfaction in being one step ahead of him by coping admirably…and then some.

The weekend loomed, with nothing planned other than her usual routine, and maybe a call to her close friend, Anja, suggesting they take in a movie currently gaining rave reviews.

Pleasant, low-key, enjoyable.

So why this sudden feeling of restlessness? As if there should be *more* to her life than a predictable pattern with little, if any variation.

She was happy with the status quo…wasn't she?

Because it's safe, a silent voice taunted.

A conscious choice, she determined. One with which she'd been perfectly content…until now.

The cause, she reluctantly admitted, was Alexei.

There. In her face. Invading her mind…her sleep, as a reminder of what they'd once shared together.

Like she wanted to be caught up in an emotional maelstrom? Alternately dismissing the secret yearning deep in her heart, and the need to rail against him for causing it.

The electric fire of his touch when their hands met on the door clasp of her car in the bowels of the basement car park, when for one wild unprincipled moment she hadn't been able to *think*, let alone move.

Had he felt it, too?

For heaven's sake, take a reality check.

Alexei's sole motivation was revenge. Hadn't he gone to exceptional lengths to ensure he'd covered every possible angle?

So why waste time trying to search for that elusive something that didn't quite gel?

Worse, why was it *she* who was paying the price for her father's indiscretions and financial misdeeds?

Enough already.

Except her weekend plans were felled in one swift stroke with a text message received at ten fifty-three Saturday morning from Alexei demanding she contact him asap.

A soft imprecation escaped from her lips, followed by, 'Who the hell does he think he is?'

Natalya thrust the phone back into her bag and zipped the compartment.

He could wait.

She was hot, sweaty, in need of a shower and change of clothes following a vigorous hour of squash. There was a sense of satisfaction in taking her time, and she emerged into the reception area to find Aaron waiting for her.

'Problem?'

'Is it that obvious?'

'Uh-huh. You have *the look*.'

Natalya rolled her eyes.

'Alexei,' he concluded. 'What does he want?'

'I have no idea.'

'And you're not exactly in a hurry to find out.'

She sent him a faint smile. 'No.'

'Careful, sweetheart. Don't bite off more than you can chew.'

His concern was touching, and her expression softened. 'I'm no longer the vulnerable young girl of five years ago.'

'Nor is he the same man.'

Isn't that the truth.

A faint shiver slid down her spine, only to be instantly dispelled as they exited the building and crossed to the adjoining car park.

'Thanks for the game,' Natalya voiced as they reached her BMW.

'But not the advice.'

'That, too.'

Aaron placed a hand on her shoulder. 'Travel carefully.'

She deactivated the car's locking system, and sent him a sunny smile as she slid in behind the wheel. 'Always.'

Asap equated to urgency. Yet she waited an hour before making the call. Justifying the delay as a need to stop by the food mart for grocery supplies, unpacking and depositing same into her fridge and pantry.

'Your smartphone was on charge; you failed to check for messages,' Alexei pre-empted with undisguised dryness as he picked up on the second buzz. 'Or was the delay merely sheer bloody-mindedness?'

'Good morning to you, too,' she offered with incredible politeness.

Strike one for Natalya.

'Afternoon.'

She made a play of checking her watch. 'By precisely three minutes,' she agreed. 'The nature of your call being?'

Was it possible for silence to be explosive? And why did the thought please her?

'A meeting set up in Melbourne late this afternoon. My

car will collect you at three-thirty. You'll need an overnight bag.'

'Need I remind you it's the weekend? You expect me to drop everything at a moment's notice?'

'Yes.'

'And if I decline?'

'I suggest you reconsider.' His cool, slightly acerbic response hit a hot button, and she tamped down her temper.

Of course. He held all the cards in this diabolical game, with not one in her favour.

Once, just once she'd kill to be able to upset the balance of power between them.

Not going to happen anytime soon...

'Could we make it three forty-five?' Fifteen minutes was a small concession, albeit a deliberate one.

'No.'

Well, there you go. Nice try, even if it failed. With that, she slipped into smooth professional mode. 'Any specific instructions?'

Alexei outlined them with succinct brevity and ended the call.

Hotel. Restaurant. Six for seven. Suitable attire.

Natalya extended the tip of her tongue in an unladylike gesture, then she swept into her bedroom to pack.

CHAPTER EIGHT

HIGH-END MELBOURNE HOTEL, stunning river and inner-city views, *check*.

Top floor restaurant, good table, time and number of guests, *check*.

Luxury two-bedroom suite, each with en suite bathroom, and separated by lounge, *reluctant check*. A familiar business arrangement when travelling as Roman's PA.

However Alexei was not her father.

'I'd prefer a separate suite on the same floor.'

Alexei's eyebrow rose. 'On what grounds?'

She had a few, only one of which she was prepared to voice. 'Privacy.'

The faint lift at the edge of his mouth was so fleeting, she wondered if she'd merely imagined it.

'Afraid, Natalya?'

'Of you?' Her gaze met his with cool equanimity. 'Not in this lifetime.'

'In that case, I don't perceive there to be a problem.' He checked his watch. 'Order coffee in ten. Bring your iPad.' With that he collected his bag and disappeared into the bedroom on his right.

She ordered room service, took the second bedroom, freshened up, unpacked, and re-emerged into the lounge to find him seated at a desk checking data on his laptop.

He'd removed his suit jacket and tie, released the top few buttons of his shirt, and bore a raw masculinity that tugged at her nerve-ends, heated her blood and made her aware of every breath she took.

Not fair. Any of it.

Coffee arrived, and she filled both cups, placed one within Alexei's reach, opened her iPad and went to work keying in minor and a few major alterations to contractual clauses, highlighting the changes, then sent the amended contract to Alexei's laptop and checked the evening's schedule.

Four guests…three men well known in the electronics field and a PA.

There was time to shower, change into black silk evening trousers, attend to her make-up, style her hair, then slip on a stunning red jacket with matching silk lapels. A simple gold chain at her neck, small gold ear studs, a solid gold bracelet and her watch completed jewellery. Killer black Louboutins, and she was ready to go.

At six-fifty, evening purse tucked beneath her arm, satchel in hand, she emerged into the lounge to join Alexei.

Sensation arrowed deep within her as he turned to face her, and she had no control over the heat warming her body, or the way her pulse thudded to a quickened beat.

There was nothing classical about his features. Cheekbones a little too wide, the jawbone strong and emphasised by dark close-clipped designer stubble. Broad forehead, and eyes so dark they were almost black…equally expressive and warm, or cold as Russian ice. A generous beautifully moulded mouth, groomed hair a little longer than the current conventional style, a lithe toned body, an inherent air of power, success.

Unequivocally the *wow* factor.

So what?

She'd come into contact with equally attractive men. Yet none affected her the way Alexei had...*and still did*.

An admission she refused to give the slightest consideration.

Moving right along. They had a business dinner to attend, undoubtedly a late evening ahead, and any delays could lead to a further meeting the next day.

Superb food, splendid views of a stunning nightscape. Tall brightly lit city buildings, neon billboards...and skilled high-powered business as Alexei outlined his terms for a proposed deal involving one of ADE's subsidiary companies.

Interesting and slightly amusing to intercept the occasional glance aimed at Alexei by the super efficient blonde PA, a hint of sultry in her smile, the slow sweep of perfect mascara-enhanced lashes. Little doubt an attempt to signal discreet interest.

Like she *cared* if Alexei returned it? Natalya determined, and focussed on the job at hand.

The conglomerate represented by the three men wanted concessions written into the existing contract, which Alexei refused to consider.

Negotiations moved up a notch, Natalya acknowledged as she declined a second glass of wine in favour of sparkling mineral water.

Power became an effective sword, one which Alexei chose to wield with ruthless purpose, resulting in the spokesman for the group making a calculated attempt over coffee to regain some balance in the power play.

Without success, as Alexei brought the evening to a close by rising to his feet, inclined his head in dismissal, and silently signalled Natalya.

'Gentlemen.'

Obsequiousness was out, but Natalya detected a hint of silent back-pedalling as the head partner attempted to counter. 'We'll confer and contact you tomorrow.'

Alexei didn't hesitate. 'I have another meeting in the morning at nine.'

The implication was clear. Play ball on Alexei's terms, or not at all, Natalya reflected as they rode the elevator in silence, exited at their designated floor, and headed towards their suite.

A faint element of tension curled around her nerve-ends as he used the entry card to disengage the door and indicate she precede him into the lounge.

Professional, remember?

'Goodnight.'

It was easy to turn towards her chosen bedroom, and she was almost there, her hand extended towards the door handle when the sound of his voice caused her to pause.

'I want the evening's report accessible on my laptop by seven in the morning.'

It was all she could do not to grit her teeth. Instead, she turned towards him, inclined her head and added with sweet emphasis, 'An indication of tomorrow's agenda would help facilitate a workable schedule.' A fractional pause accelerated by a steady unwavering look lent intended emphasis. 'Seven-thirty?'

She could have sworn she glimpsed a flicker of amusement in those dark eyes, then it was gone.

'We'll confer over breakfast. Order room service for two at seven-fifteen.'

A minor concession... Whether she compiled the report tonight, or rose early to complete it was neither here nor there.

Without a further word she turned and walked towards the adjoining bedroom.

'Sleep well.' His faint drawl held a tinge of amusement.

Natalya didn't miss a beat as she spared him a glance over one shoulder as she entered her room. 'I always do.'

With that, she closed the door behind her, turned the lock, and silently pumped a fist in the air.

There was something eminently satisfying in having the last word.

A victory short-lived, Natalya conceded as business ruled their early morning breakfast.

A relaxed CEO, she perceived, with the top two buttons of his shirt undone, sleeves turned back, suit jacket spread over the back of his chair.

A casual look she silently assured she was perfectly comfortable with...and knew she lied.

Five years had added a few slight changes if one looked closely enough. Fine lines fanned out from the far corners of his eyes. Close-clipped designer stubble added a ruthless quality to his facial features...and she squashed the stray thought whether it would feel soft or slightly bristly on a woman's soft skin.

Are you insane?

Just...curious, she hastened silently, and filled her cup with coffee. It said much for her level of control that her hand remained perfectly steady. So what if she took the coffee black, strong and unsweetened for the maximum caffeine hit?

Cool, professional, as they ran an updated check on the day's schedule. Tight, Natalya perceived, with little wiggle room for any unforeseen delay.

Vastly different from the leisurely meals she'd shared with her father during his regime when the first business meeting of the day began with an extensive lunch and rarely concluded until late afternoon. Dinner inevitably morphed into a social event with a well-imbibed Roman generously picking up the tab.

Chalk and cheese, she perceived as she drained the last of her coffee, slid the iPad into her satchel, and waited dutifully as Alexei buttoned his shirt, fixed his tie before shrugging into his jacket.

Attired in a black pencil-slim skirt and fitted jade-coloured jacket, killer heels, she felt ready to deal with whatever the day would bring as she preceded Alexei from their suite.

It didn't help that the elevator doors opened to reveal an almost full occupant capacity entailing up close and personal contact with her nemesis. Nor did it aid an increased pulse-beat as unwanted awareness unfurled deep within.

Natalya stood rigidly still, consciously ensuring her breathing remained even, measured, and didn't pound to a rapid beat as it threatened to do.

In a few short seconds the elevator would reach ground level, release its passengers...and she'd be able to breathe normally again.

Did he have any idea how his presence affected her?

Or how hard she fought against it?

There were many reasons to hate him, and she did... vehemently. So why did the light musky drift of Alexei's cologne tease and heighten her senses?

His height and muscled frame proved a powerful force impossible to ignore. So, too, the sexual chemistry he managed to exude with little or no effort at all.

Five years ago she'd relished every stolen moment with him, no matter how brief. His touch, warmth of his smile, the knowledge of more, much more, as soon as they were alone. Did he remember, as she did? Wake in the night wanting, needing what they'd once shared?

Obviously not.

So who's the fool haunted by images of a past best forgotten?

You have a life…or at least she did have until Alexei reappeared on the scene.

Her relief was palpable as the elevator slid to a smooth halt, and she accompanied Alexei across the marble-tiled lobby to the black limousine and driver parked adjacent the hotel entrance.

Any hope she had of occupying the rear seat alone was dashed when Alexei slid in beside her, and she silently cursed his close proximity as the limousine cruised through city streets towards their destination.

'No last-minute instructions?' Natalya managed quietly, and incurred his measured glance.

'None.'

Okay. Time out from idle conversation. Which suited her just fine.

Instead she reflected on the meeting's key points, and the background research she had managed to glean on the major player in opposition.

An open mind, adhere with polite formalities, record all details from both parties…and become the quintessential PA.

In other words, be prepared for anything.

The limousine pulled into a semi-circular driveway and drew to a halt adjacent an impressive entrance lobby.

Showtime, Natalya accorded as they were met and led towards a bank of elevators, one of which transported them to a high floor where they were escorted to a designated boardroom.

There was a brief moment when Alexei's hand inadvertently brushed her arm, and she hated the way her pulse immediately quickened to a crazy beat.

In the name of heaven...*focus*.

The fact she did owed more to the experience of long practice, and she took her seat at the conference table, extracted the necessary iPad, and mini-recorder.

Playing tough in the business arena was an art form Alexei had mastered with unfailing ease as he calmly stripped negotiations to a base level of take it or leave it. Something which didn't augur well, and resulted in harsh criticism of ADE CEO's tactics.

Cut-throat didn't come close. Although Natalya had to concede the methodology worked. A break for lunch involved food eaten in one of the hotel's private rooms... and a review of key points from the morning's meeting.

High-powered, with Alexei's unyielding stance, and his superb negotiation skills.

Natalya could only quietly admire his ability to figuratively pin his business competitor to the wall...while her personal jury remained out regarding the inherent ruthlessness he managed to employ.

The pace increased during the afternoon, with Alexei adamant his terms were final, which led to a hastily arranged meeting the following morning.

'Reschedule our flight to mid-afternoon tomorrow,' Alexei instructed as their limousine took the route to their hotel.

Natalya sent him a killing look as they entered their hotel suite. 'In this technological age legal documents can be digitally signed and emailed.'

'True.' He removed his suit jacket, loosened his tie and tossed both onto a nearby chair as he sent her a piercing look. 'You're questioning my decision?'

'Merely expressing an opinion.'

'Which you feel entitled to do?'

Why did she suddenly feel as if she'd ventured onto

shaky ground? 'It wasn't specifically mentioned in my employment contract.'

Was that a faint gleam of humour in his dark gaze?

'Consult the menu and order a meal to be delivered to our suite at seven.' Alexei waited a beat. 'I'll have the sea-food pilaf.' He reached forward and collected his jacket and tie, then turned towards his room. 'I'll change and go down to the gym for an hour.'

All this *togetherness* didn't augur well, especially from her perspective. She could manage days, business lunches and dinners. It was the overnight thing that bothered her. *Especially* the sharing of a suite, despite it being a sensible business arrangement.

Hadn't she accompanied Roman to interstate meetings? Shared similar suites in several different hotels?

So why, now, did she feel wary? Defensive, on edge?

Yet she did, and it angered her that she should.

Worse, a full-blown suspicion Alexei took pleasure in figuratively ruffling her feathers.

Civil during business discussions in the presence of others, yet when alone with him she detected a watchful element, almost as if he was deliberately intent on…*what*?

There had been a time when she could read him well. Yet the passing of time had wrought changes. Few of which she could condone. For even now, her heart ached for the loss of the love they'd once shared. The pain of him leaving her so suddenly without a word and no further contact, despite all her efforts, still existed…like a wound that had never completely healed.

So go do something constructive, an inner voice urged. *Check out the hotel boutiques. Or better yet, go swim laps in the hotel pool and work off some pent-up angst.*

The pool won out, and she quickly rang Room Service, placed an order, then retrieved a one-piece from her bag, changed, caught up a towelling robe, popped the suite swipe card into one of two capacious pockets, and took the elevator.

Most of the guests were readying themselves for drinks at the bar or in the lounge, and Natalya felt a sense of relief on discovering she had the pool to herself.

The water was enticing, crystal clear and sparkling. Without hesitation, she shrugged off the robe and dived in.

It felt so good as she rose to the water's surface and began stroking laps, one after the other, steady at first before picking up speed. After a while she lost count, content simply to power up and down the pool's length, varying strokes as the whim took her, until she simply rolled over and lazily backstroked to the pool's edge.

How long had she been in the water? Half an hour?

A quick glance at the wall clock revealed longer, and she hastily emerged, dried off, then pulled on the towelling robe. Ten minutes should be sufficient to return to the suite, shower and dress before room service delivered their evening meal.

Alexei was already seated in one of the lounge chairs as she entered the room, and she met his gaze, rolled her eyes, lifted a hand in a silent gesture and hurried towards her bedroom.

Oh, hell, emerged as a silent condemnation as she caught a glance at her mirrored reflection. Bright lights enhanced her damp hair...rats' tails was an apt description...bare face...great!

So what? He's seen you in less...a lot less. But that was years ago when things between them had been different.

Way different.

Suck it up, girl. Take the fastest shower ever, dress and wind wet hair into a knot on top of your head, add lip gloss and go.

Food, perhaps a shared wine, followed by coffee and a recap of the day's business at hand. An hour, maybe two. Then she could escape to her room, duty successfully executed for the evening.

Three hours, slightly more to be exact, Natalya perceived, as she checked her laptop, read and discussed pertinent points, gave her opinion when asked, and provided a requested overview from her perspective.

'Honesty? Or circumspection?'

Alexei leaned back in his chair. 'Both.'

'They want the deal on their terms.'

She was good, he conceded, aware just how well she'd covered for her father during the past few years. Without her, Roman's business would have crashed and burned way before it had become vulnerable to a takeover.

Family loyalty...or desperation? Maybe both.

'Not going to happen.' A statement, no wiggle room.

Of course not. Alexei held the power, and was unafraid to use it.

'You've decided on a predetermined figure,' Natalya ventured. 'I imagine they will offer ten percent lower, then prepare for you to negotiate.'

'Astute.'

She inclined her head. 'Thank you.'

'Did your father request your opinion on any of his business dealings?'

Now there was a question. 'Occasionally.' In a befuddled alcohol-infused state, only to resort to something totally different in the light of day.

'Yet he rarely implemented them.'

The truth hurt, in more ways than one. At peak, Montgomery Electronics could have sold at almost double what ADE had paid for it. 'No.'

'Did you resent that?'

This was becoming upfront and personal. She was a daughter, not the son Roman envisaged Ivana would dutifully bear him.

'Is there a point to this?'

His eyes took on a watchful quality. 'It fills in a few blanks.'

She drained the coffee in her cup, closed her iPad and stood to her feet. 'I think we're done for the evening.'

Alexei silently commended her efficiency, enjoyed the challenge she presented...and wondered what it would take to crack the shell she'd erected to protect herself.

From him? Or men in general?

It shouldn't bother him.

Yet it did.

She offered a polite goodnight and crossed the room to her bedroom suite.

'Sleep well.' His faintly mocking voice curled around her nerve-ends as she reached for the door handle.

What she wouldn't give to best him at something...anything, just for the satisfaction of doing so.

A feeling which continued as she undressed and made ready for bed, rearranged pillows and settled comfortably with a current paperback.

Two chapters, then she'd close the bed lamp and sleep.

Except an escape into blissful oblivion didn't appear to be happening anytime soon, as Alexei's compelling image filled her mind and refused to disappear, no matter how hard she fought to dispel it. Nor her ability to evade dreams of their shared past. The intimacies...erotic, all-encompassing, as she became alive beneath his touch in a mutual gift of passion in all its guises. Lost, so completely lost she had no recollection of anything other than Alexei.

Magical. Transcending to a place where heart, body and soul became one...until the dream began to fade into a reality where she slowly woke to discover her body damp with sensual heat. Bereft, wanting…with silent tears slowly drifting down her cheeks.

Her breath hitched for a second before she caught hold of the now, and the need to shower, dress and face the day ahead. As well as the man who managed to slip through her subconscious and invade her heart.

Their shared morning breakfast was interrupted by the ring tone of Alexei's smartphone, and Natalya lifted her head to witness his eyes darken.

Trouble?

Undoubtedly, as Alexei's voice hardened during a conversation with, she assumed, a spokesman representing the group with whom they'd shared dinner the previous evening.

It didn't sound promising, as Alexei firmly refused to consider any further negotiation.

He ended the call, calmly drained the rest of his coffee and refilled his cup. 'They've requested a two-hour extension. A delay with their bank.'

'In a bid to gain more time.' She made it a statement, not a question.

And you have no intention of playing into it, Natalya conceded. Nor would I, in your position. 'So we wait.'

We…a slip of the tongue, and a throwback to the days when she prompted her father, whenever he required it… more frequently than it should have been.

'They have my number, flight departure time,' Alexei stated. 'The ball is in their court.' He checked his watch. 'I'm catching up with a friend for an hour or two. During which time I need you to complete a few shopping items on my behalf.'

Natalya's eyes widened. 'Shopping?'

'Is that a problem?' There was a hint of wry amusement in his voice, and she met his gaze, held it.

'I gather you intend to supply a list?'

'Note it will be business combined with family while we're in New York,' he enlightened, as she retrieved her iPad.'

Natalya attempted to ignore the slight blip in her heartbeat, and stilled the temptation to tell him to choose his own gifts.

Yet if she displayed the slightest hesitation…

'I guess I can add it to my job description.' Just don't make a habit of it, she added silently. Helping the boss choose family gifts came under personal…and personal wasn't ever going to be in the picture.

'Your mother?'

'Books.'

'That's really not helpful,' Natalya offered. 'Fiction? Fact? Romance…modern, historical, suspense, crime? Shall I elaborate further?'

'Romantic suspense.'

This could go on for a while. 'Favourite authors? Or don't you know?' She named a few, which presumably didn't strike a chord.

'Scarves,' he added. 'To add to my mother and sister-in-law's existing collection.'

'Any particular designer?'

He named a few, then handed over a credit card.

Safe choices, Natalya mused, and two hours later she had acquired numerous gifts beautifully wrapped and placed in a clutch of glossy carrier bags.

Ignoring the occasional brief…very brief moment, she recalled other occasions of shared shopping excursions. A time when Alexei would place an arm across her shoulders and catch her body close to his own. The dark emotion evident in his eyes, and the silent promise of how the day would end.

The memories shouldn't affect her...except they did, and she mentally struggled to put them back into a figurative box, and throw away the key.

She re-entered the hotel foyer to find Alexei standing to one side, newspaper in hand as he appeared seemingly engaged in reading an article.

Alexei's smartphone beeped as she drew close, and he moved aside to take the call, kept it brief while Natalya checked her watch, noted they had an hour and a half to pack, check out, and reach the airport to make their flight.

'The deal has been accepted,' Alexei relayed as he returned to her side.

Of course, she acknowledged silently. Had there been any doubt?

CHAPTER NINE

A FEW HOURS later they disembarked at Sydney's major airport, collected their bags, and were met by Paul in the passenger lounge.

'Welcome back,' Paul greeted with a smile. 'A successful trip?'

Natalya inclined her head as Alexei answered in the affirmative as Paul took hold of their bags, and began leading the way towards the exit.

Confirmation documents digitally signed in ADE Conglomerate's favour had been recorded. Another deal settled, Natalya acknowledged as Paul eased Alexei's limousine away from the terminal.

No matter how many domestic and international flights Natalya had made over the years, the return to Sydney inevitably invited the pleasure of familiarity, the buzz of city traffic, famous landmarks.

Mission accomplished, she acceded...admitting it was good to be back. Within half an hour of her own home, free of an insidious awareness pervading her senses with every passing day.

A temporary madness, she dismissed, due to being in Alexei's presence a minimum of eight hours five days a week...more, if you counted business dinners, travel.

She didn't feel comfortable with it. Didn't condone he

had managed to manoeuvre her between a rock and a hard place by robbing her of choice…aware there was only one choice she could make.

It made her want to rail her fists against him…except she didn't *do* tantrums. Couldn't remember throwing any, even as a child. Not that there had ever been a reason for her to do so.

A faint smile curved the edges of her lips. Except one incidence as a child in first grade when a boy…she couldn't even recall his name…grabbed hold of her single hair braid and pulled it so hard her eyes had watered. The taunt of 'cry-baby' had made her so mad she didn't hesitate to kick him…inadvertently where it hurt him most. An act which earned both children a demerit point, a lecture, and a phone call to each of their parents.

A forgotten incident…until now.

The limousine eased to a halt outside her home, and she emerged from the door Alexei held open while Paul removed her bag.

It was a simple expedient to offer Paul a polite word in thanks, reach for her bag, only to have Alexei collect it and accompany her to the front door, wait as she extracted her keys.

'I can take it from here.'

For a brief moment she imagined she glimpsed a tinge of amusement in his dark eyes. The temptation to execute an expressive eye-roll was uppermost. She selected the appropriate key, unlocked the front door, reached for her bag…missed by a mere second or two as Alexei placed it in the hallway before exiting without so much as a backwards glance.

An unladylike swear word slipped quietly from her lips, followed by another as she transferred her bag into her bedroom, tossed her satchel, then dug out her smartphone and rang Ben.

'Okay if I call over and collect Ollie?'

'Sure. He's antsy. I think he heard the car and your key in the door.'

'On my way.'

And there was Ben waiting for her with Ollie in his arms. 'Good trip?'

The fluffy cream seal-pointed cat squirmed with delight at the sight of his mistress, purred as Ben transferred him to Natalya, and she smiled as Ollie smooched his head into the curve of her neck, lightly nipped her earlobe in mild protest at her absence and followed it with another smooch.

'You missed me, huh?' Natalya acknowledged, and received a soft plaintive meow in return.

'Thanks, Ben. I appreciate you taking care of him.'

'No problem. Any time.'

He was a great neighbour, and looked out for her like the brother she didn't have. 'We'll catch up. Soon,' she added, meaning it.

'No rush. Whenever.'

She smiled, aware his life was even more hectic than her own. 'We're good.' And they were, for the pet minding thing was reciprocal... Ben owned an adorable sad-faced pug named Alfie, whom she looked after on occasion. 'Talk soon.'

'Look forward to it,' Ben bade as she crossed to her adjoining apartment.

Time spent with Ollie, smooches, head-butts...the feline equivalent of an adoring, *Welcome home. I missed you*, and food...always a clincher.

After which she changed into comfortable sweats, unpacked her bag, set up her laptop, checked the agreement, itemised the salient points and sent the data to Alexei. Resisting adding an expressive emoji...only to send it separately minutes later.

Time for a light meal, shower, then hit the bed with Ollie curled up beside her, maybe view a television programme.

Surprisingly she slept well, woke early, checked her email…no response from Alexei…then fed Ollie, collected the morning newspaper, made breakfast, then she poured a second cup of coffee and began skimming the daily headlines.

Normally she might have missed the article, except the bold print caught her eye. So, too, did the capitalised name—ADE CONGLOMERATE SCORES MEGA DEAL—together with a photograph of ADE's CEO, followed by brief details.

An approved press release from ADE? Doubtful, given she would have known about it. Unauthorised, damage control would ensue via a statement from Alexei in the late afternoon news.

Exactly as Natalya predicted, followed by a phone call from her father voicing a conspiracy rant, insisting she must have had advance knowledge the deal was about to go public. Concluding with a spiel alluding to the victory should have been his.

Any attempt to defuse the situation proved unsuccessful, and Natalya simply concluded the call, aware a reality check would prove a wasted effort.

Their return resulted in invitations to social events supporting various prominent charities arrived, requesting Alexei Delandros' presence and partner.

Back in the day of Roman's excesses and largess, almost all such invitations were accepted, including Natalya's attendance with her parents from the age of eighteen when she'd adapted to sharing the glitz and glamour as the social elite worked the ballroom.

Natalya checked each of the invitations, listed a few she

warranted would benefit from Alexei's presence and probable donation, and placed them on his desk.

'I'll organise for an acceptance when you've made your choice.'

Would he decide to appear solo...and if not, whom would he choose as his partner?

Like she cared?

Yet deep down she did, and for a brief few seconds she considered attending with her parents...just *because*.

Only to have the decision taken out of her hands when Alexei summoned her into his office prior to an event.

Natalya took a seat, opened her iPad with her fingers poised to tap in an update, schedule or reschedule a meeting...and glanced up when he failed to begin.

It was the end of the day, and he'd removed his jacket, loosened his tie, aiding a casual look that succeeded in ruffling her composure.

'Ensure you're available for Thursday evening's charity event,' Alexei began.

She schooled her expression and met his steady gaze. 'I'm sure you have a few young women on speed dial who would jump at the chance of an invitation.'

'None of whom possess your observation skills and diplomacy.'

'Assuming their total focus would be on charming *you*?' Natalya queried sweetly, sure she caught a faint smile at the edge of his mouth.

'Consider your presence a necessity as my PA.'

Be seated at his side throughout a lengthy dinner? Play nice, when privately she wanted to hit him? An inconceivable action in public view. Something more subtle...an elbow in his ribs, perhaps? *Accidentally*, of course.

'Business-oriented,' she clarified in droll tones. 'I'll ensure the mini-recording device will fit in my evening purse.'

'You've attended several events in the past. I doubt to-morrow evening's event will be any different.'

A number of the people present were repeat guests at several of the city's charity events throughout each year. Wealthy, influential, dedicated in donating funds to worthy causes, active on the social scene…and most familiar with Roman Montgomery's fall from grace in the finance sector.

The fact Roman's daughter would be seated next to, and to all intents and purposes partnered by, Alexei Delandros would be viewed with interest and a degree of speculation.

Poise and sophistication were an acquired façade, and qualities in which Natalya excelled…on the surface. Education in one of Sydney's highly respected private schools and world travel had ensured she could handle almost any situation without falling in a heap.

This evening's charity event would be no different. So why the edgy onset of nerves as she put the finishing touches to her make-up prior to Alexei's timed arrival at her home?

Her expressed insistence she meet him at the hotel venue had been dismissed out of hand, and for twenty-four hours she'd considered defying his edict with a last-minute text…only to abandon the tempting plan.

Instead she visited one of her favoured boutiques and purchased a new gown in champagne silk with an over-lay of matching lace.

Dressed to kill, she observed as she added a diamond pendant on a slim gold chain, attached a single diamond tennis bracelet to her left wrist, adding discreet diamond ear studs…each of which had been gifts over time from her late grandmother.

Natalya ran her fingers over her hair, plumping the loose

waved tendrils touching each collarbone, and reached for her evening purse.

Good to go, with a few minutes to sparc.

Alexei's limousine slid to a halt at the prearranged time, and she drew in a deep breath as the doorbell rang.

Nervous tension, Natalya excused, and sought to steady the increased pulse-beat at the base of her throat as she opened the door.

He had presence, an elusive quality that set him apart from most other men. Difficult to define in mere words, but there nonetheless.

Dark eyes that could sear the soul; a mouth which held the promise of sensual sin...and delivered.

Stop, a silent voice echoed inside her brain. Remembering how it had been between them served no purpose.

As an escort he ticked all the boxes. Appearing even more devastating in impeccable evening wear, he could easily have passed as a male model in a photo shoot for Armani. The epitome of the man he'd become...assured, comfortable in his own skin. The acquisition of the fine things in life, its influence and power. An added quality he bore with ease.

The limousine purred silently through the city streets, entering the inner city perimeter until they reached the hotel where the evening's event was being held.

Assembled media, photographers were positioned ready to capture the arrival of well-known guests, and flashbulbs popped as the cream of Sydney's society descended from a moving procession of limousines...women offering practised smiles, should their photograph be one of a chosen few to make the following day's social pages.

Alexei's light touch at the back of Natalya's waist was a courtesy, although only she was aware of the flare of sensual electricity coursing through her body.

Her role was strictly business-oriented. Definitely not personal. She should have organised a pin discreetly emblazoned with PA to clarify her presence.

Natalya offered a slight smile as she accompanied Alexei into the large atrium where guests were gathering for pre-dinner drinks prior to a bank of doors being opened to allow access into the formal dining room.

Waiters circled the atrium offering flutes of champagne as guests mingled with fellow associates and friends, increasing the noise factor as the numbers swelled to capacity.

Natalya offered a smile in silent acknowledgment as she recognised friends among the crowd, aware they'd be able to connect throughout the evening, and when a few scions of industry approached Alexei she achieved each introduction with practised ease.

It became increasingly obvious Alexei garnered attention. His takeover of Roman Montgomery's firm had become a lingering buzz among those in the financial sector, fired by successful deals Alexei had achieved worldwide.

There was media interest in his background, together with any information investigative journalists could dig up about his personal life.

Until now Alexei had declined to give interviews, sanctioning only information his media personnel were instructed to release. Fine in theory, but the gutter press possessed few scruples, and a grain of truth embellished with innuendo could increase sales of varying tabloids tenfold.

'Natalya.' The sound of Ivana's voice captured her attention, and she greeted her parents with affection, formally introduced Alexei to her mother, who offered him a gracious smile and shook his hand.

'You've already met my father,' Natalya indicated, sensing the tension beneath the obsequious smile as Roman extended his hand.

'Indeed,' Roman expressed. 'So pleased you've taken Natalya on board. She's an excellent PA.'

Proficient at covering your back…words which remained silent.

'Ivana, darling. We're seated together.' Aaron's mother, Elvira, Natalya perceived, aware both women were long time friends. 'Roman. Natalya.' Her gaze shifted towards Alexei. 'Alexei Delandros, of course. You photograph well. I'm delighted to meet you.' She turned towards Natalya. 'Aaron is parking the car. Al has been shanghaied by a client. I'm sure he'll manage to escape soon.'

Interesting didn't begin to describe the seating arrangement. Aaron, the gay son whose parents were in ignorance of their son's sexual proclivities; Alexei and Roman… which member of the committee thought to put the fox and the rabbit together? Each table seated twelve. Who were the remaining five?

'Ah, they're opening the doors,' Elvira declared. 'Shall we go in?'

Moving within a crowd involved some inadvertent contact with other patrons, and she stiffened as Alexei placed an arm along the back of her waist…and kept it there until they reached their table, choosing to position her chair as she graciously took a seat. The gesture polite, impersonal…so why did his touch affect her body as much as it did?

A temporary madness, and one which she'd avoid by maintaining a reasonable distance between them. Which worked until a complement of five guests soon joined them. None other than Lara and Richard Tremayne, their two daughters Abby and Olivia, with son Jason bringing up the rear.

Like she needed *awkward*?

Nothing she couldn't handle…and she did, with grace and politeness, expressing amusement at the right intervals, while easing her way through three courses of beautifully presented delectable food.

'Champagne, Natalya?' Alexei queried, and she spared him a polite smile.

'Thank you.'

Definitely a departure from her usual preference of sparkling mineral water, and she caught Aaron's faintly raised eyebrow in silent askance.

On the surface all twelve patrons at their table appeared to be sharing a pleasant evening. Perhaps they were, and she was the only one present who sensed an edge of tension.

It was a relief when the wait-staff began clearing tables in preparation for serving coffee. An action which usually pre-empted a series of announcements, speeches offering thanks for generous donations, the evening's success, followed by music and the voiced encouragement for guests to enjoy the dance floor.

Roman stood to his feet and crossed to Natalya's side and extended his hand. 'Shall we?'

At least her father employed a little circumspection in leading her part-way through the waltz before he lowered his head a little and quietly demanded,

'What in hell are you thinking?'

She didn't pretend to misunderstand. 'I'm Alexei's PA, and seated with him in a professional capacity.'

'Darling girl, he's merely using you to highlight his success over my business failure.'

Natalya looked at him, glimpsed the anger, the frustration evident, and sought to alleviate it. 'Why would he do that, when the media have already printed the coup in various newspapers?'

Roman snorted in derision. 'Didn't you learn anything five years ago? The man upped and left you without a word.'

'That's not relevant to the current discussion.' Her voice was firm as she refused to placate him. 'Shall we rejoin the others?'

Coffee, hot, black, with no sugar helped, Natalya admitted, and she offered a smile as Roman swept her mother onto the dance floor, which left Natalya, Alexei and Jason Tremayne the only occupants at the table.

Not the best scenario, she perceived, wondering if she could escape to the powder room. However luck wasn't on her side as Jason rose to his feet and approached her.

'Our turn, I think.'

'Mine actually,' Alexei intervened smoothly as he rose to his feet and placed a hand on her shoulder. 'If you'll excuse us?'

She could refuse him, plead the need for a coffee refill, and attempt to relax. Instead she inclined her head towards Jason, offered a faint smile, and accompanied Alexei onto the dance floor.

'That wasn't necessary,' Natalya said quietly as she matched his steps with familiar ease.

'No?'

What could she say? If in doubt, don't, and in this instance silence was the better option.

The music slowed, and Alexei pulled her in as they adjusted their steps to a softer beat. The top of her head barely reached his shoulder, and he fought the urge to wrap an arm around her slender body, brush his lips to her temple…as he had done in the past. Enjoy the light floral perfume she wore, aware of his body pulsing with need, and the promise of how the night would end.

He'd been so sure of their relationship, of *her*, envisaging they'd grow old together, having raised a family, and enjoy grandchildren. Until Roman Montgomery had employed strong-arm tactics to ensure Alexei's swift departure from Sydney *and* the country.

Five years on, Alexei had changed, so too had his life.

The human psyche had intrigued him to such a point whereby he'd studied psychological behavioural patterns, mannerisms, characteristics that would provide insight to figurative red flags during his business dealings.

Qualities that had led to his success.

Had it hardened him? Undoubtedly.

His late father would have been proud.

'We should return to the table,' Natalya indicated as the music sped up to a modern beat. 'Considering the duty dance is done.'

'Duty?' Alexei queried as he released her. 'Is that what it was?'

'Of course,' she dismissed. 'What else would it have been?'

Indeed. If he hadn't noted the fast-beating pulse at the base of her throat, felt the throb of it beneath the palm of her wrist, he might have believed her.

The evening eventually drew to a close, with the final speech, the lucky door ticket prize, with guests lingering in the adjoining atrium as they waited for taxis, private limousines, while others continued on to a nightclub.

There were hugs, air kisses, voiced promises to do lunch or coffee…the usual pattern following the end of an evening's social event.

'The limousine will be here within a few minutes,' Alexei indicated.

'I can easily take a cab.'

'But you won't.'

Her lips parted with the intention of arguing with him,

only for her to decide against it. Besides, taxis at this time of night were in short supply.

'Compliance, Natalya?'

She spared him a glance. 'Only because it makes sense.'

And if you *dare* smile…

He didn't, or else she missed it as Paul eased the limousine to a halt at the kerb. The late evening flow of traffic was intense as patrons vacated cinemas, cafés and restaurants until they cleared the inner city and crossed the harbour bridge.

'I trust you both enjoyed a pleasant evening?' Paul queried, and it was Alexei who responded,

'Successful.'

The context had to relate to the capacity crowd, donations raised, and Natalya added, 'Very much so.'

There was a sense of relief when the limousine drew to a halt in her driveway, her set of keys in hand as she released the door clasp and stepped out in one fluid movement, pausing to offer, 'Thanks for the ride, the evening.' She held up her set of keys. 'I'm fine. My porch light is on a timer.' She closed the rear door, then turned towards the gated path, unaware Alexei had joined her.

'I'm quite capable of walking unaccompanied to my front door.'

'I was unaware I implied otherwise.' His voice was a musing drawl, and she was conscious of the sharp tug of awareness, the unbidden heat flooding her body…and silently damned her own vulnerability, choosing to glance at the lit window on the far left of the house.

'You share the house with someone?'

Not an unusual question, given its spacious size.

'It's a large family home divided in half to incorporate two separate units. I occupy one. Ben leases the other.'

Alexei's eyes narrowed. He had no recollection of her

mentioning anyone by that name. And he would have. A sharp memory was one of his talents. 'Since when?'

'Two and a half years ago.' She deactivated security, then inserted her key into the lock and heard Ollie's pathetic wail. 'My cat,' she enlightened as she opened the door, whereupon Ollie leapt into her arms and began purring as he affectionately butted his head against her chin.

Feline love, gifted unconditionally. If only human emotions were as uncomplicated…

Except they weren't, and Natalya offered Alexei a polite goodnight, entered the spacious hallway, then with a brief smile she closed and locked the door. Less than a minute later the veranda light faded, and she released her breath.

'Bed, hmm,' she murmured against Ollie's furry head. But sleep came without success, as she tossed and turned for what seemed an hour or more, only to check the illuminated hands on her watch to witness only thirty minutes had gone by.

Ollie protested and resettled his furry self at the base of the bed as Natalya punched her pillow, counted to ten, and sought a more comfortable position.

But there were too many images filling her mind of the times when she and Alexei were so attuned to each other there had been no need for words. Magical, engaging, special…so much so, she would have wagered her life nothing, no one, could tear them apart.

Yet someone or something had.

CHAPTER TEN

NATALYA MUST HAVE SLEPT, for when she woke Friday morning the sun was filtering through the bedroom shutters, and a quick glance at the bedside clock revealed she had plenty of time to shower, dress, linger over breakfast, flip pages through the daily newspaper and feed the cat, ready to face whatever the day might bring.

But something in the press changed her light mood to one of outrage as she caught a newsprint photo on the social page featuring Alexei handing her into his limousine. Taken on angle the photographer had managed to imply an intimacy that didn't exist.

Worse, the caption—MOGUL AND FORMER LOVER TOGETHER AGAIN?—was endorsed by a brief paragraph beneath the photo.

Without hesitation she tore out the page, folded it and thrust it into her satchel.

Seconds later the phone rang, and she bit back an unladylike curse as she saw the ID.

'Hi, Dad.'

That was as far as she got, before her father launched into a diatribe, which in essence demanded to know what was going on between her and Alexei.

Soothing him down took several minutes, until she cut his words short with the excuse she had to leave for work.

She was barely a kilometre from her apartment in heavy morning traffic when her cell phone beeped with an incoming text.

WTH? Aaron.

Her staunch and loyal friend who'd supported her through the worst of times had clearly seen the same photograph too.

Worse, she garnered a few speculative glances as she rode an elevator to the high floor occupied by ADE Electronics.

All it took was one vigilant employee to start the gossip mill…and who better the focus than Natalya Montgomery, daughter of the fallen Roman Montgomery *and* former lover of the new head honcho, Alexei Delandros?

Dammit. This had to be stopped *now*.

She ignored her own office and in one swift action she retrieved the newsprint page and marched directly into Alexei's office…which probably wasn't the best idea, but she was so angry she didn't care.

If he was surprised, he failed to show it, and she hated that he'd leaned back in his chair seemingly intent on regarding her with detached interest as she crossed to his desk.

Natalya drew in a deep breath, then released it slowly. 'Let's get one thing straight,' she stated firmly. 'I'll act the polite efficient PA in all matters business. Anything alluding to *personal* is off the table.'

He waited a beat. 'Clarify *personal*?'

'Placing me in an invidious position.'

'Apropos of?'

Natalya extracted the page she'd torn from the daily newspaper and placed it on his desk. *'This.'*

She watched as he skimmed the offending caption…and waited for his reaction. Except there was none.

'I have no control over the media's agenda.'

Had the light touch of his hand at her waist been deliberate? Or was she simply being super-sensitive?

It irked he had the power to tie her emotions in knots… She hated that she actively looked for and subsequently judged his every word and action, silently seething if she imagined they crossed the line…*her* self-imposed line.

Her eyes darkened measurably. 'I want a retraction printed in tomorrow's edition.'

Alexei leant further back in his chair and regarded her thoughtfully. 'Don't you think that will only exacerbate the situation?'

Natalya drew a deep breath, then released it as her eyes darkened with anger. 'There is no *situation*.'

He lifted one eyebrow. 'Perhaps you'd care to inform the media of that?'

She pursed her lips, then opened her mouth to deliver a volley of words best left unsaid. Instead she directed him a glare which had no visible effect whatsoever, much to her annoyance, leaving her little option except to turn on her heel and sweep out from his office.

Her silent frustration with the media's intrusion continued throughout the morning, while she fought to qualify they were only doing their job. Not that it helped much. Nor did she feel comfortable with a part of her private life being played out in the public domain.

Natalya ordered lunch in, despatched a text to Ivana, and cursed beneath her breath when Reception notified several calls representing the media had not been redirected to Alexei Delandros' PA.

Like she *needed* this?

Late afternoon a text arrived on her smartphone.

Flight Monday a.m. Sydney/NY. Details laptop. Confirm. Alexei.

Two weeks? Natalya silently queried when she checked her laptop and read Alexei's schedule.

The expected meetings, a few business lunches, three business dinners. Family.

Alexei's family. So, not all business.

Which meant she'd have free time to check out a few upmarket boutiques, enjoy a leisurely coffee in any one of numerous cafés. Me time.

She sent off a text in confirmation, then she turned her chair towards the plate-glass window, momentarily took in the harbour view, and smiled.

Suddenly the day appeared a little brighter.

The weekend involved a close inspection of her wardrobe, a list of items to pack, the need to check with Ben if he could look after Ollie, a phone call to Ivana, who listened, wisely chose to relay a simple, 'Take care, darling,' instead of a litany of words attributed to caution of the personal kind. So not Ivana's style.

When the persistent beep of the alarm woke her the next morning, Natalya had an urge to push the off button, roll over and grab another hour's sleep, only to groan... *not going to happen*.

There was a need to be ready on time. Alexei's text stating she be ready for pick-up at seven-thirty a.m. ensured she was waiting on the front veranda with her luggage, overnight bag and satchel.

Sure enough the limousine slid to the kerb with Paul at the wheel. Within minutes the driver transferred her luggage while she joined Alexei in the rear passenger seat.

'Good morning.' Pleasant, she could do pleasant...which he responded to in like manner.

There was no need to run through their immediate agenda. They could do that once they were in the air.

Not a passenger jet, Natalya discovered, but a private one. Expensive, luxurious and essentially an office in the air with cabin staff who provided coffee, offered a light meal be served once they reached cruising speed.

A review of their agenda required a few adjustments, and their first appointment in New York required only a minor amendment.

'There's a sleeping compartment with a comfortable bed adjoining the en suite bathroom,' Alexei relayed as he retrieved a set of earphones. 'I suggest you get a few hours' rest.'

'What about you?' The query was out before she'd given it any thought.

'I'll take the second shift.' He paused, and his eyes met her own. 'Unless you suggest we share?'

'Not going to happen.' Her response was instant, and his mouth curved a little.

'Relax, Natalya.'

She hadn't been able to completely relax since the first day he'd reappeared in her life.

The bedroom compartment was more spacious than she expected, containing a bed with fresh linens, a small wardrobe, appointed mod-cons, and a comfortable chair.

It took a few minutes to discard her outer clothes, remove make-up and don a wrap, then she turned back the bedcovers, settled comfortably, and much to her surprise she slept for more than four hours and woke feeling refreshed. Suitably clothed, she applied moisturiser, added a touch of colour to her lips, then she returned to the cabin, accepted fruit and coffee while Alexei sought the sleeping compartment.

Which became more restless than restful as the light

floral perfume Natalya used lingered to taunt him with memories of shared passion, and what he'd believed to be unconditional love.

Elicited fact appeared to prove him wrong.

Yet deep in his gut there was a kernel of doubt based on the occasional unguarded moment during the past few weeks…when he was able to catch a glimpse of the young woman he'd known so well. A momentary warmth in her smile. A faint wistfulness, only for it to quickly disappear.

The slight change in her breathing when he'd held her in his arms on the dance floor. The tension evident in her stance when he escorted her to the front door of her home. There was a degree of vulnerability evident he found intriguing…a quality she endeavoured to disguise. And almost succeeded.

A stopover in Los Angeles for the jet to refuel, Customs, before boarding for the final leg of their flight to New York…where a uniformed chauffeur was waiting for them in the Arrivals lounge.

A service Alexei had obviously used on prior occasions, Natalya observed, given the ease of friendship between both men, and with smooth economy of movement their luggage was cleared from the carousel, carried through the terminal and deposited in the boot of a sleek black limousine which had slid smoothly to the kerb.

A driver *and* a bodyguard?

Elevated status…or a necessity?

New York contained a variety of differing vibes…from extreme wealth and luxury to the opposite end of the spectrum. Alive with a mix of cultures, from traditional to the exotic. A city which moved to a certain beat, glamour, pizzazz, to the bleakness of the Projects. A familiar vibe she recalled from previous business trips she had shared as her father's PA.

Music was key to the difference in attire and speech, and Natalya breathed it in as the limousine traversed the distance between airport to the high-end hotel in the vicinity of Central Park.

Classy, Natalya determined as they rode the elevator to a high floor, with stunning views over the city that never slept.

For the following few days they attended meetings, while maintaining a painstakingly professional façade.

Each day became mission accomplished. The nights, not so much.

Arranging business dinners didn't faze her, nor had attending them when the CEO had been her father. Alexei was someone else entirely.

Five years had wrought changes in Alexei she'd thought she'd known so well. Eyes dark, gleaming, sensual, conveying with just a look how the night would end.

The antithesis of the man he'd become…hardwired, ruthless—*driven*.

Except she was no longer the biddable young girl with stars in her eyes, imagining love would overcome everything.

How wrong had she been? she reflected as she dressed for the evening ahead. Formal, Alexei had forewarned, and she selected a red gown with a high neck artfully draped to cover each breast, leaving her shoulders and arms bare, nipped in at the waist to fall in a swirl of soft material at her feet. Subtle make-up, emphasis on the eyes, bold red lip gloss, her hair styled in large soft waves which fell past her shoulders and curved forward to partly frame her face, a touch of jewellery, she gathered up a wrap in matching red, slid her feet into red stilettos, took a deep breath, and

emerged into the adjoining lounge to find Alexei conduct-
ing a conversation on his smartphone in a language she
failed to comprehend.

Black evening suit, white shirt and black bow tie did
much to emphasise his European features, impossibly dark
eyes and wide mobile mouth. A mouth that could wreak
mindless havoc…as she knew too well.

His cologne held a subtle blend of musk and something
she failed to define…a soft sensual whisper that teased,
taunted and made her think of the forbidden.

Each breath she took in his presence became measured,
controlled, as every muscle in her body slowly tightened.
In the close confines of the limousine she felt as brittle as
the most delicate piece of Venetian glass.

One touch, and she'd shatter.

CHAPTER ELEVEN

THE EVENING AHEAD was a formal occasion. *Very* formal, Natalya noted, given the venue, the sumptuous grand dining room, the quality linen covering the many tables, exquisite crystal, cutlery and tableware.

Security was evident, invitations carefully checked, and guests personally escorted to their tables.

A gala event of note.

'Why me?' she had queried quietly, and incurred his studied look.

'Why not you?'

'This is social, not business.'

'The lines between the two are blurred, are they not?'

Anything else she might have added remained unsaid as a stunning blonde, who appeared out of nowhere behind him, snuggled close against his back, wound her arms around his neck.

'Guess who?'

Natalya caught a glimpse of diamond rings, a diamond necklace, sensed a drift of exotic perfume, heard the sultry in the young woman's voice, and felt her stomach plummet.

A friend? Lover? Mistress?

'Stassi,' Alexei acknowledged with a tinge of amusement as she released her hands and stepped to face him. 'Your signature perfume is unmistakable.'

There was a light tinkle of laughter followed by a staged *moue*...belied by the sparkle in Stassi's eyes as she stood on tiptoe to brush a light kiss to his cheek before turning towards Natalya. 'And you are?'

'Natalya,' Alexei drawled. 'Let me introduce you to my irrepressible cousin, Stassi.'

'Family,' Stassi declared. 'So Alexei is off limits, unfortunately. Although he does duty as a partner on occasion.' She glanced from Natalya to Alexei. 'And you are Alexei's...?'

'Friend,' Alexei declared.

'Uh-huh. Euphemism for...?'

'Friend,' he drawled, undeterred by his cousin's inquisitiveness.

'PA,' Natalya corrected.

Stassi smiled. 'Business *and* pleasure. Interesting combination.' She offered Alexei a teasing grin. 'You do realise your mother is planning a family dinner in your honour? She'll be delighted to welcome Natalya.'

Family? No, not happening. 'I don't think my presence would be appropriate.'

'Alexei will do his persuasive best,' Stassi stated with a light laugh. 'He's very good at it.' A slow smile curved her lips. 'I really must return to the parents. They have plotted to introduce me to a gorgeous man who, according to my darling mama, displays excellent potential as future husband material. Should be a fun evening.' She kissed her fingers and playfully touched them to Alexei's cheek. 'Take care.'

She turned towards Natalya. 'I'll look forward to catching up with you again.' With a mischievous smile she began threading her way through the numerous guests.

'Your cousin is delightful,' Natalya ventured politely, and caught his musing expression.

'Yes, she is. She's also intelligent, with a degree in criminal law. Loves life, has no intention of marrying, now or in the near future. Much to her mother's despair.'

'She obviously hasn't met the right man.'

'Is marriage so important?'

Sticky question, and not one Natalya was prepared to answer. Five years ago she would have said marriage represented a lifetime commitment, enduring love, growing a family…including qualities such as trust, faith and respect. Sharing the good and the not-so-good times together, without blame or regret.

'No comment, Natalya?'

She managed a credible smile. 'Much depends on one's life plan, don't you think?'

'And yours is?'

'Personal.'

For a moment she glimpsed a slight change in his expression, then it was gone, and she was left to ponder if her imagination was playing tricks.

'Perhaps we should take our seats,' Alexei indicated smoothly, inclining his head to a staff member waiting to escort them to their reserved table.

Society's glitterati at its finest, Natalya noted, as she sipped an excellent French wine. Similar to, but different from, she perceived, other charity functions she'd attended in the past. For there was ample evidence of extreme wealth apparent in the women's designer gowns, and their jewellery alone could have funded housing and food for a poor nation.

Cosmetic enhancement appeared to be *de rigueur* for the mature women, varying hairstyles combed and teased to within a whisper of perfection.

Nor, she suspected, was it confined to the women.

It was akin to viewing a movie on screen, where the

majority of guests were actors playing a part, prepared by stylists, make-up artists, such was the achieved element of perfection.

The ballroom was enormous, and soon seated to capacity. Soft background music became almost lost to the chatter of voices as stylishly clothed wait staff ensured champagne and fine wines were replenished with reputed flair.

'Darling Alexei,' a female guest seated opposite at their table inclined with exquisite poise. 'I heard you'd touched down in this part of town.' All that was required to complete the woman's image was a long cigarette holder, for she had the pose down pat of the lead actress who played the original role of Auntie Mame in an old movie. 'So delighted you could grace us with your presence. But then, you have a vested interest in the nominated charity.' Her smile held graceful interest as it settled on Natalya. 'You've brought along an interesting new friend. Natalie, I believe?'

'Natalya.' It was easy to smile as she offered the correction.

'Of Russian origin?'

'It was my great-grandmother's name.'

'How interesting.'

Her great-grandmother's history *was* interesting...the story of a family who escaped a life of poverty to settle on a distant relative's farm in northern Europe. As a young girl of eighteen, she'd entered into an arranged marriage and bore four children...the youngest of which being Natalya's grandmother, who'd fled to America as a teenager, found work and lodging in a Californian vineyard, borrowed a sewing machine and made children's clothes long hours into the night. Embroidery was her specialty, and at first her exquisitely embroidered gowns sold by word of mouth, until she was encouraged to sell direct to a childrenswear shop in a nearby town. In storybook style, her grandmother had married the vintner's son, bore two children, a girl and a boy. Sadly her husband and young son were killed in an accident together with her husband's parents. Stricken with grief, Natalya's grandmother attempted to run the vineyard, only to sell it within two years, and start a new life with her daughter Ivana in Australia, settling in Sydney, where she set up shop, employed minimum staff, and gradually expanded over time to export her childrenswear overseas.

Natalya's cherished Babushka…so morally and emotionally strong. A woman who had worked every day of her life and for whom family was everything, and who left behind so many memories of love, wisdom and laughter.

'More champagne?'

The sound of Alexei's voice intruded, and the ballroom with its numerous guests returned in sharp focus as Natalya offered a polite smile together with a quietly voiced refusal.

Background music faded, and there was the introductory speech of welcome, followed by the purpose of the charity in question, funds raised, together with a plea for guests to be generous with their donations.

In terms of success, the event topped the scale, given the plaudits offered throughout the evening. Guests appeared at their sparkling best, the food superb and the champagne flowed.

Polite small-talk appeared to be the order of the evening…the best party a few of the society doyennes had attended, who were present, snippets of gossip, and descriptions of apparel…designer of course, and who wore it best.

Different country, another major city…familiar scenario, merely on a larger scale.

Natalya briefly compared the evening with some she had attended with her father; the increasing tension as his alcohol intake rose, and her attempt to minimise the fallout. The relief when the evening came to a close and they could leave.

Now there was tension of a different kind, arising from her emotional reaction to Alexei's presence. Sexual sensuality…a heightened awareness that threatened her sanity. The question being…what was she going to do about it?

'We'll be dining at my mother's home this evening.' Alexei's seemingly normal statement following breakfast the next morning caused Natalya's breath to momentarily catch in her throat.

We?

Her fingers momentarily paused from keying words into her laptop.

Surely she'd misheard?

'I'm sure you'll enjoy spending time with her,' she offered with genuine sincerety as she set her fingers tapping on the keys.

There was a need to transcribe recorded notes from the previous day's meeting, prior to lunch and a mid-afternoon consult…when casual attire would be exchanged for suit, heels to present a more professional image.

Vastly different from his current casual attire of black fitted jeans and black tee shirt which emphasised the breadth of his shoulders, powerful flex of toned forearm musculature…the taut stomach, narrow waist and six-pack abs. The fact he worked out was evident in every move he made.

It made her want to explore. To track every muscle, the hard flex and tone with her hands. Purr with pleasure at the thought of dragging the tee shirt from his body, to tease and caress his bare skin...with the familiar touch of a lover.

Exult in his response, the faint catch in his breath when she unbuckled the belt at his waist, slid the studded button free, then slowly freed the zip of his jeans in a slow sensuous play that could only have one end...almost crying out as he mimicked each movement she made, slowly, with exquisite care. The almost reverent touch as he cupped each breast, lowered his head to taste one nipple, and drove her wild as he used his mouth to draw it deep and suckle, before slowly withdrawing to shift focus to its twin.

The way she trailed a hand over his stomach to trace the extended length of him, feel, rather than sense his indrawn breath, the shift in his body as he lifted his head and claimed her mouth in erotic possession...until extended foreplay wasn't enough. Nor the whispered words inciting the sensual promise of sexual pleasure.

Stop right there, a silent voice echoed in Natalya's mind. Mentally reliving an erotic memory of what they'd once shared served no purpose.

Almost as if Alexei knew, his dark eyes lifted and held her own for what seemed to be a long minute, when it could only have been a few seconds.

She couldn't move, nor did she have the power to utter a word.

A lost moment in time, brief...but it took an age before she managed to gather herself together and gain a sense of focus on the prosaic...laptop, transcribing notes.

Yet her mind lingered... Five years on there was a maturity evident, an innate knowledge of the man he had become. A certain ruthlessness apparent that almost alluded to an element of danger should anyone be sufficiently foolish to attempt to thwart him...on any level.

He possessed charm, respect, loyalty, and employed

each characteristic facet with ease. Yet he possessed the ability to freeze an opponent with a mere glance, the power to walk away from a prospective deal without so much as a second's hesitation.

Was that how he treated his women?

Don't go there.

'The invitation includes you.'

Natalya's fingers inadvertently touched a wrong key, and a silent epithet echoed inside her head as she turned towards him.

Professional, she could manage. Sharing dinner with Alexei's mother was in a different category entirely.

'Will I be required to take notes this evening?' The query held polite civility, and one as his PA she was entitled to ask.

Alexei's expression remained unchanged. 'Possibly, given my two brothers and I form part of a European-based business partnership. Although primarily the evening will be a family gathering.'

Her stomach executed a slow roll of discomfort. She didn't do family...specifically not an ex-lover's family.

A slightly hysterical laugh rose and died in her throat. Like she'd had more than one lover?

A couple of close encounters that hadn't ended well, when there had been the expectation of more than she was prepared to indulge.

'Given the evening is family-oriented, and any business matters are unlikely to be discussed on a level requiring my presence,' she inclined, 'I'll—'

'Pass?' Alexei lifted one eyebrow. 'My mother is expecting you. My sister-in-law will be delighted to have you there to tone down what she refers to as excessive male testosterone.' A faint smile curved the edges of his mouth. 'Despite qualifying affection for her two brothers-in-law.'

'I don't think it's appropriate.'

'What are you afraid of, Natalya?' His eyes held a glimmer of dark humour. 'We might be issued an invitation to stay overnight?'

In the same bedroom? How much of her former relationship with Alexei was his family aware of?

Almost as if he knew the passage of her thoughts, he offered quietly, 'Any fears you might have are completely groundless.'

Were they? So why this feeling of heightened awareness? She didn't want or need a reminder of what they'd once shared. She'd dealt with the past, moved on, created a pleasant life for herself.

Who do you think you're fooling?

'I agree,' she managed firmly. 'For each of us.'

Alexei moved in close before she had time to draw breath and laid his mouth over her own in what began as an explorative kiss that soon changed and became something else.

She wanted to protest, and lifted both hands to create a distance between them, only to have them falter as the years melted away as she was transported back to a place and time where everything was right between them.

She had no recollection of the passage of time...only the assault on her senses as he brought her emotions alive in a manner that tripped her heart into rapid beat.

Heaven, and then some, as she began to respond, uncaring at that moment where it might lead...and if it did, would she gain the emotional strength to step away?

Then he released her, and the room came into focus... together with reality.

There was a need to breathe in a conscious effort to still each throbbing pulse in her body...acutely sensitive to the once familiar touch personally geared to send her totally undone. As it had in the past.

'An experiment, Alexei?' She even managed to inject a shred of disdain into her voice, caught the dark glitter in his gaze before it was masked, and she valiantly ignored the sudden lump that rose in her throat.

There was only the heavy thud of her heartbeat as she sought to bring wildly swirling emotions under control. The words I hate you remained unsaid...*just*.

Or was it herself she hated? For momentarily succumbing to the special magic they'd once shared. And its vivid reminder.

'An answer.'

Which didn't sit well with her at all. 'You think?'

With forced calm she crossed to the mirror, extracted her lipstick, repaired the damage, then she caught up her satchel, included her laptop, recording device, added sundry necessities...and moved towards the front door of their hotel apartment, all too aware of his close proximity as they rode the elevator down to lobby level. Prepared, in essence, to become the quintessential PA as business meetings were due to unfold for the day ahead.

CHAPTER TWELVE

CALISTA DELANDROS RESIDED in an elite part of Georgetown.

A slender elegantly attired woman who welcomed her son with a warm hug, before extending a hand in greeting to the young woman who stood at his side.

'Natalya. Welcome to my home.' Her smile was genuine. 'The family are waiting in the lounge. Let's join them, shall we?'

Beautifully appointed, fine handcrafted furniture, framed family pictures on the walls. Warm, welcoming, Natalya perceived as Calista indicated a large comfortably furnished lounge where two men stood... Alexei's brothers, without doubt, given the likeness in height, stature, and facial features. A young woman displaying the slight emerging bump of early pregnancy held the small hand of a young girl.

'Cristos,' Alexei greeted and clasped his brother in a brief hug before indicating, 'Cristos's wife, Xena, and their daughter, Gigi. My younger brother, Dimitri.' He turned to include Natalya. 'Natalya. My PA.'

Natalya smiled...a smile was good. Polite, professional.

It was Xena's daughter who captured Natalya's attention. Petite, dark curls framing beautiful features, offering a smile to melt hearts.

'Gigi is a lovely name,' Natalya said gently.

She was rewarded with a polite, 'Thank you.'

For a few fleeting seconds it proved difficult to ignore the faint wistful ache in the region of her heart.

It was relatively easy to converse, to fit in, as the evening progressed. A skill she'd mastered since mid-teen years, together with an interest in current world affairs and a degree of genuine charm.

She accepted a small measure of wine, which she sipped as she observed family dynamics, their affection, and genuine interest in the current play in each of their lives.

Cristos headed the New York arm of the family business, while Dimitri travelled to interstate branches, and maintained an active social life...very social, Natalya surmised from the slightly wicked gleam in his eyes.

A family originating in Greece, as had Calista's late husband. Evident in some of the classical pottery on display in a few of the glass cabinets.

A faint lilt, not exactly an accent, in Calista's speech on occasion.

Xena, who was charming, and delighted the babe she carried was a boy.

The food was superb, and Natalya felt at ease...comfortable, she amended silently. Gigi began to tire, willingly retiring to bed for an overnight stay at her grandmother's home.

They were a pleasant family, Natalya perceived, extending polite interest in Natalya's role as Alexei's PA, her familiarity with the field of electronics...although not why, how or where she'd gained that knowledge.

It was after eleven when the evening drew to a close.

'You seem surprised,' Alexei drawled as the car cleared the drive and headed towards the inner city.

Perhaps because she'd expected...what? Cool reserve?

Why, when Alexei hadn't imagined it necessary to mention her existence in his life?

'In what way?' She could do cool, and tempered it with a touch of deliberate sweetness. 'Because you chose not to out me as my father's daughter?'

He shot her a quick glance before returning his attention to the traffic. 'Would you have preferred me to do so?'

'Perhaps I should thank you.'

'Give it up, Natalya.'

The atmosphere had taken a subtle change. A personal element that didn't sit well, for too many reasons she was reluctant to explore.

Consequently it was a relief when Alexei drew the car to a halt outside the hotel entrance, where a uniformed attendant hailed a waiting employee to drive the car down into the underground parking area.

A few words, a generous tip, and a leisurely pace through the foyer to the bank of lifts...one of which swiftly transported them to their designated floor.

One day led to another, as Alexei, Cristos and Dimitri conducted high-powered meetings, each with their individual PAs in attendance, as they brokered deals, added valuable real estate to their company portfolio at a pace which left Natalya in awe of their combined expertise and staying power.

Ruthless power, she added silently, at the end of a particularly fraught day...one that was far from over. Debrief, dinner, highlight pertinent points from recordings, send same to Alexei's laptop. Shower, bed, sleep...

Except sleep proved elusive, and she lay staring sightlessly at the darkened ceiling for what seemed an age before emerging from the bed to pull on a wrap and quietly emerge into the lounge, where she crossed to the wide floor-to-ceiling glass sliding doors, parted the drapes a little and looked out over the brightly lit city, lingered on the kaleidoscope of neon signage on numerous city skyscrapers.

'It's a bit late to be admiring the view.'

Alexei's quiet drawl caused her breath to hitch as he moved to stand at her side.

'It beats counting sheep.' The words were out of her mouth before she gave them thought.

'Something is bothering you?'

You, she wanted to throw at him. *There, in my face...all day, every day. A constant I don't need or want.*

Because...she didn't want to explore the *why* of it.

Okay, she totally got the business part. What she hadn't bargained for was the constant twenty-four-seven away from home bit. Far away from where she could retreat at day's end to her own home. Dammit, her own sanctuary.

'Go to bed. We have another full day tomorrow.'

'Perhaps you should take your own advice.'

Admit he couldn't sleep? Her image haunted him, firing the need to pull her into his arms, claim her mouth with his own...and let whatever would happen, happen.

So why hesitate?

With any other woman he'd play the seduction game, accept the unspoken invitation and enjoy the sexual activity...heart untouched.

Natalya...their shared history was gaining too much intrusion on his original intention to gain revenge. So why now question what he'd believed to be fact?

Something didn't add up...but *what*?

He felt compelled to do the unexpected, and lifted a hand to trail light fingers down her cheek. And felt her tense.

'Don't.'

His mouth curved a little at the slight huskiness apparent in her voice. 'No?'

If she acted on sexual need, she'd tear the clothes from his body...and to hell with the consequences.

How many nights had she lain awake restless with the aching need of wanting him? *Only him.* Fighting an overwhelming urge to stem the tears that filled her eyes, angry with herself for lapsing into an emotional watershed as she wretchedly fought for control.

Alexei watched as she turned and escaped into her bedroom suite, heard the faint snap of the door clasp...and remained where he was for several long minutes, unaware of the night skyline, the many lit buildings, flashing multicoloured neon, the traffic.

Instead he became caught up by her reaction...the faint quiver of her lips, the warmth of her cheek beneath his touch.

All too aware of his own body's damning response.

For the past five years he'd worked eighteen-to-twenty-hour days, fuelled by the need to succeed beyond measure in the name of revenge, ruthlessly crafting each move, each strategy in a personal vendetta where there could be only one survivor...*him.*

He'd won. Big time.

Satisfaction should be his...and it was.

So why this feeling a subtle shift had come into play?

The weekend provided a welcome change from the hectic week's business schedule. It was a beautiful day, and Natalya decided to revisit a few of the many glamorous stores and fashion boutiques New York city had to offer.

She was entitled to take some down time, to savour a coffee, a delicious pastry, browse a little...simply explore where the mood might take her. Sit a while, and watch the people walk by. Enjoy the cosmopolitan atmosphere.

Not to mention relax away from Alexei's powerful presence.

Something which earned a studied look from Alexei on learning her intention.

'Ensure you have your smartphone for contact, should it be necessary.'

It was simple to voice the few necessary words. 'Of course. Although I might remind you it's my day off.'

'But not the evening. The Delandros corporation sponsor an annual invitation-only dinner to commemorate my late father's love of his birthplace and Greek heritage. My mother insists you join us.'

Now there was the thing...an invitation from Calista Delandros made it difficult to refuse. 'I don't think it's...'

'Appropriate?' Alexei prompted.

'No.'

His smile held a tinge of amusement. 'Your reason being?'

'It's a significant occasion for family and friends. My position as your PA doesn't fit either category.'

'Consider it a personal request.'

'Personal is not on the agenda.'

A musing smile curved his mouth. 'The lines are becoming a little blurred.'

'Not,' Natalya confirmed, 'from my perspective.'

He wanted to change her mind, and would...soon.

Subtle persuasion was an art form, one he'd mastered at a young age. Only to realise seduction didn't equate to love, and while some women were content to play a part, he had tired of that game.

He wanted *more*.

'My mother will be disappointed if you refuse.' Manoeuvre and conquer was a skill in itself…one he owned unequivocally, and didn't hesitate to use to his advantage.

Natalya recognised it, wanted to call him on it, only to concede defeat. 'I accept, given the invitation came from your mother.'

The faint gleam of amusement momentarily apparent indicated he was one step ahead of her. 'I'll book a limousine for seven o'clock.'

'I'll ensure I'm on time.'

There was a sense of freedom as she rode the elevator to foyer level, declined the need for a limousine or taxi, and began to walk, choosing one of her favourite department stores in which to browse a while.

Coffee and a sinfully loaded pastry in a small café, followed by a gift for Ivana, a colourful top for Anja, a cute little doggy bow tie for Ben's pug Alfie.

It had proven to be a relaxing, enjoyable afternoon, and she entered the hotel suite ahead of time to discover it empty, a note in plain sight, which she quickly read before heading into her own suite.

A male could shower, dress and be ready in less time than a woman…

Nevertheless, Natalya was ahead of Alexei by five minutes, poised, attired in a tailored black skirt, matching camisole and a red silk box jacket. Stylish, flawless make-up, matching red lipstick, and diamond studs her only jewellery.

He did evening wear with superb masculine style. Designer stubble added an edgy touch that set him apart, adding to an overall masculinity impossible to ignore.

'A drink before we leave?'

Natalya shook her head, and he checked his watch, caught up door swipe cards, then ushered her out of their suite.

The evening lay ahead…different from the usual social occasion, together with the pleasure of Calista and her family's company.

A limousine took them to a private venue in the city's outskirts where cars lined the streets, and the subdued beat of Greek music resonated in the evening air, softening as the four limousines carrying members of the Delandros family drew to a halt adjacent the main entrance of a large single-storey building.

'Smile,' Alexei bade quietly as the driver opened each door and ushered them to join Calista, followed by Cristos and Xena, then Dimitri.

The guests were greeted personally by each family member, which took a while, given a numbered ticket, until everyone was accounted for, seated…and the evening began.

An evening which was a mix of formality, anecdotes relayed in turn by Alexei, Cristos and Dimitri of a much-loved father. Reminiscences of times past, interspersed with the serving of food. Specialties of the region where Calista's husband was born. And laughter.

Truly a celebration of a life well-lived. Of honour, hard work, and the joy of family.

Later there was music, gentle, like the air drifting over the seas lapping the islands that made up Greece, the fishermen who dragged the nets, and the men, like Calista's husband, who had built many fine houses and villas on his beloved Santorini.

'Nothing like you expected?' Calista queried with a slow sweet smile as Natalya shook her head. 'We share this each year, and the money raised is gifted to those less fortunate. Soon there will be dancing, the music will become a little loud as the men move to the strains of the bouzouki. Each invitation carries a number for the prize of a ten-day cruise around the Greek Islands, including a three-day stay at a villa on Santorini.'

It was a beautiful sentiment, and Natalya said as much.

'My husband worked hard to provide our sons with a good education, to appreciate the good things in life, and to always remember where they came from.'

'Their success is a testament to you both,' Natalya offered with quiet sincerity.

'Thank you.'

The music proved enticing, and couples moved onto the dance floor, initially led by Alexei and his mother, followed by Cristos and Xena.

'Our turn,' Dimitri indicated, glimpsed her faint hesitation, and smiled. 'I don't bite.'

'Good to know.'

A younger version of Alexei, tall, well-built, easy-going with a sharp legal mind. Evidenced during the most recent meeting the three brothers had held with one of their competitors.

'Will you object if I pull you in a bit closer?'

She got it…or at least she thought she did. 'You're attempting to attract someone's attention?'

'Uh-huh.'

Natalya offered him a teasing smile. 'I doubt you'd fail attracting any young woman you chose to pursue. So you want me to appear as a decoy date,' Natalya teased. 'May I ask *who* has captured your attention? The gorgeous blonde eating you with her eyes? No? Hmm… The auburn-haired angel on the next table to our left, looking to kill you first chance she gets?' Given there was more than one titian-haired sophisticate in the room, Natalya added, 'The one wearing a stunning bronze-coloured gown, with a strand of diamonds showcasing a dazzling pendant showcasing her elegant décolletage?'

'You're more than just a pretty face,' Dimitri inclined with a faintly rueful smile, and she offered a light laugh.

'I'm trained to observe.'

His eyes assumed a musing gleam. 'Something you obviously do well.'

'Are you going to tell me who she is?'

'Curiosity, or genuine interest?'

'Interest,' Natalya answered quietly.

'A corporate lawyer in her father's firm.'

She smiled a little. 'Does she have a name?'

'If I told,' he enlightened as the edges of his mouth quirked a little, 'I would have to kill you.'

She wanted to laugh. 'Got it,' Natalya offered solemnly. 'So… Alexei?'

That came out of left field…and unexpected. Dimitri's eyebrow lifted a little. 'What's with the vibe between the two of you?'

'Your misinterpretation.'

His smile widened a little. 'I beg to differ.'

The music increased in beat, as almost everyone joined in with the laughter, and those couples dancing on the floor took a few missteps…which didn't appear to matter at all.

Voices rose, and Natalya gave a startled sound as Alexei appeared at her side and led her onto the dance floor before she had the opportunity to protest.

I don't know the steps, remained unsaid.

'It doesn't matter. I'll guide you.'

He did, and she soon mastered the rhythm, laughed a little when she almost missed a step, which Alexei faultlessly covered.

For the moment she simply let go, lost in the moment, the music, ambience…and the man who led her.

Until the moment the music slowed…and Alexei drew

her close for timeless minutes, when it took all of her inner strength not to lean in against him, rest her cheek close to his heart, and just let the evening, the music, take her wherever it might lead.

Except there was an awareness of time and place, the haunting music, the slight pathos that seeped into her body, making her wish for more.

Did Alexei feel it too?

Who would know?

The sound of strings stirring from the bouzouki teased the air, and the chatter of conversation ceased as the pace lingered, dwelled, then began to quicken in tone and pitch. Stirring memories for most, of times past, and present for those who returned to revisit again and again in order to relive the magic merging of old and new, the history, the future.

Special, Natalya perceived, and felt the touch deep in her heart.

Coffee, thick, aromatic and strong, was served, after which the duplicate numbers handed out at the point of entry were presented in a circular glass tumbler, spun, and Calista, by tradition, extracted a ticket and read out the winning number.

There was a shout of victory, applause from the guests, the music lingered as the evening wound down, guests began making preparations to leave, with the sound of pleasurable laughter, affectionate farewells, car doors opening and closing, engines starting up as the streets slowly emptied.

It had been a memorable evening, and she said as much as she thanked Calista for the invitation, bade Xena, Cristos and Dimitri goodnight, before sliding into the limousine Alexei had summoned to return them to the hotel.

'You enjoyed the evening?'

Her mouth curved into a generous smile. 'It was great. The venue, the music. Uplifting to witness everyone coming together for a specific purpose. Reliving memories of times past, sharing lifelong friendships. Tradition,' she offered quietly.

Alexei shifted slightly to take in her vivacious features alight with pleasure, and held back the desire to pull her close, take her mouth with his own, and absorb her response.

There was a heaviness in his groin…needing, wanting what she could give him, as he would gift her. Sex, as a means to define love?

It didn't work that way. Love was a gift from the heart, inviolate, unconditional. A force of Nature shared by two people whose lives were inexplicably bound together for all time.

Hadn't he searched for its likeness in the intervening years? Only to despair a woman's interest was more attuned to his bank balance than his heart, his soul.

It hadn't been enough to put a ring on any woman's finger. Call him cynical, but he wanted *more* than a facsimile.

The limousine slowed and drew to a halt in the curved apex adjoining the hotel's main entrance. It was late, but the inner city remained alive with guests returning from drinks after the theatre, parties.

A city which never slept, Natalya acknowledged, as she rode the elevator to their designated floor.

The vibrant hype of the evening began to dissipate as she preceded Alexei into their suite, and she toed off her stilettos, discarded her jacket, and bade him goodnight.

He let her go.

And silently cursed…for lost opportunities.

Need…for a woman. Not just any woman…he could have any one of many who would give whatever he wanted.

A wild eroticism among tangled sheets, each aware it was merely satiation of the senses, nothing more.

To his credit, he was selective…upfront, no false hope, mutual pleasure for as long as it lasted.

Sexual satisfaction for a price.

None of which applied to Natalya. For what they'd once shared rested deep within. A memory he'd failed to expunge…no matter what method he chose to apply.

She was *there*, as much a part of him as every breath he took…every beat of his heart.

Steely control…he possessed it in spades. In the boardroom.

Only a door separated him from Natalya's bedroom. He could breach it, seduce, and maybe succeed in gaining her compliance.

So why didn't he?

Damned if he knew.

Yet he did.

Aware losing wasn't an option.

CHAPTER THIRTEEN

THE FOLLOWING FEW days were business-oriented, with meetings between Alexei, Cristos and Dimitri as they explored strategies for a major takeover of a company on the brink of financial collapse.

Natalya's recordings were lengthy, the content involved as each man added input, opinions regarding the need for further investigation, relevant sources…calling a coffee break for a short debriefing session.

A relief from the intensity of the past few hours, Natalya accorded as she placed an order for coffee.

'Amalgamated will play ball,' Dimitri projected as they regrouped. 'They don't have any option.'

'Unless United undercut you,' Natalya offered, immediately aware of three pairs of male eyes refocussing their attention.

'An interesting observation,' Cristos declared. 'Your basis being?'

'They tend to sideline, then jump in just as a competitive deal is due to be struck.'

Alexei's eyes narrowed as he leaned back in his chair. 'They're not one of the major players.'

Dimitri leant forward. 'You have experience of their tactics?'

She inclined her head. 'They know how to play the game.'

'So do we,' Cristos answered, shooting Alexei a glance.

'A back-up plan alternative, and play our hand close to our chest?'

Good thinking, aware just how well United had tied her father's negotiations in knots two years ago, and left Roman red-faced, bluffing, and totally out of his league.

'Well, there you go,' Dimitri accorded softly. 'PA is a misnomer.'

'I imagine Natalya's observation skills saved Roman Montgomery's lack of attention in the field of negotiations.'

If her father had listened, she added silently. Unfortunately he rarely did.

Natalya indicated the carafe. 'More coffee?'

Each man declined, and she bore Alexei's scrutiny with equilibrium, caught the faintly speculative gleam, and gathered the carafe, cups onto the tray and moved it to the sideboard.

The meeting continued, the pace broken from time to time as Dimitri sought to lighten proposed strategy with a little levity.

Which he did very well, causing Natalya to smile at his efforts, laugh a little at one of his witty takes on one of New York's scions of industry, known for his slight pomposity.

It was light fun, momentary, although at one point she had to stifle her laughter…which earned Dimitri a searing glance from Alexei.

The afternoon wound up, with paperwork dispensed into briefcases, with Dimitri heading out as Alexei accompanied Cristos from the apartment.

'Natalya is a highly valued PA.'

Alexei directed his brother a non-committal glance. 'I agree.'

'She is also Roman Montgomery's daughter,' Cristos

commented. 'And the young woman you were involved with during your Sydney sojourn.'

'Apropos of…?' Alexei queried. 'Besides being none of your business.'

'You chose not to elaborate why you returned to New York following your sojourn in Australia.'

'Missing home, family, was a logical reason.'

'More than that, unless I'm mistaken.' He waited a beat, then added, 'Dimitri flirted with her. You didn't like it.'

'Natalya is my PA.'

'Dimitri likes to play. We both know it's harmless. Yet you considered Dimitri's attention inappropriate.'

'Out of place during a business meeting.'

'Dimitri was bent on getting a reaction.' Cristos sent Alexei a musing look. 'That he succeeded proved…interesting.'

Alexei's dark glare was accompanied by a terse, 'Back off.'

Cristos lifted both hands in a gesture of silent compliance, offered a commiserative smile that required no words, then turned and headed towards the bank of elevators.

Natalya focussed on what she did best…encapsulating key points during the day's board meeting. Ensuring lunch reservations were in place, and displaying smooth efficiency as she dealt with unforeseen interruptions, while remaining cool, calm and collected.

Everything her position entailed and required.

By day's end, all she wanted to do was change, shower, slip into comfortable clothes…and chill.

Good luck with that, a tiny voice taunted, as a call came through stating the power brokers affiliated with the financially ruined company were ready to deal.

Chilling was out as she accompanied Alexei to the bank

of elevators, one of which would deposit them to the floor housing several boardrooms where a take no prisoners negotiation took place, which the Delandros brothers won. A deal reluctantly struck, legalities approved, paperwork signed.

A coup to add to the Delandros portfolio.

Any form of celebration would be delayed until the legal formalities were complete.

Natalya glanced at the wall clock, made an attempt to shake off the weariness creeping through her body as she followed the men from the boardroom.

She was tired, it was late, she required time to de-stress, and importantly gain a few hours' sleep before rising soon after dawn to begin dealing with the follow-on from the evening's meeting. Right at that moment she silently acceded she earned every cent of her generous salary.

'Congratulations,' she offered as Alexei closed the door after they entered their suite, watching as he shrugged off his jacket and loosened his tie.

He spared her an intent glance, noted the shadows beneath her eyes, the tense edges of her mouth, the faint droop of her shoulders...and felt a degree of empathy for the long day, the even longer night.

Without a word he tossed his jacket onto a nearby chair, followed it with his tie, then he crossed to stand within touching distance, laid a hand on each shoulder, and began massaging the tight muscles, easing out the kinks, the tightness.

Natalya didn't move, couldn't...it felt so good, as he worked his magic easing the pain, and gradually the stress began to ebb...to be replaced by something...*more*, as he removed the clips from her hair and trailed light fingers over her scalp, soothing, taking her to a place where it would be so easy to succumb.

The touch of his lips to her forehead, lingering at her temple, the gentle whisper-like touch as he reached the edge of her mouth, savoured a little, then brushed the soft seam with a wicked promise of seduction.

A slow savouring persuasion, which left Natalya spellbound, uncaring where it might lead…only to baulk as reality began to descend.

She'd been down this road before, become pregnant and suffered a miscarriage. Hadn't the obstetrician advised in future certain steps should be taken prior to falling pregnant in order to avoid another miscarriage?

Birth control…she wasn't on any. Her mind spiralled… what if Alexei wasn't prepared? And even more alarming…what if she fell pregnant?

She closed her eyes, then slowly opened them again as a voice in her head silently screamed no.

'I don't do casual sex,' she managed carefully.

'I want you in my life,' Alexei said quietly.

She took care to meet his eyes, unsure what to say…or whether to say anything at all.

He lifted a finger and traced a gentle path over her lips. 'Is it too much to ask we share what we once had?'

She was willing to swear her heart took a downward flip. Lover? Mistress?

She closed her eyes, then slowly opened them again.

'I don't do the mistress thing,' she said carefully.

At that precise moment she hated herself for letting her guard down. Tempted, just once, to have him take her mouth with his own, to feel sensually alive. To accept whatever he offered, and to hell with the consequences.

She almost succumbed, knowing how easy it would be to lose herself…and that made her angry beyond measure.

Without thinking, she wrenched herself out of his arms, grabbed her jacket, the suite's swipe card and walked out of the door, uncaring of anything other than the need to get away from him, the hotel suite…to be *anywhere* but here.

Instead of summoning a lift, she chose the stairwell to the next floor down, made it to an elevator about to close, and took it down to street level.

The air was crisp, and she pulled the edges of her coat together as she exited the foyer.

The area was well lit, traffic moved quickly, and right at this moment she was too angry to consider the wisdom of walking alone late at night in a city not her own.

One block, crossing on to the second, becoming increasingly aware she should turn back.

Fool, she silently berated. What would this achieve?

Nothing. Other than reveal her lack of common sense.

One more block, then she'd turn and retrace her steps.

By which time her anger would have lessened, together with the dawning reality of place, time and the foolishness of walking alone on a New York street, prey to… whatever, whoever.

Enough.

Quickly followed by the realisation she'd left so quickly, she didn't have a bag, money…just the hotel swipe key.

Angry tears filled her eyes, and she brushed them away, turned…and witnessed Alexei closing the distance between them.

'You were *following* me?'

'A few metres behind you.'

'That's…' Words temporarily failed her as he moved in close and silenced her with a savage kiss, before easing into something else, gentling as his hands moved from her shoulders and slid down to cup her bottom, lifting her against his hard arousal, holding her there, his mouth softening to tease a little, then tangle her tongue with his own, sensuous, arousing, until she became lost to his persuasive touch, unaware her hands had crept unbidden to clutch his face, holding him close.

The sharp blast of a car horn, followed by a male cat-call and a laughing voice demanding, *'Get a room!'* acted like a bucket of icy water, and Natalya released her hands and wrenched her mouth from his.

Her eyes changed from slumberous to startled fury as she began to struggle free...only to fail miserably.

'We're going to talk.' His eyes became dark ominous pools. 'Back at the hotel.'

Without warning he turned to face the opposite direction, holding her hand, pulling her along with him as he began walking, not even so much as flinching as she curled her fists and hammered his shoulder-blades...anywhere she could reach with as much force as she could muster.

Alexei just kept walking.

She bore his silence for several long minutes, then she launched a punch into his ribcage...with no physical reaction whatsoever.

'Alexei, slow down,' she demanded. Causing a public scene had never been on her agenda...waiting a beat before adding, 'Please.'

'Will you behave?' His anger was quiet...too quiet. She drew in a deep breath, aware in a moment of clarity just how ridiculous it was to attempt to best him.

Temporary capitulation was the only option as she released her breath and briefly inclined her head. Relieved as he finally slowed down and released her hand.

There was wisdom in silence, and she refrained from uttering a further word until they reached their hotel. Together they crossed the marble-tiled foyer to the bank of elevators, all too aware the air between them could be cut with a knife.

Tall, dark, and silent, Alexei resembled a dangerous

force as electronic doors opened, and two other couples
followed them in.

Natalya deliberately looked straight ahead, ignoring
him until the elevator reached their floor, choosing to walk
ahead of him along the carpeted passageway to their suite,
swiped the room card and she took three steps into the
lounge before swinging round to face him.

'I want *out*.' Anger was a palpable entity she barely managed to control. She indicated the desk. 'My formal resignation will be there in the morning.' It provided a measure
of satisfaction to turn her back and walk towards her suite.

Right at that moment she didn't give a *damn*.

She was *done*. With *him*, the situation she'd been manipulated into...all of it.

'I didn't figure you for a coward.'

Alexei's voice reached her as she was about to open the
door to her suite, and she turned to spare him a scorching glare.

'Why? Because you kissed me?'

'You were with me every step of the way,' he offered
quietly.

'I'm no longer the girl you once knew,' she retaliated.

'No?'

'You saw to that.'

His eyes darkened, sharpened. 'Enlighten me...how?'

'There's no point to this conversation.'

His entire stance stilled. 'I think there's every point.'

Natalya suddenly felt as if she was standing on the
edge of a precipice, poised between the need to lash out in
anger...or live to regret not imparting fact...as she knew it?

She tensed, every muscle in her body tightening as she
recalled in minute detail the devastating discovery he'd
disappeared out of her life.

'You left without a word. I called you. Many times. I

made enquiries… *"The line has been disconnected."* I checked your apartment, hospitals, any and everyone I could think of who might have a clue to your whereabouts.' She tamped down the helplessness, and resorted to anger. 'I sent you texts. Emails. Desperately pleading for an answer. An explanation.'

She clenched each hand into a fist, felt her nails dig in each palm…and didn't even feel the painful sensation. '*Anyone* who could tell me whether you were alive or dead.'

The pain of him leaving her…even after five years, was still there…raw, aching, like a wound that had never truly healed.

Anger rose to the surface. 'Do you know what it's like to wake each day…and hope *today* a call, text or email could ease the heartache? God willing in the best way possible? Only to fade into despair? Until eventually there's a need to accept whatever path you thought your life would take no longer existed?'

'Yes.'

She couldn't stop until she said it all. 'Worse, the agony of not knowing what went wrong? Why texts and emails remained unanswered?' She took a deep breath. 'To consider the worst scenario in each of many guises?'

He moved towards her and closed his hands over her shoulders. 'Back up a little,' he demanded quietly.

Her eyes blazed in anger. *'Why?'*

The ensuing silence became electric, and she closed her eyes in an effort to shut him out…only to have them widen as he took hold of her chin and tilted it.

She opened her mouth to berate him, except no word emerged as he pressed it closed.

'I didn't receive any texts or letters.'

She tore his hand away. 'You expect me to believe that?'

He stilled, his features hardening as a muscle clenched

at the edge of his jaw. 'I left messages on your answering machine. Texts.' His eyes darkened. 'Are you saying they never reached you?'

The colour fled from her cheeks as uncertainty left her temporarily speechless. 'No,' she managed as her mind reeled. 'Nothing,' she said in a shocked whisper.

First and foremost, how it could have happened, followed seconds later by why?

She was reluctant to explore who, for it appeared highly unlikely anyone had access to her laptop, smartphone, snail mail.

Except…memory resurfaced in minute detail…her move to another apartment building, misplacing her smartphone, her father's decision to replace all their phones, both business and personal, with a different provider and new numbers. As well as a new email address for a reason that appeared valid at the time.

When?

Years ago. Her mind momentarily retraced the events back then, examined each sequence in detail, unaware of Alexei's narrowed scrutiny as he witnessed every fleeting emotion on her expressive features…and caught the moment she realised she had stepped into an unbelievable nightmare. Surely…it couldn't coincide…except it did.

Her father.

'How could he do such a thing?' Natalya's voice was an agonising whisper.

'Roman wanted you to marry up. I didn't come close to being a prospective candidate.'

'Tell me.' Her voice was calm…too calm. 'I need to hear what my father did. All of it.'

She deserved the truth…which he whittled down to essential detail. Leaving out his emotional turmoil, anger. Worse, the desperate need to discover *why*.

'Roman demanded I end my relationship with you, and presented me with a substantial cheque in a pay off. I tore it up.'

For the love of heaven. That her father would dare to go to such lengths to destroy their relationship was unconscionable. Unforgivable.

The disbelief, the silent anger.

The loss of *five years* of their lives.

Dear heaven, her miscarriage.

Natalya felt a cold hand clutch her stomach.

Sickened, almost literally, she briefly closed her eyes in an effort to retain a sense of calm. Opening them again, her eyes pierced his own, held steady, controlled…when inside she felt like screaming.

'He fired you, didn't he.' A statement, not a question. 'And threatened to make it impossible for you to get a position with any electronics firm in the country.' Her eyes locked with his own as she sought confirmation.

He didn't confirm or deny it…but then he didn't have to. The truth was there. Ugly, untenable, damning.

Did she realise how well he could read her? See the silent rage simmering beneath the surface?

She closed her eyes as Alexei reached for her and drew her close. There was magic in his touch, the way his lips sought the sensitive curve of her neck, savoured there, then he gently traced a path up to settle in the sweet hollow beneath her earlobe.

Evocative eroticism stirred something deep inside and spread through her body in sweet sorcery, dispensing with inhibitions and making her want so much more.

A faint groan emerged from her throat as he lifted and carried her into the bedroom.

He felt the warmth of her silent tears seep through his shirt, and brushed a kiss to the top of her head.

With care he slid her down his body to stand on her feet, and his gaze held her own as he carefully removed each item of clothing from her body.

She felt the warmth of his fingers as they trailed up her ribcage and unclipped her bra. Free, her breasts burgeoned in anticipation as he cupped each mound, and she bit back a gasp as his fingers sought the delicate peaks, traced them until they hardened beneath his touch.

Sensation arrowed deep inside, and she couldn't utter a word in protest as he lowered his head to one breast and took its peak into his mouth to lave it with his tongue.

Liquid fire coursed through her veins, heating her body to a point of madness.

Almost as if he knew, he lowered her evening trousers, traced a path up the inside of each thigh and sought the throbbing clitoris…brushing his fingers against the sensitive folds as she arched against him, unaware of the whispering plea emerging from her throat.

She was beyond sanity, filled with an aching need for his possession.

His clothes became an unwanted intrusion and were quickly discarded as they sought to touch, explore, as she became lost in the delight of tracing warm flesh, tight musculature, the sheer strength of his arousal.

She didn't want to wait. Wasn't aware of her soft cries as he inserted a finger into the damp warmth between her thighs and skilfully brought her to orgasm, absorbing her guttural cry as she shattered.

It wasn't enough. She needed more, so much more, and he knew, teasing a little, taking time to lay his mouth against her own in a slow kiss that became sensual foreplay as she met and matched everything he gifted…then she gasped as he used a hand to pull aside the bed covers and lower her down onto the sheeted mattress.

She kissed him, teasing as he had teased her, and explored his body with light kisses, circling the tight masculine nipples, using her teeth to nip, the slide of her lips to soothe, before trailing to his navel, delicately laved it, before she turned her attention to the thick jutting arousal pulsing beneath her touch as she stroked its length with her tongue, reacquainting herself with its shape and throbbing size…heard his husky groan, and delighted in his throaty *you're killing me* an instant before firm hands took hold of her hips and eased her onto her back, holding her hands fast above her head as he trailed a path down the quivering flesh of her stomach. Lower, and she cried out as he suckled the damp flesh, nipped the sensitive folds with care, then used his tongue to send her mindless.

Her entire body felt as if it were on fire, and she gasped as he shifted over her and drove in deep, held still as she absorbed him, then he gently rocked, lengthening his thrusts until she reached the edge and came, as he did in unison, and there was only the euphoric ecstasy of two lovers in perfect accord…mind, body, heart and soul as they gave everything there was to gift…before easing down to the sweet exhaustion of sexual fulfilment.

'Amazing,' Natalya whispered, and felt his lips drift gently over her skin, soothing her rapid pulse-beats, before exploring her lips, caressing with such tenderness she fought to hold back tears.

Lost, so completely *lost* in him, there was no sense of time or place. Only the need to cling to the pulsing thrum deep inside her body, and exult in sexual nirvana.

The musky scent of sensual heat combined with the dawning knowledge they'd just shared unprotected sex…

Dear heaven, what had she done?

They, she corrected silently. There were two of them

in this bed, two who had seduced, shared, and exulted in their mutual passion.

Alexei caught each fleeting expression as the reality widened her eyes, the brief few startled seconds as her eyelids shuttered closed, only to open again as instinct kicked in together with a sense of *déjà vu*. Unfounded, according to rapid silent calculation.

She pushed at him, endeavouring to escape without success as he caged her in, his eyes dark as the blackest slate as he took in her expression.

Without a word Alexei rolled off the bed, scooped Natalya into his arms and walked into the en suite bathroom, turned on the shower and carried her beneath the pulsing water, collected the liquid soap, and began smoothing the lightly scented fragrance over her body in a slow sensuous slide that drove her wild...wanting, *needing* to respond in kind. His mouth curved into a sensual smile. 'Patience. You'll have your turn.'

She did. Eventually. Only it took a while. And later, towelled dry, he took her to bed, drew her close in against him.

She couldn't find the words—not the right ones. The extent of Roman's intervention devastated her, and merely confirmed the extent her father was prepared to go to in order to rule not only his company, but his family.

'There's something you should know,' Natalya said quietly. At the time she'd borne the heartache in the light of day, and let the tears fall during the dark of night when she was alone. Until there were no more tears to shed, and she gathered the resolve to get on with her life.

'I discovered I was pregnant.' She faltered in an effort to find the right words, and her mouth trembled as his hands shaped her face. His eyes were dark, silently questioning, and she couldn't look away.

'Why didn't you tell me?'

Her features paled, her eyes dark with an edge of pain, and he swore softly beneath his breath.

'I drove to your apartment after work.'

A lump rose in her throat, momentarily preventing speech, and she swallowed compulsively in an effect to allow her voice to emerge. 'You weren't there.' The words tumbled out. 'I rang your phone. No answer.'

Alexei stilled, his eyes almost black. 'When did you ring?' His voice was hard, urgent. 'What time?'

'Is time so important?'

'Yes.' He bunched his hands into fists. 'Dammit.' Yet he already knew. 'Think…please,' he added in a strained voice.

'After six…maybe six-thirty.'

He closed his eyes briefly in silent anguish at the hand of Fate. Ten…fifteen minutes after the police had taken him from his apartment, arrested by the hand of her father. His phone confiscated.

'Theos.' The soft imprecation left his lips with the realisation she'd had to cope without his knowledge, or the benefit of his support.

Silent anger consumed him, together with the imminent need to take Roman Montgomery apart with his bare hands.

Her words hurt like a stab to the heart as memory surfaced in vivid Technicolor detail.

The anger…helpless rage at Roman Montgomery's manipulative machinations.

Natalya felt his lips rest against her forehead, then trail gently down her cheek to rest at the edge of her mouth, soothing the trembling seam as he held her close.

Roman, Natalya determined fiercely, was about to be called to account. She'd call and invite him to share lunch with her, then calmly…surely she could *do* calm several hours from now?

'He's going to pay.'

'Natalya,' Alexei cautioned, and she shook her head.

'You don't understand.'

But he did. All too well. The silent rage that had almost destroyed him, the desire to succeed beyond measure.

Not the least of it, to throw that success in Roman's face. As he had with deliberate intent, using his business nous to prove he could. Then plotted his revenge against the man who'd wielded God-like power…using Natalya as a weapon.

Ill-founded, as he discovered…and beat down the rage simmering beneath the surface.

How could a father do that to his own daughter?

As easily as Roman succeeded in deceiving his own wife. A self-absorbed narcissist who put his own needs first and foremost…without exception.

Alexei wanted to slam a fist against something…for a few brief seconds he almost did. Just for the hell of it.

Almost as if she knew, she lifted a hand to his cheek. 'Natalya…'

Her eyes seared his own, steady, obdurate. 'There's nothing you can say to stop me confronting my father.'

He waited a beat, then offered quietly, 'Think it through,' he advised gently, and watched her eyes narrow.

'He doesn't deserve consideration.'

CHAPTER FOURTEEN

THERE WAS A need for planned strategy. An assemblage of irrefutable facts. Cool, sans anger. Absence of a public scene.

In Roman's true sense of style, he'd vetoed a small restaurant in favour of one of his favoured upmarket haunts noted for its fine cuisine.

Natalya entered the boutique restaurant several minutes past the appointed time, for, in truth, she wanted her father to be seated and waiting.

It helped that he was there, charming the wait staff in his typical style. The smile, a flirting tease in his eyes… just enough not to offend, but holding a silent invitation, should it be accepted.

Natalya touched a hand to Roman's shoulder to catch his attention, and he turned at once, offering a warm greeting as he caught her hand and lifted it to his lips.

'Darling girl.' Ever the showman, he gave the waitress a knowing smile. 'Better late than never.'

Did he ever stop? And to think she'd always put his teasing down to his consummate charm.

'Have the sommelier choose the finest champagne and have it brought to the table,' he instructed the waitress in a grandiose manner, 'A celebration.'

He might think otherwise by the time their meal concluded.

'Problem with traffic?' Roman enquired as Natalya slid into the chair opposite.

'Parking,' Natalya enlightened, and when the champagne was presented, checked, approved and opened she instructed, 'Just a small amount. I have to work this afternoon.'

She waited, sipped superb champagne and exchanged small-talk as she selected an entree, refused a main, and settled for a lemon sorbet to follow.

The waitress served coffee, and Natalya added milk, sat back and mentally directed...*now*.

She kept it brief, citing irrefutable fact with admirable restraint...and took some satisfaction as her father stiffened, blustered a little, then paled as she relayed knowledge of each pertinent detail...the coincidence of her lost smartphone and its replacement with a different provider and new number.

Coinciding with Alexei's disappearance from her life.

'Don't,' she cautioned as he attempted to speak, 'attempt to justify your actions. Your manipulative meddling was unforgivable.'

'I wanted the best for you.'

She battled with anger, and fought to contain it.

'Without thought for my right to choose?'

'Delandros had nothing. He could never have supported you in the style you deserved.'

Leave now, a silent voice urged...before you say something regrettable.

Natalya rose to her feet, caught up her bag and walked to the cashier's desk, produced a credit card, paid the bill, then she emerged onto the sidewalk, covered the three blocks to where she'd parked her car.

Alexei was at the industrial plant, the rest of the afternoon was hers, and there was a need to occupy her mind and minimise any inclination to dwell on her father's actions.

She aimed the car remote, then slid in behind the wheel, had a flash of inspiration and delved into her bag for her smartphone. Minutes later she engaged the engine, eased out of the parking bay and headed towards fashionable Double Bay.

A relaxing facial, some one-on-one time with Anja... what could be better?

'Thanks for fitting me in,' Natalya greeted with affection as she took her place in one of the beauty rooms.

Bliss, absolute bliss to simply close her eyes and let every muscle in her body slowly relax as Anja worked her magic.

'Are you going to update me? Over the past few days a number of regular clients have quizzed me if the rumours are true about you and Alexei.'

'Which you refrained from providing.' It was a statement of fact.

'You know better.'

Yes, she did. They'd shared much over the years, and maintained a mutual trust.

Yet she hesitated...the sex with Alexei was great. Okay, *fantastic*. The question being what their future might hold. Or if they had a future.

There were words left unsaid, and while she ached for the whole package...did Alexei want the same? Or would it be her fate to remain his PA with benefits?

'Hello?' Anja prompted. 'Natalya to Planet Earth?'

'There are issues,' Natalya admitted, and glimpsed Anja's faintly wry smile.

'Resolve them. Anything less is a cop-out.'

'What would you suggest?' Natalya queried, *sotto voce*.

'Grab Alexei by the scruff of his neck, pin him to the floor, and demand his intentions?'

'That would be my modus operandi.'

Natalya bit back a light laugh. 'I'll remind you of that when the love bug strikes.'

'Not going to happen anytime soon.'

'Famous last words.'

'Keep your eyes closed,' Anja ordered. 'I'm not done yet.' Firm hands created their own magic, and Natalya uttered a pleasurable sigh. 'Something you're not telling me?'

'Nothing to tell.'

Not yet, Natalya perceived. She could wait, and would, aware there was a time and a place, and now wasn't it.

Natalya's phone chirped with an incoming text as she entered her home.

Dinner tonight. I'll collect you at six. Alexei.

She checked her watch, saw there was ample time in which to change, and then took a leisurely shower, towelled dry, stepped into her bedroom, and riffled through the contents of her wardrobe. Formal or semi-formal?

The latter appeared a safe choice, and she selected a stylishly cut dress in emerald-green.

Ear studs, a simple necklace, black heels, a black clutch with essentials, then she caught up a black wrap and she was good to go within minutes before the appointed time. On cue the security gate buzzer sounded and she crossed to the video link, identified Alexei and released the locking mechanism.

He was waiting for her as she opened the front door, attired in casual trousers, open-necked shirt and casual jacket. Tall, ruggedly attractive... Her stomach flipped as heat flooded her body as she walked into his outstretched

arms, lifted her face for his kiss and breathed him in, relishing the moment as his arms pulled her close.

Nice. She could have stayed longer…resisting the urge
to invite him in, suggest they forgo dinner, and eat later.
Much later.

Except he trailed his mouth to the sweet curve of her
neck, savoured briefly, then took hold of her hands linked
behind his neck and brought one to his lips.

'Food,' Alexei opined with a wicked smile, and led her
to the sleek Aston Martin waiting kerbside.

Natalya wondered which restaurant Alexei had chosen
as he eased the luxury car into traffic. A boutique place
in one of the suburbs, or city venue.

Not a restaurant, she discovered as the car headed towards one of the elite northern suburbs where residences
commanded multimillion-dollar prices, and were guarded
by high-tech security.

Alexei turned into a tree-lined street and slowed the car
before a wide set of high black elaborately scrolled gates,
beyond which stood a graceful two-level residence at the
apex of a semi-circular driveway.

Were they dining as guests at a private home?

His home, appeared the correct answer, as he used a
remote to open the gates and eased the car towards the
front entrance.

Immaculate lawns bearing some decorative sculpted
shrubbery, and there were borders bearing a beautiful
array of flowers lining the driveway.

The front door opened as he disengaged the engine, and
a middle-aged woman stood waiting to welcome them.

'My housekeeper, Lisette,' Alexei informed her quietly
as he curved an arm across Natalya's shoulders and drew
her forward, effecting introductions.

Together they entered a large circular foyer with a marble-tiled floor, showcasing a sweeping double staircase leading to an upper level.

Lisette greeted Natalya with a pleasant smile before turning towards Alexei. 'I expect you would enjoy a drink in the lounge. Dinner will be served at seven in the private dining room.'

'Thanks, Lisette.'

He turned towards one of four heavily panelled doors leading off from the lobby and led her into a spacious lounge, closed the door behind them, then pulled her close.

What began as a gentle kiss soon became an evocative tasting as he explored her mouth, and she met and matched him, luxuriating in his touch as she lifted her arms to link each hand at his nape.

Natalya's entire body came alive, as the kiss moved up a few levels, where the urge to dispense with his clothes... and have him remove her own, became almost impossible to ignore.

She wanted to slide the palms of her hands over his naked skin. Explore the tight muscles sculpting his body, admire the strength apparent, and savour every inch with her mouth as she drove him wild.

Then welcome him into her body as they became lost in each other...lust, avid, earthy and beyond mere words.

Love, as it had been in what seemed to be another lifetime when they had implicit trust in each other.

Alexei gently shifted his hands to cup her face. He traced her cheek with his thumb, his eyes dark as he examined her features.

'I'll get you a drink.'

Did she look as if she needed one? Probably. 'Preferably non-alcoholic.' It was a while since lunch, and she recalled she'd eaten very little. 'I'll have some wine with dinner.'

Alexei moved to the drinks cabinet, retrieved two crystal wine glasses, filled one with mineral water, the other with white wine, then he retraced his steps and placed a glass in her hand.

She avoided the prosaic, and went for the most relevant.

'I had lunch with my father today.'

His eyes sharpened. 'He upset you?'

'In hindsight…not so much.' Surprising, given how much pain Roman's actions had caused her. 'I said what I wanted to say, paid the bill, and walked out of the restaurant.'

She possessed an inner strength. Yet he sensed the hurt, her loss of trust for her father's almost criminal meddling. Worse, perhaps, for having been totally unaware of her father's other life.

Roman had created the perfect cover in choosing Natalya as his PA.

Which bore the question of Ivana's wealth and social standing…somehow it didn't add up with the woman he'd come to know. Her values, her unconditional love for her daughter.

Perhaps a woman was entitled to her reasons, none of which were his to attempt to explore.

Of one thing he was certain. Natalya's total loyalty to her mother.

'You have a beautiful home,' Natalya complimented as they entered a tastefully furnished dining room.

'Which I will show you after dinner,' Alexei said as he led her to the table and withdrew her chair.

The housekeeper had excelled herself, providing a seafood entree, followed by perfectly grilled salmon steaks accompanied by a delicious salad, with fresh fruit compote for dessert.

Later they took coffee on the terrace, relaxed following a pleasant meal. The view over the harbour to the city with its buildings lit and rising high against a darkened sky presented a superb panorama. Coloured neon signage promoting varying products, the moving headlights of passing traffic...mere pinpricks observed from this distance.

Peaceful, tranquil. A place that could be a home, filled with love, perhaps children...

A vision of which the stuff of dreams was made. Not always the reality.

So where did they go from here?

The word love hadn't been mentioned.

Alexei unwound his length from the chair, leant forward to take hold of her hands and gently pulled her to her feet and into his arms.

His touch, the brief flare of unguarded emotion in his eyes...dear heaven, his kiss...sensuality at its peak as his tongue curled around her own, tasted, teased, gentling a little at the sound of her despairing groan as he went in deep, persuasive, pervading as he gifted his heart...his soul.

It was more, so much more than she believed possible, and seemingly an age before he lifted his head, his eyes dark as he glimpsed her flushed cheeks, the soft mouth slightly swollen from his touch, and caught the faint quiver as she visibly sought control.

He lifted a hand to smooth the pad of his thumb over the fullness of her lower lip. 'Stay with me tonight.'

Her eyes lit with a tinge of humour. 'Presumably this isn't a work-related request?'

'Not even close.'

'I'll give it some thought,' she said, delighting in teasing him.

Without a word he led her inside, secured the terrace doors, set the security alarm, moved towards the beautifully curved staircase leading to an upper floor and the master bedroom.

He took it slow and easy, removing each item of her

clothing, as she unbuttoned his shirt and slipped it from his body. Loving the muscular chest, the tight abs, the strength apparent in his broad shoulders.

'Don't stop.'

Natalya reached for the belt at his waist. 'Just savouring the moment.'

'Uh-huh. You want some help there?'

She traced the bulging length of his arousal pressing against the zip, and offered him a witching smile. 'Got it covered.'

'Uncovered is better.'

'No foreplay?'

'As much as you can take.'

'That sounds interesting.'

Interesting didn't equate to what they shared as he slowly removed each item of her clothing, pausing to press his lips to each pulse, his hands intent on shaping every curve until she trembled, on fire, wanting, *needing* him inside her...so much, she was unaware of the faint sounds slipping unbidden from her throat, the way her hands moved on him...and her satisfaction as he took her mouth with his own in a kiss that sent her over the edge.

'You want to hear there has been no one who mattered since you?' Alexei queried quietly.

In one easy movement he leant forward and stripped the covers from the large bed, then he laid her down on the cool sheets and moved over her body.

Now...or she'd have to beg.

And then she did, as he trailed his lips down her stomach to the moist heat below, using his mouth, his tongue, to drive her wild.

Then he positioned himself and drove in hard, exulting in the feel of her, the way her inner muscles contracted around his length when he began to move, slowly at first, building sensation to an exhilarating peak, held them both there as an intense orgasm took them high, consuming mind, body and soul.

So excruciatingly sensual she had no memory of crying out in ecstasy...nor was she aware of his own groan of release as they lay joined together, too caught up in the deliciously slow ebb of exquisite pleasure.

Natalya didn't want to move...wasn't sure she could, until the wonderful lethargy consuming her body settled a little.

It felt good, so incredibly *right* to snuggle her cheek into the curve of his neck, to bury her lips into the hollow and savour his musky heat, feel the strong beat of his heart as he tethered her close.

Later, so much later, Alexei gathered her up into his arms and headed to the en suite bathroom, set the shower into action, and held her beneath the pulsing warm water as he smoothed liquid soap over every inch of her body with such evocative slowness it was nothing less than seduction.

With a witching smile Natalya took the container of liquid soap from his hand, moved to stand behind him, cupped a handful of soap and administered slow sweeping strokes across his shoulders, down his back, covering the taut slopes of his buttocks, then turned him round to face her.

She could do evocative slowness as well as he did, and his eyes became dark, faintly hooded, as she teased a little, plucking lightly at his nipples, felt them tighten beneath her touch, then she moved to his shoulders, his arms before trailing down his ribcage to settle a hand on each hip.

'If you stop there,' he declared with a throaty drawl, 'you will suffer.'

'I'm afraid,' she mocked quietly, and offered him a mischievous grin as he caught hold of her shoulders. 'Very afraid.'

'Witch,' Alexei accorded with dangerous softness as he lowered his head and took her mouth in a passionate kiss that robbed her of breath.

At the same time his hands slid down her back, cupped her bottom and lifted her high against him, caressed the softness of one breast, then sought her burgeoning nipple, tasted, teased, before drawing it into his mouth.

Intense sensation spread through her body, coalescing at the most sensitive part of her femininity, and she gasped as he trailed a hand over her stomach, palming the indentation as his mouth moved to render a similar salutation to her other breast, where he took her almost to the edge as he teased, tasted and lightly caught the nipple with the edge of his teeth.

Heat rose deep within, and she gasped as his hand trailed low…way too low as he sought the sensitive folds protecting her clitoris.

Her mouth parted with a soft gasp as he stroked the delicate bud until she almost reached begging point.

He slid a finger into the moist passage, heard her unbidden groan and felt the restless movement of her legs, aware she needed more…*more* than this slow delicate, exploratory, teasingly intimate foreplay.

Natalya curled her fingers around his thick arousal, squeezed a little, and sensed Alexei's quick intake of breath.

In one easy movement he carried her into the bedroom, tossed back the covers, then he sought her mouth with his own, staking a claim that seared every erogenous pulse in her body as he brought her to tumultuous orgasm, stilled a little, then he began to move, slowly at first, then with deeper intensity, driving them both towards a mutual orgasm that left her temporarily bereft of the ability to breathe. Sensual overload…and then some.

There were no words, just a whisper of a heartfelt sigh escaping from her lips.

She didn't want to move…didn't think she could as Alexei held her close for what seemed an age, until sleep overcame them both.

Only to wake in the early morning hours to the touch of his mouth against her own as he made love to her with such exquisite gentleness she wanted to weep. Lazy pre-dawn sex, infinitely sensual, Natalya managed as Alexei curved her close to his muscular frame. Exquisite and a beautiful beginning to a new day.

'Sleep,' he murmured as he pulled up the bedcovers.

The next morning, showered, dressed, they shared a wholesome breakfast together on the terrace, took a refill of coffee, after which Alexei drove her home, settled his mouth on her own, then headed into the city.

There was time to feed Ollie, exchange her clothes for office wear, a slimline skirt, silk blouse, jacket, make-up, check her satchel and head into the city.

A day where *work* took priority, which was a blessing, for it allowed Natalya little or no time to think…or in her case, over-think.

Alexei slipped easily into professional mode, moving it up a notch as he liaised with Marc Adamson, chaired an intense meeting, took a business lunch which ran over time and by day's end she required every ounce of energy in order to match Alexei's pace…while he appeared as if he'd enjoyed a good night's sleep instead of a mere few hours.

In truth, she was in a state of ambivalence. Unsure of what their future held.

One day led to another, each following a familiar pattern as Natalya dealt with everything Alexei threw at her.

While the nights were something else…spent at his mansion, her apartment. Emotive, passionate.

Until one evening when Alexei offered the words she longed to hear.

'Marry me.'

Not I love you…can't live without you.

'I want you in my life.'

Want, not need. 'In your bed,' she managed evenly, and saw his eyes narrow slightly as she slid out of his bed and began pulling on her clothes in the moonlight streaming in from the night sky.

'That, too.'

It took all her resolve to utter the one word she'd hoped never to have to say to him. 'No.'

His expression remained unchanged. 'Marriage is not important to you?'

Yes. Just not merely another merger added to your life portfolio.

'I'm content with my life the way it is.'

'What if I want more?'

Five years ago she'd believed their love was inviolate, a permanent entity that would entwine their lives for a lifetime.

'Qualify "more".'

Your heart, gifted unconditionally. Words she couldn't, wouldn't voice.

She needed her own space, her own bed. Without a word she gathered up her bag, her keys, bade him a polite goodnight…and left. Waiting until she used the remote to close the gates guarding Alexei's residence.

Fool, she silently chided as she traversed the streets towards her home.

CHAPTER FIFTEEN

NOT THE DESIRED result Alexei had envisaged.

Five years of hard business negotiations had resulted in paring details down to the bare essentials...cut-throat minimalist facts.

Successful in the business arena.

A complete failure when it came to proposing marriage.

He wanted to hit something, and almost did...except doing so wouldn't achieve the desired result.

There was a flashback to the night he'd intended to ask Natalya to share his life.

The champagne on ice. Flowers...her favourite roses, tastefully assembled in clear cellophane with a note expressing his love. The for ever, until death do us part in poetic prose. The ring, the delicate diamond, the best he could afford at the time, put on hold and paid off in increments from his fortnightly wage. Her favourite food.

The evening she didn't arrive.

Her smartphone cut off.

Alexei's arrest.

History.

Which had no part in the *present*...or the future.

He picked up the phone, punched in numbers, made a few calls, cancelled two appointments, and set the next day in motion.

A day in which Alexei spent time with Marc Adamson caught up in meetings with Marc's PA in attendance. Not entirely unusual, Natalya perceived...nor was the late afternoon text requesting her presence at a restaurant on the other side of the city.

Despite the location not being one she perceived Alexei would normally choose. Who was she to judge? Presumably privacy was key, with no intrusion from the media.

Parking wasn't difficult, and she slid in behind Alexei's Aston Martin...a surprise, given his preference for the limousine with Paul at the wheel.

Whatever...it hardly mattered. She was here in her capacity as Alexei's PA, with no time to delay if punctuality was key.

She walked through the door, and paused, initially puzzled at the lack of patrons. There was only one occupant... Alexei, who rose to his feet as she crossed to his side.

'Has there been a delay?' She glanced up as a waiter appeared out of nowhere and pulled out a chair for her. 'I take it your guests are late?'

'No guests,' Alexei said quietly as he placed a hand to the back of her waist. 'Please, sit down.'

She sank into the chair and a faint frown creased her forehead. 'There's no meeting?'

'Not tonight.'

'Then why are we here?'

It was difficult to read his expression, and her eyes widened as the lights brightened a little, and another waiter appeared bearing an ice bucket holding a bottle of champagne.

For a brief second she thought she got it...only to dismiss the possibility as a flight of fancy. Until the waiter popped the cork and poured a measure of champagne for

Alexei to savour and approve…a mere formality, given the exclusive label…before carefully pouring a quantity of the sparkling liquid into two crystal flutes.

Alexei lifted his flute, touched its rim to her own, and gently named the toast… 'To us.'

Natalya's lips parted, but no words emerged.

Light muted music wafted from hidden speakers, and a waitress appeared with a silver platter, on which lay a single red rose and a personalised card.

Natalya simply looked at him as he removed both and placed them in front of her.

'I planned a surprise evening five years ago…champagne, food,' he revealed quietly. 'A ring to seal our love.'

Her lips quivered a little, and there was nothing she could do to prevent the single tear escaping to slowly trickle down one cheek.

He leant forward and carefully brushed it away. 'I love you. For the beautiful woman you are, in heart, mind and spirit.'

Her heart stopped beating, then quickened a little as she attempted to say the words caught in her throat, only to feel the press of his finger against her lips.

'Last night…'

Natalya's eyes softened as she resisted the temptation to interrupt him. Was it asking too much to want to hear the words?

'Will you marry me? Please.'

It was the *please* that did it for her. 'Yes.'

He rose to his feet and caught her close, his mouth on hers as she clung to him. Unaware of time or place…until he gently released her, and the restaurant, the importance of the evening returned to focus.

'There are words,' she offered quietly, 'written, said, for momentous occasions such as this. Poetic prose escapes me…you're my only love. *Yours*, for as long as I draw breath.'

Alexei's eyes darkened with slumberous passion. 'I'll hold you to that.'

It was her turn to tease him a little. 'I'd hoped you might.'

He drew her apart a little and reached into his pocket, withdrew a ring, took hold of her left hand and slid a magnificent solitaire diamond onto her finger.

For a breathtaking few seconds, she couldn't find the words. 'It's beautiful,' Natalya accorded with quiet reverence. *Stunning*, she added silently. A visual testament to his wealth and power.

'But?'

'The ring you bought five years ago,' she began. 'Do you still have it?

'Why do you ask?'

The thought he might have kept it held such meaning. Bought with an emotion-filled heart…a symbol of everlasting hope, love, and the intention of them spending their lives together.

The ring he'd placed onto the third finger of her left hand flashed brilliant fire as caught by the steady flickering candle. Magnificent and ruinously expensive.

'It represents the love we shared at that time.'

'And that is important to you?'

There were words she could say, a few of which she had already expressed. 'Yes.'

A warm smile curved his lips. 'Are you going to tell me why?' A diamond worth little in comparison to the ring which now replaced it.

Natalya lifted both hands to frame his face, her expression soft with emotion, and incredibly beautiful. 'You need to ask?'

No, he didn't.

'Will you mind if I accept this ring as a commitment gift representing everlasting love throughout all the years we'll share together, and wear it on the third finger of my right hand?'

Alexei shook his head and offered a quizzical smile. 'And the original ring?' he teased.

'Suspended on a gold chain close to my heart.'

She was something else. 'If it pleases you.'

'Thank you.'

He gave a soft laugh. 'I'll commission the jeweller to craft a wide wedding band.' Encrusted with diamonds, he added silently.

He knew her so well, her values, ideals...her generous loving heart.

His for ever...all the days and nights of his life.

She reached up and kissed him. 'Perfect.'

So too was the evening.

The champagne, the food, ambience...a special memory that was theirs alone.

One, Alexei determined, they would celebrate each year for the rest of their lives.

The next thing on their agenda was to inform Natalya's parents before the ring on her finger resulted in a media article citing rumour and supposition. Even if the ring didn't appear on her left hand, the mere sight of it would draw comment, assumptions would be made...and Ivana deserved better than to hear such important news second-hand.

It was okay to be cool-headed in all things business... inviting her parents to dinner to formally announce an engagement, followed by a wedding, was something else.

Alexei and Roman in the same home, the same room? 'You're stressing too much,' Alexei chastised gently. 'Ivana will be delighted.'

'Perhaps I should pre-warn her?'

'In order for her to pre-warn your father?'

He read her too well. 'Something like that.'

Alexei touched a light finger to her cheek. 'I'm sure Roman will be the consummate guest.'

If not, he'd deal with it.

Natalya planned the menu with care, choosing each course with her parents in mind. Cuisine was one of her skills, and she made lists, selected the best ingredients, took care with the dining room setting, using the finest linen inherited from her *babushka*, a favoured dinner set, fine crystal, and silverware. Faintly scented candles.

A double-check, a change of clothes to pencil-slim linen skirt with matching silk top, make-up, hair...done.

'What do you think?'

Alexei crossed to her side and laid his mouth to the sweet hollow at the edge of her neck. 'Amazing.'

He was her rock, the love of her life...everything.

Designer black trousers, a pristine white shirt unbuttoned at the neck, the shadowed designer stubble...eyes so expressively dark as he smiled.

Hers. Truly hers...as she was his.

Together again, as they were meant to be.

Not by luck...*faith.*

'It's perfect,' he accorded quietly. 'So, too, are you.'

'Don't make me cry, or I'll have to...' she caught the musing gleam in his dark eyes '...go fix my make-up, and leave you to greet the parents.'

'For a moment I thought you might be considering an interesting diversion.'

She trailed light fingers down his cheek, the soft designer stubble to the edge of his mouth. 'Later.'

'I'll hold you to that.' He lowered his lips to her forehead. 'You're my love, my life.'

'Same goes.'

At that moment the external buzzer sounded, and she watched as Alexei crossed to release the gate mechanism.

There were hugs, a mutual handshake between Alexei and Roman, who expressed his appreciation for the invitation, while Alexei attended to serving drinks in the lounge.

Ivana's delight, her appreciation of Natalya's ring.

Warm, friendly...even Roman appeared to behave himself, and it became easy to relax a little.

Fine wine preceded the starter, followed by the main course, eaten in a leisurely fashion. Conversation flowed, as Roman made an effort to engage, sans his usual bonhomie. Dessert was a pavlova variation created by Natalya's grandmother...crisp meringue, soft on the inside, covered with whipped cream and drenched in fruit and their juices.

'Perfection, darling,' Ivana complimented, adding to Natalya's pleasure, 'Let me help you in the kitchen while Roman enjoys his customary after-dinner cigar.'

A familiar ritual following a lifetime of family lunches and dinners for as long as Natalya could recall.

Alexei stood to his feet. 'I'll join you.'

This evening's short sojourn would hopefully create an emerging bond of sorts between Alexei and her father. Each had issues to be resolved, and although the timing wasn't perfect...at least it might help both men to move forward.

Natalya waited until the men had moved out on the back terrace, and spared her mother a quick glance, received a reassuring smile. 'I'll be okay.'

Alexei closed the door quietly and indicated the decorative gazebo at one end of the terrace, waited until they reached it, and they stood facing each other while Roman extracted a cigar, expertly clipped the end, then his lighter flared, and he took the first draw.

Alexei kept it brief, merely the bare facts, and lowered his voice.

'Five years ago you went to extraordinary lengths to separate me from Natalya. You deleted text messages from Natalya's cell phone, wiped her answering machine clean and misappropriated her mail. Information I imagine you'd prefer to remain buried?'

'Are you threatening me?'

'Not at all. Merely assuming you'll want to attend your daughter's wedding and share a part in your future grand-children's lives?'

Roman closed his eyes, then slowly opened them again and inclined his head. 'Yes.'

'Then we understand each other.' Alexei extended his hand, which Roman shook, then Alexei indicated the night-scape, the sprinkling of electric lamplight in the distance, the moving vehicles along major traffic roads, and the darkness of the ocean beyond. 'An attractive view, by day or night.'

'Yes. The home which once belonged to Ivana's mother.'

'So I understand.'

'A hardworking feisty lady,' Roman imparted. 'Who spoke her mind.'

'Of whom Natalya was very fond,' Alexei reminded, which drew a nod in silent agreement.

'Shall we return indoors? Share champagne, raise a toast to the future...and family.'

In hindsight the evening proved a pleasant one, as Ivana suggested lunch to initiate pre-wedding plans.

'I don't want to diminish your enthusiasm,' Natalya offered with gentle affection. 'But we haven't discussed the when or where of it yet.'

'It's every mother's dream to help plan a daughter's

wedding. The dress, the venue, flowers…all of it.' She caught hold of Natalya and whirled her around full circle.

'Okay,' Natalya protested with a light laugh. 'I totally get it. But let me talk to Alexei first.'

There was coffee, thick, black, aromatic to provide a finishing touch to the evening, and there was time to relax a little before her parents took their leave.

'Our time, I think,' Alexei decided as he drew Natalya into his arms. 'Ivana is in her element.'

She turned her face up to him, and trailed her fingers down his cheek. 'Prepare yourself for bridal magazines, material swatches…everything that goes towards a wedding. Which we need to discuss.'

He wanted to indulge her, run the shower, share it with her, and help ease the tense muscles formed from a long day. And he would, soon.

'How do you feel about a private family-only civil ceremony, a relaxed tropical island honeymoon, followed by a formal church wedding for family and friends?'

Natalya closed her eyes, then opened them again. 'Two weddings? Are you kidding me?'

'Think about it.'

'I'm endeavouring not to.'

'Your parents, a few close friends. No fanfare, followed by lunch, or dinner if you prefer…then we fly out for a week of rest and relaxation. A private island, no tourists. I know someone who owns the perfect place.'

It sounded appealing…becoming more appealing by the minute. 'And do it all over again in style…when?'

'Six, maybe eight weeks later.'

'I think that could be a plan.' She uttered a faint shriek as he lifted her into his arms and headed for the main bedroom, helped discard her clothes and his own, then he took her to bed.

It was bliss…utter bliss, as he massaged out the kinks in tight muscles, *more* as his hands shaped her body, lingered a little, then he took her to bed…to sleep curled close in against him.

Discretion was key in planning a private wedding.

Subterfuge a given.

What should have been simple in arranging a very private wedding ceremony took effort in a bid to avoid media attention.

The preferred setting narrowed down to two venues… The gardens at Ivana's home, or the grounds surrounding Alexei's home.

Alexei's Seaforth mansion proved the ideal choice, followed by a celebratory lunch prepared by Lisette.

'I'm calm,' Natalya assured Ivana as she put the finishing touches to her make-up.

Words, which didn't hold much weight, evidenced by the slight tremor in each hand as she tended to her hair.

There was a brief tap at the door as Lisette entered carrying a tray. 'I thought tea might be a welcome distraction.'

'How kind,' Ivana assured her with a smile. 'Will you join us?'

A small window of light relief helped ease the increase of nervous tension…which was crazy.

She loved Alexei with every cell in her body, every beat of her heart. *Sure*…as every breath she took, that his love for her was absolute.

Ivana offered a faint smile in silent understanding, almost as if she knew the train of her daughter's thoughts, and Natalya returned the smile, sipped the tea, then she discarded the silk wrap-around, and selected the white fine linen mid-calf dress overlain with guipure lace, elbow-length sleeves and a wide scooped neckline, stepped into it, stood still as Ivana slid home the long zip, before stepping back to offer a smiling nod of approval.

White stilettos, a wispy white confection of a cocktail hat, completed the outfit, Ivana handed her a bouquet of white roses culled from her own garden...and it became time to join Alexei waiting in the formal downstairs lounge.

Alexei cut a resplendent figure in a dark suit, white shirt and dark silk tie.

Ivana shared the role of matron of honour and mother of the bride. Roman gave the bride into Alexei's keeping, and Cristos, who'd flown in from New York, took the part of Alexei's best man.

A simple, heartfelt ceremony conducted by a celebrant...touching in that Alexei caught hold of her hand as she reached his side and lifted it to brush his mouth to her fingers, offered a deep emotive smile, then lowered his head to take her mouth with his in a soft lingering kiss.

It added to the informality, and brought a smile to those present.

The exchange of rings, hers a magnificent wide diamond-encrusted band, while Alexei had chosen a plain gold ring.

The kiss sealing their marriage was more evocative, loving, and tears shimmered in Natalya's eyes as she whispered, 'Love you.'

Lunch was a delight, with love, laughter...laid-back and incredibly personal.

Lisette had excelled herself. Roman remained quiet, reflective, while Ivana appeared relaxed, delighted her daughter had found everlasting happiness with her first and only love.

Not journey's end, she perceived.

A beginning.

* * *

The choice of a tropical island paradise became their personal honeymoon destination.

Owned by one of Alexei's friends, it was off the tourist tracery of holiday island venues.

Small, unique, with live-in staff to cater to the smallest of any guest's whim. There was an indoor pool, private, with an electronic roof to let in the sun…if desired, or not. A lanai…with cushioned cane chairs overlooking an outdoor pool that appeared to meld into the sapphire blue ocean. A motorised yacht moored at the end of a long jetty.

Indoors a large central lounge, a home office, three large luxe bedroom suites each with an en suite bathroom. A games room, set up for billiards, table tennis. A sauna.

Together with a rich man's necessity…a heliport complete with helicopter.

Perfection, luxurious, a haven from the hi-tech world of international business. Yet everything on hand at the push of a button, if need be.

Staff quarters situated at one end of the island housed a married couple employed as caretakers, their eldest son who acted as chef when the owners or invited guests were in residence. A younger son who piloted the motorised yacht and helicopter, and a daughter who assisted with household chores.

It was divine, an experience to remember…infinitely special—as Natalya evinced at the end of their stay.

'We can always return,' Alexei assured as they boarded the helicopter for the return home.

It was the caretaker's youngest son who took the pilot's seat, and set the engine in motion.

'Something to look forward to,' Natalya said with a whimsical smile. Maybe in a few years, with a young child to laugh at puddles, make sandcastles, enjoy the sunshine unfettered by the rush and bustle of city life. Playschool, kindergarten…

It was good to be home, to complete the final move of her belongings to Alexei's mansion. To make decisions to lease her own apartment, interview prospective tenants… only to discover Ben had a friend who was looking for an apartment, possessed of impeccable references, solid employment, whom she had already met, knew, and without hesitation she offered a lease, stored her furniture, and was grateful for the done deal.

Work proved intense during their first week, with Alexei taking up the slack from their absence, involving long hours…evenings when it was almost midnight before they each hit the shower and fell into bed.

Only for life to settle back into a reasonably familiar routine…if you factored in a formal wedding to be held with Alexei's family as guests, close friends, ADE's office staff together with top personnel from ADE's industrial plant.

A wedding planner took care of the details, liaised and approved the caterers' menu…ensuring everything went as smoothly as possible.

Eight weeks after their intimate wedding, they enjoyed the best of the best…both families together, guests they'd requested to attend, a beautiful church favoured by Ivana's mother during her lifetime, and a stunning venue for the wedding breakfast.

The bridal gown surpassed Natalya's dreams, with an exquisite bodice of intricate lace moulded to showcase her upper body, a sweetheart neckline, three-quarter sleeves in lace, with layers of silk falling from the waist beneath pale ivory silk to boost the skirt's volume a little so the hemline touched the tips of ivory stilettos. A floaty veil completed the bridal gown, and only she and Alexei knew the slender gold chain at her neck held his original gift of the simple diamond ring nestling deep within the V between each breast. On her right hand she wore the magnificent solitaire diamond Alexei had gifted her, and which she'd worn as a betrothal ring at their private wedding.

Soon he'd place the wide diamond-encrusted wedding ring on her left hand, and they would formally be named husband and wife before a church filled with family and guests.

'Tilt your head a little. I need to blend the eyeshadow just a touch more.'

Natalya obeyed, and shot Anja a faintly wry smile. 'Tell me again why I agreed to do this?'

'Ivana,' Anja reminded her gently. 'Your mother is in her element. Her smile, the soft laughter, her bond with Alexei's mother and family is a beautiful thing to witness.

'Then there's Alexei, the gorgeous man you're already married to...'

'I get it. I really do.'

'So hush... It's a lovely day, the sun is shining, the wedding planners have achieved a magnificent setting. The photographers are due to arrive any minute. Each mother of the little flower girl and pageboy have everything in hand.' She tapped a light forefinger to the tip of Natalya's nose. 'Relax.'

She was tempted to roll her eyes, and refrained...barely. 'I am perfectly relaxed.'

'Uh-huh,' Anja responded, *sotto voce*. 'Perfectly.'

'Am I permitted to say I preferred my first wedding?' It had been so intimate, so laid-back. *Special*.

'Of course. But only to me.'

Her mouth curved into a genuine smile. 'Thanks for being here. For doing what you do best. Friend, the sister I never had. All of it.'

'You're welcome. And for the record…right back at you. What you said, and more.'

It became time to shed her wrap, and step into her wedding gown…exquisite, delicate, perfect.

'You look so beautiful,' Ivana complimented gently, almost on the point of tears.

Natalya caught her mother close. 'Please don't cry.'

'I'm so happy for you…both of you.'

A special moment, encapsulating the now, the promise of the future.

'I know,' Natalya said gently. And she did. 'Thank you for everything. All of it, for as long as I can remember.'

Her childhood, the happiness, laughter, and memories of three generations…the special times influenced by a different culture from a different country.

Ivana and Natalya drew apart, smiled, touched a hand to each other's cheek…and stepped out into the sunshine together where three limousines waited to transport the bride's parents in one, Anja with the two small children in the second, and the bride with Paul at the wheel ready to complete the procession.

This was the moment, Natalya reflected as the limousine travelled the suburbs en route to the beautiful old church her darling babushka had adored. Settled back from the road and accessed via a long curved driveway shadowed by trees, it captured a timeless era of tradition, faith and something more…almost indefinable. And familiarity, for all the occasions she had attended there with her grandmother and mother.

A year, even six months ago, she could never have envisaged she would be attending her own wedding. Or that Alexei would be waiting for her at the church.

A broken dream, never imagined to be realised.

Yet there were occasions when dreams shifted, reassembled and were resolved. As hers had been…by the hand of Fate.

Paul slowed the limousine to a crawl prior to making the final turn to the street where the church's entrance lay, and slowly travelled the gently curved tree-lined driveway, where a team of photographers captured the moment of the bride's parents' arrival, immediately followed by Anja and the two children…and minutes later by the bride.

Flashbulbs popped, almost blinding as they melded with the sunshine, and the media were there to record the scoop of the day that would feature in the evening's newspapers, and probably occupy a small segment on the TV news.

As a notable event, the wedding would attract attention…and better an organised compliant willingness to share, than have the gutter press issue their dubious take filched from supposition and unsubstantiated fact.

Consequently there had been a private interview with the press, vetted and approved prior to publication. Also a sanctioned photograph…both of which had been released prior to the wedding. Now it was time to seal their love sanctioned and blessed in the church of their choice.

Today would feature a touch of grandeur, of love, light and happiness…genuine, even to the most critical eye.

Nervous, much? A little, Natalya admitted as the limousine eased to a halt outside the main entry. She knew enough not to look directly at the flashbulbs, to smile, and appear composed.

To pause long enough for Ivana and Anja to straighten her veil, ensure the gown's hemline wasn't caught up, and surprise both women with an impromptu kiss to her mother's cheek, before bestowing a similar salutation on Anja.

'My only wish is for you to be happy,' Roman said quietly as they took the first steps down the aisle.

There was a time to put her father's transgressions in the past, to move forward with the future...and this appeared to be the appropriate moment.

Natalya turned her head to offer Roman a winsome smile. 'I am...very happy,' she assured him gently.

Then she took her father's arm, leant forward and said quietly, 'Let's do this.'

The aisle seemed long, and she took the first step, then another, looked up and saw Alexei ignored tradition and had turned to watch her progress.

Natalya simply focussed on his expression as she slowly closed the distance to his side, saw the way his mouth curved into a smile, the light, the love in his eyes...for her. Only her.

And her head lifted a little, her smile faintly teasing as they shared a silent promise mere words could not convey.

Perfect, so incredibly right as she drew to a pause at his side...totally unprepared as he lowered his head and bestowed a gentle lingering kiss, sensed her response, only to reluctantly withdraw and clasp her hand within his own as they both turned to face the beaming minister, oblivious to the light laughter of the guests.

Oh, my.

Natalya was conscious of the vows spoken, the solemnity of the service, the faint tightening of Alexei's hand as they were pronounced husband and wife.

The kiss was a mutual benediction, and they turned to face the guests, to the hand-clapping and the smiles as they slowly stepped forward, paused for Anja to set the flower girl and pageboy in their positions, then began the slow walk down the aisle…only to hear a child's startled cry, and turn to see Gigi had tripped and become momentarily disoriented, bent on ignoring Anja's soothing voice and helping hands…as the little girl turned and ran towards the closest person she recognised… Alexei.

Without hesitation he scooped her into his arms, soothed her tears, and touched his lips to her small forehead as she curled her arms round his neck.

Xena rushed from her seat, only for Gigi to shake her head and cling to Alexei.

'It's okay,' he offered gently as Xena looked distressed.

And it was. Gigi simply buried her head against Alexei's neck, and didn't lift it until they reached the vestibule where Cristos waited to extricate his daughter.

Natalya felt her heart melt at the sight of Alexei cradling his niece as if it was the most natural act in the world.

Aware he would do the same with their own children, be a hands-on father who would gift his heart, everything he had, to the well-being of his children…and for her.

There, whenever, wherever he was needed.

Because it mattered. As she mattered.

Evident in everything he did, the words said and those not needed to be voiced.

Love. Theirs alone.

Now, she waved aside Cristos's attempt at an apology. 'It was delightful,' she assured him with a genuine smile.

It became a talking point among the guests, who collectively accorded it a touching moment.

There were photographs, professional, the media, family, video cameras recording the ceremony, before and after wedding snaps, laughter, smiles, the beautiful bonding between Calista and Ivana.

It was, in retrospect, a very special wedding. A blend of grandeur and contemporary…of love, family and friends who each came together to celebrate the joining of two people who had loved, lost, and found each other again.

The moment when Natalya and Alexei were alone, Alexei took hold of her hand and lifted it to his lips, then kissed the tip of each finger in turn.

It was the wedding waltz which almost brought her undone as she circled the floor in Alexei's arms. The lowering of his head as he brought his lips close to her ear and said, 'You're the love of my life. You…only you complete me.'

Uncaring of time or place, she reached up and touched gentle fingers to his cheek, caressed the groomed stubble, and rested fingers to the edge of his mouth.

'There are the words I could say,' she said quietly. 'And I will, because I need you to hear them. I want to touch you, to show you you're the other half of me. My love, soul-mate…my everything.'

He pulled her close against him, held her there…his arousal a potent force. 'Let's get out of here.'

It was easy to smile, to tease a little. 'It's our night. We get to choose.'

They finished the bridal waltz, circled the room with unhurried steps, pausing to thank their guests individually for attending the wedding celebration, spent a little time with each of their parents and family, then slipped away from the venue to a waiting limousine with Paul at the wheel. For he, too, had been a valued guest.

'Home?'

'Yes. Please,' Natalya added, as she nestled her head into the curve of Alexei's shoulder. Perhaps the best gift she could give him was the one she'd been waiting days for the right moment. When would be better than now?

There was more. Just a few words, and she offered them

later…much later after they'd made love, tears gathering at the edge of her eyes as she relaxed in his arms.

'This morning I took a pregnancy test.'

She didn't make him wait.

'It was positive.'

EPILOGUE

LIFE WAS GOOD, Natalya reflected as she carefully eased the sated babe from her breast. The night was still at this pre-dawn hour.

'There we go, my little darling,' she murmured with a loving smile as she hugged Nikos close and brushed soft lips to his forehead.

This was their time, so precious and special, and she quietly began singing a soft lullaby of a small babe falling asleep in a cradle as she gently rocked him in her arms, smiling at the sound of his customary burp.

She wanted to hold him a little longer, to stroke light fingers over his soft cheek, and to give quiet blessings for the miracle of life. And she did, silently, with all the love in her heart.

Then she carefully placed him into his crib, reached out and lowered the baby night lamp, paused to double-check he was sleeping, then she turned to leave the nursery…and saw Alexei's tall frame leaning against the door frame.

'How long have you been standing there?' Natalya queried quietly as she drew close, and in the dim light she caught his slow smile.

'A while.' He lifted a hand and curved it beneath her chin. 'I like to watch you both together.' He pressed his thumb-pad to her lips. 'Share the bond between mother and child.'

A lump rose in her throat, and she swallowed it down. 'You're a great father.'

A wonderful support during the initial few months of her pregnancy, when he took time out to accompany her to every appointment—there at her side through every injection, each examination. Marvelling at each sonogram as they watched their son develop in the womb. Counting fingers and toes, the moment when it appeared the unborn babe turned and appeared to look at them.

Choosing a name, agreeing on his late grandfather's name... Nikos.

Alexei touched his mouth to hers, gently at first, then he curved an arm around her shoulders.

He was a good babe, suckled well, only woke once through the night for a feed, then slept until the early predawn hours. He tended to smile...although Natalya felt sure it was simply wind.

Natalya cast Alexei a musing glance. 'This is one of the best times of the night. The day is done, Nikos is sleeping, and...'

'It's our time,' he assured her quietly and pulled her into his arms and deepened the kiss before raising his head to touch his lips to her temple. 'I love you.'

Her eyes filled, and she blinked to hold back the tears. How could she not know?

'You touch a hand to my cheek, and my heart begins to dissolve,' she said gently.

'You're the other half of me.' His lips traced her own, nibbled a little, then soothed. 'I sense every move you make during the night, and draw you close.'

She held back the threat of tears. 'Returned in kind. Every word. All of it.'

How could she not, when he'd read everything available

on pre-natal care, gowned in the operating theatre during the caesarean section?

His was the first face she saw after the birth. The gentle kiss he bestowed as she offered him a wondrous smile as she was given their son to hold for the first time.

Now, she reached up to cradle her husband's face. 'Let's go to bed.'

His smile almost undid her. *Love*...all of it, and more, clearly evident. For her.

'You need a few hours' sleep before Nikos will want his next feed.'

'Uh-huh.' Natalya pulled his head down to hers. 'And I'll have them.'

A touch, the light drift of fingers over sensitised skin.

All consuming, captivating as the senses coalesced in the joining of mind, body and soul.

The completion of the circle of love. Sensual magic.

'But first,' she teased gently, 'I want to make love with the main man in my life.'

Alexei smiled in the dim moonlight filtering through the shuttered windows. 'I have no problem with that, *agape mou*.'

* * * * *

LOCKED DOWN WITH THE ARMY DOC

SCARLET WILSON

This book is dedicated to all the loyal readers of
Medical Romance all over the world.
Thank you for letting me write for you and for
enjoying Medical Romance.

CHAPTER ONE

AMBER BERKELEY LEANED against the wall of the elevator as it descended to the ground floor. The doors reflected a kind of odd image. She'd forgotten to check in the mirror before she left. Her half-up-half-down hair looked like some kind of bewildered lost animal on her head. She let out a laugh. She didn't even want to know what her bright pink lipstick looked like. Truth was, she didn't really care.

Tonight's ball was bound to be full of specialists and consultants who were all too important to breathe. She loved her job, but some doctors just seemed like a different breed entirely. Self-important. Self-interested. Amber didn't waste much time on people like those.

Tomorrow she was lecturing at one of the most prestigious conferences in the world. And she couldn't pretend she wasn't nervous. Hawaii was a magnificent setting. One hundred per cent more gorgeous than most of the places she visited. The Disease Prevention Agency tended to send their staff to investigate outbreaks and try and prevent the spread of infectious diseases.

Most of her time was either spent in the main base at Chicago, or on one of many expeditions as part of a team, generally to places with few or poor facilities.

This five-star hotel in Hawaii was like something out of

a dream. She'd even been greeted by the traditional colorful leis on check-in. And, corny or not, she'd liked them. The beach outside had perfect golden sand with sumptuous private loungers and straw parasols complete with serving staff. This part of the main island near Kailua Kona was a perfect piece of paradise.

Her first-floor room had a gorgeous view of the Pacific Ocean, which seemed to change color depending on the time of day. So far today it had gone from clear turquoise blue to light green. Shimmering like a tranquil soft blanket stretching to infinity.

As the doors pinged and slid open, the noise and the aromas of the food surrounded her. The room was full of people talking, a sea of dark tuxedos with a smattering of colored dresses in the mix. She threaded her way through, keeping her chin raised as she glanced from side to side. She had to know someone here. But the sea of faces didn't reveal anyone familiar. Amber's nose twitched. She wanted easy company. A chance to share a few drinks, grab a few snacks and get rid of the butterflies in her stomach for tomorrow.

She stared at a sign on the wall. Ah…there were two conferences on in the hotel—not just the one she was attending. It seemed that a world of business and economic experts were here too.

Just before she'd left, the director of the Disease Prevention Agency had called her into his office. She'd only seen the inside of his office walls on two previous occasions. Once, on the day she'd started. And second, on the day she'd received her promotion.

"Dr. Berkeley," he said solemnly. "I wanted to wish you well for tomorrow. There's been a lot of interest in our contribution to the conference. Thank you for presenting the meningitis research for us."

Amber gave a nod and a smile. "I've loved being part of the meningitis work. I'm honored to present on it."

The director nodded. "And you're confident you can answer any questions?"

Amber held up the list in her hand. "I've spent the last few months eating, breathing and sleeping meningitis. I think I've got it covered."

The director didn't even blink. "Oh, I'm not worried for you." His eyebrows rose as she stood from her chair. "I'm worried for them. Let's hope they're ready for you, Dr. Berkeley."

She'd smiled as she'd left. It seemed that her take-no-crap attitude was getting a reputation of its own. She wasn't embarrassed by it. Not at all. She'd never seen the point in beating around the bush. She'd always talked straight, to patients and to colleagues. Medics could be notoriously sexist. And Amber could be notoriously blunt.

Had it cost her a few jobs? Maybe. Had it earned her a few others? Definitely.

A guy with a paunch belly and gaping shirt approached her, beer sloshing from his glass. "Hello, gorgeous. Where are you going to?"

She didn't miss a beat. "Away from you." She didn't even glance at the lanyard round his neck. She had no intention of finding out his name.

She'd always vowed never to go out with a fellow medic. Life experience had taught her it wasn't a good idea.

She glanced around the room again. This was probably her worst-case scenario, wall-to-wall fellow medics, with copious amounts of alcohol flowing.

A few seconds later she met another charmer who refused to let her step around him. "We must stop meeting like this." He grinned as his hand closed around her forearm and his eyes ran up and down her body.

She didn't hesitate. She flipped his arm up and twisted it around his back, catching him completely by surprise and thrusting him in the other direction as the woman next to her laughed out loud. "Yes, we must," she said sharply.

The main bar in the center of the room was currently three people deep. Her chances of getting a drink were slipping further and further away.

Her eyes homed in on another bar on the far side of the room and through a set of doors. It looked much more sedate. She could have a glass of wine, check out the list of bar snacks then head back to her room and enjoy the view.

She threaded her way through the rest of the crowd. There were a few people who obviously knew one another sitting around tables. Even from here she could recognize the medic talk.

Right now she couldn't stomach that. So she headed directly over to the stools at the bar. There was a broad-shouldered guy already sitting there. He looked as if his whiskey was currently sending him into a trance.

Perfect. Too drunk to be a pest.

Or if he wasn't? She could deal with that.

She smiled as she sat down, crossed her legs and leaned her head on one hand. He might be tired but he was handsome. Actually, he was more than handsome. He was good-looking with an edge of ruggedness. His dark hair was a little rumpled and his suit jacket had been flung carelessly onto the bar stool next to him. She couldn't get a look at his eyes as his head was leaning forward toward the glass. But she could see the lean muscle definition beneath his pale blue shirt, the slight tan on his skin and the hint of bristle around his jawline. She smiled and just couldn't help herself. "Well, aren't you just the original party pooper?"

Jack Campbell blinked and blinked again. Nope. It had definitely happened. Or maybe he was just hallucinating. He stared into the bottom of his whiskey glass again and clinked the ice.

The warm spicy aroma emanating from the woman sitting next to him started to surround him, just as she crossed her long legs on the high stool, revealing the daring split in her floor-length black dress.

Even from here, he'd noticed her the second she'd appeared at the entrance to the ballroom. She was taller than most women, but wasn't afraid to use her height, combining her black sheath dress with a pair of heels and piling her dark hair with pink tips on top of her head. He'd watched her survey the room, ignore a few admiring glances, give short retorts to two men who dared to try and approach her and, now, she'd just crossed those exceptionally long legs and given him a clear view of them. Her black heels had ornate straps and crisscrossed up her calves.

At least he thought he'd watched her. Maybe he was dreaming. Truth was, he was so tired the only reason he still awake was that his body was craving food. Food he seemed to have been waiting an eternity for.

He gave himself a shake. Maybe he needed another whiskey. The first one was putting him in that strange state between fact and fiction. His stomach rumbled loudly, so he lifted his hand to grab some nuts from a bowl on the bar. Quick as lightning, someone gave his hand a light slap.

For a second he was momentarily stunned. Then he shook his head and gave a smile of disbelief as he turned in his chair.

She was staring straight at him with a pair of bright blue eyes. He couldn't help himself. It was as if the fatigue coupled with a dash of whiskey had reduced all his usual politeness and social norms to a scattering of leaves beneath his feet. "Did you really just hit me? For trying to eat a peanut?"

She gave a shrug. "Yeah, sorry about that. Force of habit."

He raised his eyebrows. "You don't look too sorry."

She pulled a face and waved her hand. "Actually, I've just *saved* you."

Now he was amused. "Saved me from what?"

She shook her head and pushed the bowl away. "Probably some kind of horrible death. Best way to catch some kind of disease." She shuddered. She actually *shuddered*. "If I sent those to a lab I could horrify you."

He deliberately leaned over her, ignoring her orange-scented perfume, and plucked a nut from the bowl, holding it between his fingers. "One tiny little nut is going to fell me?"

She arched her eyebrows and blinked. There was black eyeliner flicked on her eyelid, enhanced by her thick extra-long lashes. With those blue eyes she really was a bit of a stunner.

"If I could put that in an evidence bag right now and send it to the lab I would." She shrugged. "But, hey, it's your poison. Your stomach."

"This is how you meet people? You attack them at the bar and steal their food?"

For a second she looked momentarily offended, but then she threw back her head and laughed. She put her elbow on the bar and rested her head on it. "Actually, my ambition this evening is not to meet anyone—I just wanted to grab a drink, some food and get out of here."

He gave a slow nod. "Ah, great minds think alike, then."

She looked a little more conciliatory. "Maybe. Sorry about the slap. Bar snacks make me testy. It really is an automatic reaction."

He laughed. "How many states have you been arrested in?"

She sighed. "More than you could ever know."

He could see the way her careful eyes were watching him, obviously trying to size him up. He liked her quick answers and smart remarks. He mirrored her position, leaning his head on his hand for a second as a wave of tiredness swept over him.

And then she spoke. "I'm trying to work out if you're drunk or just in a coma. I'm warning you—I'm off duty tonight."

The corners of his lips headed upward. Maybe he was imagining all this? Maybe he was already dreaming? Or maybe the jet lag was making him see things. If this was a hallucination, those words were *so* not what he was expecting. He let out a laugh. "I could actually be a bit of both. Jet lag and drinking—" he held up the whiskey glass "—are probably not the best idea in the world. But do I care right now?" He shook his head as he downed the remains at the bottom of the glass. "Not really."

Now she laughed as the bartender came over and set a coaster in front of her. "Well, the jet lag explains the accent. But not the complete disregard for your fellow man."

The bartender caught her eye. "What can I get you?"

She looked at his glass. "I'll have what Mr. Happy's having."

Jack raised his eyebrows at the bartender. "Better just put both on my tab."

She drummed her fingernails on the bar next to him. "Who said I wanted you to buy my drink?" Her overall presentation was quite glamorous but her nails were short and clean. Curious. Most women these days tended to have glittery painted talons.

"Don't drink it," he said smartly. "I can easily drink both."

She smiled. A genuine, wide smile. The pink tips of her hair matched the bright pink on her lips.

"You are easily the most crabbit man in the room." She gave a wink. "Is that Scottish enough for you? I learned that from a Scottish colleague."

He tried not to smile as he nodded his head and furrowed his brow. "It's a well-used word. My granny might have called a few people crabbit in her time."

She gave a smile. "Yeah, crabbit. I like that. It means you won't be a pest."

"But you will be."

"Ouch," she said as the bartender brought over the drinks.

She lifted the glass to her nose and sniffed. "What is this, anyhow?"

"Guess."

She tilted her head to the side. "Oh…guessing games. I know it's whiskey. I've just no idea what kind. And here was me thinking tonight was going to be totally boring."

He liked her. He was actually beginning to wake up a little. But that still didn't stop him putting his head on the bar for a few seconds. He closed his eyes and murmured, "I'm dreaming of snacks. I've only eaten airline food for the last twenty-eight hours. And you've stolen the peanuts."

She was still sniffing the whiskey but laughed anyway and grabbed a bar menu. "Haven't you ordered?"

He sighed as he lifted his head again. "I think I ordered around ten hours ago. Apparently the kitchen is busy, but—" his fingers made the quote signal in the air "—it'll get here soon."

She set down the whiskey glass and gestured to the bartender. "Actually, can you give me a glass of rosé wine instead, please?" She gave Jack a sideways glance as she pushed the glass toward him. "This is too rich for my tastes."

He was still leaning on his hand. After a few hours in a fugue, his brain was kick-starting again, along with his dormant libido.

"I've never really met anyone like you before," he murmured.

Her eyes narrowed. "Is that a pickup line?"

He laughed. "I'm too tired and too lazy to try and pick you up, right now. But, hey, look me up tomorrow. I'll probably have a whole new lease of life."

"With those circles under your eyes, I doubt you're even going to see tomorrow. I bet you sleep right through."

He shook his head. "Oh, no. I have to see tomorrow. I'm speaking—at the conference." He gestured behind her. "I should probably be in there right now, trying to charm my way around the room and into a new job."

"You're looking for a new job?" She gave a half smile. "What? Been fired from everywhere in Scotland?"

The bartender set down her wine in front of her, along with the biggest burger and plate of fries Jack had seen in forever. He couldn't help it. "Praise be. Food of the gods."

She sipped her wine and he could feel her watching him with interest as he snagged a fry. "I'm warning you. Try and put any of this in an evidence bag and I'll have to wrestle you to the floor."

She pushed up from her bar stool, leaning over to steal one of his fries. "You Scots guys. You think you're tough. You ain't got nothing on a girl from Milwaukee."

She bit into the fry and nodded. "Better than it looks. And, because it came fresh from the kitchen, I won't tell you any horror stories about it. I save them for the bar snacks."

Her stomach growled loudly and he couldn't help but laugh again.

He picked up his knife. "Okay, then, mystery woman. Since you're obviously the least boring person in the room, I'll make a deal and share with you." He waved the knife at her. "But let's be clear. This isn't normal behavior for me. I'm just too tired to fight."

He cut the burger in half and pushed her half toward her. "But no more insults. And—" he looked down at her long legs "—I still think I could take you."

She picked up her half. He liked that. A woman who didn't pussyfoot around her food. "Okay, then. Because I'm starved and can't be bothered to wait for room service, I'll take your offer." She gave him a sideways look. "You haven't even told me your name."

He nodded as he poised the burger at his lips. "Kinda like it that way."

Her eyes sparkled. "Me too."

She waited a second then added, "Are you really here looking for a job?"

He waited until he'd finished chewing. "I'm still officially in employment for the next two weeks. After that?" He held out one hand. "The world is my oyster. I've had a couple of offers. Haven't decided whether to take them up or not."

"Don't you need a paycheck?"

He paused for a second. "Of course I do. But right now, it's more important I take the right job, rather than just the first one that comes along."

She studied him for a few seconds. He could see a whole host of questions spinning around in her brain, but she was far too smart to ask. Instead she grinned as she stole another fry. "Makes you sound old."

"You think?"

"Definitely."

He shook his head. "I'm not old. I'm just...well-worn."

She laughed again as she took another sip of wine. "At what? Thirty? Thirty-five?"

He choked. "Thirty-five?" He patted one of his cheeks. "Wow. I was really conned by that moisturizer. I wonder if it's got a money-back guarantee."

He leaned a little closer. "I'll have you know I have a whole ten days before I reach the grand old age of thirty-five."

He narrowed his gaze as he looked at her again. "But two can play at that game." He gave a slow nod and took his time letting his gaze go up and down her length. "I'm guessing, forty? Forty-six?"

She let out a little shriek. "Forty-six! Oh, no way, buster. You've had it now." She leaned over him again, her soft skin brushing against his as she lifted the whole bowl of fries out of his reach.

"Not the fries!"

She perched the bowl in her lap and nodded solemnly.

"Surely you know a woman of my maturity needs to keep her strength up."

He liked her. He liked her a lot. The room opposite was full of anxious glances and too much "my qualifications are better than yours." Too many people wanting to talk about how wonderful they were as loudly as they could.

Jack was here for one reason. To present his research. To let people know he'd found something that had made a huge difference in a wartime setting. The difference between life and death.

That was the privilege of being an army doctor. He got to try things—sometimes out of desperation—that private clinics and hospitals around the world would throw their hands up at in shock.

But, so far, some of the best medical inventions ever had come from the battlefield. Freeze-dried plasma, handheld inhalers for pain relief, a specially designed applicator for ketamine to treat trauma casualties, and his own particular find—a type of wound dressing part clay, part algae that stopped severe bleeding in under twenty seconds. It had already saved over a hundred casualties who would have surely died. If they started using it in trauma bays around the globe, it could potentially save millions.

Ms. Mystery next to him leaned over and put her hand on his arm. "Hey? Everything okay?"

The feel of her warm hand sent pulses up his arm. He blinked. "Yeah, of course."

She gave a gentle smile. "Thought I'd lost you for a second there. Maybe the jet lag is getting to you after all." Her tone had changed a little. It was almost as if she'd just had a look inside his brain for a second and seen what he'd been lost in.

He gave a small sigh and tried to imagine meeting her in any other set of circumstances than these. "If I was any kind of gentleman, I should be trying to charm you and be swirling you around the ballroom floor in there."

She leaned her head on her hand. "But that's what I like. You're not trying to charm me. In fact, I should be insulted, because it seems as if you couldn't care less." She wrinkled her nose. "I did hear that Scots guys could be grumpy."

He straightened up. "Hey, that's the guys from Edinburgh. Not the guys from Glasgow." He tugged at his shirt, trying to make himself look more presentable. "And anyway, I have charmed you. I bought you chips."

She stared down at the bowl. "Chips?"

He shook his head. "You call them fries. We call them chips."

She pointed to a box behind the bar. "Oh, no. Those are the chips."

He smiled and leaned a little closer. "No, no. They're crisps. And I was just being polite earlier, calling them fries. Didn't want to confuse you."

She threw back her head and laughed, revealing the pale skin on her long neck, then shook her head and leaned a little closer. "The more tired you get, the stronger your accent gets. Any more Scottish and I'll need a translator."

His brow furrowed. "Nothing wrong with my accent. You just need to pay attention—concentrate a little more."

"Says the man who is sleepwalking at the bar."

He waved a fry with his fingers. "I'm not sleepwalking—I'm sleep-*eating*. There's a difference."

She leaned over and snagged another fry. They were dwindling faster than should be possible. This woman was smart, confident and full of sass. He liked that. "So, what brings you here?"

She waved her hand nonchalantly. "Yeah, yeah, I should be in there too. Schmoozing. But the truth is, I'm not much of a schmoozer."

He raised his eyebrows in mock horror. "You don't say?"

"Hey." She smiled. "It's my one and only true failing as an adult."

"You'll admit to one?"

She nodded solemnly. "One, and only one." Then she laughed and shook her head. "But you? I bet I could write a whole list."

Her stomach gave a little grumble and she started, putting one hand on it as a little pink flushed her cheeks. "Oops, I guess I'm hungrier than I thought."

He looked down at the plates. All remnants of the burger were gone and there were only a few fries left in the bowl.

"I could eat the whole thing again." He sighed.

She looked a little sheepish. "Sorry, I just stole half of your dinner." She waved over the bartender. "Can we order the same again, please?"

The bartender leaned closer. "I have to be honest. The kitchen is a little slow this evening and bar food is even slower. Between you and me, the quickest way to get served is to order room service. You'll get it in half the time because they prioritize those orders."

Jack paused for only a few seconds, and then he stood up. He nodded to the bartender. "You know my room number—can you put it through as a room-service order?"

The bartender glanced between them briefly then nodded. "Of course, sir. Any drinks to go with the food?"

Jack leaned on the bar. "Any drinks for you?"

Ms. Mystery looked stunned for the briefest of seconds. Then he saw that sparkle in her eyes again. He wasn't propositioning her—not tonight at least. He was still hungry and she was good company. He had no qualms about inviting her to his room.

"Diet cola," she said quickly as she stood up from her bar stool. There was a hint of a smile on her lips. He hadn't even had to make the invite; he'd just worked on the assumption she would join him. And it seemed she was taking up the challenge.

He turned back to the bartender. "Make that two, thanks."

The bartender disappeared and he crooked his elbow toward her. "Looks like I'm about to buy you dinner for the second time this evening." He glanced toward the packed ballroom, then paused. "You okay with this?"

Her eyes scanned the ballroom too and she gave the briefest shake of her head. "I have the strangest feeling I might be in safe hands with you, Mr. Grumpy Scot. I think I can take the chance." She laughed. "And to think, I took this position at the bar because you looked like the least trouble in the room."

As they headed toward the elevators, he couldn't resist. "Honey, I'm more trouble than you could ever imagine."

CHAPTER TWO

AMBER GLANCED AROUND the foyer and tugged nervously at her black suit jacket. She rubbed her cheek self-consciously, wondering if the imprint of her Scotsman's shirt button had finally left her skin.

It was embarrassing. One minute they were laughing and joking, legs stretched out on the bed after they'd shared the second burger; next she was blinking groggily, aware of the rise and fall of a muscular chest beneath her head. She'd peeled herself back oh-so-carefully, removing the arm and leg she had draped around his sleeping form.

For a few seconds she lay rigid on the bed next to him, her mouth dry, trying to work out what had happened. But it only took a few seconds to orientate herself. Nothing had happened. Nothing at all. She was still fully dressed—the only items missing were her shoes, which were strewn across the floor alongside her bag. He was minus his jacket and shoes too, but his trousers and shirt were still firmly in place.

She took a few steadying breaths. His room was almost identical to hers, so she slid almost in slow motion from the bed, gathered her things and tiptoed to the door. It was ridiculous. All that had happened was they'd fallen asleep. Now she thought about it, he'd fallen asleep first and she'd been so relaxed and so tired; she'd meant to get up a few minutes later. Instead it seemed she'd snuggled up for the night.

As she closed the door behind her while holding her breath, she wondered if she should be offended. They hadn't even kissed. And he was more than a little hot. Maybe he hadn't been attracted to her?

By the time she'd reached her room she'd started to get mad. Irrational and pointless, but, hey, that was just her. Half an hour later she was showered, hair tied back and looking as pristine as she could. She grabbed some coffee and fruit at the breakfast buffet and sat down at a table for a few moments.

This presentation was important. She was representing her agency to more than five hundred delegates. She could make connections today that could help her career. Not that she had ambitions right now. She loved her job. But the work the Disease Prevention Agency did was international. Having contacts across the world was always helpful. Last night had thrown her off balance a little. And she couldn't afford to be distracted right now. Nerves weren't usually a problem for her but she couldn't pretend her stomach wasn't currently in knots. She stared at the huge breakfast buffet then back to her untouched fruit. Apple. She picked a few pieces of apple out of the bowl with her fork then followed up with a large glug of coffee.

There was a rumble around the room immediately followed by heads turning. It was almost like being in a room of bobbing meerkats. Her eyes flickered out to the horizon. The ocean looked a little darker and there were some black clouds in the far-off distance. There were a few nervous laughs around her. "Maybe it was one of the volcanoes telling us all to behave," said someone close to her.

"I don't know," said one of the women close by in a tone Amber didn't quite like. "I wonder if it could be something else."

Just then the doors to the main auditorium opened and people started to file inside. Amber glanced at her program. It was over an hour until she had to speak. The conference organizers had already told her the presentation was prepared. All she had to do was stand at the podium and talk. She'd initially planned to wait outside and practice, but her churning stomach told her that probably wouldn't do anything to quell her nerves. Maybe listening to someone else would be enough distraction to keep her calm.

She picked up her things and let herself be carried in with the crowd, taking a seat near the aisle in a row close to the back of the auditorium. Within a few minutes the lights dimmed and a professor from one of the national organizations delivered the introductory speech. "Our first speaker is Jack Campbell, Senior Medical Officer in the Royal Army Medical Corps. Dr. Campbell has just finished his second tour of duty. As many of you will know, some of our most widely used medical products were first introduced on the battlefield—and it looks like we're about to hear about a new revolutionary product that could help save lives across the globe. I give you Dr. Jack Campbell."

There was a round of applause in the room as a man in uniform walked across the stage to the podium. Amber blinked. Then blinked again.

A medic. He was a medic.

As he started to speak, her skin tingled almost as if his familiar accent were dancing across it. Jack. His name was Jack. The man she'd spent the night wrapped around was delivering one of the keynote speeches of the conference.

Every hair on her body stood on end. Nothing had happened last night. Nothing. But…it could have, if they both hadn't fallen asleep.

Her stomach did a flip-flop. She'd spent the last ten years avoiding any close relationships with fellow medics. And now she'd just accidentally spent the night wrapped around one. Hardly her most defining moment.

Why hadn't she asked more questions? The truth was, as soon as she'd realized he was Scottish she'd assumed he must be part of the business and economic conference. The UK had the NHS—a government-run health service. Her brain had automatically told her that it was unlikely the NHS would send a doctor to the other side of the world for a conference. But a private business—they probably sent employees to international conferences on a weekly basis. And she'd just automatically put him into that slot.

She gave a tiny shudder. That was what happened when you made assumptions. She lifted her head and looked at him again, angry with herself.

She'd found him attractive. She'd liked flirting with him. The truth was, more than she'd expected to. And now he was here. Standing right in front of a room full of professionals and addressing the room.

And boy, could he speak. She sat mesmerized along with the rest of the audience as he described his time in Afghanistan and the sometimes limited resources. He showed a new wound dressing he'd developed—a mixture of clay and algae that could stop severe bleeding and form a clot within twenty seconds.

Amber could almost see the ears pricking up in the room and people sitting a little straighter in their seats.

Those twenty seconds could be the difference between life and death.

His accent drew the audience in—as did his demeanor. He was a commanding figure, especially in uniform. He spoke with passion about his work, but was also realistic and even a little self-deprecating. All things that had drawn her to him last night. He acknowledged everyone who'd worked alongside him, fellow doctors, surgeons and army medics. He showed pictures of some of the soldiers who had been treated and had their lives saved by this dressing that had been used in the field. Finally he showed cost pricing for the wound dressings along with approximations of lives that could be saved across the world. She could sense the buzz in the air; it was almost infectious.

Then he just stopped.

After a few seconds people started glancing nervously at each other. The presentation had finished and his image was now being shown on the large screen behind him in intimate detail. As she watched she could almost swear she saw a little twitch at his right eye— those brown eyes that had almost seemed to bewitch her last night. She gave herself a shake. Where had that come from?

His eyes seemed to focus and he started talking again. "This product was conceived in a place of war. It was needed. It was essential to save lives—and it will be essential to saving lives in the future. War is never a situation you want to be in. People die. Families are devastated and lives change…forever."

He took a deep breath. "What makes me sad is that we need something like this. I'm sad that, even though we're no longer in a time of war, because of gun and knife crime, this product will continue to be needed."

His words echoed across the room. It was the way he said them, the change in timbre of his voice. She could hear the emotion; she could almost reach out and touch it. Even though the temperature in the room was steady, she could swear that a cool breeze swept over her, prickling the hairs on her arms.

People around her were openmouthed. Then slowly, but surely, applause started throughout the room. Within a few seconds it gathered pace and Amber couldn't help but smile as she glanced at the nods of approval and the conversations starting around her.

"Do you think we should get it?"

"It would be perfect for paramedics."

"What an investment opportunity…"

The professor crossed the stage again, shaking Jack's hand enthusiastically. He then launched into the next introduction. "Our next speaker is a doctor from the Disease Prevention Agency."

Amber felt a wave of panic.

"Amber Berkeley has been working there for the last five years. She specializes in meningitis and will be presenting some of the latest research into emerging strains. Please welcome Dr. Amber Berkeley."

Darn it. She stood up quickly. She'd come in looking for distraction and Jack Campbell had certainly met the criteria. Usually she would spend the five minutes before a presentation going over things in her head and taking some time to do controlled breathing. But she hadn't even thought about the presentation the whole time she'd been in here. Somehow her attention had all been focused on her mystery almost-suitor from last night.

She walked smartly down the auditorium, climbing the steps and shaking the professor's hand. Her heart was thudding so loudly she almost expected everyone else to hear it.

She glanced at Jack, who was giving her an amused look. Rat fink. Could he sense her panic? "Dr. Berkeley," he said with a nod of his head as the corners of his lips turned upward.

"Dr. Campbell," she answered as coolly as she could, trying not to take in how he filled out his army fatigues. She was sure he could have worn his more formal uniform for an event like this, but somehow the fatigues suited him—made him look more like Jack.

Her hands were shaking slightly as she set them on the podium, waiting for the professor and Jack to leave the stage. She tried to still her thoughts and let her professional face slide into place. She'd always been bothered with nerves. It was weird. Put her in a clinical situation— even an epidemic—and she could deal with the pandemonium of that no problem. Put her in a classroom setting, or even an interview setting, and her heart would race at a million miles an hour, making her thoughts incoherent and her words even worse. She'd had to work at this. She'd had to work hard.

She took a few deep and steadying breaths. Truth was, she could do this presentation in her sleep. She knew the information inside out. But could she present with the commitment and compassion that Jack just had? He was a hard act to follow.

A horrible queasiness came over her. That familiar feeling of not being good enough. The way she'd constantly tried to prove herself to her father by getting perfect grades, being the first in her class, qualifying for med school—all just to gain a second of his attention. Those memories ran deep—even though her father was gone.

She hated feeling this way. And as she looked out over the sea of expectant faces, she felt her anger spike.

She looked up as Jack descended the stairs to her right. At the last possible second he turned his head, gave her a cheeky grin and winked at her. *Winked at her.*

A little spurt of adrenaline raced through her body. The cheek. Right now, she could cheerfully punch him. Anything for an outlet to the bubbling frustration she was feeling inside.

She lifted her head and looked out at the still-waiting audience. She could do this. She could. She could be good enough. She could deliver her presentation with the same passion and commitment as he had. She would deal with Jack Campbell later. She tilted her chin upward and plastered her most professional smile on her face. "Thank you so much for inviting me here today…"

So her name was Amber Berkeley. It suited her. A tiny bit quirky, with a hint of grace.

He'd had no idea she was a speaker at the conference. That was the thing about not sharing names and trying to be a little mysterious—it made you miss out on other things.

He'd left the stage and stood at the back of the auditorium listening to her. Her nerves were clearly evident. Her hands had been shaking and she'd been white as a ghost as she'd stepped up to the podium. Last night she'd been brimming with casual confidence. He'd liked that better.

But as he'd stood and watched, the woman he'd met last night had slowly emerged. It was clear she knew and understood her subject matter. She spoke eloquently about meningitis and its spread, the way that the different viruses adapted and changed and the problems that could cause. He was impressed with the way she handled random questions that were thrown at her about the new emerging types of meningitis and the difficulties in diagnosing quickly enough for appropriate treatment.

He'd learned something new. And as she stepped down from the podium and walked back up the aisle toward him, he waited for her at the door, pushing it open as she approached.

The light in the foyer was bright compared to the auditorium. She stepped outside, blinked for a few seconds then unfastened her jacket and breathed a huge sigh of relief.

"You winked at me, you cheeky…" She left the last word missing.

"Did I?" He raised his eyebrows.

She shook her head and sagged against the wall for a second. "Thank goodness that's over."

He looked surprised. "You were good. What on earth were you worried about?"

She arched an eyebrow at him. "Who said I was worried?"

"Do your hands normally shake?"

Her tongue was stuck firmly inside her cheek. She waited a second before replying, then pulled her shoulders back and started to walk past him. "For that, you owe me breakfast. I couldn't eat anything earlier but right now I could probably eat the entire contents of the kitchen."

He held his arm out, gesturing toward the nearby hotel restaurant, trying not to fixate on the swing of her hips in that skirt. "Your wish is my command." Then he gave a little smile. "I seem to buy you a lot of food."

She tutted and shook her head as she walked past him, letting one of the waiters show them to a table looking out over the Pacific Ocean. The wind had whipped up outside, bringing the earlier dark clouds closer and making all the parasols on the beach shake.

Amber glanced outside. "What's that all about? I came here for sunshine and good weather."

Jack shrugged. "Almost looks like a day in Scotland instead of Hawaii. Must just be in for a bit of bad weather."

Amber sat down quickly as the waiter showed them to a table. She didn't hesitate to order. "Can I have coffee, please? Not just a cup—a whole pot. And some eggs, sunny-side up, and some rye toast, please."

Jack gave a nod and tried not to smile again. "I'll have what she's having—and some orange juice, please." He waited until the waiter had left. "So, you didn't want to hear the next speaker?"

She laid her hand on her stomach. "Are you kidding? If I'd stayed in there I'm sure all five hundred delegates would have heard my stomach rumbling. I had to eat."

Her hair was tamer today, tied back in a slick ponytail instead of piled haphazardly on top of her head. The pink tips were just visible when she turned her head. The simple black suit and white shirt were elegant, but as they sat at the table, she pulled off her jacket and rolled up her shirtsleeves midway, revealing a host of gold bangles.

"You ducked out on me."

She looked up quickly. For the briefest of seconds she looked a bit startled, but he could almost see her natural demeanor settling back into place. "How do you know I ducked out? You were too busy snoring."

He shook his head. "I don't snore. You, however..."

"You never told me you were a doctor." The words were almost accusing.

"Neither did you."

For a second she didn't speak. It was almost like a Mexican standoff.

He could see her swallow, and then she gave him a haughty stare. "I don't mix with fellow doctors."

Jack leaned forward. "What does that mean?" He held out his hands. "And what do you call this?"

"This," she said firmly, "is breakfast. Breakfast is fine."

He kept his elbows on the table, wondering if he could lean even closer. "Oh, so I can buy you food. But you can't spend the night with me?" He wanted to laugh out loud. She sounded so uptight, and that seemed a total turnaround from the woman he'd met last night.

But now he was curious. "So, what exactly is wrong with doctors? After all, you're one."

She gave an exasperated sigh. "I know. It's just…" He could see her try to find the words. "It's just that I don't like to mix work with…" She winced.

"Pleasure?" He couldn't resist.

She closed her eyes for a second.

He sat back in his chair and folded his arms. "So, if I'd told you last night in the bar I was a doctor, you wouldn't have come back to my room with me?"

She bit her bottom lip. He could tell she knew she was about to be challenged.

"Well, yes."

He held open his arms. "It's a conference full of medical professionals. The hotel is full of them. Who did you think you might meet in the bar?"

She shrugged. "There's more than one conference on in this hotel. I thought you were maybe one of those—" she waggled her hand "—business, economic-type guys."

He let out a laugh. He couldn't help it. From the second he'd started studying medicine it had felt as if he practically had *doctor* stamped on his forehead. He put his hand on his chest. "Me? You honestly thought I was some kind of accountant, computer, business-type geek?" He shook his head. "Oh, my army colleagues would just love that."

She looked distinctly uncomfortable and he tried to rein in his amusement.

"Why are you getting yourself so worked up? Nothing happened. You know it didn't." He gave her a kind of sideways glance. "Maybe...if things had been different and jet lag hadn't been involved then we could be having an entirely different conversation today."

He was probably pushing things. But it was true. There had been a spark between them last night. He wouldn't let her try and deny it.

Her face was pinched; there were faint wrinkles along her brow. He couldn't actually believe it. She really, really did have an issue with the fact he was a doctor.

He'd worked with colleagues in the past who didn't like to mix work with relationships. It wasn't so unheard of. Maybe if he'd adopted that rule he wouldn't have ended up losing someone. He wouldn't have felt the need to shut himself off entirely from the rest of the world.

But even as he had that thought he knew it was ridiculous. Relationship or not, they would still both have been posted to Afghanistan. He'd been tortured with what-ifs for a long time before he realized nothing would have changed.

He saw a glimmer of something in Amber's blue eyes. A spark at his words. Baiting her was easy.

She flung her paper napkin at him. "No way."

He raised his eyebrows. "Purely because I'm a doctor?"

She neglected to answer that part of the question and gave him a long stare. "Let's just say had you been some mysterious businessman…" She leaned back in her chair and crossed her long legs. "It's a bit insulting, really."

Was she changing tack? He mirrored her actions and leaned back in his chair. "What is?"

"A man inviting you back to his room, then promptly falling asleep and ignoring you."

He squirmed. When he'd woken up this morning he'd cringed. He remembered sitting up in the bed together to eat their second burger and fries. He also remembered watching some old movie with her and laughing along at the lines. And he could just about remember a warm body wrapped around his in the middle of the night. He'd tried not to remember the fact it had felt good because that flooded him with things he didn't want to acknowledge.

He lifted his hands. "Guilty as charged. Sorry. It was the jet lag." He put his elbow on the table and leaned a little closer. "But now? Jet lag is gone. Let's start again."

Even though she'd just tried to joke with him, she still looked the tiniest bit uncomfortable. She obviously took her "no fraternization with other medics" rule seriously. He couldn't help but be curious.

He waved his hand. "Relax, Amber. This is just breakfast. Nothing more. Nothing less. What do you have against fellow doctors, anyway?"

She didn't meet his gaze; she just sucked in a breath as her fingers toyed with the cutlery on the table. "Let's just say I lived in an environment with an absentee medic who was obsessed with his work. As a child I had no choice. As an adult, it's not a situation I ever want to repeat."

He wanted to ask questions. He did. But somehow he got the impression it wasn't really the time. He was curious about this woman. And after two years, that was a first for him—one that he couldn't quite understand.

The waiter appeared with the coffee and filled up their cups. Jack decided to take things back to neutral territory. "You might have told me you were a speaker."

She raised her eyebrows. "You might have told me you were starting off the conference." She gave a thoughtful nod. "You were good. I was impressed." Her eyes ran up and down his uniform. "I can't believe I thought you were at the business conference. I should have guessed. Your suit didn't quite fit perfectly—and, let's face it, those guys probably spend on their suits what I would on a car. I should have guessed you were an army guy. I'm still surprised you didn't mention it."

"I'll try not to be insulted by the suit comment—because you're right. I much prefer to drive a reliable car than buy a fancy suit. If you want to split hairs, you didn't mention you worked for the Disease Prevention Agency. Aren't you guys supposed to walk about in giant space suits?" He grinned and nodded his head. "Now I understand the comments at the bar about the peanuts."

She shuddered. "You have *no* idea what we've found on bar snacks."

He laughed as he kept shaking his head. "And I don't want you to tell me." This was better. This was more what he wanted. He could gradually see the tension around her neck and shoulders start to ease.

The waiter appeared with their eggs and toast, and Amber leaned over the plate and inhaled. "Oh, delicious. And just what I need."

She ate for a few minutes then looked back up at him. "Your wound dressing. It looks good. How on earth did you discover the science behind it?"

Jack was spreading butter on his toast. "There's been quite a bit of work on clot-forming dressings. My problem was they just didn't work quickly enough for the situations we were in. But—" he gave her a smile; she was watching him with those big blue eyes "—the Internet is a wonderful thing. I contacted a few people who'd led other studies and asked if we could try a combination. I knew the specifics of what I really needed. I needed something so simple that it could be slapped on by anyone—and so quick acting it could stop bleeding within twenty seconds."

The glance she gave him was filled with admiration. "I heard people talking after you finished. They think you're sitting on a gold mine."

Jack shifted uncomfortably in his chair. "It's not about money," he said quickly.

Amber didn't even blink, just kept staring at him with that careful gaze. "I know. I got that."

He picked at his eggs with his fork. "I know that for a lot of people medicine is a business. Britain isn't like that. The army isn't like that. Our health care is free—always has been and hopefully always will be. I'm not sure I can exist in a climate where every dressing gets counted and every profit margin looked at."

She took a sip of her coffee. "You've already been approached, haven't you?"

He bit the inside of his cheek, unsure of how much to tell her. Jack liked being straightforward. And from what little he'd seen of Amber, she seemed to operate that way too. That thing on the stage had just been a wobble—he was sure.

"Right from the beginning we had a contract arranged and a product license developed. It was developed during army time, so they have a part ownership, as do the original creators of the components." He sighed. "I knew this could happen. As soon as I realized how good it was, I wanted to make sure that it wouldn't end up being all about the money. That's not why I did this—it's not why *we* did this. And I know it's good. I know it could save lives around the world, and that's what I want it to do."

She tipped her head to the side and studied him for a few seconds. "I like that." The color had finally returned to her cheeks and she seemed more relaxed.

He gave her a smile. "Your presentation was good too. I know the basics about meningitis but not the rest. I had no idea just how quickly the strains were mutating."

She pushed her plate away. "Thank you. The presentation was important. I'm the only person here from the DPA this time, and I wanted to be sure that I gave a good impression." Her fingers were still wrapped around her fork, which she was drumming lightly on the table. "Monitoring infectious diseases is all about good international working." She let out a little laugh. "Let's just say that some of our counterparts have been a bit reluctant to share information in the past. In a world of international travel it makes contact tracing interesting."

"Ouch." Jack wrinkled his brow. He couldn't imagine trying to contact trace across continents. It was bad enough on the few occasions he had to make an urgent call to a far-off relative, and that was with all the army resources at his disposal.

He topped up his coffee. "Want anything else to eat?"

She shook her head. "I think I'm done. Thank you for this."

She kept staring at him, with a hint of a smile around her lips. He waited a few seconds then couldn't help himself.

"What?"

This was odd. It was the most relaxed he'd been around a woman for a while.

But he liked this woman's sense of humor. He liked her sassiness. And he was curious about the hint of vulnerability he'd seen on the stage. Not that it had stopped her—she'd gone on to deliver an impressive talk.

And he couldn't help but be curious about the No Doctor rule she'd obviously decided to follow.

There was a rumble outside and they both glanced out at the darkening and choppy ocean. "I thought Hawaii was supposed to be sunshine, sunshine and more sunshine." He frowned.

"Not forgetting the killer surf waves," she added as she kept her eyes on the ocean. "I think you were right. It looks like you brought Scotland's weather with you."

He shook his head. "Believe me, you wouldn't go into the sea in Scotland when it looks like that. Even on a roasting hot day, the sea still feels like ten below zero. On a day like today? You'd be a frozen fish finger."

She burst out laughing. "A what?"

He wrinkled his brow and drew a tiny rectangle on the table with his finger. "You know, cod or haddock, covered in bread crumbs. For kids. They're kind of rectangular."

"Oh…" She nodded. "You mean a fish stick."

The wrinkles grew even deeper. "A fish stick? What's a stick about it? It's a rectangle."

She folded her arms across her chest. "Well, what's a finger about it?"

He waved his hand in mock exasperation. "You Americans."

"You Scots," she countered just as quickly.

"Is this what we're going to do?" He couldn't help himself. He lowered his voice. The look she gave him through her thick lashes sent tingles across his skin.

"What do you mean?"

He gestured to the table. "Eat food and argue about words. We're starting to be a habit."

She glanced at her watch. "A habit? After less than twenty-four hours? Has to be a new world record."

He leaned his head on his hand. He really should go back in to the auditorium and listen to some of the other talks. He should be thinking about his career, and be circulating and making contacts the way he'd failed to last night. But somehow, like last night, the only contact he was interested in making was right in front of him.

Three days in Hawaii. That was how long he planned to be here. He could easily lose himself in three days with a woman like Amber Berkeley. She was smart. She was fun. And he could sense the spark between them.

In a way he was glad nothing had happened last night. It meant their flirtation could happily continue and he could find out a little bit more about her. All within the confines of the conference. Whether they attended any more talks or not was entirely a different story.

As for her No Docs rule? Rules were made to be broken. And they didn't work together—never would. Maybe she could be persuaded to spend some more time together. His stomach gave the weirdest little lurch. He couldn't believe he'd actually just thought like that.

He'd imagined landing in Hawaii to scorching sun, colorful flowers and interesting birds and wildlife. That was the picture he'd always had in his head.

He'd lived so long in his own little bubble that finding someone to exchange anything other than clinical findings with was odd. But odd in a good way.

He looked her straight in the eye. "You've never just met someone and clicked?"

She blinked for a second as if she wasn't quite sure how to answer. "Is this a trick question?"

He shook his head. "What? No."

Then she tapped her fingers on the table slowly. "Okay,

since you found out my name, did you look me up on-line?" She looked a little anxious.

He shook his head again. He was getting more confused by the second. "No. Why, should I?"

She hesitated for a few seconds then rolled her eyes and waved her hand. "There's no point hiding it. If you search up my name you'll find the whole news headlines. A very long time ago, when social media was a mere babe, and I was working as an intern, I met a fellow medic." She lifted her fingers. "And I clicked."

He folded his arms across his chest. "You clicked? Oh, no. You're not getting away with that. What happened to the No Doctors rule?"

She sighed. "Let's just say this was a huge contribution to the No Doctors rule."

"Tell me more."

She gave a slow rueful nod and held up her hands. He couldn't quite work out the expression on her face; it was a mixture of sad, exasperated and just…tired. "I was duped, I admit it. Or I was *charmed*."

"How charmed?" He was definitely curious. Amber didn't seem like the kind of girl to be either duped or charmed. Maybe there was a reason for the slightly brash exterior?

"Charmed enough to plan a wedding." She stopped for a second. "My father was a very accomplished surgeon, notorious for only picking the best of the best for his residents. He was also notoriously sexist. There were no women on his team. Charles used me, to get to him." The words were matter-of-fact, but the way that she said them wasn't.

"He did?" Jack couldn't help the wave of disgust that swept over him and the way his heart twisted a little for her. "So what happened?"

She shrugged. "I found out on the morning of the wedding via an overheard conversation in the local hairdresser that he'd been boasting about getting on my father's team, and worming his way in through me."

"I thought women were supposed to drink champagne on the morning of their wedding."

"Oh, I was drinking champagne as they pinned my hair up. I thought about it all the way home. I thought about it all the time I stepped into my dress and little things came into my head, like a giant jigsaw puzzle slotting into place. By the time I reached the church and saw him standing at the top of the aisle, the smug expression on his face told me everything I needed to know. I turned on my heels, picked up my dress and ran."

"You ran?" He couldn't actually believe it.

She gave a small nod. "Do an Internet search of Milwaukee Runaway Bride. That's me." A long slow breath hissed out from her lips. "Not really something I want to put on my résumé." Her eyes looked up and met his. She gave a half shrug. "I hate the thought of people reading that about me online. It's like a permanent stain on my character."

She put her hands up to her forehead as if it ached, closing her eyes for a second. It was obvious she found this hard.

But she was being honest. He appreciated that. What would he have thought if he'd read this online? Probably, that she was a bit of an idiot, or that she was an attention seeker. Hearing it in person from her was an entirely different experience. He could tell that the whole experience had changed her.

"Regrets?" The words were out before he really thought about them, but Amber quickly shook her head as she lifted it from her hands.

"No. My father never spoke to me again. Nor did Charles. But then again, Charles lost his job the next day."

"You never spoke to your father again?"

She shook her head again but didn't look sad. Her words were more assured. "No. I was the ultimate disappointment. But then again, no matter how well I did, I'd always known that."

He could almost see her physically bristle.

"What kind of surgeon was he?"

"Renal. Top of his game—until the day he died."

"He wasn't proud that his daughter was a doctor too?"

"Don't think he even noticed." Her answer was short and snappy. "Truth was, I wasn't a boy. By the time I realized how little respect my father had for me, and my mother, I was done with him anyhow. He died a few years later and it actually set my mother free."

Jack was a little surprised at her words but at least now he had half an understanding about her No Doctor rule. Of course, it didn't make sense. But in her head, it did.

Then she took a deep breath and shook her head. "Let's change the subject." It was clear there was a lot more to this, but he could tell that she'd shared enough, and he respected her for that.

Her blue eyes met his and she sat up a little straighter in her chair, tilting her head at him. It was like a shock wave. When the anger and resentment left her face, Amber Berkeley was stunning. "You said last night you should probably be schmoozing. You're almost not in the army now. What's your plans, soldier?"

He raised his eyebrows. "Why, are you offering me a job?"

She straightened her back and narrowed her gaze, imitating some kind of stern interviewer. "Well, let's see. I know your qualifications. I know you're from Scotland. I know you appear to be quite bright, and maybe even a little bit of a humanitarian." She put her elbows on the table and leaned toward him. "Think you could cut it at the DPA?"

He gave a lazy kind of smile. "Not if you call chips fries."

She sighed and waved her hand. "Oh, well, that's it. Interview fail. I'm sorry, Dr. Campbell—looks like you have to work on your interpersonal skills."

He nodded in agreement. In the corner of the room one of the conference staff had a phone in her hand and was talking quietly to one of the waiters and pointing toward their table. After a few seconds she approached. "Dr. Berkeley?"

Amber turned around in surprise. "Yes?"

"Would you mind taking a call from one of your colleagues from the DPA?"

Amber stared down at her bag for a few seconds, and then her face crumpled. "Darn it. I switched off my phone before I came down because I knew I'd be in the auditorium. I hope nothing is wrong."

She held out her hand for the phone. "This is Dr. Berkeley." He heard it instantly. The change in her tone, her professional persona slipping back into place. He wondered if he should move to let her take the call in privacy, but she didn't seem to mind the fact they were still sitting together.

"Hi, Warren. Yes. No. Really?"

He watched as he could see her concentrating. After a few seconds she fumbled around in her bag. Jack reached into his fatigues and pulled out his pocketbook and pen, pushing them across the table toward her. She nodded gratefully as she flicked open the book and started to scribble. "Yip, what's the name? Oh…how awful. Which strain? Yes. Do you have a contact at the local agency? At the admitting hospital? Okay. Can Drew give me a lab contact I can work with? I might have more experience at identifying the strain. Sure, no problem." She glanced outside at the darkening sky. "No." She gave a little smile, then met his gaze. "Things have been a little different than expected. Let me get on this." She clicked the phone and sighed as she set it down on the table.

"Something wrong?"

She nodded. "A new unidentified strain of meningitis. One affected teenager. A request for assistance has been made to the DPA and since I'm here…"

She let her voice tail off. Jack spoke carefully. "It's your specialty area—of course they should call you."

She nodded. "I know. I'm lucky it's meningitis. In the DPA you have to do a bit of everything. I've been in Africa looking at polio and sleeping sickness, Chicago, when we thought we might have a smallpox outbreak, and Washington and Texas for flu." She gave a resigned kind of smile. "We get all over." She stared over toward one of the windows. "Let's just hope it's only one case. I'm here by myself. If there's any more and it turns into an outbreak, contact tracing could be a nightmare."

It was all he needed to hear and he made his mind up instantly. Jack was never going to schmooze his way around this conference trying to find a suitable job. No matter how much his head told him he should, it just wasn't in him to do it. He couldn't do it. He was far more interested in finding out more about the woman sitting opposite him. It had been so long since he'd felt like this. She was sparking his interest in so many ways—so many ways that he hadn't acknowledged in such a long time. He stood up. "Okay, then, let's go."

Amber's eyes widened. "What?"

He shrugged. "No point in you going alone. And I guess you could always do with another pair of hands even though it's not my specialty. If it turns into more than one case, you'll need help. I can be that help. Why don't you change, I'll grab a few things from my room and I'll meet you back down here in ten minutes?"

Amber looked a bit lost for words. She waved her hand toward the doors to the foyer. "But don't you have to work the room, find a job?"

"I just flunked my last interview." He gave her a wink. "I've been told I need to work on my people skills. No time like the present to start."

She stood up and picked up her bag. "Are you sure about this?"

He gave the briefest of nods. "Let's face it. You're the most interesting person I've met here. Better stick around."

He could swear that was relief on her face. "Okay, then, Dr. Campbell. I'll meet you in ten."

She'd never changed so quickly—just kicked off her heels and let her expensive suit crumple across a chair. She pulled on a pair of stretchy dark trousers, a short-sleeved shirt and a pair of flats. Because her wardrobe was mainly formal clothes for the conference—none of which she wanted to wear to the local hospital—she grabbed her least formal jacket, a khaki military-style one. She shook her head as she pulled it on. At this rate, she and Jack would look like a matching pair.

She dumped her purse and stuffed her wallet, phone

and notebook into a small backpack. She'd learned over the years to travel lightly.

She still couldn't believe he'd volunteered to come with her but she was secretly pleased. It didn't matter that she was confident in her practice. It didn't matter that she'd handled contact tracing for meningitis on numerous occasions. This was the first time she'd actually represented the DPA on her own. And it made her a tiny bit nervous. But from what little she knew of Jack Campbell, she hoped he would have her back.

He was already waiting as she walked back out to the main foyer. It was busier than she'd expected. Filled with anxious faces. Jack was standing among some other people.

"What's happening?" she asked.

"Look at that rain."

"What did they say about a weather warning?"

"I've never seen black clouds like that before. What happened to the sun?"

Jack was still wearing his fatigues; for the second time she tried not to notice how well they suited him. He smiled as he noticed her similar garb. "Are we ready to get started? I think we should move. Something seems to be happening."

She nodded. "We need to go to the Hawaii Outbreak Center and Lahuna State Hospital."

They walked across the foyer and out to the hotel main entrance. Both of the suited doormen were standing inside. They looked at her in surprise. "What's your destination?"

Almost immediately the sharp wind whipped her ponytail around her face and she had to brace her feet to the ground. She glanced around as her jacket and shirt buffeted against her. Rain thudded all around her, bouncing off the ground. The streets were almost empty and she could feel the stinging sand on her cheeks picked up from the beach across the road. All of the straw beach umbrellas had tipped over and were rolling precariously around. No one seemed keen on rescuing them.

Hawaii had never looked like this in any of the photographs she'd seen.

The doorman looked down at the deserted street. When she'd arrived the day before it had been packed with cars and taxis.

He gave a wave. "Come back inside and I'll call for a car. It may take a while. We've just had a six-hour emergency hurricane warning. The hotel is just about to make an announcement. All residents are going to be asked to stay inside. Could your journey wait? It's unlikely flights will be taking off anytime soon."

"What?"

"What?"

Jack's voice echoed her own. A wave of panic came over her. Did this mean she couldn't get to her patient?

She shook her head. The doorman was obviously assuming the only place people would try to get to right now was the airport. "I'm a doctor. I have to go to the Hawaii Outbreak Center then Lahuna State Hospital. I have to consult on a meningitis case."

The doorman gave her a solemn nod and didn't try to put her off any further. "Give me five minutes. I can get my brother-in-law to pick you up." He drew in a deep breath as he picked up a phone at his desk and dialed the number. "You might have to be prepared to lock down wherever you reach. Once we're on hurricane alert everyone is instructed to stay safe."

Jack stepped forward. "I knew that the weather was

looking bad, but when did they issue the hurricane warning?"

"Just in the last ten minutes. It seems to have picked up force somewhere in the mid Pacific. Apparently the hurricane has taken an unexpected sharp turn. We usually have more time to prepare. All hotels have been contacted and the news stations are broadcasting instructions."

"Is it normal to be so late letting people know?"

The doorman shook his head. "We usually have between thirty-six hours and twenty-four hours to prepare. We have statewide plans for hurricanes, but the truth is, Hawaii has only been affected by four hurricanes in the last sixty years. Tropical storms? Oh, they're much more common."

Jack met her worried gaze. She'd been in crisis situations before, but usually for some kind of an infectious disease—not for a natural disaster. It was almost as if he could sense her fleeting second of panic. He put his hand at the back of her waist and nodded toward the doorman. "Thank you so much for doing this. We're only going out because we have to and we'll be happy to lock down wherever appropriate."

Ten minutes later a taxicab appeared. They watched as a few large gusts buffeted it from side to side on the road. The doorman handed them a card with numbers. "We'll be keeping an inventory of guests in the hotel as we do the lockdown. I've noted where you're going and here's some contact numbers if you need them. Good luck."

They climbed quickly into the back of the cab and Amber leaned forward to give the driver instructions. The roof of the hotel pickup point rattled above them. The driver listened to her then rapidly shook his head, gesturing toward the empty streets. "No. Pick one or the other. Which is the most important? We don't have enough time to take you to both."

Amber blew out a breath and turned to face Jack. "If the phones are still functioning I could call the Outbreak Center. It's more important to be where the patient and lab are, particularly if I want to try and identify the strain."

She didn't mind batting off him. It was always useful to throw ideas back and forward with another doctor and he had a completely different kind of experience from her—one that was more likely to be suited to this.

He nodded seriously as his eyes took in the weather around him. "Sounds like a plan."

She leaned forward to the driver. "Can you get us to Lahuna State Hospital?"

The driver nodded. "It's near the city center. We should get there soon."

The cab wove through the streets and high-rise buildings. There were a few people practically being carried along by the wind as they rushed to get places. Some stores were already closed, shutters down and all street wares brought back inside.

A large white building with dark windows emerged through the rain. The main doors and ambulance bay had their doors closed, with security staff visible through the glass. They unlocked the door as Jack and Amber jumped from the cab.

"We've had to close the automatic doors," one told her. "The wind is just too strong and a member of the public has already been injured."

Amber gave him a grateful smile as he locked the door behind them. "Can you direct me to Infectious Diseases? I've been called about a patient."

"Third floor. Elevators at the end of the corridor. Take a right when you get out."

The hospital was eerily quiet, the main foyer deserted as they made their way through. But as they reached the corridor in the heart of the hospital they could see uniformed staff swiftly moving patients and talking in hushed, urgent voices. "I wonder if the windows will be okay?" said Jack thoughtfully as they reached the elevators.

"What?" She pressed the button to call the elevator.

"The windows." Jack looked around him even though there were no windows nearby. "A place like this? It must have around, what—three hundred windows? How on earth do you police that in the middle of a hurricane?"

Amber blinked. She hadn't even thought about anything like that at all. "The hotel too. Do you think they'll tell people to leave their rooms?"

The doors slid open. "They must all have disaster plans. Won't they just take everyone to a central point in a building, somewhere they can hunker down?"

He could almost read her mind. Both of them had rooms at the hotel that they'd literally just abandoned with no thought to the impending hurricane. If they'd had a bit more warning she might have closed her curtains and stashed her computer and valuables somewhere safer. Who knew what they would return to later?

They stepped inside and she pressed the button for the third floor. It only took a few moments to reach there and the doors to the infectious disease unit. Amber reached for the scrub on the wall outside before she entered, rubbing it over her hands.

She could already see through the glass that the unit looked in chaos.

She turned to face Jack before she pressed the entrance buzzer. "Ready?"

She felt a tiny glimmer of trepidation. She was it. She was the sole representative for the DPA. Was she asking him, or herself?

But Jack didn't hesitate for a second. "Absolutely. Lead the way."

CHAPTER THREE

FROM THE SECOND she walked into the unit she was in complete control. He couldn't help but be completely impressed. Whatever the little waver was he'd glimpsed outside, it seemed to have disappeared. There were actually two infected patients. It seemed that they'd been brought in only a few hours apart. Was that the start of an epidemic?

Amber took it in her stride and reviewed them—Zane and Aaron, both eighteen, who were clearly very sick. Then she phoned the Hawaii Outbreak Center and liaised with their staff, and then asked for some instructions to find the lab.

Her face was a little paler as they headed to the stairs. "I need to find out what strain of meningitis this is. These kids have got sick really quickly."

The lab was down in the bowels of the hospital and they had to change into white lab coats and disposable gloves before entering. It was a modern lab, with traditionally white walls, an array of machinery and computers and wide work benches. But somehow it wasn't quite as busy as he might have expected.

"Where is everyone?" he murmured.

Amber shook her head as they walked through. "Maybe

they've sent some staff home because of the hurricane warning."

The head of the lab was an older man, tall but thick and heavyset; he already knew they were on their way and walked over with his hand outstretched. "Mamo Akano. I take it you're my meningitis doctor?"

Amber nodded her head. "Amber Berkeley from the Disease Prevention Agency. Any further forward in identifying the strain?"

Mamo had deep furrows in his brow. "Maybe. The DPA just sent me some files over for you to consider. Come over here. I've opened them on the computer next to the microscope."

Amber hurried over and pulled up a stool next to the microscope. She glanced over her shoulder toward Jack. "Ready for this?"

It was the first time since he'd got here that Jack had felt out of his depth. This wasn't his forte. But he was always willing to learn. He gave a nod and pulled up a stool. "Tell me what you need me to do."

Three hours later her neck ached and her brain was fried. She'd spoken to her contacts at the Hawaii Outbreak Center, and her colleagues in Chicago. Their strain of meningitis seemed to be unique. It was definitely bacterial meningitis. The cerebral spinal fluid collected from both boys had been cloudy. But the gram stains hadn't given them the information that they needed. There was nothing like it on file—which was not entirely unusual, but just made things more difficult. It was closest to a previously identified strain of meningitis W135, but seemed to have mutated slightly. "What do we do now?" asked Jack.

Mamo sighed. He'd been by their side the whole time. "In theory, now we wait. But we can't really do that."

Jack frowned. "What do you mean?"

Amber gave a slow nod. "Mamo will need to see what the most effective antibiotic for treating this strain is. But sometimes we don't know that for up to forty-eight hours—even seventy-two hours. We can't wait that long. Both of these patients are too sick. I need to try and treat them now."

Pieces clicked into place in Jack's brain. "So, you guess?"

"Yip," said Mamo, "Amber has to guess." His voice didn't sound happy.

Amber straightened up. Her voice was confident and her manner methodical. "Zane was already started on a broad-spectrum antibiotic—Penicillin G—when he was admitted. But it already looks like it hasn't started working. Neither of these boys was immunized. So, we immunize against Men W, and we treat them with something more specific—more than likely chloramphenicol—and hope the strain's not mutated too much." She pointed to the phone. "Let me make one more phone call. Then I'll go back up to Infectious Diseases to speak to the consultant. Then..." She turned to face Jack. "Then we're on a race against time. We need to contact trace. If there are children involved they may already have been immunized against meningitis W. But because this strain is slightly mutated, I still want to give them antibiotics. I can't take any chances with this."

"Meningitis W is one of the most dangerous strains, isn't it?"

She nodded. "That's why it was included in the immunization schedule in lots of countries only a few years ago. These kids really should have had this vaccine.

But not everyone agrees with vaccination. Not everyone takes their kids for them, even though they can get them for free." She shook her head and turned to Mamo. "I need supplies. Where can I get oral supplies of antibiotics?"

Jack couldn't help but be impressed. She was on fire. This was her specialty and it was clear she knew the subject matter well.

Mamo walked over to another phone. "I'll talk to the hospital pharmacy. It's emergency circumstances—in more ways than one. Being part of the DPA will give you visiting physician credentials. You'll be able to get what you need."

She nodded again in grateful thanks. Jack got that. He was a medic too and part of the army. And, although he was confident in his abilities and credentials, it didn't matter where you were in the world—most countries had their own conditions and registrations for being a doctor. The US had different regulations for each state, so sometimes it made things difficult.

She nodded and laid her hand on Mamo's arm as he waited for someone to answer the phone. "Thank you," she acknowledged. He nodded as they made their way back out of the lab and to the elevators.

She leaned against the wall as the elevator ascended. A few strands of her dark pink-tipped hair had fallen around her face and shoulders, and he could practically see the tension across her shoulders and neck.

He leaned forward and touched the end of one of her strands of hair. "I never asked last night. Why pink?"

She blinked for a second as if her mind was racing with a million different thoughts, then glanced sideways as she realized he was touching her hair. "Why not?" she replied simply.

There was something about the expression on her face that made him suck in his breath. She appeared calm and methodical. He was seeing Amber Berkeley at her best.

He was so used to being in charge. But here? Here, he was just Jack Campbell. This wasn't a trauma situation. Here, he had to let the person with the most experience lead the case. And that was hard for him. "What can I do?"

He had to ask. He wanted to help. He'd help any colleague who needed it—whether it was his specialty area or not. The army had made him adaptable in more ways than one.

She fixed him with her steady blue eyes and gave him clear instructions. "I need to get histories. I need to find out where these boys have been in the last few days in detail. I need to know every contact. I need names, addresses, dates of birth—contact details if they have them."

Jack licked his lips and asked the first question that had danced into his brain. "And if they are too sick to tell us?"

She grimaced. "Then we ask their family. Their friends. Whoever admitted them. This is a potentially deadly strain. We can't wait. There isn't time." She shook her head. "I don't even want to think about what doing this in the middle of a hurricane means."

He gave a swift nod and reached over to give her arm a squeeze. "I can do detailed histories. I haven't done any for a while, but I still remember how. Let's split it. You take one, I'll take the other and then we can check if there's any crossover."

She looked down at his hand on her arm and gave a weary kind of smile. "Thank you for this, Jack. You didn't have to offer, but I'm glad you did. Usually I'm part of a team. So outside help is appreciated."

"You okay?"

She nodded. "The meningitis stuff? I can do it in my sleep. The hurricane stuff?" She shook her head. "I don't have a single clue. I feel completely thrown in at the deep end."

She gave a smile as the elevator doors slid open again. "Remember your first shift as a resident when it seemed like everyone on the ward was going to die simultaneously?"

He let out a wry laugh. Everyone felt like that their first day on the ward. "Oh, yeah."

"It feels a bit like that all over again."

He gave her a smile. "Well, think of me as your backup plan. You lead, I follow. Brief me. What do I need to know?"

She glanced over the notes she had. "Okay, these two kids were both part of a surf club. Zane became sick first, exhibiting some of the normal meningitis signs— high temperature, fever, signs of an early chest infection and, a few hours later, some confusion."

"So, there are at least a few hours between the disease progression in these kids?"

She gave a slow nod. "They were worried they might have to sedate Zane, but the lumbar-puncture procedure went smoothly and they started him on IV antibiotics straightaway."

"And the second kid?"

"Aaron came in a few hours after Zane with symptoms of shock. One of the other young guys had gone to see why he hadn't joined them and called 911 when he found him still in bed. The ER physician connected the cases pretty quickly. Neither of them had been vaccinated against Men W, and both had been bunking down at one of the local student residences."

Jack let out a slow breath. "Darn it. Close contacts?"

She nodded. "Close contacts. We need names and to find the rest of the kids who were in that residence."

"What else should I be looking for with close contacts?" He realized he was firing questions at her but he couldn't help it. He wanted to make sure he covered everything.

"The rules are generally people who've slept under the same roof, nursery or childcare contacts, and anyone they've shared saliva or food with. Dependent on age, they all need a two-day course of rifampicin."

Jack pulled a face. "Shared saliva with? You mean anyone they've kissed? For two teenage boys at a surf school we might have our work cut out. How far back do we need to go?"

"Seven days from first symptoms."

"Let's hope the surf school kept good records, then, and let's hope the boys know who they kissed."

The lights around them flickered and they both froze. "Please don't let us lose power," said Amber quietly. "This could be a disaster."

Jack sucked in a breath. He could tell the thought of the hurricane was making her nervous. Truth was, it made him slightly nervous too. But he had to believe that the authorities would have plans in place to take care of things. They couldn't control the weather. They also couldn't control time, and it was rapidly slipping away from them. "We have two cases. We can contact trace for these two cases and try and get antibiotics to anyone we think could be affected. Hopefully any younger kids will already be immunized."

Amber pulled a face. "Usually we would spend a few

hours discussing this with the local outbreak center and the DPA. The impending hurricane doesn't help. What if we can't get to the people that need antibiotics? We can't ask people to leave their homes as a hurricane is about to hit. And who knows how long it will last?" She shook her head.

"It's a disaster," he said simply.

"Just pray it isn't an epidemic," she said swiftly. "Then it really would be a disaster."

By the time they reached the infectious disease unit again it was in chaos. Bed mattresses had been piled against the windows. The curtains around the beds had been taken down and also stretched across the windows with large Xs taped on the glass. A few of the patients who'd been there earlier had been moved out, but Zane and Aaron were still attached to all their monitors.

There was only one adult walking between both beds. Amber and Jack walked over to meet him. "I'm Amber Berkeley with the Disease Prevention Agency. Are you Zane or Aaron's parent?"

He shook his head. "Ty Manners from the surf school. They've both been with me for the last ten days. I can't believe they're both sick."

He glanced toward the covered windows and put his hands on his hips. It was clear he was stressed. "Everything has just happened at once. I should be down at the surf school making it ready—and sorting out the other kids."

Jack saw Amber word her question carefully. "Ty, I'm sure you're worried about all the kids in your care, and the surf school. Do you have any records? Do all the kids that go to the surf school stay in the same place? We really need to trace all the contacts that Zane and

Aaron have had for the last seven days. It's really important we find out if other people have been immunized, and that we get some antibiotics to them if appropriate."

"It's definitely meningitis?"

Amber nodded. "It is. Both of their lumbar punctures were positive. And it's important that we treat things as quickly as possible. We don't want anyone else to get sick."

One of the nurses came and stood at Amber's shoulder with a clipboard in hand. "I've contacted both sets of parents. Zane's mother stays on Oahu. There's no way she can get here with the imminent hurricane weather but we're keeping her as up to date as we can. Aaron's mother and father live just outside Hilo. That's a two-hour drive to Kailua Kona. State police have told them not to leave their home but I have a horrible feeling they won't listen."

Amber walked over to the window and peeled back a tiny corner of the curtain. "Oh, my," she breathed as she looked outside.

The wind had picked up even more. Enormously tall palm trees were bending in the wind like drinking straws. Public trash cans were rolling down the street like empty soda cans. She watched as an awning at the café opposite was torn away before her eyes by the force of the wind and the red and white material disappeared like a kite being ripped from its string.

It made her heart beat a little faster. She turned to face the nurse. "How soon is the hurricane due to hit?"

The nurse glanced at her watch, then over to a TV screen they had in the corner of the unit. "In about an hour or two. It won't just be the winds. It will be the rain too. It's already started but this is nothing. Once it really hits we usually have floods. No one should be out there."

This was nothing? The rain she'd witnessed as they'd left the hotel had been bad enough. Even with the wipers at maximum their driver had barely been able to see out of the windscreen.

Amber spoke slowly. "But tell that to a parent that thinks their child is at risk." She closed her eyes for a second. "I wish I'd got a chance to speak to them. Maybe I could have played things down. Given them enough reassurance to wait."

Jack's voice was low. "But is that actually true? You suspect that this is an unknown strain of meningitis. The first antibiotics tried don't seem to hit the mark. Now it's up to the second. Are these boys really safe?"

Amber blinked back the tears threatening to appear in her eyes. "No," she said quietly. "Particularly when we don't know if our treatment is the right one. There's still a chance they could die or have lifelong aftereffects."

She could see Jack's brain was trying to make sense of this all. His natural instinct as an army doc would be to prioritize. For a second there was a flash of something in his face. Something that made her step back. He looked as if he was trying to suppress his urge to take over. It was only the briefest of glances. But it brought back a surge of old emotions that she constantly felt around her father—as if she wasn't good enough for this. As if she couldn't possibly be good enough and someone like Jack, or her father, would have to step in and take over.

Her skin prickled. She hated that. Hated associating someone she'd just met with her father.

It wouldn't be the first time. She'd often met other doctors—particularly surgeons—who had the same old-fashioned attitudes and opinions. People who wanted to be in charge of everything—including her. These were the people she avoided wherever possible. Was Jack one of them?

Even that tiny flash of recognition in her brain would usually be enough to make her turn in the other direction. But in the circumstances, that was hardly possible.

The nurse interrupted her thoughts. "We're actually going to try and move these guys. They've done that in some of the other wards. Most of the corridors and central areas are full—and we have a lot of equipment we need to take. Someone is preparing a space for us down in the basement."

Jack's frown deepened. "Okay. We could help here. We should prioritize. Should we really be taking patient histories for close contacts right now when we might have no hope of reaching any of these people in the next few hours?"

Anger flared in her and Amber swallowed. She knew he was right. But she also knew how sick people could become with meningitis. She spoke in a low voice. "Jack, you offered to help. Not to take over. This is my specialty area, not yours. Of course I know this might be futile. But up until a few hours ago the hurricane wasn't heading in this direction. It might still turn. The prediction could be wrong."

Jack held his hands out. "Does it feel wrong to you right now?"

She held her nerve. She wouldn't let him tell her how to do her job. "Maybe not. But what if something happens to one of these guys? This might not be an epidemic yet—but it could be. It has the potential. And we have two young guys who've become really sick in only a few hours. What if something happens to one, or both, of them, and we've lost the opportunity to find their close contacts? What if we leave those people at risk? We also know this strain is slightly different. This could be the start of something." She pressed her hand on her heart. "I can't let the threat of a hurricane stop me from doing my job to the best of my ability. I have to take the histories. I have to collect the antibiotics and I have to try and talk to as many people as I can." She took a deep breath and her voice gave a little shake. "If the phone lines go down after this we could be in trouble. People might live near to medical centers. We can adapt. We could arrange for them to collect what they need from there."

His hands were on his hips. For a second she wondered if he was going to argue with her. Maybe bringing him here hadn't been a good idea after all. What did she really know about Jack Campbell? The army were used to being in the thick of things; maybe he was struggling with a back-seat role?

"I don't have time to fight with you about this, Jack. What are you going to be, a hindrance or a help?"

She could tell he was annoyed but she didn't have time to care. He had to do it her way, or no way.

There was a pause, and then he let out a sigh and gave the briefest shake of his head. "Let's be quick."

He grabbed a pile of paperwork and walked over to Aaron's bed. There was no chance of Aaron talking. He was ventilated with the briefest hint of a purpuric rash on his tanned skin. The new antibiotics were feeding into an IV line. If they were going to make a difference they would have to start working quickly.

Jack looked up at Ty. "We're going to have to ask you questions because you've spent the last few days with these guys."

Ty gave a nervous nod. "Can't go anywhere anyhow. What do you need to know?"

Amber started firing questions at him. "Where did they sleep? How many other people are there? Do you have names, ages and contact details? Have any left in the last few days? How many are still there? How many people work at the hostel and at the surf school? What have they been doing at nights?"

Once she started she didn't stop. Every now and then Jack quickly interrupted with the words "And what about Aaron?" ensuring that Ty was answering for both teen-agers.

It seemed that there were around twenty people at the surf school. Things were pretty informal. Most had traveled to get there—some from the other Hawaiian islands. The people who worked there were all local. Timescales were important. Two teenagers had traveled back to other states in the USA yesterday, and a third had left for New Zealand in the early hours of this morning.

While all this was going on, hospital staff worked around them, attaching the two boys to portable ventilators that could be pushed out into the corridor with them; oxygen cylinders were attached to the sides of the bed and a portable emergency trolley was positioned near to the door.

One of the hospital administrators appeared and spoke in a low voice. "The patients in Surgical have been moved. The hospital front entrance has been completely cleared." Of course, it was covered in glass. "Medical CCU is the safest. It's right in the middle of the building with no windows, but we've already moved the sickest of our elderly patients in there. Pediatrics have been moved down to the theaters."

"Is the basement ready? Do you have the equipment that will be needed?" asked Jack. Transporting these patients would take more than the few nurses that were left in the department.

The administrator looked a little worried. "The staff room down at the laboratory has been cleared in the basement. The corridor down there is one of the most shielded in the building." The lights flickered around them again.

"As long as we don't have a power cut," said Jack warily.

"Let's go," said the head nurse smartly as the windows started to rattle around them. "I don't think it's safe to wait. We've packed up the equipment that we need."

She gestured to the nurses who were left. "You two with Zane." She looked at Amber. "You go with him too."

"Myself, Ty and Dr. Campbell will take Aaron down in the other elevator."

There was only one hospital orderly to assist—the rest obviously deployed to other parts of the building. How on earth did you lock down a hospital and keep all patients safe from a hurricane outside? She didn't even want to think about it.

They wheeled the bed out to the elevator, along with the portable ventilator, tanks and emergency trolley. The progress was slow; it was almost like a juggling act getting all the equipment they needed inside the elevator.

A few minutes later they arrived in the basement. This time she was familiar with the surroundings and backed out of the elevator first, pulling the bed with her. The lab staff must have been warned because a room to the right had been cleared. It looked as if it had been the large staff room, as a pile of chairs and large table were at the bottom of the corridor. The nurse guided the bed into the space and they quickly connected monitors to plug points and checked the ventilator was working properly.

It was weird. Amber actually liked being back in a hospital environment—even though this was a makeshift one. It always reminded her of why she did this job. Sometimes being stuck in an office at the DPA was tough. Only communicating with patients and fellow doctors by phone and email wasn't really how she preferred to work. She liked this. She liked being in the thick of things. She liked to see the patients, talk to them, be on hand when treatments were being tried and tested. A bit more like the role Jack had just done...

There was a weird sound from the corridor. The nurse looked up and frowned as she fiddled with some cables. "Go and check that, will you?"

The lights flickered again as Amber walked swiftly down the corridor. She automatically looked over her shoulder. It was like being in an old-style horror movie—never her favorite kind of entertainment.

The metal doors of both elevators were still closed. Shouldn't Jack be here by now with Aaron?

The lights flickered once more then went out completely.

Black. Everywhere.

She automatically sucked in a breath and held it.

"Darn it," came the shout from further down the corridor, followed by the flickering of some kind of light. Must be from a phone.

"You okay, Amber?" shouted the nurse. "We have a backup generator. It should kick in any second."

Something flooded into her brain. Keeping her hand on the wall, she walked quickly back to the room she'd just come from. The nurse had her phone in her hand and was using the light from it.

"Are the ventilators still working? Do we need to bag him?"

Even though it was dark, Amber moved to the bed, watching for the rise and fall of Zane's chest. The nurse was at the other side. She shook her head. "We should have three hours' worth of battery power. Honestly, the backup generator should kick in. Give it a few minutes."

There was a large thump from the corridor and some muffled voices shouting.

"Oh, no," said the nurse.

"What?" asked Amber.

"The elevator. I think your colleague's stuck in the elevator with Aaron."

Amber's heart started to thud in her chest. She lifted her hands from the bed. "Okay, you're okay here? I can go?"

The nurse nodded. Amber pulled her own mobile from her pocket and flicked the switch on as she walked back down the corridor.

The shouts were getting louder. "Jack? Are you okay?"

"Amber? Is that you? The elevator's jammed and the emergency phone isn't working!"

Amber ran over to the doors. It was ridiculous. She tried to pull them apart with her hands but it was obviously no use.

Mamo appeared from the lab. "Problems?" He shook his head. "Can't do much without power down here."

She pointed to the doors. "We've got one of the kids with meningitis attached to a portable ventilator in there."

Jack shouted from inside. "Is there anything outside you could use to try and pry the doors apart? I can try from in here, but I think I need you helping on the outside."

There was a strange sound from inside. Almost a whimpering. Oh, no. The nurse inside must be freaking out. Being trapped inside a black box wouldn't be most people's idea of a normal working day.

"Hold on." Amber held her phone up and tried to scan the corridor around them.

Something seemed to flick in Mamo's head. "Over here. I think there's an emergency fire ax next to one of the exits. Maybe we could use that."

Sure enough, on one of the walls there was an ax mounted in a red box behind a breakable panel. Mamo pulled his lab coat over his fist and broke the glass, grabbing hold of the ax.

"Give us a minute, Jack," Amber shouted. "Mamo is trying to pry the doors from this side." Something flashed through her brain. "Where's Ty?"

The reply was slightly muffled. "He stayed upstairs to make a few calls to the surf school. He wanted to check all the kids had been taken to an evacuation center."

Prying the doors apart was more difficult than it looked. Mamo put the edge of the ax into the gap at the doors and tried to turn it sideways to widen the gap. After a few minutes he turned to Amber. "You keep holding it," he said gruffly as he slid his hands and foot into the space that was only a few inches apart.

Amber kept trying to turn the head of the ax wider, while keeping it in the space. Her shoulder muscles ached. Her jaw was tight. From the other side she could see a flash of light. The nurse inside must be using her phone. White knuckles appeared on the inside of the door. She could hear the grunts and groans from Jack. "Grrr…"

After a couple of minutes the doors started to release a little further, both Mamo and Jack stuck their shoulders and body weight in the doors, using their feet to push the opposite door apart.

The elevator wasn't completely aligned with the floor—probably the reason they'd had so much difficulty prizing the doors apart.

The nurse looked numb. Amber ducked inside and grabbed the end of the bed. "You get the ventilator," she said to the nurse. "There will be a bit of a bump as we push out."

Mamo and Jack stayed at their doors, holding them back with their body weight as they guided the bed through between them. The nurse jerked as the bed thudded the few inches to the floor, then steered the portable ventilator alongside. The lights flickered in the corridor again.

"Got everything?" checked Mamo. Jack nodded as he pulled out the emergency trolley and let it roll across the floor. The two of them glanced at each other, then gave a nod and both jumped. The doors slid back into place swiftly just as the lights flickered back on in the basement.

"Thank goodness," breathed Amber.

Mamo gave a nod of acknowledgment as he glanced at Aaron in the bed. "Everyone okay? I need to go back to the lab and check the machines."

Amber, Jack and the nurse pushed Aaron into the room in the basement. It only took ten minutes to make sure he was safely set up alongside Zane and that the power supply was working as it should be. The IV infusions with fluids and antibiotics stopped pinging, as did the cardiac monitor and ventilator.

"We're good." The nurse nodded. "I've phoned one

of the ICU doctors and they're going to base themselves downstairs with us." She gave a rueful smile. "Don't worry. I've told them to take the stairs."

Amber walked back over to where she'd abandoned her paperwork. She had to get back on task. Time was ticking.

This was her responsibility and she was in charge. "Jack, how do you feel about making some calls? Let's do the international ones first. I can give you numbers for the public health agencies in the countries our patients are heading to. Following the patients up will be their responsibility."

Jack gave a nod. That tiny little feeling she'd had that he might want to take over seemed to flutter away. "Yeah, I'm not sure how long our phone lines will work. Let's try and do these as quickly as possible. Then we could look at the people who've returned to any of the surrounding islands. See if we can get someone local to prescribe and supply the antibiotics."

She was pleased. He was methodical and logical. Definitely what she needed right now. It was odd to think that last night she'd fallen asleep next to a man she barely knew and now she was working with him in a virtual blackout.

One of the nurses gestured to them. "There's an office over there. Why don't you go and try the phones?" She pulled her watch from her pocket. "According to this, we have about ten minutes before the hurricane hits."

It was like a chill rushing over her body. Should she be scared? Should she actually be terrified? She'd faced plenty of disease disasters, but never a natural one like this. "What happens next? What happens to everyone out there?" she asked the nurse.

"They've moved most of the tourists from the beachfront hotels into emergency shelters. Hawaii has a hurricane preparedness guide. Unfortunately we've not had the warning time that would normally be in place. Things have changed quickly."

There was a tiny wave of panic. "Is there anything else I should know about a hurricane?" She hated the fact her voice sounded high-pitched.

"There's a standard set of instructions." One of the nurses pulled a leaflet from her bag.

Stay indoors away from windows, skylights and glass doors.
Secure and brace exterior doors. Store as much water as you can.
Close interior doors and take refuge in a small interior room, like a closet or hallway, on the lowest level of your home.

Jack pulled a face. "How do these apply to a hospital?"

The nurse gave a nod. "We've moved all the patients away from windows, mostly to the central corridors, and we've evacuated the top floor and ground floor. We're filling the baths and sinks with water to keep the toilets flushing, but the kitchen says it has ample supplies of drinking water." She closed her eyes for a second. "After that—we pray. This hospital has been standing for thirty years. We've had a few hurricanes in that time. We just hope that it will hold together again."

Amber gulped. "What about the staff? Do you all have to stay?"

She wasn't thinking about herself. She was thinking about all the local staff that might have families of their own close by to worry about. With the emergency warning coming so late, most of them might not have had time to make plans.

The nurse held out her hands. "We'll manage. The hospital has an emergency plan. Extra staff get called in as relief. They help transfer the patients and stock the ER. Some of the rest of the staff had to go home to sort out family issues. I came in early to let my friend go home to her disabled mother." She pointed at the nurse dealing with Aaron. "Nessa only started here a few weeks ago. Her family are on Oahu. She wouldn't have time to get there, so decided just to lock down here where she could be useful."

She gave an anxious glance between Amber and Jack. "No matter what your experience, after the hurricane hits, we'll need doctors. Probably more than you know."

Jack gave the briefest of nods. His face was serious, but he didn't seem intimidated at all. "I'd rather be working than holed up in the hotel. Let us sort out what we can about these meningitis cases. After that, put me where you need me."

The nurse gave a nod. "I'll phone up to the ER and let them know we might have some additional help." Her eyebrows rose a little in question. "What will I tell them?"

His voice was firm. "Tell them I'm an army doc and can deal with whatever they need." His eyes met Amber. "Dr. Berkeley works for the DPA. She'll help out where she can."

"Great." The nurse picked up the phone and turned her back on them.

Amber gulped. For infectious diseases she was fine. But she wasn't quite as confident as Jack at being thrown in at the deep end. It wasn't that she didn't feel capable. She would always help out in an emergency. She wasn't sure how qualified or equipped she'd be to deal with things. She'd never really worked in an ER setting. She'd been part of team expeditions for the DPA. But she'd never been in charge. Never had the full responsibility herself. But those expeditions had been more co-ordinated. She'd always ended up working in pre-ready emergency clinics or vaccination hubs.

Her director had already mentioned he thought she was ready to try her hand as a team leader on a field mission to further her experience. But this was entirely different—totally out with her normal expertise. It was almost as if Jack sensed something from her. He leaned over and whispered in her ear. "Don't worry. I've got your back."

Then he did something completely unexpected. He turned her toward him and lowered his forehead onto hers. It was a gesture of security. Of solidarity. Of re-assurance.

Warmth spread through her. She looked up and met his gaze. His dark brown eyes were fixed on hers. They were genuine and steady.

She pressed her lips together and took a deep breath, so many thoughts flooding into her mind. Her brain was such a mess. All she could concentrate on was the feel of his hands on the tops of her arms and the gentle way his forehead pressed against hers. His warm breath danced across her skin. Her gaze was naturally lowered and she could see the rise and fall of his chest.

He was a doctor. The type of guy she'd spent most of her life trying to avoid any romantic entanglements with. And this was crazy. She'd already seen a flash of something in him that reminded her of the focused way her father used to be.

So, if she already had alarm bells flashing in her

head, why wasn't she running for the hills? She could pretend it was the hurricane. That the only reason she wasn't moving was because she was stuck here.

But that wasn't what was anchoring her feet firmly to the ground.

That wasn't what was letting the heat from the palms of his hands slowly permeate through her jacket and trickle its way through her body. Her last few boyfriends had been as far removed from medicine as possible—a landscape gardener, then a chef. But somehow she hadn't felt this. This connection.

And she couldn't understand it. She'd only met Jack last night. And yes, they'd clicked. There was no doubt the man was attractive. There was no doubt her mind was imagining so many other places they could go.

But the timing wasn't right. It wasn't right at all. Her mother's face flashed into her head. The tired, weary look that had always been visible. The sadness when she'd glanced at a clock and realized Amber's father wouldn't be home that night. The endless amount of wasted dinners scraped into a trash can. The times when Amber had sat at the dinner table, desperate to tell her father about her day, and he could barely pay attention—talking over her as he launched into yet another story about work, or surgery, or research. Or when he left the table again as soon as the phone had begun to ring with another call from the hospital.

She'd spent her whole life feeling like an unimportant spare part. Constantly trying to earn the approval of a man who barely knew she existed. When Jack had spoken on the stage earlier on today, he'd had the same conviction, the same passion and dedication as her father.

She sucked in a breath as she realized the similarities between them both.

Having any kind of relationship with Jack Campbell was a complete nonstarter. She'd already lived part of her life being second best in someone's life. She was determined never to allow herself to be in that position again.

She wanted to step away. She should step away.

But for the briefest of seconds her eyes just fixated on the rise and fall of Jack Campbell's chest under his fatigues. She tried to focus. She had a purpose. She was a physician. She was here as the representative of her agency. She had a job to do. She could continue to monitor Zane and Aaron to try and keep them stable. To chart the progress of the infection and its reaction to treatments. Information like this was vital right now— nearly as vital as stopping the potential of any spread.

Aaron's parents might be on the road here and in the path of the hurricane. Her skin prickled. The logical part of her brain told her that these people were Hawaiians. They would know all the emergency plans for hurricanes. They would know how to keep safe. But would they follow their heads or their hearts?

Two years ago she'd had to make a heartbreaking call to another parent. She'd been called to an ER overwhelmed with flu patients. A small child had been admitted straight from school with a history of asthma, difficulty breathing and a high temperature. She'd called the parents and told them they should attend as quickly as possible. They never got there. In their sense of panic they'd been involved in a car accident and it had etched a permanent memory in Amber's brain and a scar in her heart. If she'd said something different, maybe if she hadn't let them know the urgency that she was feeling, they might have taken more care.

But the truth was, in the midst of a chaotic ER, she'd held that little girl's hand—angry that the parents hadn't got there in time—and tried to assist as they'd attempted to resuscitate her. They'd failed. And then she'd got the news about the parents.

No one had blamed her. No one had needed to. She'd blamed herself.

There were always going to be tough times being a doctor. She knew that. She expected that. But this one had hit her harder than others.

And it had affected her more than she'd realized. Her confidence at work and around others was mainly just bravado. It also helped her erect a shield around herself.

Her heart wasn't safe. She didn't feel in a position to form relationships. Not while she felt like this. Not when she couldn't open herself up to others. It was safer to be single. Safer to surround herself with colleagues who didn't seem to recognize her detachment, but, instead, thought of it as self-assuredness and confidence.

She told them she didn't date colleagues and let them think that her life was full of a hundred other potential suitors at any time of the day.

She didn't tell them that she'd run out of series to watch on her paid Internet TV.

For the briefest of seconds earlier today she'd thought she'd recognized something on Jack's face.

That expression. That look. A flashback—a haunting. It was momentary. Only lasting a few seconds.

But it made her feel *something*. A connection.

And even though there was a hurricane outside, that scared her more than anything. So she turned on her heel and walked away.

CHAPTER FOUR

HE WASN'T ENTIRELY sure what was going on. Maybe he'd been too forward with the woman who'd shared his bed last night. He'd wanted to envelop Amber in a hug, but her demeanor had told him not to, and he'd ended up just pulling her toward him and gently touching heads.

He still couldn't work out what had possessed him. He hadn't held a woman that close in…how long?

Two years. Two long, hard years.

One minute she was there. Next minute she was gone.

Jill Foster had been a bright-eyed medic he'd met in Afghanistan. She was one of the best he'd worked with. As a teenager she wanted to be a doctor but couldn't afford to go to university, so she joined the army instead. Her skills and natural talent were picked up and she excelled in her role.

They worked side by side for six months. And as soon as he got home he missed her. By the time they redeployed again they were dating. Right up until the day he was felled by abdominal pain. The bothersome ache that had been distracting him had turned into an acute pain and he'd collapsed after finishing a long emergency surgery. Twelve hours later he'd woken up and life had changed.

Life had changed completely.

He'd had an appendectomy. It seemed that the army doc hadn't recognized his own appendicitis. But in that twelve hours there had been an emergency—a group of soldiers had been caught in some cross fire and had needed to be retrieved. He was usually part of the emergency call-out team. But, when he'd been under anesthetic, Jill had taken his place. And it had cost her her life. While going to pick up their injured comrades the vehicle had driven over an IED, the effect instant.

Gone. Just like that.

He'd never forget the face of the base commander who'd been there to tell him as soon as he came around from anesthetic. The guy looked ill, his face pale underneath his tanned skin. The other soldiers had been retrieved, but Jill and three other members of the team Jack normally worked with had been wiped out.

The numbness spread through his body immediately. He pushed up from the gurney, ignoring any wound pain, and staggered across the compound toward the mortuary. Two squaddies saw him and ran over to help, throwing their arms around his waist to keep him steady.

But no one would let him see Jill.

And he knew why. He did. Surgeons knew better than anyone what the effects of an IED could be.

So, he sat on the floor of the mortuary for the next six hours and vowed to make his time in Afghanistan meaningful.

Everything after that became about the wound dressing.

Wartimes were tough. Surgeons dealt with explosive injuries that no normal surgeon would ever see. And because of his postings he'd grown familiar with the faces around the camp. The cheeky squaddie in the armory. The quiet Yorkshire lad who liked to read books. The gung-ho female sergeant who could give any guy a run for his money. All of them had ended up on his table.

Not all of them had lived. But Jack had done his best. He agonized over any person that he lost. Replayed everything in his mind, wondering what he could have done differently—could have done better.

Once he was in the desert setting, work was everything. He became almost obsessed. The research too was entirely in his focus. He quickly realized how good their dressing worked and what the life-saving implications were. It was everything to him.

It gave him something to focus on. It allowed him to build a shell around himself and close out the rest of the world. He still went above and beyond for his colleagues—he always would. But he'd lost the connection, he'd lost the emotion and empathy that he'd always had within the job.

He'd lost a little part of his heart.

And now? He had no idea what he was doing—in more ways than one. He wasn't worried about helping after the hurricane. The infectious disease stuff was beyond his professional expertise. But if he had to hunt down people to deliver emergency antibiotics, he could live with that.

What he wasn't so sure about was the fact that the first woman he'd held in two years had just blanked him and walked away. Was his heart so numb that he couldn't pick up on female cues anymore?

Amber looked as if she was sucking in some deep breaths as she scrubbed her hands at one of the sinks. The noise seemed to echo around them in the basement. He couldn't stand it. Should he apologize for holding her?

He shook his head and stalked across the corridor to the other room. The IV antibiotics were feeding slowly through to both Zane and Aaron. Both of them were still sedated and ventilated. He glanced at the monitors and then at their charts. The nurse came over and stood with him at the end of Zane's bed. She gave her head a slight shake. "I still don't know if he's reacting to the medicines. He still seems so flat." She gestured toward the rise and fall of his chest.

Jack nodded. He understood what she meant. All of Zane's accessory muscles were working around his chest area. With ventilation and sedation he should be in a much more stable position. It was almost as if his body was fighting against everything.

Aaron seemed much more settled. His heart rate, temperature and blood pressure were good. It seemed that he was reacting better to the treatments and medications.

The lights flickered again and the television monitor in the room across the hall shorted out. The nurse's face paled. "This is it," she said warily. "The TV signal is gone. The hurricane is about to hit."

Amber appeared back in the doorway. She looked awful. "What do you do next?"

The nurse gave the briefest shake of her head. "Hunker down."

For the next four hours they held their breaths as they waited to see if they would come out the other side of the hurricane. It didn't matter they were in the basement with no windows or possibility of flying glass. At times the whole foundation of the building seemed to shudder and Jack wondered if the whole hospital could end up on top of them. Doors and windows throughout the hospital must have been affected as the doorway to the stairwell at the end of the corridor continued to rattle incessantly. It was impossible to stay still for four hours. They had patients to look after, and Jack couldn't help but worry about the patients above them and the people outside. They tiptoed around each other in a kind of unspoken frustration. The phone lines had died. Between them they'd managed to reach fourteen of the local people who had stayed overnight in the same accommodation as Zane and Aaron.

"I thought the eye of the hurricane was supposed to be silent. Quiet even," he said to one of the older nurses.

She shook her head. "Maybe in a movie. Or in a fairy tale. I've only seen two hurricanes. And there was no silence. Except when they were over. We're being hit by the fiercest part of the storm right now. Anything or anybody out there right now probably doesn't stand a chance. Anything not anchored or cemented to the ground will likely never be seen again. Or end up on one of the other islands." She sighed, and he realized she must be thinking about her family on Oahu. He put his hand on her arm.

"I'm sure they're safe. Just like we are."

She gave the briefest of nods and then marched over to the monitors and started pressing buttons again. Jack was exasperated. He needed to be doing something. Anything. But he'd done everything he could down here.

Ty had been started on the antibiotics too. And he, in turn, had been concerned about his employees with young families.

Amber took the time to explain how meningitis passed from person to person and how, at the moment, unless an employee showed signs themselves, their families weren't at risk.

She seemed to circumvent Jack wherever he went. And that was fine. If he'd overstepped he was glad of the message.

They monitored Zane carefully, watching his limbs

closely for any visible signs of septicemia. Eventually, Jack finally made his way up the stairwell to see if he could be of assistance in any other part of the hospital. He'd only made it to the first floor before he could hear the rattle throughout the building. The door at the stairwell had been juddering loudly, obviously being buffeted by wind that had found a way inside the hospital.

Jack stuck his head through tentatively. No patients should be on the first floor or the top floor. Flash flooding and roof damage were two of the major probable issues. The evacuation plan dictated that most patients were moved to central areas on the second and third floors.

"Hello?" he shouted. He concentrated and listened hard. All he could hear was the wind whistling through the building and the sound of thudding rain.

He pulled his head back in and started up to the second floor. There definitely would be patients and staff up there. There was a crowd of people in green scrubs standing at the entrance to the stairwell on the second floor. A few glanced in his direction as he pushed through. He held out his hand to the nearest member of staff with a stethoscope around his neck. "Jack Campbell, Senior Medical Officer, British Army. Can I do anything?"

He could see a myriad people in the corridors with swabs held to arms and heads. The man gave a brief nod. "Oh, yeah, the army guy. I heard about you. I'm Ron Kekoe. Head of the ER. We've had to move upstairs in case of flash flooding." He glanced at his watch. "We're going to give it a few hours then move back down, and send out teams as required." He pointed toward a makeshift desk just along the corridor. "Phones are down but we've got radios to contact other emergency services and the evacuation shelters," His face was serious. "We've already had a few reports of winds up to one hundred and eighty miles an hour and roofs being torn off buildings. There will be casualties." He frowned for a second and Jack realized someone had appeared beside him.

Amber, breathing heavily. She must have run up the stairs after him. His first thought was for the teenagers. "Zane? Aaron?"

She shook her head. "No. They're just the same. But I realized I probably wasn't much use down there. One of the residents is staying with them. I thought I should probably come and help."

He could hear it. That little edge of nerves in her voice. It was clear, however, that Ron didn't hear it. He just gave a nod. "The infectious disease doctor?"

Amber didn't seem to mind the label and held out her hand. "Amber Berkeley, DPA."

Ron gave her a half-suspicious look. "Someone mentioned you wanted to take antibiotics out." He shook his head fiercely. "No way. Not anytime soon. First vehicles that go out will be heading up portable trauma bays. If it's near to where you need to be, you're welcome to tag along—provided you do some doctoring."

He didn't even wait for Amber's reply. Jack got that. Everything about this was familiar territory to him. This was all about triage, all about prioritizing. Ron gave them both a nod. "Can you deal with some minor injuries? There's nothing too threatening. Just flying glass and debris. A few staff were caught. If you could clean and stitch that would be great."

Amber gave a quick nod of her head and walked around Jack, heading toward the first person with a bloody wound pad pressed to their forearm.

He watched for a few seconds as he could see her

swallow nervously. This was different for her. And he got that.

He moved on over and started treating the next member of staff who had a cut on their forehead.

He was methodical. And he was quick. All the injuries were relatively minor.

But as he worked steadily he noticed the continued chaos around him. Although the external phone lines weren't working, the internal phones rang constantly. Staff seemed to be disorganized, and Ron, as Head of the ER, seemed out of his depth.

Jack couldn't help himself. He walked over. "How about you let me do some of this?"

Ron looked up from a prescription he was writing. Three other members of staff were waiting to talk to him and the radio was crackling constantly on the table.

"What can you do?"

Jack pointed to the desk. "I have experience of crisis triage. How about I field all the radio calls? I can take the details and liaise with the other agencies. We need to know what's needed and where. As soon as the winds die down we could have teams packed up and ready to go. What do you say?"

He was trying so hard not to overstep. He could see Ron was struggling with the volume. He might not know Jack, but surely he would let him help?

Ron only paused for a few seconds as the radio continued to crackle.

"Perfect. Let me know if there's anything major."

"You got it." Jack settled at the desk and picked up the radio. There were a few notes already about building damage—but no reports about casualties. There was a footnote querying whether a home with disabled residents had been evacuated, with a note to check with the nearest evacuation center. There were a few other notes from a care agency who had several housebound residents that they hadn't been able to get to. Chances were they were safe. Most Hawaiians knew about the potential threats and what to do. But the infirm or frail would probably not have been able to put all preparations in place without assistance.

There seemed to be no standard way of keeping track of all the information, so Jack added all the names and addresses to a list for checks and pulled out a citywide map to start charting where everyone was.

Some staff were reporting that the sky was almost black now. No one with any thought to safety could possibly go outside.

The chatter on the radios was constant, along with the background noise of the hammering winds. Even though they'd been told not to, some of the staff squinted past mattresses at the windows and let out squeals and gasps. "Did you see that?"

"That car just flipped!"

"Oh, my, look over there. The roof's coming off that building like a tin can!"

"Those trees are bending like drinking straws."

"That one's going to snap for sure!"

The rain thudded off the windows, battering down in among the wind's fury. Debris flew through the air, randomly hitting windows and shattering glass.

Jack tried to tune it all out, focusing on the task he'd been given and trying to keep a clear head. But even though he tried, his eyes were distracted by the woman who'd pulled her hair back into a ponytail and seemed to be cleaning and stitching wounds precisely. She had a quieter nature when working with staff who were patients, and, even though he'd seen a smattering of nerves earlier today, he would never question her clinical skills.

Reports continued to come in and his list grew longer and longer. By the time Amber came over and sat down next to him, he'd started to separate out all the calls by seriousness and area.

She looked down at the lists and charts he had spread across the table. "Wow. You're really keeping on top of this. How many teams do we have?"

"Probably less than we actually need." He didn't mean his answer to seem quite so brusque.

Amber shot him a strange sideways glance. "Do you know how many staff we have, and how many transportation vehicles?"

He glanced over at Ron, trying to hide his frustration. "Ron hasn't told me yet. Search and Rescue say no one leaves unless they deem it necessary. There can be risks of flash flooding."

Ron appeared next to Jack and blanched when he saw the list and map covered in colored dots. Jack stood up. "The eye of the hurricane has passed. How about we send staff back down to the first floor to reopen the ER? It's important that people have a central point to come to."

Ron nodded in agreement.

"Makes sense." Amber pulled a crumpled piece of paper from her pocket and smoothed it out in front of her. "So, do any of the areas where teams will be sent have patients we'll be looking for?"

He could tell she was trying to sound reasonable. He knew perfectly well that as soon as the winds died down she wanted to find a car and get around all the contacts immediately.

He pulled out his own list. He hadn't forgotten that he'd offered to help her. "Trouble is, it's so dark out there now. With all the debris, the roads will be hard enough to maneuver along. What with no street lighting, things will be much worse." He pointed to colored dots he'd stuck on the map. "The blue dots are addresses where we need to give people antibiotics. What complicates things is that some of these people might not have stayed in their own homes. The statewide evacuation shelters are all based in high schools or elementary schools. Chances are, some of them might have gone there."

"We have no way of telling?"

Jack shook his head. "Not right now. There could be thousands of people in each of the evacuation shelters. With limited communications, there's no way for us to find out."

"Any news about Aaron's parents?"

Jack shook his head again. "I've not heard a thing about them. If I do, I'll let you know."

He could see her swallowing nervously as she pointed to another part of her notes. "These people, there's fourteen of them. That includes the three close contacts who had traveled internationally. We've contacted Florida, Texas and New Zealand. It's up to their own public health departments to make contact and issue the antibiotics. We also had four kids go back to Oahu. Honolulu staff are coordinating for them. Another two kids are on Maui and one more on Kauai. Local doctors will deal with them."

"So that leaves us the kids and staff from the Big Island. How many do we need to still track down?"

"Four. That's not too many. Hopefully we can coordinate with any team that's going out." She was toying with a strand of her hair. It must be a nerves thing. But it made him feel instantly protective.

"We still have the other six teenagers that were still staying at the surf school. Ty hasn't been able to get hold of anyone else, but he's pretty sure they'll have been evacuated to the Deltarix High School. Six close contacts in one trip. That should make things a bit easier."

Amber bit her bottom lip. She looked over at the map. "So the red dots are the reports of damage or destruction, and the blue dots are the places we still need to go for contact tracing?"

"Yellow are the people that need to be checked on. That doesn't necessarily need to be medical personnel, but since that information is being passed between agencies, I thought it wise to keep it up there." He sighed. "We still have no idea if there's a threat of flooding, or what the roads will be like."

Ron pointed to a part to the north of the city. "During the last tropical storms, these roads were impassable between mudslides and flood damage."

There was a blue dot very close to that area. Jack leaned forward. "Where's the nearest evacuation center to there? Maybe because of what's happened in the past, the residents will have evacuated anyway?"

The radio next to Jack crackled and he picked it up. "Reports of major incident at Deltarix High School."

Amber glanced at the list on the wall and her face paled. "That's one of the evacuation centers. The one we were just talking about."

Jack's pen was poised. "Can you give us some more information?"

"Roof's been torn from the high-school gymnasium where hundreds of the evacuees were waiting out the storm. Reports of serious injuries and multiple minor injuries."

Jack glanced over toward Ron. He waved his hand to attract his attention. "Do you have any idea of numbers?"

The voice crackled at the end of the radio message. "Around six serious. Two head injuries, three with chest injuries or breathing difficulties and another with multiple fractures. Also a number of children with fractures, and another child reported to be seizing."

Jack ran his fingers through his hair and looked at Ron. "It's time. We've got to load up and get out there." He didn't want to be at the end of a radio, manning a desk. He'd never been that type of guy. He'd been asked to triage. Well, the time for triage was over. It was time to get out on the ground and use the skills that he'd been trained in.

Right now he wasn't afraid of the hurricane. Right now he was afraid that people would die if they couldn't get the medical attention they needed—people like Jill.

And no matter what, he couldn't let that happen.

He was trying so hard to give Ron his place. He handed the lists he'd made to him. Jack had been watching the staff in the department for the last two hours and could guess exactly who'd be sent on the teams. "How about you call everyone together and let them know?"

It was the first time since she'd got here that Amber's head had really cleared. She'd stopped thinking about Aaron's parents. Her brain had already worked overtime on that one, imagining a million different ways they could have been injured trying to get to their son. She hated the way her stomach churned over and over. The logical part of her brain just couldn't override the emotional part.

She had patients to seek out—people who were at risk of developing meningitis. And she had other patients to help. Cleaning and stitching had almost felt therapeutic. Getting back to basics. She'd even reviewed a few elderly patients on the medical ward who had taken a downward turn in the last few hours. She was almost sure one had a chest infection and the other a urinary tract infection. Because of the hurricane, X-rays and lab tests would likely be delayed, so she'd ordered antibiotics and IV fluids for them both.

She'd felt useful. She'd felt part of something. And it had sparked something inside her. Which was why she'd finally found the courage to sit down next to the guy who had sparked something else inside her earlier.

Now was not the time to get freaked out. Now was not the time to worry about someone breaching her inner shell.

There was too much else to worry about. There was too much else happening. She wanted to move back into the tough and sassy woman he'd met at the bar last night. Was that really only twenty-four hours ago?

Jack grabbed some tape and put up the map on the closest wall. He started moving sticky notes around at lightning speed. Ron was at his shoulder.

"We definitely need a team at the high school. There are twenty known casualties, with probably more." Jack looked over his shoulder at the melee of staff. "Another team here." He pointed at a care home. "We know that seven elderly residents were unable to be evacuated along with three members of staff. Red Cross have reports of injuries of a group of tourists on a bus tour."

There was a flash of frustration across Ron's face. "Why on earth didn't they take shelter as instructed?"

"The radio on the bus wasn't working, they didn't

hear the alerts, and once the driver realized there was a storm, he pulled over to the side of the road. That bus has overturned just outside Kona."

Ron threw his hands up. "Well, too late now. Any more information on the numbers?"

Jack shook his head. "No. The mobile masts must have gone down just after it was called in. Apparently the caller was given standard advice about sheltering, but there wasn't time for anything else."

Ron had his hands on his hips as he shook his head. "The tour buses are pretty standard—usually single-deckers with around fifty passengers." He ran his fingers across the map, paying attention to the notes Jack had given him and then looking back among his staff and nodding. Jack pressed his lips together. It was hard not to try and take charge. His army ranking meant he was usually the one in charge of any emergency planning.

It was almost as if Ron sensed his thoughts as he gave Jack a sideways glance. "Okay, army doc. Which team do you want to lead?" Jack felt Amber flinch next to him. He knew that her eyes were currently fixed on the blue dots on the map, while her brain did the countdown in hours. The residential home was closest to a few addresses they had to visit, but the nearest evacuation center could also house some of their close contacts. No matter the temptation, he kept his mouth closed.

He wasn't the boss. This time he was only here to assist. He didn't know the area and he didn't know the skills of the staff. This was Ron's team. Not his. He turned to face Ron. "I'll go wherever you need me. Just let me know how I can help."

There was a glimmer of amusement on Ron's face—almost as if he knew Jack was trying to resist interfering.

Ron glanced around, whistled and then put his hands

about his head, clapping loudly. "Right, everyone—pay attention. We have work to do, so listen up, people. Okay, Marie Frank, Akito, Sarah, Leia and Tom, I want you all back in the ER with the doors open to receive casualties as soon as we have the all clear. Abram, Jess, Sito and Amal, you'll be team one." He pointed to a position on the map. "I want you out here. Collect your emergency kits. There's an overturned bus with an unknown amount of casualties. Coordinate with the Red Cross. They gave us the initial information. They may also have some staff that can assist."

He turned to face Jack and held his hand above his head. "People, some of you might have already met this guy. This is Jack Campbell, an army doc from Scotland who has offered to assist at this time. In an emergency, we take all the international help we can get. Follow his instructions as you would mine."

He turned toward Amber. "And this is Dr. Amber Berkeley from the Disease Prevention Agency. We have two teenagers in the basement with a strain of meningitis W. Before the hurricane, Dr. Berkeley identified a number of key contacts who require antibiotics. At the moment we only have a rough idea of where those people might be. Dr. Berkeley will give you a list of names and addresses, and some spare antibiotics. If you come across any of these people at evacuation centers, or you are near to the addresses and it's safe, feel free to try and make contact. In the meantime—" his pale gray eyes turned to Amber "—Dr. Berkeley will also be assisting in the field."

Ron pointed to two other members of staff. "Dr. Campbell will be leading team two along with Dr. Berkeley and Lana and Jamal. Guys, show our new doctors where they can pick up supplies and radios. You guys will be covering the high school where the roof has been damaged. Team three."

He pointed to some other staff and shouted names. "You'll be covering the elderly care center, and also check on the additional needs facility nearby. After that, head to the high school with team two." Ron stopped and took a deep breath. "As soon as we get radio confirmation it's safe to go outside, the police will be here to assist us. Chances are, none of us are going to get any sleep anytime soon. Stay safe, people. Now, let's do what we're trained to."

Amber hadn't even realized she was holding her breath as Ron spoke. It was almost as if he flicked a switch. The buzz began immediately. But instead of more bedlam, it was like a weird kind of organized chaos.

She'd recognized something in Jack during Ron's talk. She could see how hard he found it to defer to someone else. How had that really worked for a guy in the army? An army was all about rank and discipline.

But she'd seen him swallow and tell Ron that he'd go wherever he was needed. Ron must have recognized the struggle too, because he'd almost laughed out loud, then decided they should go to one of the most challenging areas.

It was clear he had faith in the skills of an army surgeon.

But would he have the same kind of faith in her? Her stomach twisted. That awful feeling of having to prove herself all over again.

"Let's go," said Jack. He was already following the two staff they'd been assigned to work with. Amber gave herself a shake and pushed everything else from her head. They followed Lana and Jamal tentatively down the stairs, and after a quick check through the doors, they braced themselves against the continuing wind sweeping through the building and headed toward the ER.

All the staff who arrived in the ER moved seamlessly, locating emergency packs and handing out tabards for all staff. Amber found herself wearing a bright orange vest over her jacket with the word "DOCTOR" emblazoned across it in fluorescent white letters.

It was odd. She'd thought she might feel more awkward than she did. But she seemed to find her place and slot into it. Maybe it was the complete air of calm around Jack. Or the sideways glances he kept shooting at her when he thought she wasn't watching. She tried to keep her professional face in place. There was so much going around about her, it was easy to follow every instruction given and pay attention to the briefings about equipment they could carry, potential patients and what they might face outside.

Lana and Jamal seemed confident in their roles. Lana showed Amber where everything was in her pack and handed her an emergency supply of drugs. They'd moved down to the ER and other staff ensured the department was ready to open. The wind was still fierce outside but the intensity had started to diminish. Eventually, they heard a set of sirens outside. Jack appeared at her shoulder, stuffing something in the bag on her back. She tried to turn around. "Wh…what?" she asked.

"Extra pads," he said casually. Somehow the sense of him beside her was reassuring. It didn't stop her head going to the place it wanted to be—finding a way to the patients she was supposed to see. Finding out where Aaron's parents were. Keeping to her mission.

Amber was nervous. She couldn't help it. What she really wanted to do was find a working phone and contact the DPA to see if someone else could coordinate information on her patients. Jack seemed a little distant. He did things automatically, almost without any thought. He'd seemed so passionate about his work, it was weird to see him behaving in this oddly detached way. What was it like to do things on automatic pilot?

And her stomach was still twisting in knots about Aaron's parents. Information seemed a bit chaotic right now. She so wished she'd had a chance to talk to them. Maybe she could have persuaded them to stay at home until after the storm. Her gut told her that most parents would have got behind the wheel of a car if their child was at risk, but somehow it just made her feel worse. She hadn't even had the opportunity to try and stop them. That was the thing that frustrated her the most.

The bright orange pack on her back wasn't light. It was jam-packed with just about everything she could need. Her hand still held a copy of the list of patients they hoped to find. As she heard the sound of sirens outside, her heart gave a little lurch. She stepped back over to a desk and picked up an internal phone. "May I?"

The nurse at the desk gave a nod and she quickly dialed the room downstairs. "It's Amber. We're just about to leave. How are Zane and Aaron?"

The nurse gave her a quick rundown. "Holding steady" seemed to be the most appropriate phrase. One minute later the doors were pulled open and some of the Fire and EMS personnel came in. All were wearing heavy gear, helmets and visors. They started handing out similar headwear to the emergency teams. One of the guys shook hands with Ron and had a quick conversation. He turned to face the waiting teams.

"Okay, people. Remember, hazards will be encountered after a hurricane. Live wires, gas leaks, building fires, unsafe structures, flooding, hazardous materials, victims of the trauma and displaced animals. No one travels alone. Everyone keeps in radio contact. If the wind speeds increase again above fifty miles an hour, you'll all be told to stand down until it's safe. All of my staff have flood maps. Listen to what they tell you. Areas may look safe but the ground under the water may be unstable. All our mobile masts are down. Several of our utilities are down. The rainfall is still heavy. Be safe out there, people."

As soon as the fire chief had finished, several of the EMS staff came forward. "Team one, over there. Team two, you're with me. Team three, let's go."

The first things that struck Amber were the wind, the noise and the driving rain. Even though the eye of the hurricane had passed, the weather was still a force to be reckoned with. It wasn't an ordinary ambulance that sat outside. This vehicle looked more like an army vehicle. It still had emergency markings, but also had bigger, thicker tires and an overall heavier build.

They climbed inside and Jack checked over the map with the driver. "Dave," he said as he glanced around at the team. "Consider me your scout. We aren't sure of all the roads as we've only come from the emergency center. It's a few miles to the school, so be prepared."

The radio was fixed to the dashboard with the channel open so they could hear any updates.

Amber stared out of the windows as the vehicle started to slowly move. Some of the trees looked permanently bent in the wind. Some shop fronts with shutters appeared undamaged. Others weren't quite so lucky with gaping holes in the front of their stores. Most of the high-rise buildings they passed were eerily quiet. The city center had plenty of offices that should have been safely evacuated. Some of those windows had obviously been hit by flying debris too, and a few curtains were buffeting in the winds from high floors.

The streets were littered with random and sometimes odd items. Signage, chairs, a table, kitchen utensils and lots of city trash cans rolled around. A few cars were turned on their sides. The wind continued to sideswipe them, but Dave held the vehicle steady. "It's like a disaster movie," breathed Amber.

"Except it's real life," answered Jack, his voice gravelly.

She could hear it. The edge of wariness in his body. He was perched on the edge of the seat, looking constantly from side to side, as if he were waiting for something to jump out at them. It unnerved her. Inside the hospital they'd been relatively safe. Out here? Anything could happen. And even though there were parts of Jack that reminded her of her father, right now she was glad he was at her side.

They turned the next corner. "Darn it!" yelled Dave, and the vehicle came to a screeching halt. They hadn't even been going fast, but Amber found herself flung forward, despite being strapped in.

Part of a building lay in front of them. It was as if the edge of the latest block of apartments had disintegrated onto the road. She looked up and couldn't help but gasp. She could see inside the second-floor sitting room. Pictures were on the wall. There was a door leading…somewhere. Half of a settee was still sitting in the room. But then? Then a whole corner of the room had just disintegrated over the road. "How on earth did that happen?"

Dave very slowly edged the vehicle around the rubble, mounting the pavement on the other side of the street, continuing to stare upward. "Has to be the roof," he murmured. "Part of it looks torn off, part of it has collapsed downward, taking the edge of the building with it."

Jack shook his head as he adjusted the backpack at his feet. "This hasn't been called in. There could be people in that building."

Amber blinked and looked at the debris on the road. It all just seemed like a pile of bricks, along with an upturned armchair, lampshade and parts of a window. Thankfully, she couldn't see anyone among the rubble. But Jack already had his hand on the door handle.

"I'm going to check the building," he muttered to Dave. "Radio in. The entranceway and stairwell look safe. I'll run up and have a shout, check there's no one stuck inside."

Amber's first thought was to say no. But Dave nodded and Jack was out of the car before she could object. He stuck his head back in the door. "Wait here, you lot. I'll only be five minutes."

"Wait. That can't be a good idea. Should he be going in there?"

Dave shook his head with a half smile. "Nope. But we shouldn't go in any building without a health and safety check after a hurricane. Do you honestly think that's going to happen anytime soon? They're sending us to a high school with half the roof ripped off."

The irony struck her hard. Of course they were. This was always going to be dangerous. Dave radioed in about the damaged building and partially blocked road, while the rest of them stared out of the vehicle windows, waiting for any sign.

A few minutes later Jack appeared with a bundle in his arms. Amber couldn't help it. She was out of the vehicle immediately, Lana and Jamal not far behind her.

"It's okay," said Jack as he strode toward them in the

strong winds. The elderly woman was huddled in toward his chest. "This is Mary," he said as he placed her inside. "She was sheltering in the stairwell. No serious injuries, just some cuts and bruises. And a whole lot of shock since she was in her sitting room as it collapsed." He gently sat her down and put his hand at the side of her face. "It's okay, Mary. You're safe now."

There was something so caring and tender about the way he spoke to her. It tugged at Amber's heart. What was it about this guy? One second he reminded her of her father and she wanted to sprint into the distance; next second he did something like that and it just melted her heart.

He looked up for the briefest of seconds and his dark brown eyes met hers. He didn't say anything. He didn't have to. Whatever the weird connection between them, it was obvious he felt it too.

After a second he broke their gaze and nodded to Dave. "Nothing serious. We can go on to the high school and tend to her there with the others."

Amber settled in the back with Mary as they set off again. Jamal patched the few small wounds Mary had on her legs and arms, then bundled her under his arm and held her tight, talking to her the whole time.

It was clear she was shocked. Her voice was shaking and tired. She'd missed the transport to the evacuation center and decided to lock down in her house until the hurricane passed. Amber's stomach turned over. Where would Mary go after the storm? Where would anyone go whose house had been damaged?

Fifteen minutes later they reached the high-school evacuation center. Half the roof was missing from the auditorium and gymnasium. Debris was strewn across the football field. There was another emergency vehicle outside, so the team piled out and headed to the main entrance of the school.

Someone with an orange tabard was waiting for them. "Are you the team from Lahuna State Hospital?"

Jack nodded and held out his hand. "Jack Campbell." He nodded over his shoulder toward the rest of them. "Amber, Lana, Jamal and Dave. We've also picked up a woman with a few minor injuries." There was no need for more formal introductions as they all had tabards too with their designation.

The woman put her hand on her chest. She looked as if she might cry. "I'm Chrissie. We have a number of injured people and a whole lot more to assess." She pointed toward one of the classrooms. "Your lady can go in here. We have a few volunteers."

"Take us to the people that are injured," said Jack.

"Wait," said Amber quickly. She handed a note to Chrissie. "Do you have a register of the people here?"

Chrissie looked confused. "We tried to do that, but things got a bit chaotic."

She squeezed Chrissie's hand with the list in it. "Please, can you check these names? It's really, really important we get in touch with these people."

Chrissie stared down at the list in her hand. "I'll do my best."

Amber followed Jack further into the building.

There were a few firefighters already in the building. They were moving debris and assessing damage. One of them shook his head as they approached. "We have a few power issues. Electrical faults. We've put tape over some of the doorways so no one goes inside."

Jack nodded and headed into the main gymnasium. Rain was thudding down onto the floor on the half where the ceiling was missing. Everyone still inside had been moved to the other side. There were a number of people lying on the floor.

Jack shrugged his pack from his shoulder and walked over, setting it down on the floor next to one of the injured. "You over there." He pointed to Amber, then turned to Jamal and Lana. "One over there, and one over there. Let me know what you've got."

Amber took a deep breath as she approached the young woman lying on the floor ahead of her. The woman looked around the same age as herself but her arm was lying at an awkward angle and she had a gash on her head.

Amber knelt down next to her, reaching in her pack for some supplies. "I'm Amber. I'm one of the doctors. What's your name?"

"Kel," she breathed.

Amber tried to do a quick assessment of the patient, pulling a small flashlight from her pack and checking her neuro obs. The woman gave a little groan and her eyelids fluttered open for a second. She attempted to move then let out a yelp. Her arm was obviously broken. Amber grabbed a dressing and covered the wound on the woman's forehead after she'd checked it. The arm was going to take a bit more than a wound dressing.

"When was the last time I dealt with broken bones?" whispered Amber to herself. She touched the woman's other shoulder. "I'm going to give you an injection for the pain," she said lowly, "before I try and move your arm." It only took a matter of seconds to draw up the injection. Amber kept talking to the woman the whole time. She gave her the injection and waited a few minutes for it to take effect. She found a sling in among her supplies. Once the woman's pain was under control, she very gently put the injured arm in a sling.

Where was Jack? She couldn't see him and there were a number of other patients to deal with. Jamal and Lana were dealing with patients of their own, checking wounds and patching dressings. Amber moved on to the next patient. Then the next, then the next. It seemed that lots of people in the evacuation center had been injured, some before the storm, some on the way to the center and some as a result of the roof being ripped off.

Eventually one of the firefighters came to her side. "Dr. Jack said to come and find you. He needs a hand, and wants a rundown on your patients."

A hand she could do. But should she be offended he wanted a rundown on her patients? She asked one of the volunteers to keep an eye on a few people and followed the firefighter outside, then followed him down a corridor into a back entrance of the damaged gymnasium.

There were a few people who looked as if they were standing guard outside one of the doors. "What is it?" she asked.

"The school janitor. He was already injured trying to help someone. Now we think he's been electrocuted."

Amber gulped. Water had seeped into every part of this building due to the roof damage and storm. One of the firefighters handed her a pair of rubber boots. "Put these on before you go any further."

She threw her shoes to the side and pulled on the rubber boots, nodding to the firefighter once she was ready.

But when he opened up the door, she realized she was anything but ready.

Jack was almost hanging from the ceiling, above a floor covered in a few inches of water, and holding on to a man who was trapped in twisted bleachers. He had a plastic portable gurney in two bits next to him.

"Great," he said once he saw her. "Amber, can you

bring an airway? I need you to maintain this guy's airway for me." His hands appeared to be on the patient. "But don't touch the floor. You'll need to climb around, across those bleachers. Get a pair of gloves from somewhere."

She tried to make sense of the room. The bleachers were twisted into an almost unrecognizable state. One of the large ceiling lights had landed in the pool of water on the floor. The firefighter next to her spoke into her ear. "The janitor pulled a kid out of here just before that light landed on the floor. He was flung up onto the bleachers with the shock. He's been groaning ever since." The firefighter nudged her. "Your Dr. Jack is quite the gymnast. He managed to make it over there better than some of our boys."

Amber was trying to plot her course along the edge of the water-lined floor then up toward the tangled bleachers. After a few seconds, she gave a nod. "Okay, I think I can do it." The firefighter handed her some gloves.

"Wait," she asked. "What's Jack going to do while I hold the airway?"

The firefighter pressed his lips together. "Oh, he's also trying to stop the bleeding."

"What bleeding?"

She looked back at the floor again and directly under the bleachers to where Jack and the patient were. The water was stained with red. This guy was bleeding heavily. However he'd landed on those bleachers, it hadn't been pretty.

She shook her head. "Don't worry. I get it."

It was obvious that Jack couldn't take his other hand from wherever the wound site was. She bent down and pulled one of his wound pads from her pack and stuffed it inside her jacket. It took a few moments to maneuver her way around the edge, taking care to avoid any hint of water, to where one of the firefighters was waiting to give her a punt up onto the bleachers.

"Ready?" he asked.

"As I'll ever be," she replied. Her hands caught on to a plastic chair and she moved from one to another, ducking between them and squeezing her body from side to side.

"Any word from the power company?" shouted Jack. "If we could be sure the power was off, things would be a whole lot easier."

"Can't even get through," replied one of the firefighters. "Ironic, really. The one place we actually want a power cut is the place we can't get it."

Another guy came up alongside him and shouted over to Jack. "We've looked for the breakers but we think the box has been covered by the debris from the roof."

Jack pulled a face as Amber continued to thread her way through the twisted bleachers. The last part was the toughest; she had to shrug off her jacket and push it through first before she could squeeze through the small space, finally ending up breathless next to Jack.

"How on earth did you get the plastic gurney up here?"

Jack raised his eyebrows. "It's plastic. We just threw it across the floor then had to work out a way to pick it up on this side without getting shocked." He gestured to the large plastic pole next to him and a thick pair of rubber gloves. As she looked down at them she caught sight of the blood on Jack's clothes.

"Are you okay?" she asked, instantly worried.

"It's not mine," he replied quickly. His jaw was tense with a little tic at the side, as if his muscles were straining. One hand was positioned at the patient's head and neck, keeping his airway propped open, the other pressed hard against the patient's side.

Something flickered in her brain. "Wait," she said quickly as she unfolded her jacket. "I brought one of your wound pads."

His eyes lit up. "Great. Thanks." He rolled his eyes. "I left my pack behind when I came in here. We thought he'd just been shocked. I didn't realize there were other injuries." She opened the wound pad and held it toward him. He grabbed it and replaced it with the one he'd been using. As he pulled it upward Amber could see that the traditional dressing had virtually disintegrated.

"Let me help," she said as she moved her position to near the head of the trolley. She pulled an airway from her pocket and worked around Jack, inserting it into the janitor's mouth. Once she was sure it was safely in position, she placed her hands carefully on either side of the janitor's head, her fingers covering Jack's. He looked up and met her gaze.

"You got it?" he asked.

There was something about his words and the expression in his gaze. All the way along she'd felt as if his natural position was to take over everything. To take charge. But now Jack was the one asking for help.

She'd thought she'd have to ask him a million questions out here—out of her comfort zone. But he hadn't been around and she'd coped fine. Maybe the director at the DPA was right—maybe she was ready for more field missions.

"I've got you," she whispered in reply.

In that second she felt a wave. A connection. An understanding of the overwhelming pain in his eyes. A deep, fathomless hurt that he never revealed or let bubble to the surface. Jack Campbell never asked for help. He never counted on anyone else. He was solitary in his life. For reasons that she couldn't even begin to imagine. It was the first depth, the first exposure she'd seen from him, and it was the truest thing she had ever felt.

Even though she'd only just got to know him, she got the overwhelming impression that he'd have her back. A warm feeling flowed through her, filling her with the confidence that she sometimes lacked. This strong, fearless army surgeon needed her help and she was happy to give it. Always. And something about it felt good. Special.

He released his hand, pulling it gently out from under her firm grip. For a second the tension left his shoulders, but a few seconds later he put his second hand down with his first on the wound.

"What's he done?" asked Amber. The sky was dark above and there were no artificial lights. From this position she couldn't really make out what was wrong.

"He's been pierced by a bit of the bleachers. From the amount of blood, I think he might have damaged his spleen."

She licked her lips. "How's your wound pad doing?"

Jack gave a brief nod of his head. He lifted one hand from the wound site. The glove he was wearing wasn't smeared in blood this time. It was more or less wiped clean. He put it back down. "I think things are clotting. The blood loss has certainly slowed. Before it just seemed like a steady flow. Nothing I was using was stemming the blood flow."

She gave an appreciative nod. "That's another life, Jack. Another life saved."

She shifted a little. Her position was awkward, her legs spread across an unstable base above the still-wet floor, her back starting to ache already. The space across the floor was vast, with easy access to the door if only there weren't a chance of water filled with electricity in their way.

"Jack, how are we going to get out of here? We might be able to clamp this gurney around him but there's no way we can fit it through the spaces we climbed through." She wrinkled her nose and stared down at the floor. "The gurney is plastic. Could we lower it to the floor and push him across again?"

Jack raised his eyebrows. "You want to take that chance?"

She pulled a face. "Not really."

"Me either."

She stared at the rope around his waist, looped around something hanging from part of the ceiling and allowing him to slightly change position as needed. "How on earth did you do that?"

He grinned. "One of the firefighters is some kind of mountaineer. At first they were worried I shouldn't actually touch the bleachers. They rigged the rope and tied it to me before I set off. Theory was it would keep me off the floor if everything else around me collapsed."

She stared down at her waist and raised her eyebrows. "Great. Where's mine?"

He nodded toward her feet. "You got the rubber boots. That's your insurance policy." He wiggled one foot at her. "I'm still on the regular army boots. Not quite the same."

She noticed he was still keeping his hands firmly down at the janitor's wound. She watched carefully the rise and fall of the janitor's chest. At least he was maintaining his airway, without any oxygen. That was good. Even if he had suffered some kind of electric shock, he was still breathing. If only she had a spare hand right now to reach for his pulse.

"Any idea about his cardiac situation right now?"

"I'd love to know about his cardiac situation. But I've run out of hands. You have too. Let's just say, due to the amount of blood loss, we know his heart has kept beating. I just wish he'd regain consciousness so I could try and assess him."

Amber shook her head. "With that wound, I'm not sure you do. How much pain will he be in? I don't know how still he would stay and we're not in the most stable of positions."

Jack gave a reassuring nod. "I know that." For a second his dark eyes twinkled. "Did you ever imagine when you met the jet-lagged Scotsman in the bar we'd end up working together in the middle of a hurricane?"

She let out a quiet laugh and shook her head. "If you'd asked me to place bets that night, I'm pretty sure this would never even have been on my radar."

"Still annoyed I didn't tell you I was a doctor?"

"Till my dying day." She laughed.

Jack's face changed. There was the briefest flash of something and Amber's insides flip-flopped, cringing. She'd said the wrong thing—but she had no idea why.

"Dr. Jack!" came the shout behind her.

She wanted to swivel around but her position made it awkward. Jack replied for them both. "We're almost ready."

"What are they doing?" asked Amber as she tried to see out of the corner of her eye.

"It's the backup plan," said Jack. "Just think really big planks of wood."

There were loud noises behind her. Scraping, thudding and the odd splash of water. She could also hear quite a lot of groans and moans behind her as the firefighters positioned the planks of wood.

After what seemed like forever, there was a voice not too far behind her. "Okay, Docs, we think we're just about ready. The wood is in place. We're on it. We're going to come toward you and help you clamp that gurney into place. Then we'll try and bring you all down together. Whatever you do, as you come down from the bleachers, make sure you step directly onto the wood. We're still not sure about the state of the electrics and the main floor is still wet. Nobody touches the floor. Are we clear?"

Jack glanced at her. "We're clear," he shouted back.

But the firefighter didn't seem to be happy with that response. "Dr. Berkeley, did you get that? I need to know you understand before anyone moves."

Amber shouted back. "Okay, I've got it. Just let me know when."

From that point, Jack was her eyes. He told her where everyone was, and how soon it was until they were at her back. And they were a good partnership. She held her hands steady, supporting the janitor's airway, even though they felt as though they could cramp. It was the longest time until she felt a pair of large hands at her waist. It made her start a little. "Right behind you, Doc," came the deep voice at her back. "I'm going to come around your side and grab one side of the gurney."

She felt his large body brush against hers as the firefighter came around her side, squeezing his body next to one side of the gurney. Another guy appeared at the other side and they coordinated with Jack and Amber.

"We'll take the weight of the gurney. Your job is to keep doing whatever it is you need to do. We're going to move slow and steady. Let us know if there's an issue. Dr. Berkeley, we know you're going to be walking backward. We're going to have someone else behind you to guide you, and make sure you don't step off the planks."

It was the first time she actually felt a bit nervous. Of course. Stepping off the planks could result in a nasty shock. Jack met her gaze again. "Okay?"

"Okay," she replied, her voice a little shakier than she'd like. She really wanted to move her hands, just for a second, just to stretch them to stop the cramp setting in. Last thing she wanted was her hands to spasm when she was holding this airway.

She took a few breaths and concentrated on the rise and fall of the janitor's chest. That was what she needed to focus on. She could do this.

The firefighter to her right started talking slowly and steadily. "We're going to take the weight on three. Ready? One, two, three."

The gurney lifted just a little under her hands. She felt another pair of hands at her waist and heard the voice of a female firefighter. "Dr. Berkeley, I'm Kate. I'm here to guide you. I want you to take one slow step backward."

It was harder than it should be. She wasn't on a flat surface. She was still halfway up the twisted bleachers. Her hands were already fixed in position. Now she was stepping downward with no weight to steady herself. But the hands at her waist were strong and firmly reassuring. Not only did they feel as though they could take part of her weight, they also felt as if they could keep her straight and steady. She felt her way with one foot, finding another part of the bleachers to stand on. Then she shifted her weight, ready to move the next foot.

The firefighters watched her constantly, as did Jack, the gurney sliding steadily closer toward her. Jack was finding it easier to move; he could put a little weight on the gurney as he found his footing to move. Amber concentrated on the firm hands at her waist and the steadying voice of Kate. When she finally felt her foot reach a thick plank of wood on the floor, she let out a huge sigh.

Kate gave a laugh. "Don't be too relieved," she said. "We've still got a bit to go. And, believe me, these guys couldn't put planks of wood in a straight line if they tried."

Slowly and steadily they moved. Jack's eyes were on hers. He didn't talk. He just kept watching her. In any other set of circumstances she would have been slightly unnerved. But it wasn't like that. It was reassuring.

Once they reached the entranceway and stepped off the wood and onto the normal flooring in the corridor outside, Jamal was waiting with a bag and mask to take her place. He gave her a gentle nudge. "Let me take over for a bit," he said as she stumbled back wearily and stretched out her aching hands.

The gurney was lowered to the ground. Jack moved instantly to the side of the gurney and lifted the edge of his wound pad. Amber couldn't help herself. She had to see too. She knelt on the floor next to him. Lana had appeared too and fixed a BP cuff around the janitor's arm, checking his blood pressure and taking his pulse with her fingers. "Can't beat old-fashioned methods." She winked at Amber.

Amber could see a bead of sweat on Jack's brow. Just how long had he been in position while she'd been dealing with other patients? "Has it worked?" she asked.

Jack gave a relieved breath. "I hope so. It looks as if a clot has formed." He looked at the readings that Lana had taken. "His blood pressure is low. His pulse fast and thready. He's not regained consciousness. He really needs to be back at the hospital."

Amber nodded. "I agree. I've got another patient next

door with a broken arm, and a possible head injury. I also patched up a woman with a shoulder injury and another with a whole array of cuts to her face and arms."

Jack sighed. "Before I got called here, I dealt with an older man with a crush injury to his lower leg. Part of the ceiling caught him when it was ripped off. And a woman who sheltered some kids and ended up with a spinal injury." Amber's eyes widened but he shook his head. "She's not paralyzed but she's got a loss of sensation in one of her legs. She needs proper assessment. We've got two kids who had asthma attacks because they forgot their inhalers. We managed to find some and they're stable now. Another kid had a minor seizure but that's stopped and he's come around."

Jamal pulled a list from his pocket. "Here. I collated some details while you two were trying to get electrocuted," he said wickedly. "We radioed in, and they're sending a few extra ambulances in our direction." He looked at Jack. "You just need to decide who goes first."

A list. She'd forgotten. She'd forgotten about her own list.

Jack must have caught the expression on her face, because he raised own eyebrow in silent question. She shook her head and stood up. "You've got this. Let me see if there's anyone else needing to be patched up before the ambulances arrive. I'll let you know if there's anything serious."

She stretched out her back for a few seconds, trying to relieve the ache she was feeling, and made her way back to the main gymnasium. There were a few more staff, helping patch patients up. She found her pack again and emptied its contents on the floor next to her, then made a quick check of Kel and her broken arm, giving her some more pain relief and checking her neuro obs again.

The evacuation center had over two thousand people in it—they were lucky there weren't more seriously injured. Lots of the people in the center volunteered to help and some had first-aid certificates or previous experience in the health service.

Jack appeared at her side. "Have you finished sorting out who goes first?" she asked him.

"We've got fourteen people who need transport to the hospital sometime soon. I found out our janitor is called Hugo. He's going, along with the lady with the spinal injury, a woman with a head injury and the older gentleman with the broken tib and fib. We only have two ambulances initially, so I've had to prioritize."

Amber leaned in a little and looked at the list in his hand. She could see Kel, the woman with the broken arm and head injury, on the second list. On any other day of the week, she would have wanted to get her assessed sooner. But things were different here. She wasn't unconscious. The other patients would actually take priority.

Jack must have noticed her expression. "You don't agree?" He seemed surprised, but held up the list for her to look at. "If you think differently, let me know."

She swallowed. She hadn't expected that. He actually wanted to know if she had other ideas—even though this wasn't her specialist area. Her fingers crumpled around the list in her pocket as she shook her head. "I don't disagree. I understand why you've prioritized them. How much longer until we get ambulances again? I'd like to get Kel checked over in the next round of patients."

He pulled out the radio from his pocket. "The first should arrive in around ten minutes. It could be an hour before they're back."

"Do we stay here?"

Jack gave her a curious stare. "You can't let it go, can you?"

"What?"

He smiled and shook his head. "Don't pretend with me. You're itching to find out about the close contacts of the meningitis, aren't you?"

He handed her the radio. "Here. Call in. Check on Aaron and Zane and see if anyone has recorded seeing any more of the close contacts."

Amber took the radio gratefully. She wanted to find out how many people were still out there without any medicines. She talked into the radio as she walked back toward the entrance point where Chrissie was based. It only took a few minutes to find out that Chrissie had managed to find the group of boys who had come from the surf school. They'd thought there were six, but it turned out to be seven. One of the boys who was supposed to go someplace else had been delayed by the weather and ended up here. Amber signaled to Lana, and she came and helped her talk to the teenagers and distribute the antibiotics.

Jack appeared at her side. "Ambulance is here. We're loading the first patients. How are Zane and Aaron?"

She gave her head the briefest shake. "Good, and not so good. Aaron has picked up. He's started to respond and come round. Zane is still the same. No change. His BP and temp are in normal limits but he's just not woken up yet."

"Has there been disease progression? Septicemia?"

"Thankfully no. But this whole strain worries me. I'd be much happier if I could find the rest of the close contacts."

Jack seemed to stare ahead for a few seconds. Then the edges of his lips seemed to hint upward. "I was going to ask if you wanted to head back to the hospital with the patients, or if you wanted to stay here and treat any more casualties that come in."

She could hear the slight edge in his voice. He was teasing her. Just a little. "Or...?"

He drew himself up and pushed his shoulders back. It was that second—that second that she saw the man who had served in the army and done two tours of duty. The man who had saved lives and had to juggle priorities in a way she probably never would.

He met her gaze with his dark brown eyes. "Or we could volunteer to stay out here. To help at the bus, or elsewhere, and see if we can drop any more of the antibiotics off."

Her heart gave a little leap. He got her. He understood her. She smiled and folded her arms across her chest. "I think I'll take option three."

CHAPTER FIVE

IT WAS DARK. More than dark—with the power cuts throughout the city it was virtually a blackout. It seemed that only sporadic places had power, so parts of the city glowed like little bulbs on a Christmas tree. Total wrong time of year.

It made Jack catch his breath. Dave, their driver, had helped take people back to the hospital and they'd coordinated with Ron in ER and managed to visit a few of the addresses in the surrounding area where close contacts resided, along with a few other addresses where they'd been asked to check on vulnerable adults.

They decided to go back to the evacuation center and help as best they could. The school kitchens had been opened and manned by a whole host of volunteers. Chrissie pressed some food into their hands and pointed them down a corridor. "We're short of space. But you'll find somewhere down there to sit down for the night."

Amber looked down as her stomach growled loudly. Her hair was pulled back from her face in a haphazard way and there were tired lines around her eyes, but somehow they still had a little sparkle. "Oops. I'd forgotten how hungry I was. It's been a crazy day." She leaned her head against his shoulder.

Jack paused in the corridor; he couldn't help it. "I feel

like we should go back to the hospital in case there are other patients to see."

She lifted her head back up. "Jack. Take a breath. We've been working all day, and if we have to pull a night shift, then we will. But let's just sit down for five minutes."

He took a deep breath. That angsty feeling that had been in his stomach all day was still there. It was constantly there. He'd just learned to live with it. Learned to live with the fact he was always looking over his shoulder, waiting for the unexpected.

Every part of his body wanted to keep living on the adrenaline. To keep going, to find the next person to help. But the truth was, his muscles ached. The aroma coming from the food in his hand was tempting. And the thought of sitting down for five minutes didn't seem quite so alien as it might have. Particularly when he was with Amber.

He nodded. "Okay, then—you win. But five minutes. There's probably still a whole host of people that need help. The damage from the hurricane seems huge."

He followed Amber down the corridor. Every room they reached seemed packed with people, some sitting, some lying on the floor. Amber frowned as they struggled to find somewhere to sit.

Suddenly Jack had a brain wave as they kept walking. He bent toward her ear. "I have an idea. Back this way, I think."

Two minutes later he found what he was looking for. The janitor's storeroom. He nudged the handle with his elbow to open the door. Sure enough, it was empty, even though it was tiny. There was a metal cage packed with supplies. A large chair in one corner and a mop and bucket in the other. Amber turned toward him. "Good call. Now let's sit down."

He thought about being polite for a second, then realized they were past that point, so he let her sit down first, then crushed in next to her.

She laughed as he joined her, giving him a last glimpse of those bright blue eyes as the door slowly closed behind them.

"Oops," giggled Amber as they sat in the pitch darkness. "I guess there's no light in the store cupboard."

"I guess not," agreed Jack. "Looks like we might need to eat in the dark."

"I can do that. I can eat anywhere. I'm so hungry," said Amber.

Within a few minutes their eyes started to adjust to the darkness, the only light being the thin strip at the bottom of the door from the corridor outside.

Amber finished eating and set her paper plate on the floor, sagging back into the chair. Jack finished too and clashed shoulders as he rested back beside her.

"Do you think this is really a chair for one?"

"I don't care." Amber waved her hand. "After the day we've had, I'm happy to share. Hey, do you think we should have gone back to the hotel?"

Jack shook his head. "I was wondering though—we weren't the only doctors at the conference. There were lots of others. I wonder if anyone has thought to draft them in to help."

Amber sighed. "Please tell me that in an emergency situation, some of them will have volunteered like we have. It can't possibly just be us."

She stretched out her arms in front of her, then clasped her hands to stretch out her fingers too.

"Are you stiff? Sore?" It suddenly struck him that

he'd asked Amber to do things today that were totally out of her comfort zone. When was the last time she'd had to support an airway? And she'd done it expertly—just like checking broken bones and assessing a potential head injury.

"I'm just trying to stretch out the sore bits," she confessed. "I thought my hands were going to cramp at one point when I was supporting the airway." She shook her head. "And we definitely didn't need that to happen."

Jack smiled at her. "You did well today, Amber. Better than others that I've worked with in the past."

It took her a few seconds to answer. "Thanks... I think. Truth was, I *was* worried. I thought I might forget everything and have to ask you to remind me. But once I started, everything just kind of fell into place." She let out a sigh. "Maybe the director was right. Maybe I should do more field missions."

"The director?"

"Of the DPA. He's been at me for a while, telling me it's time to do some more field missions."

"I thought you'd already done some."

She nodded slowly. "Oh, I have. But I've always been part of a team. I've always had other medics and nurses around me. I've never actually been the one in charge. I guess I've just been a little afraid."

Now he was curious. He shifted onto one hip so he faced her a little better. "Afraid of what? You're a capable and competent doctor."

Her head dropped and her hands kneaded together in her lap. "Amber?" he pressed.

She let out a long slow breath. "I know I am. I know that I'm capable at what I do. Infectious disease is my comfort zone. I like it—more than that, I enjoy the work. The variety. The locations." Her head lifted and even in the dark he could see her meet his gaze. "But…" Her voice tailed off.

"But what?" He couldn't understand why she would doubt herself.

She leaned her head back against the chair, her eyes staring out in the darkness. "I guess I've spent my life feeling as if I wasn't good enough."

Jack shook his head. "Why on earth would you think that?"

She blinked and he thought he could catch a glimmer of moisture in her eyes. "It was just the life I was brought up with," she said slowly. "My father was obsessed with his work as a surgeon. My mother and I barely saw him. Even when we did, he would spend his time at home, studying journals or taking hospital calls. My mother was basically a widow on the day that she had me. It was never a marriage, and he was never a father."

Jack held his breath at the intensity of her words. He could hear the pain in her voice. The rawness of it all. This obviously ran deep.

He remembered small parts of their original conversation at breakfast. He still couldn't really get his head around it. "Surely, he was proud of the results you got to get into medical school, then the fact you qualified?" He put his hand on his chest. "I don't have kids, and would never want to push them in any direction, but if any of my kids went after their dream and achieved it, I would be over the moon for them. Isn't a parent's job to be proud of their kid?"

Her voice cracked. "Maybe. In an ideal world. Instead, I had a father who never seemed to notice or acknowledge me, or my mother, and now, after he's gone, I feel as if my mom wasted forty years of her life on someone who never loved or appreciated her."

He reached out and took her hand in his. He could tell how upset she was by this. "But she got you. And I bet she's prouder than you can ever imagine. I can't second-guess your parents' relationship, but she probably has a whole host of reasons for why she never left. But now? Now she can pursue whatever she wants, and know that her daughter has her back." He squeezed her hand. "And I'm sorry about your dad. When did he die?"

Amber cleared her throat. "A couple of years ago. It was ironic, really. The surgeon had an aortic aneurysm. He could have been screened at any point, but hadn't found the time."

Jack nodded. He didn't need to ask any questions. As a fellow surgeon, he completely understood how fatal a ruptured aortic aneurysm was.

He couldn't help but try and lighten the mood. "So, runaway bride, are you still dead set against dating doctors?"

It was almost as if something in the air changed between them instantly.

Her voice rose in pitch. "Oh, we're going down that road again, are we?"

"Yeah, well. It seems I've got five minutes on my hands."

"Okay, then. So, I've had a lifetime's experience of an almost vacant father, then a follow-up with the jerk of the century."

Jack gave a little laugh. "Yeah, the guy you left in full tuxedo standing at the end of an aisle."

She gave a smothered laugh too. "Yip. But I did it because he was a butt-licking, using social climber." She turned to face Jack, their faces just a few inches apart. "It seems I have terrible taste in men."

His lips automatically turned upward. He could

smell a hint of her floral scent. It had been there earlier, but after the day they'd had, he would have expected it to vanish. But, as they sat together with their bodies pressed close, he could smell it again. If he reached up right now he could touch her cheek—the way he should have done after he'd met her in the bar. But in a way, it was probably better that he hadn't. At least now he knew why this intriguing, smart, sassy woman wanted to brush him off. And although her exterior was sassy, her interior was entirely different. How many people actually knew that about Amber?

"Hey," she said quietly. "I've spilled a whole lot more than I ever usually do. What're your dark secrets? You've just told me that you've got no kids. Well—none that you know of. But what else don't I know? After all, I have spent the night with you. Will I get messages at some point from a wife, an ex-wife, a girlfriend, and have to reassure them that actually nothing happened between us?"

He sucked in a breath. Even though his eyes had adjusted, they were still in the dark. He could see her profile, her eyes and her eyelashes, all highlighted by the tiny strip of light at the bottom of the door. There was something so private about this—even though they were in an evacuation center with around two thousand other people. They'd found a tiny little spot where they could be alone. And he was grateful for it.

Even though they were in the dark, he closed his eyes. It seemed easier somehow. "I'm single. I've never been married. I don't have an ex-wife."

Even as he said the words out loud, he knew how they sounded. As if he were telling part of a story but not it all.

"But…"

He sucked in another breath. "But then there was Jill."

Amber's voice was a little more high-pitched than normal. "Jill? Who is Jill?"

"Jill was my girlfriend. For just over a year." He let out a wry laugh. "Though she didn't like to be called that. She preferred The Boss."

Amber's voice was wary. It seemed she'd picked up on the fact he was using past tense. "Sounds like someone I would like."

The words struck a chord with him. Jill would have liked Amber. He could imagine them as friends. Jill would certainly have put Amber straight about her choice in men—him included.

"She was good. She was…great." This time it was more difficult to suck in a deep breath. He never really discussed Jill. Not with those who'd served with her, nor with her family after the funeral. It just made everything too real. Too human.

"I was sick. I was operating on a soldier who'd lost his lower limb. It was a tricky op—long—and I started to have abdominal pain. I just ignored it and kept going. By the time I finished I collapsed. My appendix had ruptured."

"What? For crying out loud, Jack, how much pain must you have been in? Wasn't there anyone who could take over from you?"

He winced. "Probably. But the guy on the table was a friend. And he'd already lost so much. I knew how he would feel when he woke up. I also knew that he'd want to get back on his feet. I had to do the best surgery I could to give him a chance of a prosthetic limb. I didn't want him to have to spend the next eighteen months needing revision after revision, when I could take the time to try and get things as good as they could be."

Amber nodded slowly as if she understood. "So what happened next?"

Jack squeezed his eyes closed again. "When I was in surgery...there was a retrieval—when something's gone wrong in the field they sometimes send out a medical team to bring back the injured. It can be the difference between life and death." They were still holding hands, but this time her other hand closed over his, holding it tight, supporting him to continue. "I was always the person that went. Except this time—this time I was in the operating theater on the table. So Jill went. She was an army-trained medic and she was good. As good as any doctor. But they never made it. Their vehicle hit an IED."

Amber didn't hesitate for a second. She pulled her hands away from his and wrapped her arms around his neck, enveloping him in a bear hug and pressing her face next to his. Her breath warmed the skin at the bottom of his neck. "Oh, Jack. I am so, so sorry. That's cruel. I can't even begin to imagine how that feels."

He stayed there. He let her hug him. He let her hug him in a way he'd never really let anyone hug him since it happened. He'd had a few awkward hugs at the funeral from Jill's mom, dad and sister. But he'd only met them on a few occasions briefly. He didn't really know them the way that he'd known Jill.

So it just hadn't felt right. Not when he was so busy building a shell around himself. One that wouldn't let him feel. One that would let him channel all his emotions and energies someplace else.

The sensation gripped him so much it was almost a physical pain. Amber just kept holding him. She didn't let go. And after what seemed like forever, the tension in all his muscles that he permanently held tight finally started to dissipate. He was so conscious of her cheek against his. She didn't seem to mind the fact his bristles must be scraping her skin.

He could feel the heat emanate from her body, and after the fierce winds of the hurricane it was like a warm comfort blanket. Only trouble was, the reaction his body was having was nothing like a warm blanket. It was more like a spontaneous firework.

And his head was trying to work out what was going on around him.

It had happened again. He'd actually *felt* something.

It had happened on the bleachers, when Amber had lifted her head and just stared at him. The connection had been like a punch to the stomach. The way she'd held his gaze, even though they'd been in the middle of something major, and just looked at him. Unflinchingly. As if she'd seen more than was actually there, and buried deep down to find the rest.

He hadn't really wanted to believe it then. He'd been holding his hands against a man's side, trying to stop him bleeding to death. For the last two years his mind had never been anywhere but on the job.

But for the briefest few seconds those big blue eyes had connected with something, tugged at something inside him, in a way he hadn't expected.

Or had he? The last few days had been crazy. He'd been attracted to her as soon as he'd seen her sashaying across the room and slaying potential suitors with a mere look. From her casual, unhindered and sparkly chat in the bar, to her professional, passionate, presenting face she'd shown at the conference. To her dismissal of him at breakfast when she'd found out he was a doctor, to the moment that he'd stepped forward and pressed his head against hers because it had just felt as if she'd needed it.

In every subtle way, he'd found himself drawn to this improbable woman. Someone who, it turned out, had just as many layers as he had.

He didn't even know where to start anymore.

But his body seemed to.

He lifted his hand to her face and touched the side of it gently, pulling back from their hug just enough to give him room to maneuver.

He should ask permission. Because his brain was so muddled he clearly wasn't thinking straight. So he just kept his hand on her soft cheek, tilted her head up toward his and put his lips on hers.

He was hesitant. But Amber wasn't. As soon as he brushed against her lips she ran her fingers through his hair at the back of his head, urging him closer, and her mouth opened to his. What started as tentative and questioning progressed quickly. Amber Berkeley knew how she wanted to be kissed. His hands tangled through her hair, tugging it from the ponytail band. His kisses moved from her lips to her ear and neck, but she was too impatient for that, pulling him to her mouth. She changed position, straddling him on the chair so she was on his lap, letting his hands run up and down the curves of her waist. Her hands moved from his neck to his chest, resting there while they continued to kiss.

There was a noise outside. A shout that permeated the dark world of the storeroom they'd claimed as their own. They both froze and pulled apart, listening to see if the shout would return.

This time it was Amber who pressed her forehead against his. She let out a light laugh. Her breath warmed his skin as she whispered, "Just so you know, I don't date doctors."

He laughed. "Just so you know, I don't kiss on the first date."

She tapped his chest. "This isn't the first date. This is about the third. And anyway, it doesn't matter because—"

"I don't date doctors." He said it simultaneously with her. "Well, that's a relief."

Amber climbed off him as another shout came from outside. "Think we should see what's happening?"

He nodded as he picked their food containers from the floor. "Let's face it. Someone's going to need something from the store cupboard eventually."

He thought for a second she was going to say something else as her hand paused on the door handle, but her head gave the tiniest shake and she pulled it open toward them.

There were more people in the corridor outside, but if anyone wondered what they were doing in the store cupboard, no one mentioned it. Jack walked over to the main entranceway. A number of firefighters and police were gathered there, comparing maps and discussing next steps.

"Give me two minutes," said Amber. "Lana's just given me a wave to check someone over." He nodded as she disappeared.

"Anything I can help with?" Jack asked as he approached the main desk.

"Oh, there you are." Jamal walked up behind them and handed over the radio. "Ron was wanting to talk to you."

Jack turned the dial on the radio and put it to his ear, checking in with Ron. "Where do you need us?"

One of the firefighters turned around as he heard the

instructions Jack was given. He waited until Ron was finished then gestured Jack over toward the main table.

"We're getting short of drivers. We can give you a vehicle. But at this point you'll be on your own." He pointed to part of the map. "There's been some flooding around the coastal areas. We're more inland here, but we think there has been around twelve inches of rainfall during the hurricane—and the rain hasn't stopped yet. There's still a chance of flooding from swollen rivers and rain coming off the hills."

The firefighter looked at Jack a little warily. "It might be better to wait until daylight."

"Wait until daylight for what?" asked Amber as she walked back up.

Jack turned to face her. He knew exactly how the words he was about to say would affect her.

"To be part of the search party for Aaron's parents. They've never arrived and are now presumed missing. It's time to go look for them."

CHAPTER SIX

ONE MINUTE SHE was kissing a man she shouldn't; next minute her heart was plummeting into her shoes.

"They haven't appeared?"

Jack shook his head. "Someone has reported a car off the road. It was an ambulance who were resuscitating another patient, so they couldn't stop. But they glimpsed a black car in the trees just outside the city. It's the road they would be expected to be on if they were traveling between Hilo and Kailua Kona."

She gulped. "Then we have to go. We have to go and see if it's them. Even if it isn't them, someone could be hurt." She looked around, trying to remember where she'd left her pack.

"Give me a minute." His voice was authoritative. It was the kind of thing she'd expected earlier from Jack. He walked back over to the table and started talking to one of the firefighters while she scrabbled around locating her jacket and pack. "Lana? Are you coming?"

Lana shook her head. "Can't. Sorry. I've got a sick kid that I'll need to transfer with to the hospital. She's asthmatic and is having problems."

"Anything I can help with?"

Lana shook her head. "I can cope. I should be gone in the next five minutes. But, hey," she said, "I've got another one from your list." She pointed to a name. "This family are here. The younger kids are nephews of Zane and had contact in the last few days. I've given them the antibiotics that they should need."

"Thank you." Amber gave her a relieved hug but Lana wasn't finished.

"Here." She bent down and pulled something from Amber's pack. "I think you should keep this handy. On a night like this, you'll need it."

Amber stared down at the heavy flashlight in her hand. Of course. Exactly what she'd need on a dark roadside. Her heart was starting to beat a bit erratically and she was starting to regret eating that food as her stomach churned.

Jack appeared at her elbow with a different dark jacket in his hand. He was already wearing one with his luminous "DOCTOR" tabards over the top. "Here, one of the firefighters gave me this for you. Apparently the rain is still really heavy and they think we might need it."

She automatically pulled her tabard over her head, shrugged off her own thin jacket and pulled on the thicker, sturdier one with a large hood. "Should I be worried that they've given us this?"

"Let's hope not," replied Jack quickly.

She'd seen him. She'd seen him at his most exposed. She'd held him. She'd kissed him after he'd told her things that could break her heart.

But right now it was almost as if that had never happened. It was almost as if he'd pulled a mask—an invisible shield—into place. Something she'd never been able to do. Everything now seemed so precise. So clinical.

"Where's Dave?" she asked as she slung her backpack over her shoulder.

"We have to drive ourselves. There are too many reports right now to deal with. One of the firefighters has given me directions. The roads were apparently passable a few hours ago. Let's hope they're still the same."

"They've been out there for a few hours?"

Jack held up his hands. "Truth is, I don't know when it was called in. All I know is we've been asked if we can go." He held up the radio. "If we need assistance we let them know. They don't have any spare people to come with us."

Amber shivered. She hated this. Everything about it made her fear the worst. But she tilted her chin and looked Jack in the eye. "Then let's go."

The road leading away from the high school started out relatively debris free. But as they started to wind further out, tree branches and bushes were scattered all around them. Jack drove slowly, taking care around corners. The wind was still strong, buffeting them from side to side, but they only passed one other emergency vehicle on the road. It seemed that everyone else had listened to the instructions to stay inside until they got word it was safe to go back out.

The rain was relentless and Amber was glad of the change of jacket. "I'm going to slow down a bit," Jack said to her. "You watch one side of the road and I'll watch the other. Hopefully we'll come across the car soon."

It was still black outside. They left the city behind and moved out more toward the mountains and green landscape. The few glimmers of light were left far behind them. It was hard trying to scan the dark landscape as they traveled forward. Trees and bushes lined the road. And on a few occasions they stopped at a felled tree, mistaking its dark outline for something else. But eventually their headlights swept over the familiar outline of the back of a car, protruding slightly at the side of the road.

"There!" shouted Amber, her heart rate quickening instantly.

Jack slammed on the brakes and they both jumped out, leaving the engine running and lights facing the foliage.

Amber's heart raced madly as she waded through the foliage on one side, as Jack strode through on the other side.

There were definitely two people in the car. There was condensation on the inside of the windows. The front end of the car had impacted on a large tree trunk and had completely crumpled. She could see where the airbags inside had deployed then gradually deflated again.

Jack yanked the door open on his side. Amber pulled at the door on her side. It had a large dent in it and wouldn't open. The ground was muddy beneath her feet and she struggled to stay upright as she put one foot on the back passenger door and pulled again at the handle of the driver's door. It finally gave and she landed in a heap in a bunch of wet leaves.

A groan came from the car and it made her heart leap. Noise was good. Noise meant that people were alive. She scrambled to her feet and leaned inside the car. Jack was checking the pulse of the woman in the passenger seat. Amber did the same with the man on her side, wrinkling her nose a little. The smell inside the car was a little unpleasant. How long had they been trapped?

Something clicked into place in her head. Top-to-toe survey. The way any doctor was supposed to assess an unknown patient. She started speaking. "Hi there.

I'm Amber. I'm a doctor. I'm just going to take a look at you."

The man under her hands gave another groan and his eyelids flickered open. She smiled at him. "Are you Aaron's parents?"

She could see the instant panic on his face. "How is he?" The words were weak and hoarse.

"He's holding steady," she replied. "I'm just glad we've found the right people." Her hands checked his arms, shoulders and chest. There was no apparent head injury, but his lower legs were pinned in place by the crumpled dashboard.

Jack had his head down low, speaking to the woman. He gently touched her arm and gave her a little shake. "Hi there. Can you hear me? I'm Jack, a doctor. How are you doing?"

His eyes met Amber's and he mouthed the words. "Color is poor."

He bent to the crumpled foot well and pulled out a purse, rifling through it until he found what he was looking for. "Bess. Bess, it's Jack. Can you open your eyes for me?" He'd pulled out a stethoscope and blood-pressure monitor from his bag and Amber did the same. She didn't want to move Aaron's dad's position in the seat, so she just had to wrap the cuff around his covered arm to try and get some kind of reading. She followed Jack's example and put her hand inside his jacket pocket, pulling out his wallet and checking for his forename. "Maleko... Maleko, can you open your eyes for me again?"

The man grunted and opened his eyes. "Can you tell me where you're hurting? Any pain around your neck or shoulders?"

He shook his head slightly, then groaned loudly and pointed to his legs. She glanced up at Jack. "It's difficult to see because of the collapsed foot well." She pulled on a pair of gloves and gently felt with her hands. When she brought her hand back out it was covered in blood.

"I think we might need some help getting him out of here. Looks like a fractured tib and fib. I'll give him something for the pain. What about you?"

Jack's brow was creased. "I could really do with some oxygen. I'm thinking she's got some kind of chest injury, either from the seat belt or from the airbag. Probably a punctured lung." His gaze met hers. "Can you give me a minute until I radio in and try and get some support from Fire and Rescue? We're going to need help getting them out of the car."

Amber nodded and edged further into the car so she could keep an eye on both of the patients. Maybe opening the doors hadn't been such a good idea. The heavy rain was driving hard against her back. She reached over and touched Bess's face. "Hold on, Bess. Aaron's waiting for you. I know he'll be so happy to hear both of your voices."

Her stomach twisted and coiled. She couldn't go through this again. She couldn't be the person who had to tell a family that their relatives had been lost in a desperate attempt to reach their child on time—particularly when she still didn't know what the outcome for Aaron would be. It was all just too much.

The hurricane. The fear. The worry about whether she was good enough. The injuries well outside her area of expertise. And Jack. The first man she'd kissed in forever. A doctor. He should have a red flashing warning light above his head to tell her to stay away. But she'd kissed him anyway. What was she thinking?

She reached into her bag to find some pain relief for Maleko, and to try and squeeze some wound pads in next to him to stem the slow flow of blood. If she knew he didn't have a spinal injury, she could help remove his jacket and get a true blood-pressure reading. But she didn't have that guarantee right now. She didn't have a cervical collar or a spinal board, let alone any cutting equipment to release his legs from the cramped space they were trapped in.

Jack was still busy on the radio. He hadn't climbed back into the vehicle and she could see the rain drenching him as he stood in front of the headlights. She sucked in a breath. From his gestures, she could tell he was annoyed. He didn't like not being in charge. He didn't like not having complete control. She could sense all these things even from here. The resolute single-mindedness and obsession with the job were written all over his face.

It was so reminiscent of her father that it almost felt like a punch to the stomach.

She closed her eyes for the briefest of seconds. She was soaked now too. The rain was running down her face and cheeks, hiding the tears that were sneaking out alongside. She'd kissed this man. For a brief second she'd felt connected to this man—even though every part of her being told her to run in the other direction.

He'd told her about his girlfriend. He'd had his heart broken. Chewed up and destroyed by a set of circumstances that he'd had no control over. That on any other day might never have happened.

How did a guy who at heart was a control freak get over that?

How many nights had he spent awake asking the what-if questions?

She ducked her head back inside the car and re-checked Maleko's obs. "We're trying to get some more help. Hopefully you'll be a bit more comfortable until we can get you out of here."

She frowned as she looked at Bess's complexion once more. Were her lips slightly more blue? She pulled out her flashlight. The headlights from the other car just weren't strong enough and she needed to see a little better.

Darn it. Bess looked terrible. She clambered through the muddy ground around the car, her rubber boots almost being pulled from her feet. Jack was still arguing with someone on the radio.

She pulled out her stethoscope and slid it under Bess's jumper. Definite decreased breath sounds on the right-hand side. It was likely that she'd broken one or more ribs. There was a good chance one had pierced her lung and caused it to collapse. Trouble was, she had no idea of Bess's medical history. She knelt down and watched for a few seconds. All of Bess's accessory muscles were trying to pull air into her body. While a collapsed lung would always cause problems, most people would still be able to get enough air through their other lung. Could Bess be asthmatic? Where had Jack put that purse?

She rummaged around the floor again and emptied the contents of the bag out onto the ground next to her, shining down with her flashlight to get a better view.

"What on earth are you doing?" came the angry voice.

"Quiet, Jack." A wallet, lipstick, credit cards, pens, a phone with a cracked screen and about ten missed calls, a strip of paracetamol, another blister pack of blood-pressure meds and, yes, an inhaler.

She picked it up and checked it, then gave it a shake. Jack sounded annoyed now. "Can you let me back in?"

It was clear he wasn't really paying attention to what she was doing—partly because the car door was blocking his view. She flipped the cap off the inhaler. "Bess, I'm going to give you a few puffs of your inhaler. I know you can't really breathe in properly, so just try and get as much as you can."

Bess was aware enough to form her lips around the inhaler as Amber administered the medication.

Jack obviously lost patience and nudged her with his shoulder as he tried to see what she was doing. But Amber wasn't having any of it.

She rooted her feet to the sticky ground and held firm. "That's right, Bess. You're doing great. Let's see if your breathing eases a little while we wait for some help."

She shot Jack a dirty look as she straightened up and pulled her head out of the car. "Back off, Jack. I'm just as capable a doctor as you. You can't be in charge of everything."

Even as she said the words, she felt an instant pang of regret. The flash of pain across his face—her recognition of what he'd revealed earlier. She understood the theory of why he had an inbuilt feeling of wanting to be in control. She just couldn't live with it.

They were incompatible in every which way.

Even though she wanted to reach up and brush some of the rain from his face right now. Even though as she looked at his lips all she could remember was that kiss.

She'd gathered confidence in the last few hours that she wouldn't let anyone take away from her—not even Jack Campbell.

An hour later Ron looked at them both as they climbed out of the back of the fire truck. The ER was swarming with people. Some clearly patients, others with a whole variety of colored tabards on. It almost made her head ache as much as her body currently did.

"Oh, my missing docs." Ron looked over as the patients were unloaded. He seemed much more comfortable now he could focus only on his ER. "What have we got?"

Amber spoke first. "This is Bess and Maleko. They were on their way from Hilo and were involved in a car accident." Ron opened his mouth to interject but Amber kept talking. "Their son Aaron is one of the teenagers with meningitis."

"Ah..." Ron's eyebrows rose.

"Maleko has fractured his left tib and fib and had to be cut out of the car. He's had ten of morphine at the scene around an hour ago. Bess is asthmatic and looks like she has a right-sided pneumothorax. Her color has only improved since she had some Ventolin, but she's been struggling with her breathing since we found them."

She was conscious of Jack standing behind her. She could almost feel him itching to talk but she was determined to do the handover properly.

Ron didn't seem to notice any issue. He just turned and issued instructions. "Him, Cubicle Three, and her, Resus Room Four. Get me a portable chest X-ray and a chest tube tray. Find me a surgeon for Cubicle Three."

He turned to face them again. "Quick question. They're expecting to have some emergency flights available tomorrow for any tourists that want to leave. I can't tell you what to do. But the next week or so will be mad. We'll move into disaster relief and emergency services mode. I still need doctors. Any kind of doctors. All kinds of doctors. And don't expect to be paid. So, do have someplace you need to be in the next few days, or can you stay?"

"I'll stay."

"I'll stay."

There was no hesitation. Their voices sounded in perfect unison. And Amber turned on her heel and locked gazes with Jack.

Both of them looked in surprise at the other.

Her heart gave a couple of flips. What had possessed her? But as she looked around the crowded ER, she knew exactly why she'd agreed.

This wasn't about her. This wasn't about Jack.

But that still didn't explain the fact she was secretly glad he'd also said yes.

CHAPTER SEVEN

BY THE TIME they reached the apartment that had been designated to emergency rescue workers, both of them were ready to collapse with exhaustion. Another emergency worker glanced at them as he was about to leave. He threw them a set of keys. "Your room is the one at the back. I hope you brought some extra scrubs. We've no spare clothes."

He disappeared out of the door and they were left staring at each other. Jack shrugged. "Your room" made it sound like one room. Amber walked down the dark corridor and pushed open the door. Sure enough, there was one—not particularly big—double bed.

"I'll sleep on the floor," said Jack quickly. He didn't want to make her uncomfortable—even though they'd kissed. It was clear Amber still had issues with him.

Amber shook her head. The moon was the only light in the room at present. "Don't be silly, Jack. I'm tired. You're tired."

She gave a half shrug. "After all, we've managed to share a bed before." She held out her hands. "We could be here for the next few days. Let's not make things difficult."

He glanced around. "It's a pretty small space." He knew exactly what she was saying. They hadn't had an official fight, but things just seemed uneasy between them.

She nodded. "It is. So let's make the best of it."

He gave a resigned nod as he stripped off his jacket. "Fine by me."

He tried to keep his face neutral. Last time he'd shared a bed with Amber, he'd barely known her, but had been acting on the flirting and glimmer of attraction between them. She hadn't known his hang-ups and he hadn't known hers. This was different. This was another step. They'd already kissed. In among this disaster there was something in the air between them. Something he hadn't quite managed to get his head around yet. He knew he acted like a control freak sometimes. He knew that Amber had her No Doctor rule in her head. But where did that really leave them?

"Fine by me." Amber's words echoed his as she sat down at the edge of the bed and took off her boots.

Jack smiled at the back of her head. They'd reached an uneasy truce, and somehow he knew he wouldn't sleep a wink.

She was sharing a room with Jack Campbell. In the midst of chaos someone had obviously decided they were together and given them a temporary room in an apartment—the hotel was literally under siege as it now had to accommodate people who had lost their homes. So it had seemed churlish to object.

Lack of power was still the main issue. The power companies were working hard to safely restore power to the island. But they were stretched beyond capacity. And safety was more important than being able to turn on your lights at night.

But it meant that nights could be long.

They'd reached an easy compromise. They worked wherever the disaster relief coordinator sent them. Her little outburst and subsequent bristliness couldn't be helped. The work was constant and exhausting. She'd managed to track down all of the close contacts for meningitis and ensure they had antibiotics. Aaron now seemed to be on the slow road to recovery. Zane's progress was picking up. For a short while there had been a question over septicemia and how it was affecting his hands and feet. But the blood flow had improved and the toxins seemed to be leaving his system.

Amber was still concerned that in among the chaos there could be more cases that might be overlooked. There were so many voluntary agencies now that coordination of information seemed nigh on impossible.

Her director at the DPA had supported her decision to stay for the next week and told her that he trusted her. That meant a lot.

"Amber, do you know if we have any food in this place?"

It had been four days since the hurricane. By the time they got back to the apartment at night they were too tired to even talk. Most of the local businesses were waiting for insurance assessments before opening again, and there was only one tiny corner shop that had managed to open its doors.

Jack was staring at a box of cornflakes they'd eaten for the last two days straight. It was empty.

"I think we had soup." She walked across the kitchen and opened a cupboard. Empty. There were four other emergency service workers sharing the apartment— any one of them could have eaten it. "Maybe not." She shrugged as she closed the door. Her stomach grumbled loudly.

She put her hands on the counter and stretched out her sore back. "I guess the only place we can go is back to the hospital, or to one of the evacuation centers. At least we know the school kitchens are open."

Jack pulled a face. "Is it wrong if I say I can't stand the noise?" He rubbed his eyes. "I've spent most of the day surrounded by bedlam. I'd kind of like five minutes of quiet."

She paused for a second as Jack's stomach grumbled loudly then burst out laughing. "Well, there's no food at the inn. So, we have to go somewhere. Hospital or school?"

He sighed. "Okay, then." He grabbed the keys for the emergency vehicle they were still using. "Let's go to the school."

Ten minutes later they reached the high school that was still doubling as an evacuation center. Although all people who were evacuated when there was a hurricane had been told to bring enough food with them for seven days, the logistics of trying to store and manage that amount of food was more difficult than anyone had previously predicted.

After two days, the high-school kitchens had been opened with volunteers and aid agencies cooking in shifts. Further emergency supplies of food and bottled water had been shipped in so that no one was left hungry or thirsty.

Jack was right. It was beyond noisy. A constant clamor of people all trying to be heard above one another. Amber noticed a little family holed up in a corner, a dark-eyed woman trying to get two small children to sleep on a mat and blankets on the floor. "What must it be like in here at night? Do you think all these people have damaged houses?"

Jack seemed to follow her gaze. "Maybe. One area had some flash flooding too. I was down helping earlier today. Some of the houses were virtually washed away."

She frowned. She'd spent part of the day in ER, part with Aaron and Zane, and part in a temporary clinic. It was hard to keep track of everything. "What were you doing there?"

"It's a bit further away and some of the people were desperately trying to salvage what they could from their homes. Lots of dirty water, some of it waist-high."

Amber nodded. "Dirty water, dirty wounds. High chance of infections."

"Exactly."

They joined the line for food at the kitchen. Jack picked up a couple of bottles of water for them both. "How much longer will you stay?"

She shook her head. "I don't know. The director was happy for me to stay for a week in the first instance. But I don't know how much leeway I'll get after that. What about you?"

"I'm officially on leave. Holidays. Then I need to look for another job. So I can stay as long as I'm needed."

She pressed her lips together and nodded. "I heard Ron asking you earlier about surgeries. Are you going to help out?"

He nodded. "Probably starting tomorrow. There are lots of bone injuries and I got loads of orthopedic experience in Afghanistan. One of the hospital surgeons was injured himself, and another's had an MI. So, they're kind of desperate."

They reached the front of the line and took the plates offered to them. Amber lifted the plate to her nose and inhaled. "It's some kind of curry. It smells great."

All the seats were taken, so they walked back through

the foyer and outside. For the first time in days the rain had finally stopped. The sky was dark again but now they could see a smattering of stars glistening above.

Amber looked from side to side. Disaster still echoed around them. Remnants of the roof were still lying on the football field. A few broken windows in the school were boarded up. But the wind that had whipped around them for days had eventually died down and the night seemed almost peaceful, even if the place around them wasn't.

They walked over and sat on one of the stone walls near the front of the school. The car park behind them was littered with emergency vehicles and cars.

They ate in silence for a few minutes. "When do you think this will ever get back to normal? I can't believe that the beautiful place we landed in a few days ago has changed so much."

Jack stopped eating and put down his plastic fork. "I didn't even really get a chance to appreciate the beauty due to the jet lag. My eyes were closed the whole way from the airport. Seems like such a waste now."

Amber sighed. "I heard in the hospital today that a hotel on one of the other islands collapsed. We're lucky that didn't happen here." She held up one hand. "But look now. The rain and wind have gone. If we were lying on the grass right now looking up at the sky, we might think that nothing had ever happened."

There was a loud clatter and some raised voices behind them. Jack smiled and glanced over his shoulder. "Yeah, and then you hear the noise."

Amber nodded in agreement. "Yeah, the noise. Or how different it is."

"What do you mean?"

She smiled. "I mean, no mobile phones. Limited electricity. No TV. No Internet. No music."

Jack groaned. "And no real water."

Four days on there were still no mobile masts and it didn't look as if they could be replaced anytime soon. None of the regular utilities were working properly and the apartment they were staying in only had water switched on for two hours a day. It meant limited showering and limited toilet facilities.

"I can't wait to get back to a hotel at some point and just stand in the shower for an hour."

Jack laughed. "I don't see that happening in the next few days. I'm not sure we'll even get back to the hotel. Did you leave anything important there?"

Amber couldn't help but pull a face. "Just business suits, other clothes and my laptop. Nothing that can't be replaced. There's only one thing I'm keen to get back and it's a locket my mom gave me for my twenty-first birthday. I'd left it in the safe." She turned to face him on the wall. "What about you?"

He blinked for a second and breathed out slowly. "Like you, clothes, a laptop."

"And?" She knew. She just knew there was something else.

He stared up into the sky for a few moments. "It's nothing that I couldn't replace. It's just…"

"Just what?"

He looked back down and stared at the plate still in his hands. "A photo. A photo of Jill from years ago. She's sitting in the camp in her army fatigues, laughing at something someone said. We had quite a lot of photos together. You know, it's a modern world. Everyone has a phone constantly. But after…the photo that made me catch my breath was this one. We're not in it together. I have no idea what we were doing at the time. Probably just taking a five-minute break between scrubbing for

Theater. But it's her. It captured her essence, the person who she was."

Amber bit her lip. Her heart ached for him. The grief seemed raw. Was that wrong two years on?

But before she had a chance to say anything, Jack continued. "I know it's stupid. It's just a photo. I don't carry it in my wallet. It's in my suitcase." He let out a wry laugh. "Jill would call me an idiot. But, sometimes, when I get carried away with things, it helps to remind me why I do this."

"You do this for her?"

He leaned forward and put his plate on the ground, then rested his head in his hands. "I do this for them all." He turned his head toward her and looked sideways through wounded eyes. "The wound dressing—the science behind it. It was all so much easier than realizing I'd lost Jill." His voice broke and he sat up and held out his hands. "I don't even know what would have happened. We might have stayed together. We may have grown apart. The one thing I am sure of is that we would always have been friends."

Her heart twisted inside her chest. She'd never felt a pull to someone like that she felt toward Jack Campbell. It didn't matter that it was all wrong. It didn't matter what her brain told her. What made her heart twist was the fact she was sitting with him and he was talking about another woman. One who'd obviously meant a lot to him.

"Friends is good," she said, trying to keep any emotion from her voice.

Jack kept his brown gaze fixed on her. "Is it?"

Her skin prickled. "What do you mean?"

"Are we friends?"

She shifted on the wall. "Well, I'm not sure…" Her

brain couldn't think straight. Was that the word she would use for the guy she'd met barely a few days before, shared a bed with, kissed and quarreled with? "Are we?"

Jack was leaning forward, his elbows resting on his knees, his gaze unwavering from hers. When he spoke his voice was hoarse. "What if, for the first time in a long time, I've looked at someone and wanted to be more than friends?"

The words swept over her skin. Half warming, half making every tiny hair on her body stand on end. Was that even possible?

Her hands automatically crossed her body and started running up and down her arms. "But I don't date doctors." It was like her default answer. She'd been saying it for so long that her brain found it easiest to resort to the familiar.

"I know. But you kiss them."

Her mouth opened. She hadn't quite expected him to be so direct. "You kissed me."

"You kissed me back." He straightened. There was a glint in his eye that seemed to be highlighted by the stars above them.

The world around them was a wreck. They were both wrecks.

But underneath them and underneath the land around them was a beauty that was hinting to get back out—to get back to the surface and let itself be revealed.

He drew in a deep breath. She tried so hard not to let her eyes fall to his broad shoulders and chest. To drink in the stubble on his jaw, and the way the expression in his eyes was so deep it just seemed to pull her in, like some kind of leash.

"I don't know what this is." The edges of his lips curled upward. "I know that our timing sucks. I know

you think you shouldn't date a work-obsessed doctor."
He put his hand on his chest. "I know that I've spent the
last two years virtually avoiding all contact with anyone
of the opposite sex. Some might call me work-obsessed."
He ran one hand through his hair. "But it's so much easier
to focus on work. To let it take over. To let it consume
all your thoughts."

She frowned. "I'm not sure you're doing a good job
of convincing me that we should be friends."

He nodded and stood up, stepping in front of her and
gently taking her by the elbows so she was facing him.
They were only a few inches apart.

"How about if I tell you that I'm confused? How about
if I tell you that my judgment may be skewed by hurricanes, lack of sleep, lack of food, forced proximity and
a hypnotic smell of rose and orange that seems to follow me around?"

Her scent. He was talking about her perfume. She
couldn't help but smile. "I'm still not sure about the
friends thing. I have standards, you know."

"What kind of standards?"

"You know, they have to like the same books, the
same movies and, most importantly, the same chocolate."

"Ah." He raised his eyebrows. "These could be impossibly high standards. I could be suspicious that you're
trying to stack the odds against me because I'm a doctor."

She smiled and shook her head. "Quit stalling for
time."

He lifted his hands and rested them gently on the
tops of her arms. "The answers would have to be crime,
sci-fi and…a kind of chocolate that is only available in
Scotland. I'm very loyal."

She wrinkled her brow and gave her head a shake. "Oh, no, we're not a good match for friends at all. It has to be romance, action movies and old-fashioned American chocolate bars every single time."

He smiled and leaned a little closer. "I have another way we can check our compatibility level."

"You do?" Now she could smell him. A mixture of earthy tones and soap.

His eyes were serious but he was still smiling. And she couldn't help but smile too. She slid her hands up his chest as he leaned in toward her, and she tilted her chin up toward him. This time there was no dark store closet.

This time there was a background of noise, and a smattering of stars in the sky. Last time around things had been more tentative. This time, Jack didn't hesitate. His lips were on hers straightaway. His fingers tangling through her loose hair, tugging her even closer to him.

She breathed in, pushing all the confusing thoughts from her head. She knew exactly where she was. She knew exactly what she was doing.

It didn't make a bit of sense to her. But she'd spent the last few days with this man at her side. And even though they weren't together, even though they weren't a couple and even though he carried a photo of someone else in his suitcase, she still didn't want to step from his arms.

His kisses were sure, pulling her in and making her want more. His body was pressed against hers; all she could feel were the strong muscular planes next to her curves. It wasn't often that she met a man who wasn't intimidated by her height. In general she could look most men square in the eyes. On a few occasions, heels had been a complete no-no on a date. But with Jack she had to tip her head upward to meet his lips. Her eyes barely came to his shoulders.

As he kissed her, his hands slid from her hair to her waist. If she were anywhere else she might be tempted to wrap her legs around him, but somehow, in the middle of a disaster, and in front of a school, it just didn't seem appropriate.

She actually laughed and took a step back.

"What? What is it?" Jack glanced around as if he'd missed something.

She shook her head and held out her hands. "We're in front of a school that's currently an evacuation center for around two thousand people. And...I'm still trying to decide if we are friends or not." She was smiling as she said the words. Parts of her brain were screaming, but other parts of her were warm.

Jack sounded ready to move on. It seemed as though he'd looked inside and realized he'd spent too long blocking out the world and just focusing on work. Maybe now he would take a breather and decide what he wanted to do next.

That could be anywhere, with anyone. But that flicker of something she'd felt that first night in the bar was igniting wildly.

So when he held out his hand toward her she didn't hesitate to take it.

CHAPTER EIGHT

HE'D KISSED HER. He'd kissed her again and again even though his brain couldn't seem to formulate any clear thoughts.

Then they'd gone back to the apartment and kissed some more.

They'd fallen asleep with their arms wrapped around each other just as they had the first night. Except Jack hadn't slept much.

He'd been too busy caught between staring at the woman in the bed next to him and looking out of the window at the bright stars above.

He felt…different. He'd spent so long focused on work and shielding his heart from any hurt that he'd never even thought about connecting with someone again.

And this had just crept up on him. Out of nowhere, really. One minute he was jet-lagged at a bar; next he was focused on the woman with the pink-tipped hair striding across the ballroom. And everything after that he just couldn't really work out.

This was a woman who had told him straight-out she wasn't interested. She didn't date doctors, ever. But the sparks that had flown at the first meeting had never died. No matter what she said.

She was a good doctor. Conscientious. Caring. Even when completely out of her depth. No wonder she was doing so well at the DPA. They were lucky to have her.

His stomach gave a few flip-flops as he thought about what came next. He hadn't been able to access emails for days. He'd been having a few tentative exchanges about job possibilities. He'd need to make a decision soon.

Amber groaned and shifted position, her arm draping across his chest. He wanted to nudge and kiss her awake. Every cell in his body was currently screaming at him. But he couldn't do that. Not like this.

They'd been pushed into a forced proximity. It didn't matter how much of a pull he felt toward Amber. After waiting two years to connect with someone, he wanted to be sure. And he wanted *her* to be sure. Because Amber Berkeley gave off a whole host of conflicting signals. Oh, sure, she kissed really well. But just because she kissed him didn't mean she wanted anything to progress between them. And how did you have that conversation with someone you'd really only just met?

Amber moved again, her lips brushing against the skin at his shoulder. Jack almost groaned out loud.

One thing was clear. Carrying on like this would drive him plain crazy.

Amber checked the obs chart in front of her. Aaron was on his way to a good recovery. Zane was finally making progress too, allowing her to breathe a big sigh of relief.

Jack came up behind her. "How you doing?"

He'd been a little awkward this morning. Not unpleasant. Just a little brisker than before. When she'd woken up and found herself wrapped around him again, all she'd been able to think of was how right things felt.

By the time she'd got her five-minute shower she'd

tried to be more sensible. In a few days she'd have to leave and get back to Chicago and the DPA. Jack still had no idea what to do next. And she'd no right to have an opinion on anything about that.

He nudged her again. "Hey? Are you with me?" His voice was soft, like velvet touching her skin, and she jerked back to attention.

"What? Yes. I've just finished checking on Aaron's mom. Her lung has reinflated and she's feeling a lot better."

Jack nodded. "I checked his dad. The pins in his tib and fib look good. He's got a walking cast on and they've had him on his feet already. Once he's mastered the hospital stairs on his crutches, he'll be good to go."

"Aaron should be ready to go in a few days. I've taken some more bloods this morning and he seems to be responding to the antibiotics well."

Jack gave a nod. "How about if I told you that I managed to find a shop that's opened?"

"Really?" That had her instant attention. She wanted to buy some toiletries and some food. Probably in that order.

He nodded again. "Apparently they had a delivery today from the mainland. They have some fresh food. I might have bought some."

"You might have bought some?" She arched an eyebrow at him. "What exactly *might* you have bought?"

"Chicken. Potatoes. Veg. Bread. Butter."

She rolled her eyes upward. "Sounds like heaven. Do we get to eat this food in a place that doesn't hold two thousand other people?" She wrinkled her nose. "And smell like two thousand other people."

"Oh, yeah," breathed Jack. "I also heard a rumor that

the utilities might be turned on for a bit longer tonight. We might get more than an hour of water."

"Now, that would really be bliss." She leaned back against the nearest wall. Then something came into her head. "Hey, tonight, who's cooking? Shall we flip for it?"

He gave a sneaky kind of smile. "Well, since I managed to find the food..."

She shook her head. "Oh, no. Oh, no, you don't. We flip for it."

"Or?"

"Or I steal the food and eat it myself."

He pulled a quarter from his pocket. "Okay, then. Heads or tails?"

"Tails."

He flipped the coin. It spun in the air and landed on his palm.

She grinned. "Tails." She lifted one finger and prodded his shoulder. "Just remember. I prefer barbecue chicken. Or maybe chicken cordon bleu."

She gave her stomach a little rub to tease him.

He shook his head. "Don't let it be said that anyone calls you Bossy Britches."

She batted her eyelashes. "Dr. Campbell, I have absolutely no idea what you mean."

He was strangely nervous. And he had no idea why. He was a perfectly capable cook. He could throw together a dinner without too many problems—even with his eyes on the clock to make sure he coordinated it with the bursts of power. The apartment they were temporarily residing in was only a few streets away from the beach. Since there were still a number of other emergency helpers using the apartment, Jack decided it might be easier to pack up the food and take it outside.

Their belongings had been dropped off from the hotel around an hour ago. In the chaos after the hurricane, the hotel was being used as a temporary shelter for some families. It seemed that his belongings had been more or less thrown into the case. But everything seemed to be there.

He undid the zipper on the inside lid of the case and slipped his hand inside. The wave of relief passed over his body instantly as he felt the battered edge of the photograph, but he froze as he went to pull it out. He knew it was there. He knew he hadn't lost it. But he'd lost her.

Did he need to keep looking at her photograph?

His fingers released the edge of the photograph as he knelt by the case. He breathed for a minute. In. Out. In. Out.

He pulled back his hand and fixed his eyes on the door. He'd used to have the picture on permanent display. That had stopped a few months ago. Would he ever get rid of it? No. Never.

He would always be respectful of Jill's memories. Her life. Her love. Her laughter.

But in the last few days it was as if the shadows had lifted from his eyes. And from his heart.

His head had stopped focusing only on the research. He'd never been interested in the business side of things. He'd only ever been interested in developing the best product that might actually save lives. Now he'd done it and he had the evidence base to prove it. But his obsession had started to diminish.

Today, he'd finally managed to access a working computer for a few minutes. Seven hundred emails. Mostly about the wound dressing.

But the only ones that he'd opened had been the

emails about job opportunities. Doctors Without Borders. Seven private clinics throughout the world. Six NHS posts highlighted to him by friends and colleagues who thought he would be suitable. Three possible aid agencies postings in far-off places that would be similar to what he was actually doing right now in Hawaii.

He'd always thought he'd know the right job opportunity as soon as it came along. But somehow, in among all of this, for the first time he was uncertain.

He'd always had a career path in his head. Up until this point it had served him well. But now? Here, in Hawaii, with his senses awakening for the first time in years, he just didn't know what path to take.

The door banged and Amber walked in. She was wearing a pair of thin blue scrubs with her hair tied up on top of her head. Her eyes widened as she saw him crouched on the floor. "Our luggage? We have our luggage?"

He nodded, and before he got a chance to point her bright green suitcase out, she'd spotted it and ran across the floor, throwing herself on top of it. "Come to Mama, clean clothes, shampoo and moisturizer." She laughed as he shook his head at her while she stayed in position.

"What? Are you trying to tell me that you haven't craved your own clean shirt and underwear in the last few days?"

She jumped up and dragged her case toward the bathroom. "Leave me alone. I might be some time." Her eyes were gleaming.

He smiled and stood up, waiting for a few seconds until he heard the inevitable signs of the shower running. He lifted his hand and knocked on the door.

"What?" came the impatient shout.

He leaned on the wall and folded his arms across his

chest as he kept grinning. "Amber? Just to let you know, you have—" he glanced at his watch "—nine minutes."

"What?" Her horror-struck face appeared at a tiny gap in the door. "Tell me you're joking?"

He tapped his watch as he walked away. "Tick, tick, Amber."

It was the quickest shower in the history of the world. She'd been vaguely aware of the smell of cooking food as she'd entered the apartment, but the sight of her suitcase had been too good. When she'd flung it open inside the bathroom there had been a note on the top asking her to collect her valuables from the hotel and to bring her passport with her. That had to mean that they'd emptied the safe in her room and taken her locket someplace else.

She ran across the hallway with only a towel wrapped around her so she could blast her hair with the hair dryer. Sure enough, in around two minutes, the lights and power flickered off. She let out a groan. Jack appeared at the door smiling, dressed in a T-shirt and jeans. "What? You didn't quite make it in time?"

She threw back her still-damp hair. "Darn it. At least I've got rid of some of the wetness." She frowned as she remembered the state of the clothes in the bathroom. "But I think I'm going to look like some kind of dishrag tonight. I wasn't able to iron any of my clothes."

Jack gave her a steady glance. "I think you'll look fine, no matter what you're wearing."

A little tingle ran over her skin. There were a few flickering candles in the main room but very little other light. She licked her lips and wondered if she could put on some makeup in the virtual darkness. It was almost as if he read her mind. He strode through the main room and walked back with a candle. "Here. You'll need it to get dressed. I'll pack up the food in the kitchen."

She was surprised. "Aren't we eating here?"

He gave her a wicked glance. "We're sharing with four other people—what's the chances of them coming in and stealing our food? The beach nearby looks safe enough. I thought we could eat down there and pretend we were still in the Hawaii we came to."

She reached out and took the flickering candle as her stomach gave a little squeeze. "Give me five minutes. That's all I'll take."

And she did. Grabbing a red beach dress from her case that she'd planned to wear for a more casual day, and a pair of flat sandals. Her hair was still damp but she left it around her shoulders in the hope it might dry in the warm evening air. Finally she slicked on some red lipstick as she squinted in the mirror in the candlelight then grabbed a light black cardigan.

When she walked back out in the corridor, Jack was standing with a package wrapped in aluminum foil in one hand and a bottle in the other. She laughed and shook her head as she walked up. "What? No wicker basket? No picnic rug or crystal glasses?"

"I'm all out." He shrugged. "This is going to be more like some high-school midnight feast than some big seduction scene."

She stepped forward, closer than she would normally dare. They were currently alone. The only light was the flickering candles. "Is that what this is?" she asked teasingly. "A big seduction scene?"

Jack's pupils seemed to dilate a little. She liked that. She liked that a lot.

He gave the slightest raise of his eyebrows and dared

to lean a little closer, letting her inhale the dark woody aftershave he'd put on.

He adjusted his package and held one hand palm up. "Let's see. We've already shared a bed—how many times? We've kissed." He gave a little smile. "Maybe twice. Do we need a seduction scene?"

She was fixed on his eyes. Had he always had such thick eyelashes? Why was she just noticing them now? She licked her lips subconsciously. "You can't seduce me," she said, her voice more hoarse than she'd expected. "I don't date doctors, remember?"

He slid his arm around her waist and pulled her closer. "Who said anything about dating?"

Maybe it was the dim lighting. Maybe it was the slow buildup of momentum in their mutual attraction. Maybe it was the combination of reasons that they shouldn't really be together.

But whatever their pasts, whatever the world had against them, it seemed that somewhere above those stars had aligned for tonight.

They walked down to the beach with her hand tucked inside his elbow. The tidy-up around them had started. There were lots of areas still needing attention. Buildings still requiring massive repairs. The path to the beach had a number of heavily bent palm trees, one appeared to have been completely torn from its roots, but other than that there were no major issues. The beach was deserted, just a pale expanse of sand and a virtually black sea.

Jack had grabbed a towel from the apartment so they had something to sit on. They settled down and he eased the aluminum foil open. The crinkling sound seemed to echo around them.

Amber bent down and inhaled, her hair falling around her and shielding her face. He resisted the temptation to reach out and pull it back. She sat back up, smiling. "You made it. Barbecue chicken." Her eyes were gleaming in the pale moonlight. "You actually made it."

"Of course I did. You requested it." He gave a simple shrug as he handed her one of the plates that he'd brought from the kitchen. It only took a few moments to share out the chicken and potato salad that he'd made. Ingredients had been few but it was still better than eating at the evacuation center. He also opened the wine he'd acquired at the nearby shop.

"Darn it." He shook his head. "We have no glasses."

Amber gave him a fake look of horror. "You mean we'll have to drink from the bottle? How classy." She shook her head as she took the bottle from his hands and expertly removed the cork with the bottle opener. "Do you honestly think I'm that kind of girl?" She winked and put the bottle to her lips, extending her neck and tipping her head back, giving him a perfect view of her profile in the moonlight.

He caught his breath. It had been a long time since that had happened—in fact, had it ever happened before? In the space of a few days Amber Berkeley had started to burrow her way under his skin. He'd found himself looking for her constantly. Picking up on the sound of her voice, even when they weren't in the same room. Wondering what she thought of him. And that last kiss—it had haunted him. In more ways than one...

Amber handed the bottle back to him, still smiling, then leaned back on her hands and sighed. "Wow."

"Wow?"

She nodded. "Yeah. Look around. From here we can hardly see any sign of the damage. Just a beautiful beach with a mile of sand, an endless dark ocean with stars in the sky above." She nodded in appreciation. "This is the Hawaii I imagined coming to. The one I had in my head. The daytime being yellow sand, bright blue ocean and a multitude of colored flowers, and the nighttime being beautiful, quiet and romantic."

Jack smiled as he shifted to face her. "Romantic?"

From here she was bathed in the pale moonlight. It caressed her skin, showing the glow and the vitality. She closed her eyes for a second and breathed again. Then turned her head to face him. "Yes. Romantic."

He paused. "What happens next, Amber?"

She licked her lips. He knew exactly what he wanted her to say.

She shifted on her hips so they were face on. She hadn't stopped smiling. "I guess I'm not entirely sure. The last few days have been...strange."

"Strange?"

She held up her hands. "Challenging. In a whole host of ways. Challenging for work. Challenging for life and...challenging for me."

He could tell she needed to talk out loud. He nodded. "It's been...different. I didn't come here expecting to find anything."

"And have you?" Her eyes were wide with expectation.

He put his hand up to his chest. "I feel like I have. I came here wondering what came next. I came here just to present at the conference—to tell the rest of the world about our product. And that was it. That was all that I was here to do."

"So what happened?" There was a teasing edge in her tone.

He met her twinkling gaze. "I met an unstoppable

force. And it made me feel as if I found a little bit of myself again."

"You did?" Her voice broke.

He nodded slowly as he licked his lips. "*She* made me feel as if I found a little bit of myself again."

Amber moved. She hitched up her dress and put one leg over him, so she was sitting facing him.

"This is getting to be a habit," said Jack hoarsely.

She slid her arms around his neck and tipped her head to the side. "I think it might be."

His hands went to her waist. "Maybe we need to re-think your rule. Don't most people say that rules were made to be broken?"

She lowered her head and whispered in his ear. "How about you convince me?"

"I think I can do that..."

And he did.

CHAPTER NINE

THE DOOR TO the room burst open. Amber sat bolt upright in the bed then remembered she didn't have quite as many clothes on as she usually did. Kino, one of the emergency workers who was sharing their apartment, only momentarily blinked. "Amber, Jack. You're needed. We've all been called in."

Jack moved seamlessly. He stood up, grabbed a set of scrubs that were lying on the floor and stepped into them. He pulled on his shoes and immediately started asking questions. "What is it? What's happened?"

Amber was still in the process of waking up and Jack was already dressed. Of course. An army doc. He was used to emergency calls. She'd never been good at the intern hours of putting your head on the pillow only for a page to sound yet again.

Kino kept talking. "A landslide. It's caught one of the villages on the outskirts of Kailua Kona. Multiple casualties."

Kino moved away. "I'll wait for you outside."

As soon as he left, Amber retrieved her underwear and grabbed a clean T-shirt, jeans and sneakers. She didn't have time to worry about appearances, so she clipped her hair up on her head and met Jack at the door.

"Ready?" His face had become almost a mask. The

warmth and emotion she'd glimpsed last night seemed to have been put back in their box. He seemed totally focused.

She grabbed her jacket and followed him out to the car. They were lucky they still had it on loan—and that their emergency packs were in the trunk. Jack handed her the radio as Kino climbed in their car. "Might as well come with you," he said as Jack nodded.

Jack started the engine. "Call in, Amber. See if we've to go to the hospital first, or straight onto the site."

Their instructions were clear. They were to be part of the first responders on site.

They traveled the rest of the way in virtual silence with only the occasional crackle from the radio. Kino was able to point out directions as he was from one of the other Hawaiian islands and was familiar with this area. Most of the major roads had been cleared of any fallen trees and debris by now.

But as they ventured nearer the village, the extent of the damage was evident. Four emergency vehicles were ahead of them, bright flashing lights causing Jack to slow down on the road. It was just as well, because the rest of the road had vanished in the landslide.

Amber had never seen anything like this before and she stepped out trying to survey the scene. "Where's the village?" seemed the obvious question.

Kino's voice was shaky. "It was there," he said, pointing to the mass of rubble and mud ahead of them.

Amber shook her head. "I don't get it. What's happened?"

One of the other emergency responders walked over. "It's because of the hurricane and the amount of rainfall. The earth around the volcanoes and mountains hasn't been able to stand the strain and extra pressure. It's always a risk a few days after any major event. It's just never happened before."

Her eyes were starting to pick out things in the debris. It was mainly mud and earth, along with a million uprooted trees. But in among the rest of it she could see a few things sticking out. Part of a roof of a house? A brick wall that seemed to have been carried away by the flow of the landslide.

"How many people?" she breathed.

"About five hundred," replied the first responder. He dug into his pack and pulled out tags. "Triage. That's your first duty. Red, amber and green. We'll set up the tarp emergency tents for first responders here. Find them, pull them out, assess them."

Jack had been silent this whole time—almost as if he was creating a plan in his head. A fire truck had just pulled up and the firefighters were out instantly.

Amber opened her mouth to shout over to them as the first responder put his hand up to her face. "Don't."

"What?" She was confused. She was only going to ask if they wanted to split into groups with the doctors.

"First rule of a landslide. The first big danger is the possibility of a further landslide. Keep noise to a minimum. No shouting. Only use the radios we'll give you." He pointed up to the mountainside. "There's always a chance that not everything has found its way down yet. There could be boulders, more trees, a million rocks, all waiting to slide back down here."

She felt her skin chill. She was walking into a situation she knew nothing about. Could she really do this? She took a few deep breaths. Jack had already started reorganizing things in his pack as some of the firefighters came over to join them, carrying radios. Another car pulled up and she recognized some of the staff from ER. They divided quickly into teams.

Her first few steps were tentative. The ground was unstable in places, and they were on an incline. But Amber followed the instructions she was given and moved as quickly as she could. Within minutes they found their first patient. A woman, who was half covered in mud and looked completely stunned. Half of her clothes were missing. Amber did a quick check and nodded to the firefighters that she was safe to move. "I was in the bathroom," the woman whispered. "I was getting dressed."

"Anyone else in your home?" asked Jack quickly.

She shook her head and Jack moved rapidly on as two of the firefighters assisted the woman back up to the almost constructed triage station.

For the next hour they worked in almost silence. Finding people trapped in the mud and earth. Some were badly injured. Others were lucky—they only had cuts and bruises. A few weren't so lucky. Amber found one man who seemed to have died of a severe head injury and another who had suffocated under the mud.

Jack was methodical and fast. He didn't waste a single second. Her stomach was in a permanent knot as she watched him. He barely acknowledged her existence. He seemed too focused on the task at hand. And she knew that was entirely how he should be. But somehow it still hurt. It still reminded her of her father. And she just couldn't shake the association.

She pulled out a child covered from head to toe in mud. But as she bent to do a quick assessment, Jack more or less elbowed her out of the way—just as he had at the car the other night. She bristled. She couldn't help it. She was perfectly capable of assessing this child. But was now really the time to fight about it?

She left him and moved on to the next spot where a firefighter was waving over to her. He pointed downward. "We've got a house buried under here." He had his ear pressed to the ground. "We think this is part of the chimney stack. Or it used to be. Is it maybe wrong way up? Who knows. We can hear them beneath us."

"Can you get them out?" She was currently up to her knees in sticky mud. The thought of being trapped underneath that made her feel queasy.

The firefighter nodded. "The space looks wide enough. I'm going to send someone down."

"Is that safe?"

His eyes scanned the surroundings. "Is anything here?"

She swallowed and stood to the side, allowing the firefighters to sort out their gear and lower their colleague. After a few minutes the guy radioed back up. "I've got four. All badly injured. Two adults and two kids. Can you lower me a cage? I'll need to strap them in one at a time."

It was a painstaking operation. The cage was carried over from one of the specialist fire and rescue trucks. First to come up was a woman whose color was verging on gray. She took the briefest seconds to assess. "Flail chest." Amber put a red tag on her. "Straight to hospital whatever way you can get her there."

The next up was a little girl with an ugly fracture of her arm, sticking through her skin. She was wailing at the top of her voice, making everyone nearby look around anxiously. Amber calculated in her head the little girl's size and weight. She hated approximating but it was the only way to try and ensure a safe dose of analgesia. Twenty seconds later she gave the little girl an injection to try and relieve her pain and handed her over to another firefighter to take her away. The next child was unconscious but breathing steadily. There was a slight graze to his head. She tagged him as amber and sent him on.

"There's a problem down here," came the crackle of the radio.

"What is it?"

"I can't move him. He's pinned down and I can't get him free. I need some assistance and he looks in a bad way."

Amber didn't hesitate. "Send me down. Let me look after him."

The firefighter frowned. "I'm not sure. Things are too unstable."

"You let your own man go down there—and you'll probably have to send another." She was determined. She was a doctor. This was her role and she wanted to play her part.

"I don't know." The firefighter hesitated.

"Well, I do. Where's a harness? Get me a harness and lower me down."

Of course she was nervous. Of course she was scared. But this was an emergency situation and she could deal with it. A tiny part of her brain objected. She could almost hear her father's condescending tone. But she brushed it away as she stepped into the harness.

"Amber? What do you think you're doing?"

Mud was streaked across Jack's face and clothes.

"My job," she replied as the firefighter clipped on her line.

"Ready?" he asked.

"Ready." She nodded.

Jack's voice cut across everyone's. "No. No way. No way is she going down there. It's too dangerous. Not a chance." His voice was louder than it should be and sent a wave of irritation over her.

She turned toward him. "Stop it, Jack. There are more than enough patients to deal with. Go and look after your own."

His hand came down on her arm in a viselike grip. "I said no." His voice was steely but it was the expression in his eyes that made her swallow. In a flash she saw a million things she didn't want to. This wasn't the man she'd laughed and loved with last night. This was a man who thought he should be in charge. This was a man who didn't believe in her as a doctor. He didn't respect her as a person and he didn't respect her as a doctor.

She turned to face the firefighter. "Tell him to get his hand off me." Her voice was shaking with rage. A few of the firefighters around them instantly stood up.

"Cool it, buddy."

"You heard the lady. Step back."

Jack's eyes flashed furiously but Amber just jerked her arm away then tugged at her harness to ensure it was secure. She grabbed a few things from her pack and stepped to the opening. "I'm ready." Her heart was thudding frantically in her chest. She felt anything but ready. But delaying now could make things more dangerous for everyone.

"This isn't finished," said Jack hoarsely.

"Oh, yes, it is," she replied as she was lowered down into the darkness.

He could barely contain his rage but he understood exactly how he'd come across. There were four pairs of eyes currently watching him with suspicion. "She's a great doctor. But she's not an emergency doctor. She's never worked in a situation like this."

One of the firefighters met his gaze. "Neither have I. Doesn't mean I won't do the job."

The words almost stung. The guy had a point. But had that guy lost a woman before that he'd loved? Jack should be down there. Jack should be the one in the position of risk. It shouldn't be Amber. She hadn't asked to be here. She'd just volunteered her services. He didn't doubt she could deal with whatever she might find down there—he didn't doubt her medical abilities at all. What he did doubt was his ability to survive if something were to happen to her.

From the second she'd stepped into that harness, his brain had had to remind himself constantly he wasn't allowed to shout. Because shouting was exactly what he wanted to do right now. Amber didn't need to be at risk. She didn't need to be in a situation that could rapidly go out of control.

He felt himself start to shake. And he couldn't stop it. It was like being dunked in a giant bowl of ice. He wanted to grab that line and haul her back up here. Back up here into his arms where she might actually be safe. Back up here where he could tell her he loved her—despite it only being a week, and despite the fact she still wasn't sure about dating a doctor.

He didn't want to date her. He wanted to marry her. He wanted to tell her that he could find a job anywhere so long as he was with her. He wanted to tell her that life was too short to wait. That when you knew, you just knew—no matter how hard you tried to fight it.

He lifted his shaking hands to the guys around him. "What can I say? I love her. I don't want anything to happen to her."

There was momentarily a flicker between them all. Then one guy put his hands on Jack's shaking arms. "Then I guess when she gets back up you should tell her."

Jack nodded and took a deep breath. "I guess I should."

* * *

She could barely breathe. What should be the inside of a home was a strange hotchpotch like one of those upside-down houses they had at an adventure park. She thought she'd come down the chimney but now she wasn't quite sure. What she was sure of was that the man on the floor beside her was barely alive. She needed oxygen. She needed a chest tube, and any longer and she'd need a defibrillator too. She had to concentrate right now, so why was her head so full of Jack?

She'd been a fool. She'd spent the night with a guy that every warning flag in her brain had told her to stay away from. But she'd done it. She'd let him in. She'd started to believe that all her previous fixed beliefs had been irrational. She shouldn't judge anyone else because of her father. Now the first time she'd opened her heart a little, he'd stamped all over it.

She was more than a fool. She was a stupid fool. And she hated herself more than anything right now. That look he'd given her. As if she were incapable. As if he had a right to tell her what to do.

She couldn't live like that. She *wouldn't* live like that.

There was a loud creak around her and the sound of shifting. A cloud of dust surrounded them and mud was seeping through a gap in the wall near to them—indicating what was waiting. The firefighter on the floor next to her looked up with his eyes wide. "Darn it. We need to move."

The second firefighter who'd come down just behind her was trying to find a way to prop up the huge boulder that had pinned their man to the floor. She finished fastening a collar around her patient's neck. His blood pressure indicated massive internal bleeding. His pulse rate was over one hundred and thirty. She slid her arms under her patient's shoulders. "Okay. Guys, is there any way you can take a bit of the weight even for a few seconds? If you can, I'm going to just yank him out of there."

The two guys nodded and attempted to slide some kind of wedge under the boulder. "You'll have a few seconds. This has an emergency inflatable action. But it won't hold—not with this weight. We'll fire it on three and try and take some of the weight too. Are you ready?"

Amber looked at the strange wedge-shaped contraption that after much manipulation was barely shoved under the huge boulder. Of course it wouldn't hold but it might give her a few seconds. She pressed down low to the floor behind her patient. All she had to do was pull. "Okay."

"One, two, three, *go!*"

She pulled with all her might. There was a tiny explosion followed by a colossal boom. She landed backward on the floor with the patient's head and shoulders planted between her legs. The two firefighters were covered in gray dust and choking madly. The boulder was back squarely on the floor where her patient had just lain.

The creaking sounded again and both guys exchanged a glance. "Let's get him into the cage." Amber didn't have time to recheck his obs as they bundled him into the cage and yanked the cord sharply to get him pulled up. She could hear frantic voices above her as the patient blocked their little light as he was pulled up. Seconds later three lines were dropped down. She didn't even have time to think as one of the firefighters clipped her harness instantly, then yanked her line.

She jerked roughly upward through the thin gap above, banging her shoulder. Arms grabbed her and threw her to one side. The noise was massive. Like a roaring in her ear. She didn't even have time to make sense of any of it. She saw the flash of orange and yellow as the firefighters were pulled up alongside her. "Take cover!" came the shout.

She still hadn't caught her breath when Jack landed on her, covering her body with his. He had his jacket pulled over his head, which in turn covered hers. Seconds later the ground moved beneath them, then over them, tumbling and tumbling around. Rocks pounded her body. Trees scratched her face and legs. Dirt crowded around her, and when she tried to inhale, mud slid over her mouth, choking her completely. Over and over they went like tumbleweed on a desert landscape. Jack's arms were around her, holding her in place. Nausea washed over her. Her head was spinning.

Finally, the tumbling seemed to slow. She was able to snatch a breath along with a mouthful of leaves. Every part of her ached. She tried to pull her hands up to protect her head, clawing at the jacket that had partially protected her. Jack's.

They finally stopped moving. She wheezed, then choked, spluttering up mouthfuls of dirt and mud. As she turned onto her hands and knees, there was a wave of pain from her ankle. But breathing came first. There was a heavy weight on her back. She pushed up, struggling to move. She tried again, ignoring all her pain and putting all her energy into curling her back around. Dirt and earth moved around her. She coughed, as she burst up through the mounds of debris. Her breathing was stuttered, her head still swimming.

Another landslide. They'd been caught in another landslide. She looked around, trying to work out where she was. Trying to work out where *anyone* was.

At the top right of her vision she could see the flicker of dark green tarpaulin. The triage tent. It seemed a million miles away now.

She shook her head, pulling twigs and leaves from her hair. She blinked. Something warm was beneath her palm.

She looked down, her eyes taking a few seconds to focus.

Jack. It was Jack.

She shifted her hand. "Jack? Are you okay?"

He'd dived on her. He must have realized the landslide had started. He must have known she was about to be caught in it.

Why hadn't he moved away? Why hadn't he got to safety?

She blinked again. He hadn't moved. More important, his chest wasn't moving. His lips were distinctly blue.

She felt a wave of panic. He'd tried to save her. He'd tried to shield her from the landslide. He'd put himself in harm's way deliberately for her. But at what cost?

"Jack! Jack!" She started thudding down on his chest. Trying desperately for any kind of reaction.

Nothing. Nothing at all. She thrust her fingers in at his neck, trying to locate a pulse. Nothing. She moved them again. Still nothing.

Panic gripped her. No. Not Jack. Not now.

"Help!" she shouted, waving one hand frantically in the air. "I need help!"

She started doing chest compressions, letting her doctor mode send her into automatic pilot while every other part of her being screamed out loud.

She loved him. She hated him. She couldn't possibly be with him. But did she really want to live without him when he'd connected with her in ways she'd never felt before?

The pain in her chest was immense. Stress, fear and terror all at once.

She could feel the movement of his chest beneath her palms. His color hadn't improved. He wasn't breathing. She couldn't feel the beat of a heart beneath her hands.

A tear dripped down her cheek and landed onto his chest.

This couldn't be how this ended. It just couldn't be.

She wouldn't let it.

She *couldn't* let it.

CHAPTER TEN

ONE SECOND HE was trying to contain himself; next second he was watching the mass of boulders and tree slide toward them as he dived on top of Amber.

He couldn't remember anything after that.

Except that his chest hurt. *A lot.*

And so did his shoulder. And so did his head.

He blinked, then squinted at the bright white that met his eyes.

A face appeared above him. "Oh, you're back to the land of the living. About time. I know someone that will be pleased."

His brain was still trying to focus. She was vaguely familiar. "Please don't make me do neuro obs on you, Jack. You haven't exactly been the easiest patient these past few hours."

She winked at him and something flooded into his brain. "Lana?" The ER nurse who had been sent out with him and Amber.

Amber. This wasn't a flood; this was a tidal wave. "Amber? Where's Amber?" He tried to sit up in the bed, yelping as his shoulder let him know who was in charge.

Lana smiled. "Oh, good. No neuro obs. You do know who we are." She pointed to his shoulder. "You dislocated that. It will probably be sore for a few days. And you've got a few cracked ribs where someone got a little overenthusiastic when you needed CPR."

"What?" He sagged back on the bed and put his hand on his chest. That was why it was so sore.

"As for Amber." Lana nodded over her shoulder. "Don't let it be said we're not accommodating. She's just back from Theater. Her ankle needed to be pinned. She's just about ready to wake up."

Jack turned his head to the side. There, in the bed next to him, lay a very pale-faced Amber, her dark hair fanned around her, doing her best impersonation of Snow White.

He shook his head, but, no, even that hurt. Lana walked over and lifted a cup with a drinking straw. "Try some water. Then we can chat. Do you need some more analgesia?"

He shook his head. "What…what happened? Last thing I remember was the landslide."

Lana nodded. "I think I'll leave Amber to discuss that with you. She used a few choice words." Lana laughed; her eyes were twinkling. "Give me five minutes to wake her up."

Lana pressed a button and the top of Jack's bed rose behind him, giving him a better view of the room. From the noise outside, the hospital was still crazy. He should be helping. He shouldn't be in here as a patient.

But he couldn't deny the pain in his chest. His heart gave a leap as he heard a few quiet words from the bed next door. He could hear Lana speaking to Amber. "Yeah, I'm the girl with all the gifts. I've been in the ER, Maternity and Surgical in the last day. I just go wherever I'm needed." Lana glanced over her shoulder and gave Jack a wink. "Here, have a little drink and I'll sit you up. Your partner in crime has woken up too."

"He has?" Jack's breath caught at the tone of her voice. She sounded almost...happy?

Lana stepped back and glanced from one to the other as she placed a buzzer next to Amber's hand. "Okay, people, things to do. Ring if you need me." She was laughing to herself as she walked out of the door.

For a few seconds there was silence. And Jack was glad of it. He was just so glad to see her there. Seeing that giant amount of earth moving toward them had terrified him. There had been no chance to move Amber out of its path. He might have had a chance to run for it. The firefighters next to him had run like lightning, carrying the patient in the rescue litter. He only hoped they'd managed to get out of the way of the landslide.

"You made it," he finally said, his voice breaking a little.

"Of course I made it," she snapped. "I haven't finished being mad at you yet."

He rested his head back against the pillow, closed his eyes and smiled. Just the way he liked her.

"What are you smiling at?"

He put his hand to his chest. "I'm just thanking someone up above that we're both still here." He opened his eyes again. She was too far away to reach out to. But that didn't stop him wanting to.

She cleared her throat. "I'm still mad at you."

He met her gaze. Somehow he'd never seen anyone look quite so beautiful. "I get that. Do you think being mad could last a lifetime?"

Confusion swept her face. "What are you talking about?"

He breathed slowly, then winced. He should have remembered about the ribs.

"Are you okay?"

He shook his head. "Just feels like someone has been tap-dancing on my chest. I broke a few ribs, and dislocated a shoulder. I still have no idea how we got out of that."

She blinked. Her eyes looked wet. "Sorry. My technique might be off."

Something clicked in his brain. "You did CPR on me?"

She let out an exasperated laugh. "Well, you'd shielded me from a landslide. It would have seemed kind of bad to leave you there when you—" her voice broke "—you weren't breathing." He saw her try to take a deep breath. "Blue really isn't your color."

His brain was trying to compute. He'd just figured that one of the search and rescue guys or gals had pulled him from the landslide.

She kept talking. "How could I walk away? You tackled me to the ground like you were some kind of superhero. Then you just threw a coat over us and didn't let go all the way down the mountainside."

He wasn't imagining it. A tear was sliding down her cheek.

"Some people are worth holding on to," he said softly.

Amber shook her head. "But we're wrong for each other. You don't believe in me. You second-guess me. You make me feel as if I have to prove myself around you." Her head-shaking got fiercer. "That's not what love is about. That isn't how someone who loves you should make you feel."

He could see it. The pain on her face that had been etched there since he first met her—always just hiding beneath the surface as she slipped on her bravado and her game face.

"Is that how I make you feel, or is that how you already feel, Amber?" he probed gently. "Because I think you're a wonderful doctor. I've seen you in situations that should be completely out of your comfort zone and taking it in your stride. Am I a control freak? Yes. I've lived the past eight years in a place where discipline and control is everything. But where acting first is sometimes the only chance you get. I know that. I recognize that.

"I've had a situation where everything was out of my control and I woke up the next day having lost someone that I loved. How do you think I felt when I saw you put yourself in danger? Did I overreact? Probably, yes. Will I do it in future? Maybe. It doesn't make me a bad person. It makes me know that I feel again. That I love again. Do you think I could bear waiting to see if something might happen to you? I saw that ground start to move, felt the rumble beneath my feet, and there was no way I was letting go of you." He could feel his hands start to shake again. It was almost as if all his emotions were finally coming to the surface.

"Love isn't perfect, Amber. I don't even know if I'm any good at it. I just know I want to try. And I want to try with you. I know we're right at the beginning. I know anything can happen from here. I just want you to give me a chance. I just want to try."

"You love me?" She said the words in disbelief.

"Of course I love you. What's not to love? You fight with me. You tell me I snore. You tease me. You make me work harder. You challenge me at every turn." He gave her a smile. "I don't think I've ever met anyone so perfect for me in my life."

Tears were tumbling down her cheeks. "But…but…"

"But what?"

He fumbled around the edge of the bed until he found

the button that lowered the side. He swung his legs to the edge of the bed and waited a few seconds while his head spun, then yanked the blood-pressure cuff from his arm.

The first step was shaky. The second was determined. Nothing would keep him from being by her side. He reached the edge of her bed.

"Tell me how you feel, Amber. Tell me how you feel about me. I might be completely crazy here." He lifted his hand to the bandage on his head. "Maybe I've got a head injury." Then he took his hand back down to his chest. "Or maybe I'm finally listening to my heart." He reached over and brushed one of the tears away from her cheek. "I've spent the last two years focused on work. Locking myself away from everything and everybody." He held up his hands and smiled. "Here. This place." He laughed and shook his head, ignoring the pain. "We came here expecting a busman's holiday. Expecting the beauty and wonder of Hawaii. Instead we got this. A hurricane. Chaos. A landslide." He moved closer and took one of her hands in his. "I'm glad, Amber. I'm glad. Because something brought us together. And whatever you want to do in the future, wherever you want to be—" he smiled at her "—I'm just praying you'll let me tag along."

He moved his other hand over hers too. "I'm not your father, Amber. I'm not your ex. I'll never be those people. I'm Jack Campbell from a tiny mining village in Scotland. Auchinleck. I'll teach you how to say it. I'll take you there. I can promise I'll introduce you to things you've never seen before." As his mind filled with the thoughts of his village back home and the characters it was filled with, he couldn't help but laugh out loud. "They'll love you. Just like I do."

Amber's tears were flowing; she started to laugh. "I

wanted to shout at you. I've wanted you to wake up so I could tell you how mad I was at you."

He leaned one arm on the side of her bed. "And what exactly were you mad about, Dr. Berkeley?"

It seemed as though all her emotions welled up at once. "I…I was mad because you put yourself at risk to try and save me." She was struggling to get the words out. "I was mad because you were trying to stop me doing something dangerous… I was mad because I was scared to do it…but I didn't want to be. I was mad because I constantly felt as if I had to prove myself to my father. To earn his respect. To earn his approval. To show him I could do it. To show him I was capable. And…I… I…" She stopped talking and sucked in a deep breath. Her tear-filled eyes met his. It was almost as if something had just clicked into place. He could see the glimmer of recognition in her gaze. She squeezed his hand. "And…I don't need to do that with you."

He could see her whole change in stance. Her shoulders went down as if the tension had left her body. "I don't need to do that with you," she repeated in a whisper.

"No." He smiled. "You don't, Amber. I've got your back. I'll always have your back. You specialize in infectious diseases. How much of that have you got to do in the last seven days? Have you complained? Have you said no? Not once. You've put your head down and got on with it. And have you stopped when you were scared? When you put yourself in a situation where you could be electrocuted? When you put yourself in the path of the landslide?" He cupped her cheek. "Who would do that, Amber?" Then he laughed again. "What normal, sane-minded person would do a thing like that?"

She started laughing too. "Jack Campbell, I do believe you may be a bad influence on me."

He fumbled around, looking for her button to lower the bedside. "Where is this dang thing? Ah...finally." He put the side down and moved closer, wincing as his ribs let him know he wasn't quite as healed as he might want to be. He put one hand on his side. "Dr. Berkeley, I believe we may need to talk about your technique."

"Hang the technique." She smiled as she put her hand around his head and pulled him closer. "You're alive, aren't you?"

He moved closer, inches away from her lips. "I believe that might put me in your debt."

She licked her lips. "You bet it does. You don't think I saved the man I love for anyone else, do you?"

Before he could ask her to repeat that, she kissed him.

And he had absolutely no intention of stopping that...

EPILOGUE

One year later

EVERYTHING WAS PERFECT. The beach was perfect. The brightly colored flowers in her wedding bouquet were perfect, and the overwater bungalows in the perfect green sea in front of them were perfect—especially when she knew one of them had their names on it.

"Ready?"

Her mother stood in front of her dressed in a bright orange dress, complete with an over-the-top hat on her head. So right for the mother of the bride.

Amber stared down and wiggled her pink-painted toenails in the yellow sand. They were always going to come back to the place they'd met to cement their union. Hawaii had recovered well and returned to the beautiful lush state it had been on the morning she'd first arrived. She ran her hand across her pale cream wedding dress. She'd opted for a three-quarter-length dress, lightweight, with lace across her décolletage and shoulders with cap sleeves. Covered enough for a bride but quirky enough that she could get away with being barefoot. Her only jewelry was her gold locket.

She nodded and breathed slowly. "Oh, yes. I'm ready."

Her mother stepped in front of her and put a hand on

each shoulder. "I always wondered if I'd have to tell my daughter not to make the same mistakes I did. You have no idea how happy I am that I don't need to do it. I love Jack. He's perfect for you. Grumpy sometimes. Doesn't let you get away with anything. But most importantly he adores you, Amber. I see it in his eyes every time he looks at you. Work hard at this marriage, honey. You found a keeper."

Tears threatened to spill down her cheeks. She leaned forward and hugged her mom, almost sending the bright orange hat tumbling down the beach in the light winds. "Thank you, Mom, for everything. You've always been my biggest supporter and I love you."

"Come on, Amber! Are you stalling, girl?"

The broad Scots voice of Jack's dad drifted down the beach. His family were waiting in the shaded area, tugging at the collars of their shirts in the searing heat. They'd been ecstatic to come to Hawaii for the wedding, even though it was a long flight. It was a small wedding with only a few other members of Amber's family, and a few of the residents they'd met in Hawaii. Lana, Jamal and Ron were all waiting patiently for things to start, as were Aaron and Zane—who'd both made a good recovery from meningitis—both with their respective parents.

Amber laughed and turned around, catching her breath at the sight of Jack waiting for her in his kilt. "Oh, wow."

Her mother gave her hand a squeeze. "Yip. Wow. Let's not keep your handsome man waiting. These Scots guys can't seem to manage the heat," she joked.

Amber met Jack's gaze. She'd never been so sure of anything in her life.

He gave her his trademark cheeky grin. His heavy dark kilt was swaying in the breeze from the ocean and his cream open-necked ghillie shirt outlined his muscled chest. As she walked toward him, he held out his hand to her.

She handed her flowers to her mother and he took both her hands in his so they were facing each other.

"You've still got a few seconds," he whispered. "If you want to do the runaway bride, you should do it now."

She smiled at the celebrant who was waiting to start the ceremony as she let go of Jack's hands, slid her hands around his neck and stepped closer.

"Where would I run to? I'm exactly where I want to be, with exactly who I want to be with. Now and always."

The celebrant gave a short laugh. "Hey, folks. Aren't you supposed to wait for me?"

Jack winked. "Just give us a minute. We'll be right with you," he said as he bent to kiss his bride.

And the guests all applauded, even though they weren't quite husband and wife.

And everything was just as it was destined to be.

* * * * *

LET'S TALK
Romance

For exclusive extracts, competitions
and special offers, find us online:

- facebook.com/millsandboon
- @MillsandBoon
- @MillsandBoonUK

Get in touch on 01413 063232

For all the latest titles coming soon, visit
millsandboon.co.uk/nextmonth

MILLS & BOON
A ROMANCE FOR
EVERY READER

- **FREE** delivery direct to your door

- **EXCLUSIVE** offers every month

- **SAVE** up to 25% on pre-paid subscriptions

SUBSCRIBE AND SAVE

millsandboon.co.uk/Subscribe

MILLS & BOON
MODERN
Power and Passion

Prepare to be swept off your feet by sophisticated, sexy and seductive heroes, in some of the world's most glamourous and romantic locations, where power and passion collide.

JOIN US ON SOCIAL MEDIA!

Stay up to date with our latest releases, author
news and gossip, special offers and discounts, and
all the behind-the-scenes action
from Mills & Boon...

 millsandboon

 millsandboonuk

 millsandboon

It might just be true love...